The only child of a circus ringmaster and a glamorous clown, Christina Jones has been writing all her life. As well as writing novels, Christina contributes short stories and articles to many national magazines and newspapers. Her first novel was chosen for WH Smith's Fresh Talent promotion, and *Nothing to Lose*, was short-listed for the Thumping Good Read Award, with film and television rights sold.

After years of travelling, Christina now lives in Oxfordshire with her husband Rob and a houseful of rescued cats.

Find out more about Christina Jones and her books by visiting her website:

www.christinajones.co.uk

Hubble Bubble

Christina Jones

PIATKUS

Copyright © Christina Jones 2004

First published in Great Britain in 2004 by
Piatkus Books Ltd of
5 Windmill Street, London W1T 2JA
email: info@piatkus.co.uk

The moral right of the author has been asserted

A catalogue record for this book is available from the British Library

ISBN 0 7499 3497 2

Set in Times by
Action Publishing Technology Ltd, Gloucester

Printed and bound in Great Britain by
Bookmarque Ltd, Croydon

As this isn't the Oscars, I've had to cull the list of thank-yous as they could – and should – have gone on forever. However, I must give a huge vote of thanks to everyone at Piatkus for not giving up on me, especially Gillian Green, my wonderful editor, who never, ever nagged, screamed or cried when I gave her ample opportunity to do all three. And to Emma Callagher for being equally wonderful and for steering me towards HUBBLE BUBBLE as a title instead of the awful one I'd come up with.

Thanks, of course, to Rob who never stopped supporting me in spite of everything. And to Laura, whose butterfly career changes gave me the insider low-down on the paramedic and dentistry backgrounds. Also, to all my friends who gave non-stop encouragement and who, to a man, believed HUBBLE BUBBLE would be written when I didn't.

Thanks also to the lovely staff and customers at the Weasel and Bucket who thought me being a novel-writing-barmaid was a good laugh and never complained about my spilling things on them; and my Nan (the herbal poisoner of Wessex Road) for giving me the HUBBLE BUBBLE idea and the inherited information, and last but by no means least, Nora Neibergall (Brit-Fic supporter extraordinaire) for kindly allowing me to nick the name of her feisty cat to become Mitzi's ex-husband. Lance – you're a feline star!

Chapter One

Peering through her farewell bouquet of mop-headed chrysanthemums, Mitzi wondered if it might just be worth serving ten years in prison for slaughtering Troy Haley.

True, it was neither the time nor the place: mid-afternoon in the foyer of the bank, surrounded by Chardonnay-clutching colleagues and customers – not to mention minor dignitaries and a smattering of the local press – was probably not the best venue to turn into an assassin. A dignified, middle-aged assassin, true, but an assassin nevertheless – and surely she'd be doing the financial world a kindness?

Troy Haley, looking about eighteen with his spiky gelled hair and acne scars, was peacocking – much to the apparent delight of every female employee under the age of thirty – around the nineteenth-century vaulted and chandeliered interior of the Winterbrook branch of the bank as if he owned it. Which, Mitzi supposed gloomily, was not too far from the truth. He was the new manager after all.

Mitzi shook her head in disbelief as she watched him – confident, laughing, joking and shaking hands. Troy Haley was far, far too young. Oh, not that she had anything against youth in general, of course. She had always been proud of her own youthful appearance and outlook, and enjoyed the company of younger people; she admired their optimism while at the same time pitying their misfortune to

1

be struggling through to adulthood in the uncertainties of the current climate.

She'd always considered herself doubly blessed, so much luckier than today's generation, having had a secure and snug 1950s childhood followed by the fabulous teenage freedom of the 1960s. It was all so austere now, grim and sort of scary for young people. But her overall empathy with youth still didn't detract from the fact that Troy Haley was surely far too immature to be in charge of anything. He was probably about the same age as her daughters.

Mitzi winced at the thought. Her daughters, Lulu and Doll, were scarcely able to manage their own lives, let alone the financial dealings of a high street bank. Yet somebody, in all their fiscal wisdom, had given this boy the chance to play God with the lives and accounts of hundreds of customers.

But then Troy Haley, Mitzi knew only too well, had been fast-tracked. She'd heard the term often enough since his shock appointment had been announced, along with her own early retirement, a month earlier. She'd gathered it was corporate speak for 'business graduate with loads of qualifications but sod-all experience'.

Whatever had happened to working your way slowly up the ladder? Learning your trade rung by rung? What had happened to earning promotion, not to mention gaining knowledge and dignity and respect as you went, and what sort of name was Troy for a bank manager, anyway?

Mitzi bit her lip and almost laughed at herself. She was in very grave danger of wandering into Victor Meldrew territory here – she who prided herself on her flower-child take on life and her equanimity. Equanimity was fine in its place, she decided, but when it encroached on one's own survival maybe it was another matter altogether.

She could see herself reflected in the bank's darkening windows, with the crystals of the chandeliers casting small flattering shadows. Trim and neat, and with her fashionably choppy hair gleaming in a dozen shades of dark red, she surely didn't look old enough to be someone about to retire. Didn't retired people wear a lot of buff and shuffle?

Was this it, then? The end of life as she knew it? Were daytime telly and pensioners' luncheon clubs the only thing left for her?

'That's lovely! Smile!' A girl from the *Winterbrook Advertiser* suddenly clicked a camera inches from Mitzi's face. 'Now, would you like one of you and Troy together?'

'I don't think so, thank you,' Mitzi moved the chrysanthemums to her other arm. 'After all, I'm on my way out. I think your readers will be far more interested in the New Order. Perhaps one of – er – Troy with my replacement would be more appropriate.'

'Yeah, right. Ta.'

Without apparently noticing the irony, the girl pointed her camera towards Troy and Tyler, his freshly appointed, equally gelled and spotty assistant, who was allegedly incorporating Mitzi's redundant post with Personal Banking, but who, as far as she could gather, had never taken shorthand or made coffee or organised a conference in his life.

Troy and Tyler! They sounded like presenters on a children's TV programme – and all the bank's recently installed nasal-voiced, call-centre girls seemed to have names like Chantal-Leanne and Lauren-Storm . . . and . . . Mitzi snorted fiercely into her bouquet, making the tissue paper rattle.

'Are you all right, my dear?' Mr Dickinson, the outgoing manager, touched her arm gently. 'Not too upset?'

'Upset, not really – angry, very.' Mitzi shifted the chrysanthemums again and flicked at the wrappings. 'I was just contemplating garrotting the sad little squirt with my stylish and trendy raffia tie thingy. Look at it. Not even a decent bit of ribbon.'

'At least you didn't get a bloody clock,' Mr Dickinson sighed. 'Why do they always give you a damn clock when the last thing you want to do is watch time slipping away?'

3

They looked at one another and pulled synchronised, sympathetic faces.

'Hi,' Troy Haley seemed to have shaken off the press, the fawning customers and his posse of mini-skirted admirers. 'Are you enjoying yourselves?'

'You really don't want the answer to that question–' Mitzi glared through the flowers '–do you? No, let me put it another way. How exactly do you think we're feeling after giving the last thirty-five years of our working lives to this bank? Put out to grass while we're still in our prime? Pensioned off while we still have years of useful life in us?'

Troy Haley shrugged. 'Tough one. Yeah, at the end of the day I know how you must feel about all that, but it's a whole new ball game, you know. Youth is the key. Technology is the new rock 'n' roll. Times they are a-changin'. What with call centres and computer banking and everything, no one wants banks with face-to-face one-to-ones – er – well, you get the picture.' He slapped Mr Dickinson chummily on the shoulder. 'Anyway, Nev, it'll give you lots of time to potter in your garden and play golf, won't it?'

Nev? *Nev?* Mitzi almost choked. In all the years she had been Mr Dickinson's right-hand woman she had never once called him Neville – let alone Nev. Even when they were mere youngsters, and she was starting out as a trainee bank teller with Mr Dickinson as the senior clerk, they'd always called one another Mr Dickinson and Mrs Blessing. How dare this crass, arrogant child take such liberties!

'I have no interest in gardening or golf,' Mr Dickinson said stiffly. 'I may find a little more time to do *The Times* crossword now, but even that seems a small recompense for being forcibly retired.'

Troy Haley grinned. 'Look on the bright side though, Nev. At the end of the day you'll have your pension before they all go tits up, and your lump-sum payment, and the world will be your oyster, so to speak. I'm looking forward to retiring, me. I hope to be able to pack all this in before

4

I'm forty. There's no way I want to sit at my desk until I'm
– er—'

'I'm fifty-five and Mr Dickinson isn't much older,' Mitzi
said, her voice ominously steady. 'We're probably the same
age as your parents. How do you think they would feel
about being put out to grass at our ages?'

'Actually, my parents are younger than you are and
they're already planning to step off the wage-slave playing
field, thanks to their well-handled ISAs,' Troy said happily.
'You're nearer my grandparents' age – and they're having
a ball on the Costa Dorada. Why don't you look into retirement homes in sunnier climes, Mitzi? At the end of the day,
you've only got yourself to consider now, haven't you? No
point in wasting the rest of your life hanging around a dead-
end hole like Winterbrook when you don't need to, is
there?'

Mitzi took a deep breath. 'Mr Haley, you know nothing
about me. You know nothing about my hopes and dreams,
my personal circumstances – nor my family, nor my
responsibilities, nor my home life. You know nothing.
Period. And if you find Winterbrook such an unappealing
town why, may I ask, are you here in Berkshire?'

Mr Dickinson chortled into his clock.

Troy, clearly not offended, beamed. 'Hey, chill out.
Winterbrook is just a stepping stone to bigger and better
things. Start off in the Berkshire sticks and aim higher. The
bank's new policy is for a swift staff turnaround. Eighteen
months max in one branch, then onwards and upwards . . .
You won't catch me or Tyler still being here, stuck in the
same old rut, when we're your age.'

'No, I don't suppose we will,' Mitzi nodded slowly. 'So
we must be thankful for small mercies.'

'Er, yes . . .' Troy looked uncertain. 'Anyway, must get
on. People to see and schmooze with.' He held out his
hand. 'Have a long and happy retirement, both of you.'

Fighting the urge to ram her bouquet as far down his
throat as possible as it would really not be the action of a

5

'love and peace' person, Mitzi glared with hatred at Troy's retreating, reed-slender, pinstriped figure. No doubt he worked out. All young people seemed to overeat on junk food and then work out as justification. Under Troy's regime they'd probably introduce a gym into the bank vaults. And a juice bar – whatever one of those was – and probably an Internet cafe.

Mr Dickinson was already shuffling towards the door clasping his clock. No one took any notice of him. No one said goodbye.

Picking up her sheaf of relentlessly cheerful cards and her other retirement presents – a rather pretty crystal vase and a quite substantial cheque – Mitzi suddenly wanted to be as far away from this party as possible. There was no point in staying. She didn't belong here any more. She simply wanted to go home.

Home offered its usual warm welcome some twenty minutes later, in Winterbrook's neighbouring village of Hazy Hassocks. Unlocking the door of the pre-war red-brick terraced house, as she had done daily since arriving there as a bride thirty-five years earlier, Mitzi stepped into a world of sumptuous colour, and bejewelled and beaded opulence.

The hall, midnight-blue and gold, hummed gently to the welcome refrain of the central heating. Picking up the morning's post from the fluffy cobalt doormat, Mitzi leafed through it – circulars, junk, and a free-sheet – and instantly discarded it into the wastepaper basket as she pushed open the living-room door. Easing off her stretchy ankle boots on the blackberry and damson hearth rug and hurling her wool jacket over the back of the plum velvet sofa, she gazed at her living room with sheer pleasure.

The plush, voluptuous cosiness of her house was a source of constant delight. Of course, it hadn't always been like this. When she and Lance were married it had looked much like everyone else's house: nice magnolia walls, a Dralon three-piece suite in taupe, Cotswold stone-clad fireplace, beige carpets, Royal Doulton figurines tastefully arranged.

Only since the divorce, ten years earlier, had she decided to turn *their* house into *her* home.

The October afternoon was closing in, hinting at a chill night to come, and she switched on a selection of crimson-shaded lamps before clicking on the flickering flames of the almost-real-logs gas fire. The glow was immediately reflected in the profusion of jewel-bright glass ornaments and candles which adorned every surface, illuminated the row upon row of books on the floor-to-ceiling shelves and dripped from the exotic rainbow blooms of a proliferation of dried-flower displays.

Mitzi sighed contentedly as she always did in this room and pulled the deep-purple velvet curtains against the twilight. Autumn had always been her favourite time of year – the richness of the colours outside her window were echoed throughout the house – but would she love it quite so much now? With all day, every day, alone, and the uninviting prospect of the short dark days of winter only a few weeks away?

'Get a grip, for heaven's sake,' she said sharply to herself. 'You've coped with massive life changes before. You can do it again. You don't really have much choice. And anyone who can handle being told about her husband's mistress at her own silver wedding party can deal with a bit of early retirement, so there!'

Immediately after the divorce she'd felt bereft and afraid of the future without Lance, but of course Lulu and Doll had lived at home then too, and she'd had the bank. These had been constants in a world that had been rocked by Lance's infidelity. Her daughters, the bank, her friends, and her daily routine had given her purpose and stability, and gradually she'd rebuilt her life over the next ten years, enjoyed her freedom, and eventually thoroughly relished living alone.

From today though, everything was going to be very

7

different. The girls now had their own homes with their partners, and without the bank, without working, without a real reason to get out of bed each morning, she was left to her own devices. What on earth was she going to do to fill the hours? She tried not to think about the glaring difference between being alone and being lonely. She had a feeling this might just become all too apparent before very long.

With a snort at her own self-pity, Mitzi padded into the kitchen with her new crystal vase and the chrysanthemums. The flowers would look nice here, she decided, splashing water into the vase and snapping the woody stems, releasing their cold, bitter scent. The golds, bronze and russet shades of the tightly packed petals matched her kitchen perfectly. She plonked the vase in the centre of the kitchen table, which should, as in all good country kitchens, have been ancient pine, scrubbed white, but was actually MFI and covered with a vivid yellow cloth.

'The fire's on in the living room,' she spoke to the washing basket.

The washing basket said nothing.

'And in a minute, when I've changed, I'll do supper. Okay?'

The washing basket didn't reply.

Mitzi peered at it. 'Yes, I know this is a bit out of routine, me being home early, but you'll just have to get used to it. I'm going to be around all the time from now on ...'

The washing basket rustled a bit. Two grey, fluffy, feline heads emerged from its depths. Four pale-green eyes blinked at her. Richard and Judy, almost-but-not-quite Blue Persians rescued by Mitzi when they were tiny, scraggy, half-starved kittens from the garage next door to the bank, stretched themselves, spilled slinkily from the basket and rubbed against her in delight.

Mitzi stroked each of them, loving the feel of their fur, soft like liquid silk beneath her fingers. The purrs became loudly competitive.

'Okay, I was wrong about being alone,' she kissed the tops of their heads. 'I've got you two ... and who knows, I might learn to cook, or find myself another job – or even another man to while away the hours.'

Richard and Judy narrowed their eyes at this and the purring halted.

Mitzi shrugged. 'I agree, it's not likely – but a girl can dream, can't she? Now, give me a few moments to turn into Mrs Slob At Home and then we'll find something suitable for a lonely celebration supper.'

Showering and changing into jeans and a multicoloured sweater took Mitzi less than half an hour. She surveyed her deliciously golden boudoir-for-one bedroom which had, during Lance's time, been as bland as the rest of the house but now was rich apricot and honey, with low lighting, and layers of sensuous fabrics trimmed with beads and sequins, and provided sheer, unadulterated, tarty luxury – and decided that a wardrobe purge would be high on her things-to-do agenda. She'd donate all her business outfits to the charity shop, and a major junking-out of her old life would be at least something to keep her occupied for a while. And why stop at the bedroom? Why not the whole house? Why not go for the full life-laundry treatment?

Feeling slightly more positive about filling at least the next few days, she padded downstairs, fed and watered Richard and Judy, then gazed at the stack of dinners-for-one in her freezer.

The phone rang just as she'd decided on Fiesta Chicken with a glass of something dry.

'Hi, Mum,' Doll's voice echoed cheerfully in her ear. 'How did it go? No, don't tell me, I'll be round later as soon as I've finished work. We've only got a couple more patients, so it'll be in about half an hour or so. Shall I bring fish and chips?'

Mitzi grinned. 'Fish and chips would be lovely – but won't Brett be expecting you home?'

'He'll be asleep as usual,' Doll's voice was still cheerful.

'He won't know if I'm there or not. I didn't want you to be on your own – not tonight. Shall I bring a bottle or two as well – to toast your new-found freedom?'

Mitzi smiled fondly into the phone. Her elder daughter was a perpetual optimist. 'That'll be lovely, too. Thanks, love. I'll warm the plates, chill the glasses and see you soon.'

As she was shoving the Fiesta Chicken back into the freezer, the phone rang again.

'We've got a bloody great big sausage casserole on the go,' Flo Spraggs from next door barked into her ear. 'I know you never cook for yourself. Me and Clyde thought you might like to pop round – it being a bit of a sad day and all that. He's uncorking some of his elderflower and rhubarb, special like. After all, you don't want to be on your own tonight, duck, do you?'

'Oh, Flo, that's really kind of you, but Doll's coming over as soon as surgery finishes and bringing fish and chips. Will my share of the casserole keep for you until tomorrow?'

'Bound to,' Flo said stoically. 'We always does too much. That's fine, duck, as long as you're not on your own. Tell you what, you can nip round here for elevenses in the morning, all right?'

'Lovely,' Mitzi smiled. 'I'll bring the biscuits. Thanks Flo.'

'You're welcome, duck. We just didn't want you to be lonely tonight.'

'No, well, it's going to be a bit strange of course, but – oh, there's someone at the door ... I'll see you in the morning – and thank you so much.'

Still clutching the phone, Mitzi opened the front door. Her other next-door neighbours, the emaciated elderly spinster sisters Lavender and Lobelia Banding, were standing on the doorstep in the dusk clutching small tea plates covered in tinfoil.

'We wanted to make sure you were all right,' Lavender said. 'Didn't we, Lobelia?'

'We did,' Lobelia confirmed. 'We know what it's like to be cast aside. We didn't want you to be doing anything foolish, did we Lavender?'

'You're at a funny age, young Mitzi,' Lavender said. 'Withering hormones and what have you. They can play havoc. You've been abandoned once by that philanderer you married, and we thought that losing your job might push you over the edge. Lots of people commit suicide at your age you know, especially when they find themselves unwanted.'

'So we're here to cheer you up,' Lobelia beamed. 'And keep an eye on you – oh, and we've made you some nice sandwiches. Fish paste.'

Mitzi chewed the insides of her cheeks to prevent herself laughing. 'Thank you ... oh, you're lovely – but honestly, I'm fine. And Doll's on her way over with fish and chips, so I won't be on my own. And I'm not suicidal, honestly. A bit sad, of course, but otherwise I'm coping.'

'That's the shock.' Lavender nodded, peeling back the tinfoil and chewing on a paste sandwich with relish. 'You'll be running on adrenaline right now, but you wait until the reality kicks in.'

'Um – yes, I'll bear it in mind ... look, why don't you come in? It's cold out here and—'

The Bandings needed no further invitation. In a scuttle of drab drooping skirts and much-washed cardigans, they hurtled past Mitzi and positioned themselves in front of the fire.

'Don't shut the door, duck,' Flo's voice echoed over the fence. 'I've put the casserole on the back burner. Me and Clyde thought you might like a bit of the elderflower and rhubarb to go with young Doll's fish and chips.'

Slightly stunned, Mitzi waited until Flo and her husband had sprinted up the garden path.

'Tell the truth, we saw Lav and Lob arrive,' Clyde said gruffly, kissing her cheek through his bristly moustache and clanking together an armful of wine bottles. 'We thought you might need someone to tip the balance away from the wrist-slitting.'

'Lovely and warm in here, Mitzi,' the Banding sisters twittered happily as the Spraggs trooped into the living room. 'Mind, you'll have to watch the pennies now you're out of work. You won't be able to have the heat on like this for much longer. We know what it's like to have to wrap up warm indoors and not turn the fire on until after *Coronation Street* ... Ooooh, Mr Spraggs! Some of your home-made wine! Lovely!'

'I'll get some glasses,' Mitzi said faintly. 'And maybe I'll ring the surgery and get Doll to bring some more fish and chips since this seems to be turning into a bit of a party.'

'That would be a rare treat,' Lavender pushed the last sandwich into her mouth just as Lobelia reached for it. 'We don't ever eat out. Can't afford it on our pensions. As you'll find out, Mitzi dear. You make the most of it.'

In the kitchen, Mitzi grinned at Richard and Judy who had retired to the washing basket and who were staring at her with orb-like eyes. 'Yes, I know. I know. And I thought I was going to be lonely ... Goodness me, now what's that?'

The front door had crashed open. The chatter from the living room had died.

Mitzi stepped into the hall and gazed at the heap of bags now completely blocking the doorway and then at her younger, Afghan-coated daughter leaning red-eyed against the front door.

'Hi, Mum,' Lulu sniffed tearfully through a mass of blonde braided hair. 'I've left Niall. This time he's gone too far – I'm never, ever going back. Never! I hope you won't mind but I've come home – to stay.'

Chapter Two

Mitzi stared at the bulging sports bags, several bin liners and a couple of overstuffed Waitrose carriers strewn across the hall with a real sense of déjà vu.

'Oh, dear – not again,' she smiled cheerfully at her younger daughter. 'Of course you know you're more than welcome to stay, love. Your room is all made up – but we both know you'll be back with Niall before tomorrow, so why not leave the luggage where it is and come and join the party?'

'Party?' Lulu swept back her beaded braids with a clatter and peered at Mitzi through heavily kohled eyes. 'Oh, bugger – it's not your birthday, is it?'

Mitzi shook her head. 'That was last month. You bought me a loofah and a book on transcendental meditation.'

'So I did,' Lulu looked relieved. 'So, what's this for then?'

'Oh, it's just a small impromptu bash, thanks to the neighbours, to celebrate the little matter of my enforced retirement. The end of my life. Being officially one of the oldies. Out to grass. No longer needed.'

'Shit!' Lulu looked stricken and hopped across the baggage in the hall to hug her mother. 'Is that today? Oh, Mum – I'm so sorry! I should have remembered.'

Mitzi hugged her back, aware, as always, of her daughter's slender fragility. It was like hugging a baby bird. Lulu

13

smelled of old clothes and mysterious unidentifiable musky things and dust. Mitzi wouldn't have expected Lulu to remember. Lulu had never remembered anything at the right time in her entire twenty-eight years.

'It doesn't matter, honestly. You're here now – whether by design or accident – and Doll's on her way over with fish and chips. Which reminds me, I'd better ring her and tell her to get some extra and—'

Lulu peeled off her Afghan coat and threw it across the banisters where it hovered for a moment before slithering onto the stairs. 'There! Doll knew it was today! She should have reminded me, she knows what I'm like and–' she regarded her mother fiercely '–I am not going back to Niall. Not this time. Not ever.'

Mitzi smiled gently. 'No, of course you're not. Now you go into the living room and chat to Flo and Co. I'll give Doll a ring for the extras and we'll talk about it later.'

Picking up the phone, Mitzi closed the kitchen door behind her. Richard and Judy popped neatly out of the washing basket and twisted themselves round her legs. While the phone rang on Hazy Hassocks's dental surgery reception desk, Mitzi fondled the pair of fluffy grey heads, and pondered on her daughters, wondering not for the first time how she and Lance had produced two such different children.

The phone was suddenly answered with a dragonish roar making Mitzi jump.

'Oh ... yes, hello Viv. It's Mitzi. Yes, Doll's mum. Is she still there? Oh, good, good – look, can you tell her to make it fish and chips for five this end – and for herself, of course? Oh, and can she get a veggie burger for Lu, too? Tell her I'll pay her back when she arrives. Thanks. What? No it's not my birthday. No, nothing like that. No, no celebration at all really ... What? I retired today, that's all – yes, today. Yes, it has come round quickly, hasn't it? No, I haven't got a clue what I'm going to do with myself. The church flower rota? Really?

No, that hadn't been uppermost in my mind ... no, nor the bowls club nor the Evergreens' coffee mornings – or what? Cricket teas? Good heavens ...'

She clicked the phone off before Viv could depress her even further. The church flowers, the Evergreens, the bowls club and the cricket teas were all policed and championed by old ladies. Really old ladies. Like Lobelia and Lavender. All of whom wore knitted waistcoats and kept their hats on indoors without their coats and turned first to the obituary column in the *Winterbrook Advertiser*.

Surely, surely things hadn't come to this. Not to her. Not when she still danced around the kitchen to the Rolling Stones on Radio Two and remembered doing exactly the same thing, barefoot in Hyde Park in 1969, and felt not a day older.

She scooped up Richard and Judy and kissed them both. 'It looks as though I'm now officially regarded as one of the Hazy Hassocks wrinklies. Hey-ho ... But if you ever catch me wearing the tea cosy as a hat or wandering around the garden at midnight pruning things or starting every sentence with "it wasn't like this in my day", you're perfectly at liberty to look for new lodgings, okay?'

'You want to watch that, duck,' Flo Spraggs pushed open the kitchen door. 'Talking to yourself is one of the first signs. I've just come in for some glasses for our Clyde's elderflower and rhubarb. Young Lulu's drinking it from the bottle. Says she's emotionally disturbed.'

'When isn't she?' Mitzi sighed, reaching for a selection of mismatched glasses from the cupboard over the cooker. 'She and Niall are always volcanic. Not like Doll and Brett.'

Flo took the glasses. 'Ah – but maybe it's better to be a bit sparky. Sometimes I look at your Doll and Brett and feel sorry for 'em.'

'Do you? I've always thought they were—'

'Bored to tears,' Flo nodded. 'You mark my words. They've been together since they were kiddies at school –

15

what fifteen years? Not married, just fifteen years of the same old routine. Where's the excitement in that?'

'Maybe they don't want excitement. Maybe they've found what they're looking for and have settled for contentment and familiarity. Maybe they're just happy with one another.'

'And maybe they ain't,' Flo clanged the glasses together. 'Still, you'll have plenty of time on your hands to sort both your girls out now, won't you?'

'Yes, I suppose I will.' With a last gloomy glance at Richard and Judy, Mitzi picked up the remaining glasses and followed Flo out of the kitchen.

In the living room, the Bandings were still hogging the fire, standing cheek by skinny jowl with their backs to the flickering flames, their drooping skirts lifted to allow the warmth to soak into their spindly, lisle-stockinged legs.

Clyde was talking earnestly to Lulu on the plum sofa, who, by her crossed eyes, looked as though she'd already had several glasses of elderflower and rhubarb. Mitzi hoped Doll would hurry up with the parcels of fish and chips – Lulu was definitely going to need a massive intake of saturated fat and carbs to soak up the alcohol. Clyde's home brew was almost 100 per cent proof. Rumour had it that Flo ran her moped on it, and they'd always used it to kick-start the Hazy Hassocks bonfire every November the fifth.

As Flo busily filled glasses, Mitzi smiled fondly at the odd assortment of people in the living room. They were there – with the exception of Lulu, of course – because they cared and didn't want her to be alone. Maybe it would be okay. Maybe she'd get used to all the WI-ish occupations and the cheap pensioners' lunches at The Faery Glen, the only pub in Hazy Hassocks, and not having to remember to pluck her eyebrows and shave her legs and have clean shoes ...

'We were just saying, Mitzi dear,' Lavender grabbed at her glass of wine, not moving a millimetre from the fire, 'that you'll have to find some little pastimes to keep you

16

from going – well – funny. Weren't we Lobelia?'

'We were,' Lobelia drained her glass in one gulp and without so much as a cough or an eye-watering blink. 'Being alone and being unwanted can bring untold misery. It's one of the blessings that Lavender and I have, being spinsters. We may have no money and no hope of anything wonderful happening, but we have each other. There's always someone to look out for you on the mornings when sticking your head in the gas oven looks like a good option.'

'Er – yes, yes – I can see the advantages . . .' Mitzi stared hard at the floor.

Lavender noisily sucked the last drops from her glass and held it out for a refill. 'There's some of us gets together in the select bar of The Faery Glen every Thursday afternoon, after we've collected our pensions, for a nice game of housey-housey and a schooner of Amontillado. You'd really enjoy it. Shall I put your name down?'

Not meeting Lulu's shocked gaze, Mitzi nodded. 'That's – um – very kind of you.'

'And,' Lobelia continued as both glasses were topped-up by Clyde, 'you might like to think about knitting some squares for our Christmas blankets. We always do lots and lots for the lonely old folks in the village.'

Mitzi nodded again. How long would it be before some fresh-faced forty-something knocked on her door with a festive blanket cobbled together in fawn and lovat?

'And if you find you can't make ends meet,' Lavender swayed unsteadily towards the fire, 'you could always take in a lodger. We're going to let out our spare room to eke out our pensions, aren't we, Lobelia?'

'We are,' Lobelia confirmed. 'We've put an ad in the doctor's surgery. And we'll be offering breakfast as well. Cornflakes *and* toast. We wanted a nice young professional lady. Someone who understands how things should be done – but that damn surly leftie of a doctor says we couldn't stipulate the – er – sex.'

17

'Gender,' Lavender looked shocked. 'She means gender. But no, apparently we couldn't because it's not politically correct – tosh! – so we had to leave it at "person". Most unsatisfactory. Still, at least we'll get someone medical who can help us with our little ailments.'

Mitzi privately thought that by advertising in the doctor's surgery Lav and Lob were far more likely to attract someone who was even more unstable and infirm than they were. And that any lodger unfortunate enough to take up residence would starve to death within a fortnight. She smiled encouragingly. 'It's a lovely idea, but I like to keep the girls' rooms ready for them – just in case – so I don't have room for a lodger.'

The Bandings clicked their dentures in sync at this short-sightedness.

'Oh, you'll find plenty to keep you amused without all that old duck's nonsense,' Clyde said quietly. 'Far better things to spend your time on. There's a fair bit of scandal and skulduggery afoot in Hazy Hassocks that you won't have noticed being a nine-to-fiver and away from here most of the time.'

'Really? Are Otto and Boris watering down the beer in the pub, then? Or is Mrs Elkins at Patsy's Pantry over-charging for the iced fancies?'

Clyde stroked his moustache. 'Oh, you may mock, my girl, but the village isn't the little haven of tranquillity it looks on the surface. There's a lot of bad stuff going on. You could do worse than to get yourself elected to the parish council and start sorting out the wrong 'uns.'

'Me? But I've never been political—'

'And you've never been unemployed neither,' Clyde said stoically. 'The council could do with fresh blood to purge the backhander brigade and you'll probably be glad of something to get your teeth into, seeing as you'll have—'

'—so much time on my hands,' Mitzi finished for him before he could possibly send the entire room to sleep with stories of Hazy Hassocks's similarity to Watergate. 'Yes, I know. Oh . . . that sounds like the front door opening. Must be Doll with the chips. Excuse me . . . '

Practically sprinting out of the living room and across the hall, Mitzi tugged her elder daughter through the half-open door. The dark chill evening rushed in behind her, accompanied by a spat of rain and a flurry of dead leaves.

'My saviour,' Mitzi kissed Doll expansively, kicking the door closed. 'You've just rescued me from promising to dedicate my declining years to knitting and bingo, and taking in lodgers, and boring the socks off myself on the council, and cleaning the sleaze out of Hazy Hassocks and—'

'Have you been drinking?' Doll surveyed her mother as she shed her suede coat and long woollen scarf and carefully hung them on the hall stand. 'You have, haven't you? God – not one of Clyde's concoctions?'

'Well, yes, but only a little glass. And I'm not drunk, honestly, although I can't say the same for Lulu.'

'Blimey,' Doll grinned. 'Is she here? Did she remember all on her own?'

'Not exactly,' Mitzi admitted, leading the way into the kitchen. 'She's left Niall. Again. Oh, those chips smell so good! I didn't realise how hungry I was. Shall we have plates or eat them out of the paper?'

'Paper, definitely. It'll save washing up and it always tastes better. Oh, nice flowers – chrysanths. Very funereal. Very fitting.' Doll grinned as she opened a separate parcel of piquant, steaming cod and distributed it into the washing basket. The purrs and squeaks indicated that Richard and Judy found it more than acceptable. 'So why have Lu and Niall split up this time?'

'No idea. We didn't get that far. Probably something to do with her forgetting to remember something vital as usual.'

Doll leaned against the gaily coloured kitchen table. 'More likely something to do with Niall being a Grade A prat. And before we go in there and start feeding the five thousand, are you okay? Really?'

Mitzi looked at Doll, neat in her dental nurse's uniform, her blonde hair in short no-nonsense layers – two years older and as far removed from Lulu's second-hand grungy look as it was possible to get – and nodded. 'I'm fine, love. I had a wobbly moment when I first came home, but it seems as though everyone in the village has found me something to do with my golden years. If I do all of it I won't have a minute to myself to wallow in self-pity or resentment. No, seriously, I'm perfectly okay. We both know I've survived worse.'

Their eyes met. The silver-wedding-party revelations would remain as one of the all-time awfuls in the annals of the Blessings' family history.

'And on that happy note,' Doll grinned, 'has Dad rung to see what retirement is like?'

'Not yet. But no doubt he will when he gets a private moment away from The Harpy. Now, let's feed the starving hordes ...'

The fish and chips were greeted by squeals of hysterical delight from the Bandings, gruff thanks from Clyde and Flo, and total silence from Lulu who had slid from the sofa and was curled on the floor, fast asleep.

By the time the paper had been scrunched into balls, Lulu had woken up, the bottles of wine emptied, and the neighbours despatched, it was half-past ten.

Mitzi stretched luxuriously in front of the fire, trying hard not to disturb Richard and Judy who had wandered in for the leftovers and settled on her lap. There really was something rather pleasant about the fact that she didn't have to rush off to bed, and tomorrow morning wouldn't have to be getting up at 7 for another day at the bank. She might even set the alarm as usual, then have the exquisite luxury of turning it off and cuddling down beneath the duvet for another hour or so.

She looked across the hearthrug at Doll. 'Won't Brett be wondering where you are?'

'Doubt it. He'll have fallen asleep in front of the telly, woken up about an hour ago and gone to bed. Sometimes I think he wouldn't notice if I never came home for a week.'

Mitzi raised her eyebrows. 'Well, he does work the most awful hours ...'

'True,' Doll nodded. 'And I'm used to his routine as he's used to mine. We're used to each other. There's no aggro.'

'I think me and Niall have got your share,' Lulu mumbled from the depths of the sofa. 'We're aggro personified.'

'That's because he's a poseur and a prat and you're a messy grunge babe,' Doll said cheerfully. 'And it's your fault for forgetting your station and abandoning your principles and going for a status-seeker rather than settling for a normal, horny-handed son of the soil.'

'Don't go all *Socialist Worker* on me,' Lulu glared at her sister. 'Just because I set my romantic sights a little higher than Postman Brett.'

Doll poked out her tongue and Lulu retaliated by flinging a shocking pink fun-fur cushion across the room. Mitzi smiled happily. It was lovely having them back together. Just like old times.

'Actually, I always thought that you'd both chosen the wrong men. It seemed to me that if you'd swapped partners you'd fare better—'

'Mum!' Doll and Lulu howled in harmony. 'Pul-ease! No way!'

Laughing, Mitzi shifted Richard and Judy on to separate knees and looked at Lulu. 'So what was this particular row about, then? I mean you don't have to tell us if you really don't want to—'

'Yes she does,' Doll interrupted. 'We've missed *EastEnders* – Lu and Niall are the next best thing. Have you set fire to his designer arrangement of minimalist twisted willow with your joss sticks again?'

'He said I had to give up work.'

'What?' Doll exploded. 'Oh, God – not the giving up

21

work and becoming a mother routine?'

Lulu shook her head in a castanets clack of beads and braids. 'No, of course not. He just wants me to have a proper job. One where I can wear a suit and drive a hatchback and produce business cards from my designer wallet and—'

'And pigs might!' Doll snorted into the fun-fur cushion. 'If he wanted to shack up with the businesswoman of the year he should have thought of it long before he moved you into his yuppie barn.'

'It's a loft,' Lulu said. 'A young executive's loft apartment. I think he saw me as a challenge and thought he'd convert me in time.'

'Like the loft,' Doll giggled. 'No, sorry ... go on then – why does he want you to give up your job? Apart from the fact that you spend all day in that weirdo animal charity shop amongst other people's junk and dirty clothes and earn slightly less than a paper boy.'

'That's about it really,' Lulu sighed. 'He says he's had enough of me earning a pittance and not contributing enough to the communal outgoings and always being out on protests. And when we go to his business functions he says I look like a bag lady. And he said I wouldn't know a designer label if it sat on my shoulder and introduced itself. And he says I fill his space with clutter and forget everything ... All of which is true and I'm fed up with arguing about it – so I think we've just got to accept that we're incompatible.'

'And it's only taken you three years to realise this, has it? Everyone else knew it straight away. I never understood why you got together with him in the first place. You were always chalk and cheese – me and Brett reckoned you'd end up with a *Big Issue* seller, which would have been far more acceptable. It's not even as though Niall's good looking. A good-looking prat would at least have some advantages.'

Lulu shrugged. 'I think I was a bit impressed by him. He was so – well – different from the other blokes I'd been out with. At least he had a job ... no, a profession. As a recruitment consultant he's a few steps up the status ladder than a bloody postman.'

'Ooooh! Hark at you! You who swore to forgo all material things in the worthy pursuit of animal welfare. And what the hell is a recruitment consultant anyway? He's just another flashy suit in an office trying to keep his own job by putting other poor sods into unsuitable occupations and—'

'It's better than riding a bike and carrying a sack and stuffing things through letter boxes!'

'Girls ...' Mitzi intervened as she had for more years than she cared to remember. 'Before we get too far down this well-trodden path and you start pulling one another's pigtails, does anyone fancy coffee?'

'Not for me, thanks.' Doll uncurled her long black-stockinged legs and stood up. 'I ought to be going. It's early surgery tomorrow and I'll be up to my elbows in decaying molars before you know it.' She leaned over the back of the sofa and tugged a couple of Lulu's braids for good measure. 'Cheer up, Lu. If you've really left him this time and are moving in, at least you can help Mum choose her tank tops and fluffy slippers and advise her on the pick of the daytime telly programmes—'

Mitzi beat Lulu to the fun-fur cushion by a nanosecond and hurled it at Doll's departing back.

Having made sure that Doll was safely in her car – not that there was really any likelihood of her being abducted on the front path – and waved until the tail lights turned the corner, Mitzi shivered and locked the front door behind her. The house snuggled and settled round her in cosy warmth. It was her cocoon. Once the novelty of endless days with no work had worn off it might well be different, but for the first few weeks she could surely convince herself she was on holiday, couldn't she?

Lulu's bags had disappeared from the hall and the living room was empty. There was to be no return to the minimalist loft or the unlovely Niall tonight, then. Mitzi switched off the fire and the lamps and wondered if Lulu's heart would be broken by the end of the relationship as her own had been. Probably not. She sincerely hoped not anyway. That sort of pain was something she wouldn't wish on anyone.

'Night-night,' she called to the washing basket as she turned off the kitchen lights.

Richard and Judy didn't reply, but she could hear them making cosy whimpering noises in their sleep. It was all a ploy, of course. Part of the nightly routine. They gave her half an hour to warm up the bed, then they shot upstairs and squirmed their way beneath the duvet, spending all night curled against her, as comforting as matching grey silky hot-water bottles.

All in all it had been a lovely evening, she thought, as she climbed the stairs, crossed the landing noting that the light was on in Lu's room and opened her own bedroom door. Mitzi nodded sagely to herself as she dragged on her pyjamas. Tomorrow was the start of a whole new life ... that was obviously the way to look at things. As a challenge. Setting herself new targets. New goals. Something new each day until she felt as though there was a purpose and ... the shrill of the telephone interrupted her life-plan.

'Bugger ...' She scrabbled around on the dressing table for the upstairs handset. 'Okay, okay ... Where the hell is it? And if it's Niall ringing to speak to Lulu then he'll get damn short shrift – ah!' She rescued the phone from a jumble of make-up, moisturisers and cotton-wool balls. The life-laundry was clearly well overdue.

'Hello? Oh, it's you ...' She pulled a face as she recognised her ex-husband's voice.

'Mitzi, sorry it's so late,' Lance whispered. 'But I had to call to see how you were.'

'It's nearly midnight,' Mitzi hopped around with only one leg in her pyjama trousers. 'And if you're whispering because Jennifer might hear you then it's probably better that you didn't ring at all.'

24

'Don't be like that, love. You know Jennifer doesn't like me calling you, but she's asleep – I think – and I couldn't let today go by without seeing if you'd survived.'

'Of course I've survived. And don't call me "love",' Mitzi muttered with the handset lodged beneath her chin as she finally managed to pull her pyjama trousers on. 'It was fine. It is fine. It will be fine—'

'Give the bloody declensions a break,' Lance chuckled. 'I would have come over but Jennifer didn't go to the gym and I couldn't get away.'

'For heaven's sake! Listen to yourself. You make me sound like some sort of mistress. We had a great night – the girls were here, and Flo and Clyde, and Lav and Lob came round, and we had a bit of a party.'

'Oh – good . . .' Lance sounded wistful. 'As long as you weren't alone.'

'No, I wasn't – but even if I had been it's hardly your responsibility any more is it? Look, I appreciate you phoning but everything's okay. Now hang up before Jennifer wakes up and demands to know who you're talking to. Oh, and by the way, Lu's here. She's left Niall. Goodnight.'

With a smug smirk, knowing that Lance would be rattled, and probably Jennifer wouldn't have been asleep at all and would ask probing and awkward questions all night, Mitzi clambered into bed and reached for her book. Richard and Judy soft-footed into the bedroom and landed on either side of her, making a huge fuss of trampling the duvet into the correct shape and purring loudly before settling down with twin feline sighs.

Mitzi stroked them both and smiled. She was safe and warm, Lulu was tucked up in the next bedroom, Doll was at home with Brett, and the cats were happy. What more could she ask? Okay, so now she was retired life was going to be pretty boring, but she could cope with that.

She started to read, listening to the wind spattering the rain against the window outside. The book was a blood and

25

guts crime novel, with all sorts of mayhem being thrown at the poor heroine and the tension being ratcheted up in every paragraph. Mitzi settled happily and sleepily into her pillows to enjoy the second-hand thrills. It was clearly the only way she was going to get any sort of buzz now. After all, nothing exciting was ever going to happen to her in Hazy Hassocks, was it? She'd just have to get used to being bored rigid for the rest of her life. She sighed and turned another page.

Chapter Three

It was still raining when Mitzi woke. She opened her eyes, sleepily stroked Richard and Judy and realised that she didn't have to get up. Not this morning or any other morning. With a small grunt of pleasure she hauled the duvet further over her shoulders and closed her eyes again. Another five minutes' sleep would be blissful.

An hour and a half later, staggering downstairs just in time to see a far more perky Lulu off to work, Mitzi enjoyed the lazy luxury of three cups of coffee in front of the television while still in her pyjamas. Then, having fed Richard and Judy, she showered, dressed quickly and popped next door for the promised elevenses with Flo.

As this involved four more cups of coffee, a packet of Viennese Whirls, and the Spanish Inquisition on Lulu's defunct love life, by midday Mitzi was both jizzing with caffeine and rather shell-shocked by her first self-indulgent morning.

She stood dithering on Flo's front path beneath her dripping umbrella as the burnished leaves flapped and slapped damply round her feet. Should she go home straight away and start the life-laundry? Or should she go into the village and find out exactly what was on offer for a lady of leisure in Hazy Hassocks?

It seemed so odd not only to have a choice, but also to have all the time in the world in which to make it. Used to running to a tight schedule with her day neatly mapped, this endless stretching ahead of time seemed a bit daunting. So, why not put all these extra hours to good use and do both things? Village first, and then she'd come home and have a late lunch and make a start on clearing out the years of accumulated tat. Lulu could then take it all to her animal welfare charity shop, so they'd both be happy.

Delighted that she'd made two major decisions in a matter of minutes and therefore wasn't losing either her business acumen or her marbles, Mitzi turned up the collar of her trench coat, pushed her umbrella into the wind and headed towards Hazy Hassocks's high street.

From the dental surgery at one end to The Faery Glen at the other, the high street wove its sinuous way through a random planting of stately sycamores and a mishmash of shopfronts. A few of the buildings, skew-whiff and half-timbered, dated back centuries to the original village; others had been added on and embellished over each decade since. Between them they offered practically everything anyone could wish for, if you looked hard enough. Hazy Hassocks residents only ever needed to make sorties into Winterbrook – or further afield to Reading or Newbury – for things like personal banking and superstores and the joys of Marks & Spencer.

The first thing that struck Mitzi was how many people there were. Not shoppers as such, more moochers. People, even on this wet and blustery day, drifting from shop window to shop window, simply staring. As if being buffeted by a chill north-westerly and having raindrops trickling down their necks while window-shopping on the high street was preferable to being somewhere else doing nothing at all.

And the second thing she noticed was that they were all about her own age.

Were there really that many baby boomers either out of work or retired? Had she just been added to the tip of a growing middle-aged redundancy mountain? Was every

28

industry being taken over by youthful Troy and Tyler clones?

It was thoroughly dispiriting to think that she was now part of this unseen grey army, although she realised she was luckier than most financially, at least in the short-term. Early retirement meant she'd receive her small monthly bank pension in full. Several of her kept-on colleagues had muttered jealously that their pensions would probably be worthless in ten years' time. And of course there was also the leaving present cheque which she was about to deposit in the building society. And, thank heavens, the house was paid for – the last mortgage payment had been made merely weeks before she and Lance celebrated their silver wedding.

She quickly pushed aside the other less-savoury silver-wedding memories, but once Lance had decamped with the vacuous Jennifer to her maisonette on the far side of Hazy Hassocks, he'd been very good about still paying his share of the bills while Lu and Doll had lived at home.

No, while money wasn't abundant, losing her job in the bank hadn't rendered her immediately destitute, and if she was extremely careful she might even manage to survive without working full-time.

But she didn't want to. It came as quite a shock, standing there outside Patsy's Pantry with its pyramids of fairy cakes and iced buns just visible through the steamy windows, that she actually was going to miss being useful more than anything at all. She didn't want to become invisible, another early retiree statistic. She wanted to do something with the rest of her life.

Having paid the cheque into her savings account and exchanged damp pleasantries with the three cashiers in the building society, Mitzi headed towards the library. If there was anything at all on offer in Hazy Hassocks then it was sure to be posted on the library's notice board.

There was a bit of a scrum in the doorway. As the library was housed in a long, low ex-Nissen hut, going in and coming out became somewhat confusing during busy periods. Eight people with buggies, shopping trolleys and umbrellas were thrusting out as a similar number, equipped much the same only wetter, were thrusting in.

Mitzi stepped back to let the mêlée sort itself out.

'Right old bugger, this, eh?' the man in front of her, muffled up to his dripping trilby with various scarves, muttered. 'You can go in front of me if you like, duck. If you've got books, that is. I ain't got books. I'm just going in for a bit of a sit down and a read of the paper.'

'Oh, right – no, I haven't got books either.'

The dripping trilby turned to look at her. 'You're a new one, then? For the table by the radiator? Hmmm, we might be able to fit you in. Mildred dropped dead in Big Sava last week – them queues can be the very devil – and I don't think we've replaced her yet.'

'Oh, God, I mean – er – how sad ... that is, about Mildred ... and that's very kind of you, but I was just going to have a look at the notice board.'

'Why d'you want to do that, duck? There ain't never anything of interest on there – not unless you want to go to a piano recital back in 1999, or think you might be eligible for free milk for your kiddies, or want to know how to stop thieves nicking your Ford Capri.'

Mitzi felt urgent questions needed asking, but as the ingoing crowd surged forward at that moment, she found herself suddenly propelled through the door in a sea of humanity, far closer to Trilby Man than she would have chosen, and popped out between Astrophysics and Astrology.

'Notice board's over there through the children's section, for what it's worth,' Trilby Man said helpfully. 'We'll be beyond the Mills and Boons, round the corner by the returned non-fiction trolley when you've had a look. I'll keep Mildred's chair for you and get you a paper. What do you want? Mind, you won't get the *Sun* or the *Mirror*, there's always a waiting list for them – what about the *Telegraph*?'

30

'Oh – um – well, probably not, but thank you for the offer.' Mitzi was touched by this show of friendship.

'That's all right, duck. We old-timers have got to stick together.'

Instantly incandescent with indignation and still fuelled by far too much caffeine, Mitzi growled under her breath and rather clumsily negotiated an adenoidal child who was stretched out on the floor with Jacqueline Wilson's entire backlist.

Depressingly, Trilby Man had been right about the notice board. It clearly hadn't been updated since Millennium Eve.

'Excuse me.' Mitzi had caught the eye of a very young lycra-clad librarian who was plodding round with an armful of returned celeb biogs. 'Can you help me?'

The librarian who — if her smudged make-up, body glitter and thigh-skimming frock was anything to go by — had come to work straight from clubbing, blinked sleepily. 'Yeah, of course. Well, I'll try. Just, could you make it easy and like, not shout?'

Having seen Lulu and Doll in similar states on many occasions, Mitzi nodded sympathetically and lowered her voice. 'It's about the notice board. Do you put up information about clubs and activities?'

The librarian shook her head and clearly wished she hadn't. 'We would if we were asked, but no one asks so we don't. There's nothing going on in Hazy Hassocks worth advertising.'

'So—' Mitzi indicated the drooping posters attached to the board with solitary drawing pins '—this is the sum total of recreational activities available in the village, is it?'

'Yeah. Reckon so. Sorry.'

It was all very gloomy. Mitzi murmured her thanks and being more careful not to trample on the youthful readers this time, wandered back into the grown-ups' section. Sadly Trilby Man had spotted her.

'Over here, duck!' He waved the *Sun* above his head.

'We've kept Mildred's chair!'

With a huge sigh, Mitzi headed towards the table in the corner.

There were eight of them poring over the newspapers, and the one symbolically empty chair. They were all, with the exception of Trilby Man, probably about her age. And they all looked grey faced, slightly unhealthy, very, very miserable, and – Mitzi peered closer.

'June? June Barlow? And Mick? And Sally?'

She felt almost faint with shock. She knew some of these people. They'd been friends in the village for years and were all, surely, still in full-time employment. They raised their heads and smiled at her in welcome.

'Didn't take you long to suss out the cosy corner, did it?' Mick Thornton grinned. 'I heard you were only pensioned off yesterday.'

'But ...' Mitzi was perplexed. 'Surely you're still working for the Pru? And June is in the accounts department at Boseleys, and Sally—'

'We've all been made redundant in the last few months,' June Barlow said sadly. 'Just like you. And for probably the same reasons – either replaced by younger members of staff who will take on three jobs for less money, or computers, or call centres in India.'

'Not sure which is worse,' Mick Thornton sighed. 'They package it up as downsizing, of course, but it still hurts.'

Declining Trilby Man's invitation to take up the recently deceased Mildred's place, Mitzi looked down at them all with a sense of mounting doom. 'And do you do this every day?'

'No, of course we don't.' A thin-faced woman adjusted a pair of bifocals and carefully folded the *Daily Star*. 'Not on Sundays. The library's closed on Sundays. I do my housework on Sundays.'

Sally Carey shrugged. 'You'll soon find out that the days seem to go on for ever once you get to our age, Mitzi, and you've got no career left. Things like dusting and

32

hoovering and ironing don't hold you in thrall, and there are no jobs for the over forty-fives – unless you want to go to B&Q in Winterbrook, and they've got a three-year waiting list. You can't spend all day every day making a cup of tea last for hours in Patsy's Pantry.'

'And a couple of pints in The Faery Glen soon stops being a pleasure and becomes part of the routine,' Mick nodded in agreement.

Mitzi exhaled. 'But if there was anywhere else to go or anything else to do, would you do it?'

'Of course we would,' June said vigorously. 'But there isn't. There's no evening classes any more, not even in Winterbrook, since the cutbacks. There's nothing at all. Unless you count the WI – but then that's only on once a week and isn't any use to the boys . . . so, we meet up here and—'

'Wait for death?' Mitzi was appalled. 'Surely there has to be more to the rest of our lives than this? What about voluntary work? Or, well, I don't know – but there has to be *something*.'

Trilby Man laid down the *Sun* and narrowed his eyes. 'You're not a bit of an agitator are you, duck? I wouldn't have offered you Mildred's place if I'd thought you was going to stir things up.'

'I'm not stirring things up,' Mitzi said crossly. 'But there must be even more of us than this hanging around wasting time and being unhappy in Hazy Hassocks. Surely we can do something about it?'

They looked at her expectantly. She whimpered under her breath at the futility of it all. Were they really that apathetic and despondent now? These people who had all held responsible positions and been vital members of society? These people who were still *young*? And were they, by the way they were looking at her – God forbid – for some reason expecting her to be their salvation?

'I can't help you . . . I can't even help myself . . .' she shook her head. 'No, what I suppose I mean is, we have to help ourselves. I came in here to find out what was on offer in the village for me. Clubs, societies, things to do during the day. Maybe, as I said, even voluntary work – but there doesn't seem to be anything at all.'

'Kids like your Lu have even snaffled the low-paid charity shop jobs,' June said. 'I've had my name down at Oxfam for months – and I'm prepared to work for nothing just to get out of the house. And there aren't any clubs or anything. I'd love to learn to dance properly, you know . . .'

'My brother in Bournemouth, he's older than me,' Mick leaned forward, 'and he belongs to an over-fifties football team. There's a league. And they play competitive cricket in the summer. That'd be great . . .'

'A film club or a reading group would be lovely too,' Sally said quietly. 'But they're all out of the question.'

'Why?' Mitzi frowned. 'They all sound like great ideas to keep people like us occupied and fit and interested. And we could surely organise stuff like that in the village. I'm surprised no one's thought of it before.'

'They have,' Mick said. 'We have. But it never gets anywhere.'

Mitzi frowned. 'Why on earth not? There must be funding available somewhere if money was needed, and premises – the village hall is ideal – and there must be more than enough people who want to do things. So what's stopping them er – you?'

The group round the table looked at one another, then at Mitzi, and answered in unison, 'Tarnia Snepps.'

Mitzi sucked in her breath. Tarnia Snepps. The self-styled Lady of the Manor. Hazy Hassocks's answer to Margaret Thatcher, Joan Collins and Cruella de Ville all rolled into one. 'What the hell does Tarnia have to do with any of this?'

'She's chairman of the parish council. The village hall is on her land. She runs the village.'

'Yes, yes,' Mitzi said impatiently. 'I know more than

34

enough about the Botox Queen – but you mean she won't allow the village hall to be used for any of these activities? She turns things down when they're suggested at council meetings? Why on earth would she want to do that?'

'Search me,' Mick said. 'But she does. And I know you and Tarnia have crossed swords more than once, Mitzi, but if you'd like to have another word or two with the old bat . . .'

Mitzi laughed. 'Oh, it would give me great pleasure – no, seriously – I certainly will, but in the meantime has anyone got a pen and a piece of paper?'

There was a lot of scrabbling in bags and pockets, and eventually a sheet of Basildon Bond and a dryish felt tip were produced. Mitzi scribbled her poster quickly, watched by eight pairs of doubting eyes.

'There!' She held it up. 'Now I'll stick this on the notice board and see what response we get – and I'll give Tarnia a ring, too, and find out what her particular problem is. No, no thanks—' she beamed at Trilby Man '—I don't want Mildred's chair or the *Daily Telegraph*. I'm not stopping – but I'll be in touch and let you know what I've managed to achieve.'

Before any sort of self-doubt could creep in, she practically bounded across the library and pinned the impromptu note on to the board:

> *Calling All Hazy Hassocks Baby Boomers!*
> *Bored? Lonely? Time on your hands?*
> *Feeling that your talents are being wasted?*
> *Want to learn/teach something to put the*
> *oomph back in your life?*
>
> *Ring Mitzi Blessing on HH 501 and find out more.*

Enduring the same sort of crush getting out of the library as she had experienced getting in, Mitzi eventually staggered out into the high street. She sighed with satisfaction. God

35

only knew whether her poster would bring any responses and what she'd do if it did, but at least she'd tried. And having a showdown with the despicable Tarnia Snepps was something she'd relish. Now all she had to do was go home and make a start on the life-laundry and today's tasks would have been more than satisfactorily completed.

It was growing cold in the loft. Up to her armpits in early 1970s memorabilia that had belonged to her newly married days and had elicited much oohing and aahing and some shrieks of solitary laughter during the course of the afternoon, Mitzi's life-laundry hadn't progressed very far. Richard and Judy had negotiated the loft ladder behind her, and were curled purring on top of a jumble of orange and brown geometric curtains that had once graced the living room and were now on the lopsided charity shop pile.

Mitzi stood up, brushed the dust and cobwebs from her jeans, and stretched.

'Another couple of boxes, then we'll go down and have something to eat.' She peered at her watch in the dim light of the single 40-watt bulb that dangled unattractively on a twisted flex above her head. 'And I suppose Lulu will be home soon, if she hasn't decided to return to Niall, of course.'

Richard and Judy made little snorting noises of disgust at this suggestion.

She hadn't intended to clear out the loft at all. She'd intended, after the library, to start on her bedroom. It was only while walking home, with the rain drumming on her umbrella, thinking about June and Sally and Mick and the others, that she'd realised an hour or so of throwing clothes out of her wardrobe simply wasn't going to kill enough time. And as she really didn't want to spend all her days reading papers she didn't like in the library simply to while away the boring hours, she'd decided to go for the clearing out in a big way. The whole house. Organised. Top to bottom.

The loft had always been Lance's province. Over the years he'd put things into it, and very rarely taken things out, and Mitzi had seldom ventured up the aluminium ladder. Mainly because of the spiders. This afternoon, she'd stoutly ignored the cobwebs in the dark corners and opened each box at arm's length just in case something the size of a dinner plate scuttled over the lid.

There was stuff up there which would stay forever, of course: Doll and Lu's toys and baby clothes, the slithering piles of old photographs, the oddments of furniture which had come from her parents' house and wouldn't fit into hers but had far too much sentimental value to be thrown away.

She crouched down again and blew the dust from a cardboard box which proclaimed it contained 24 packets of Rinso at 9*d*. Most of these boxes, she knew, had come from her parents' and their parents' before that. They contained the sort of personal paraphernalia that was worthless to everyone except the family concerned. Boxes and boxes of memories. It seemed sad, she thought, that by the time they'd been passed to Lu and Doll and their children, these people and their possessions would be merely remote, unknown, historical figures and have no sentimentality attached to them at all.

Mitzi lifted the lid of the Rinso box and gave a little cry of pleasure.

Granny Westward's treasure trove!

There were necklaces and bracelets of jet, strings of faux pearls, paste diamond brooches in the shape of lizards, piles of once-white lace doilies, postcards and letters, shells and pebbles collected from long-forgotten beaches: they'd all kept Mitzi amused through many a childhood illness.

'Mum!' Lulu's voice wavered from the landing. 'Are you up there?'

'Come on up, love, and see what I've found . . .'

With a lot of rattling, and to the amusement of Richard and Judy, Lulu hauled herself through the loft hatch.

'Wow!' She looked at the pile of discarded curtains. 'Cool.'

Mitzi laughed. 'I had a feeling you'd like them – and there's a lot of other tasteless stuff you can look through in a minute. How have you been today, love? Feeling better? I wondered if you and Niall—'

'I'm never going back to Niall,' Lulu hauled up her smelly Afghan coat and various layers of second-hand skirts, and knelt beside her mother. 'It's over. Really over. No doubt we'll have to have a face-to-face about it at some time, but for the moment I'm happy keeping out of his way. And yes, I've felt okay today – quiet liberated to be honest. Anyway, what about you? Have you found things to do today?'

'Surprisingly, yes. I've been really busy. It's been okay – now, come and look at this.'

'Oh, neat!'

Lulu had lifted out some of the jet jewellery and was letting the delicate black tracery spill through her fingers. Mitzi watched with pleasure as Lu delved further into the box, her eyes shining. Doll, she knew, was nowhere near as sentimental, and it was lovely to see these ancient possessions giving so much delight.

'We never get anything as beautiful as this at the shop ... and blimey, look at this!' Lulu pulled a battered and tattered book from the depths of the box. 'Is it a diary? Could it be Great-Granny Westward's secret confessions? Maybe she had a royal lover or something really scandalous.'

'I don't think so,' Mitzi removed Richard and Judy from the box and took the book from Lulu. 'She was a bit of a tearaway by all accounts, and there have been one or two dubious stories about her, but – crikey!'

'What?' Lulu stopped stroking the cats and looked over Mitzi's shoulder. 'What is it? Are you ninetieth in line to the throne or something?'

Mitzi grinned. 'It's not a diary full of salacious secrets at all. It's a cookery book – it must be all her home-made things – look, all the recipes are handwritten and they all have funny names.'

38

'No good to you then,' Lulu teased. 'You only know about M&S ready-made meals and how to defrost pizzas.'

Mitzi nodded ruefully. The art of cooking had passed her by. Like most people she had been inspired by Jamie and Nigella making it look so damn easy-peasy on the television. She'd rushed out and bought all the books. They stood, untouched, in pristine rows on their shelf in the kitchen. The recipes had sounded mouth-watering, the photos looked good enough to eat, but when it came down to actually *making* any of them, it was a different matter.

'I could learn,' Mitzi carefully turned the brittle, yellowing pages covered in dark-blue looping handwriting. 'I've got loads of time now, and I really should be able to cook properly. I could start with these – after all, they're clearly family recipes ...' She grinned at Lulu. 'I know, I'll have a bit of a practice and then I'll get Doll round and you two can give me your verdict. We could have a girlie dinner party courtesy of Granny Westward.'

'Yeah, right,' Lulu looked dubious. 'And I'll bring the Alka-Seltzer and keep the number of Pizza Express to hand. Good God – you can't cook that one, I don't even recognise the names ... what the hell are Grains of Paradise? And I bet Big Sava doesn't sell Job's Tears.'

'Hmmm ...' Mitzi ran her finger down the list of ingredients. 'Maybe you're right – but I can get pomegranate and dandelion and sunflower and walnut.'

'It's hamster food,' Lulu giggled. 'Granny Westward must have been having a laugh.'

'No, I don't think so – I think these are all old names for herbs and garden plants and things. I'll look them up and try to find modern equivalents.' Mitzi was suddenly fired with enthusiasm. Here was something she could really get her teeth into – in more ways than one. 'You never know, I might find I've got a flair for making these old dishes.'

Lu pulled a face. 'Or you might just earn yourself a new reputation as the Hazy Hassocks poisoner. I don't suppose Granny Westward was a sort of hooky-nosed, warty-faced, cauldron-owning, old biddy, was she?'

'For heaven's sake,' Mitzi laughed, 'Granny Westward was a down-to-earth soul who lived in a council house in a nice little cul-de-sac in Hermitage – not a broomstick-riding witch! Anyway, we'll have to give this one a go first, Lu – look what it's called . . .'

'Wishes Come True Pie,' Lulu peered over her mother's shoulder. 'Well, yeah, okay,we could all do with some of that.'

'Right,' Mitzi closed the book and stood up. 'Wishes Come True Pie it'll be. Next Friday night. Just the three of us. I'll stick faithfully to the recipe and we'll see what happens.'

Lulu picked up Richard and Judy and scrambled to her feet. 'Okay, but we'll all have to remember the old saying: be careful what you wish for because it might just come true.'

Mitzi laughed as she negotiated the ladder. As long as she managed to cook Wishes Come True Pie without burning the house down on Friday night she'd be more than happy.

Chapter Four

WISHES COME TRUE PIE

A good handful of sunflower seeds
A pestle of pulverised walnuts
A sprinkling of desiccated dandelion (sun-dried)
A handful of pomegranate seeds
A good pinch of sage
Small chunks of root vegetables – onions, carrots, swedes,
  turnips
A few grains of ginseng
A little chopped bamboo root
Job's Tears to taste
A handful of Grains of Paradise
A pinch of Tonka
Two teaspoons of liquid amber
Salt and pepper and powdered mustard in equal quantities
  to taste

Short-crust pastry rolled with chopped endives

A rich thick gravy made from kitchen stock

Must be served with white and green vegetables – white
  for lasting happiness, green for luck.
Mix all ingredients in a large bowl.

Add gravy/stock.
Mix well.
Cover with endive pastry.

Cook in a moderate oven for one hour and a half or until
pastry golden brown and ingredients softened.
Serve immediately with vegetables.

Note: For wishes to come true, the wishes must be made
while eating the first mouthful. The wishes must be
personal. Against all folklore traditions, the wishes in this
case must be spoken aloud. This pie will always make
wishes come true, so a warning – be careful what you wish
for.

'Spit – er – sorry, rinse please, Mrs Clackett.'

Swivelling away from the patient, Doll free-wheeled
across the dental surgery on her neat little chair to tap the
updated notes into the computer.

Mr Johnson, the dentist, was helping Mrs Clackett to her
feet with great solicitude, as well he might, Doll thought,
seeing that the extraction had just cost her not only an
incisor, but also an arm and a leg.

As Mrs Clackett was the last patient of Friday afternoon,
there was an end-of-term atmosphere in the surgery.
Fortunately for Doll's social life, Hazy Hassocks didn't
subscribe to weekend emergency dental treatment, so if the
villagers couldn't confine their toothache to Monday to
Friday, they had to seek relief elsewhere.

'Got anything nice planned for the weekend?' Mr
Johnson was rinsing his hands with relish. He asked her the
same question every Friday. 'You and Brett doing anything
special?'

'Just the usual.' Doll whizzed round the surgery, shoving
instruments in the steriliser and wiping up any traces of
tooth chippings, blood spatters and encrusted amalgam.
'We'll be wining and dining with the A list, and then

42

clubbing all night in London's latest hot spots.'

Mr Johnson kindly laughed at her oft-repeated response. 'The celeb lifestyle must get so boring. So, it's a swift Saturday night pint at The Faery Glen and hours of telly, is it?'

'Actually, there is a bit of a break in the routine – I'm going to my mum's for dinner tonight.' Doll pulled on her coat. 'She's cooking.'

'Bloody hell. Retirement is clearly taking its toll. I've always told your mum that half her plaque problems are due to her constant diet of ready-made meals. She reckoned it was better than poisoning herself with her own culinary efforts.' Mr Johnson flicked off the lights in the surgery. 'Has she been taking lessons in her spare time?'

Doll shook her head. 'She found an old family recipe book in the loft – traditional country cooking stuff. She's wants to try it out on me and Lulu. We're not overly optimistic.'

They stepped out into the blustery darkness. Doll shivered. Sad to think that an evening of Mitzi's iffy cooking was preferable to an evening of watching Brett snoring beside the fire.

'Well, good luck with it.' Mr Johnson hurried towards his latest retro toy, a British racing green Jensen Interceptor. 'Rather you than me. And if you're not in on Monday I'll know the reason why – oh, and don't forget, Mr Earnshaw starts on Monday, too. I'll probably put you in with him, and have young Tammy nursing with me. You know how Tammy tends to scream when things go a tad awry. Best not scare him too much on his first day.'

Doll nodded. The new dentist, Mr Earnshaw, was to replace old Mr Wiseman who had mercifully been retired before his personal fondness for Novocain had led to criminal proceedings. She and Tammy and Viv the receptionist had hoped that the new dentist would be sex on legs. It would, they'd asserted during many a tea break, liven things up a bit.

Sadly, on the day that Joe Earnshaw had been appointed, Viv had been at lunch and Doll had been in Winterbrook at the denture cast manufacturers returning a full set of false teeth allegedly tailored for Miss Fenwick, which had, when inserted, made her look like an extra from *Night of the Living Dead*.

Tammy, who had been entrusted to report back on Joe Earnshaw's phwoar rating, had wrinkled her snub nose. 'Ancient!' she'd said scathingly. 'Dead old! Nearly as old as Mr J and Mr W!'

'He can't be that old,' Doll had frowned. 'He's fresh out of college.'

'Yeah, but only after a mid-life career change,' Tammy had said. 'He used to be a brickie.'

Mr Johnson leaned from the window of the Jensen. 'Enjoy your meal, then. And don't forget to floss afterwards! Toodle-oo!'

Doll watched the Jensen roar away into the darkness of Hazy Hassocks. Mr Johnson updated his classic sports cars on a regular basis. As she wrestled with the door of her elderly Polo she pondered as always on the huge anomaly between the joint incomes of a dentist and a solicitor, as the current Mrs Johnson was, and a dental nurse and a postman.

Not that she was materialistic, she thought, chugging away from the surgery. Oh, she had a few more material needs than Lulu – everyone had more material needs than Lulu – but nothing more than the basics. It would be so lovely to be able to afford a bit more than the basics . . . a proper holiday . . . a wedding and a baby.

The bungalow was in darkness when she pulled up outside. Sighing, Doll unlocked the door and stepped into the chill bleakness. Brett hadn't remembered to fix the timing on the central heating again. He'd be asleep in front of the full-bore electric fire, with the living-room door closed, leaving the rest of the house to shiver.

As she'd suspected, the living room was like a blast

furnace. The television chattered to itself in the darkness and Brett's snoring drowned out the manic screeching from the cartoon characters. Turning down the television and switching on the lights, Doll looked round in dissatisfaction.

Brett was very much magnolia-man when it came to interior decor, as Lance had been. The bungalow was clean, neat and paid testimony to a bland lack of imagination. Not, Doll thought, that she'd ever go quite as mad with colour as her mother had, but a few soft edges, a touch of cosiness – pictures, cushions, plants – surely wouldn't hurt? Brett, sadly, considered such fripperies far too girlie. He became quite sulky and dogmatic when Doll suggested making changes and she'd long become too apathetic to insist. At the tender age of thirty, Brett was a bit of a dinosaur really.

He snored and stirred in his armchair as Doll looked at him, not with passion, but with an almost motherly affection. He was tallish and slimmish and fairish. Not ugly, not handsome, not anything particularly outstanding. He was hardworking and stoic and simply part of her life.

They'd known each other since they were fifteen. Neither of them had had anyone else. They shared a history, and rubbed along okay. The spark, such as it had ever been, had spluttered and died years before, but she still couldn't imagine her life without him in it. Sad then, that they had probably stayed together out of habit and fear of the unknown.

Hurrying across the hall and into their icy bedroom, Doll pulled off her uniform, changed into jeans and jumper, and pounded across the hall again. Making a cup of tea and beans on toast, she elbowed her way back into the living room with the tray.

'Brett . . . Brett . . . wake up. I've made your tea.'

He stirred and blinked at her. 'What? Oh, I must have dropped off.' He hauled himself upright and took the tray. 'Thanks. Where's yours?'

'I'm going to Mum's, remember? She's cooking for me and Lulu. A sort of girlie supper party.'

Brett attacked his beans on toast and didn't look up. 'Oh, yeah. Okay. I'll probably be in bed when you come home, then.'

In bed and asleep, Doll thought sadly. As always. She longed for a baby, but to have a baby you had to have sex, and to have sex it helped if you were both awake at the same time.

When she pulled up outside her mother's house she'd almost expected to see the emergency services already in situ. It seemed impossible that Mitzi could cook an entire meal without setting fire to something or poisoning herself while tasting her concoction.

'In the kitchen, Doll!' Mitzi called. 'Come on through, love.'

'Jesus!'

Doll inhaled the fumes emanating from the cooker – unknown aromatic herbs and spices served to produce a rich exotic fug which wreathed and swirled round the kitchen – blinked at her mother and then, finally, at the devastation.

Mitzi, with a towel tied round her waist, and her sleeves rolled up, was red faced, and her hair was standing on end. The kitchen looked even more scary. Not a work surface was visible, not a pot, pan or spoon appeared to be unused. Heaps of dried leaves, unidentifiable lumps of vegetation, and small bowls of peculiar-smelling unguents were scattered across the table top. Saucepans bubbled happily on the hob, the oven was radiating heat, and Richard and Judy were peering nervously over the top of the washing basket.

Fondling their grey heads, Doll tried not to laugh. 'Um – how's it going?'

'Great, love. Great.' Mitzi blew a strand of hair away from her face as she peered at the ancient recipe book. 'I've no idea why I didn't crack cooking before. It's child's play.'

46

Doll looked at the ingredients with mounting trepidation: bamboo, ginseng, pomegranate, sage, sunflower seeds and walnuts, she recognised; others she simply didn't. 'Er – is it going to be a sort of soup?'

Mitzi shook her head. 'No, love. It's a pie. A Wishes Come True Pie – served with fresh greens, because according to Granny Westward's notes green brings luck, and mashed potatoes because there has to be a white veg for lasting happiness. Lu was right of course, I couldn't get all the right stuff from Big Sava, but Herbie's Healthfoods helped a lot – and I've sort of improvised a bit with substitutes for things like the liquidamber and the tonka . . .'

'Oh, good,' Doll said faintly, now wishing she'd had beans on toast with Brett. 'Is there anything I can do?'

'No thanks. I'm all under control.'

Doll grinned. 'Glad you think so. Where's Lu? Still at work?'

'No, she's popped over to the flat to pick up some more of her stuff. It's Niall's night out with the boys so she reckoned she'd manage to avoid him – again. I've told her dinner will be ready at eight-thirty-ish.'

Doll pulled a face. It looked as though Lu and Niall were really kaput this time, then. Poor Lu. She'd had such high hopes. Doll had never thought the snobbish, desk-bound and upwardly mobile Niall was right for her sister, but at least their relationship was emotionally explosive. Volatile. All Lulu's affairs had been pretty lively. Unlike her and Brett.

The phone shrilled in the hall.

'Can you get that, love?' Mitzi waved a wooden spoon like a baton. 'And if it's for me can you say I'm busy and I'll ring back?'

Doll picked up the receiver, listened to the babbling voice, then put her hand over the mouthpiece. 'I think it might be a funny phone call, you know. It's someone called Christopher who says he's replying to your advert and that he's keen to meet up and – Jesus! You haven't put a Sad

47

Singles ad in the *Winterbrook Advertiser*, have you?'

Mitzi waved the wooden spoon a bit more. Some green gunge dripped glutinously to the floor. Richard and Judy pounced on it, sniffed it, then retreated growling. 'Don't be daft – it's for my BBC – Baby Boomers Collective, Doll, love. Remember? Can you just take his name and number, what he's interested in, and write it in that little book there and tell him I'll give him a ring tomorrow? Ta.'

Doing as she was told, Doll added Christopher – pyrotechnics and heavy metal, beneath Avis – light opera, Dorothy – snooker, Ronnie – exotic dance, and James – needlework.

'Blimey, there are loads of them in here!' She flicked through the notebook in amazement. 'Just what are you going to do with them all?'

'Goodness knows,' Mitzi grinned. 'I'm going to book the village hall and get them all together to start with, and then see where we go from there. Oooops – this doesn't look quite right. Can you give me a hand? Grab this . . .'

Hurrying back into the kitchen, Doll grabbed. The suppurating saucepan smelled like burnt socks. With her eyes watering, she sat down at the table and peered at it. 'What the hell is this?'

'Desiccated Lady's Mantle.' Mitzi elbowed a lot of clutter from the table top and sat opposite her. 'Herbie's Healthfoods said it was used in love potions in ancient times, which is why I'm using it in place of the Grains of Paradise, which again probably explains why it hasn't – er—' she consulted the recipe book '—coagulated, quite as it should.'

Doll watched with amusement as her mother propped Granny Westward's book in front of her then carefully selected a handful of bamboo, a pinch of sage and a few walnuts, and hurled them into a small bowl. Clearly not having the required pestle and mortar, Mitzi was improvising with the bowl and the ubiquitous wooden spoon. The violent crushing motion seemed to please her.

'I'm imagining that this is Jennifer . . . and this bit is that appalling Troy-the-Bank . . . and this, oh joy, is the adenoidal Tyler,' she said happily. 'It worked a treat with the pomegranate. I pretended the pomegranate was Tarnia Snepps's head.'

Doll laughed. 'You and Tarnia are going to cross swords over the village hall, you know that, don't you? She won't be happy at all about you organising activities without her calling the shots.'

'I'll deal with that when it arises. Right now I've got other things to think about . . .' Mitzi's tongue just protruded as she concentrated on adding the right amount of powdered ginseng to the bowl. She gave it all a rather haphazard beating then stopped and peered at it. 'Do you think it needs an egg?'

'I think it needs a decent burial,' Doll said dubiously, watching as her mother crossed the kitchen, removed some speckled ready-rolled pastry from the fridge and slopped it into a shallow dish before spooning the various concoctions into it, slapping the pastry lid on the top and hacking away at the ragged edges. 'Why is the pastry spotty? And if you're only just making the pie, what's in the oven?'

'The pastry isn't *spotty*.' Mitzi opened the oven and gave a little shriek as a red-hot blast shot out into the kitchen. 'It's *textured* – with chopped endive. Granny Westward's book says that endive is helpful in matters of the heart. Not clear on whether she meant circulation or love actually . . . and this—' she tugged a bubbling dish from the cooker '—is a bit of an extra just in case anyone wants seconds.'

'Er – right.' Doll stood up. 'As it looks like a battle zone out here, I guess we're eating in the living room, so I'll just go and set the table then, shall I?'

With the table laid with rainbow plates, blue-handled cutlery, three odd champagne flutes, four purple candles in pink holders, red paper napkins left over from last Christmas, and a centrepiece of the orange and yellow chrysanthemums remaining from Mitzi's leaving bouquet, Doll thought it set the room off a treat.

Putting a Mott the Hoople CD on the player and leaving Abba for afters, she turned off all but one of the table lamps, and with the candle glow and the fire's flickering flames, the living room looked wonderfully cosy. If only the bungalow could be half so welcoming.

'Right,' Mitzi bustled in carrying a steaming vegetable dish, 'Lulu's just come in, and everything's ready – so I'm prepared for the moment of truth. No, you sit down love – I'll bring the rest in.'

As Doll sat, Mitzi and Lu passed in the doorway. Richard and Judy shot into the room between them and settled down for a happy reciprocal grooming session in front of the fire.

'Wow.' Lu looked around with pleasure as she plonked herself opposite Doll, shaking her beads and braids away from her face. 'This all looks gorgeous. And it's so lovely and warm. I've just come back from Niall's bloody freezing loft and it looked so stark and harsh after being back at home for a while.'

'Just what I was thinking about the bungalow,' Doll reached for one of the many bottles on the table and scrutinised the label. 'Oh hell, it's one of Clyde's. Well – are you ready for this?'

Lu grinned, helping herself to a hefty glass of parsnip and raspberry. 'More or less. We'll have to eat it anyway so as not to hurt her feelings, and at least the veg smells okay.'

'And so does the rest of it,' Mitzi backed into the room carrying a loaded tray, 'even if I say so myself. I'm really proud of the way this has turned out.'

'So you should be . . .'

Doll and Lu surveyed the pie with ill-disguised astonishment. It appeared perfectly normal – and smelled wonderful. Still, Doll thought, the proof of the pudding and all that.

Mitzi, her hair still awry, but looking a little less harassed, dished up three portions. Doll continued to look at her plate in surprise. Considering she knew more or less what was in it, it had turned out looking like one of those 'and here's one I made earlier' jobs that the telly chefs served up. However, as you could never be too careful, she topped up everyone's glasses with Clyde's toxic home brew.

'To my first venture into cookery—' Mitzi looked more amazed than any of them '—and to making our wishes come true . . .'

Giggling, they clinked glasses in the firelight as Mott the Hoople crooned in the background.

'And yes, it's entirely suitable for vegetarians.' Mitzi beamed at Lulu as she reached for the greens. 'Granny Westward must have known. Right – gravy anyone? More potatoes? Okay – so now for the good bit. The Wishes Come True only works if you wish when you take the first mouthful, or so it says in the book.'

Lu poured more wine. 'What are we all wishing for? Weekly lottery wins and size ten figures for ever?'

Mitzi laughed. 'No way. And none of the Miss World universal peace and health and happiness for man, woman and animal-kind, either – we all want that anyway. According to Granny Westward's notes, the wishes must be personal and contrary to tradition, spoken out loud. So, who's going first?'

'You must,' Doll said. 'You've done all the work. Go on then.'

Mitzi sat back in her chair, her loaded fork hovering. 'Well, as I've been feeling a bit lonely and adrift since being forced into retirement, I'd really like to feel needed and useful again. I want a purpose in life and I want to be loved. For myself. I'm going to wish for that. For someone to really need me and love me.'

Doll pulled a face. 'That's so boring, Mum! Everyone loves you and needs you anyway – me and Lu and the

51

neighbours and your friends – and look at all those people who've been ringing up for your baby-boomers thing ... Nah, you should wish for something much more personal.'

Mitzi pushed the forkful of food into her mouth and chewed. 'Far too late, I'm afraid. I've done it – oh, and this tastes okay. Now you two ...'

Lu topped up her glass again and lifted her own fork. 'Easy-peasy. I wish someone would give me Heath Ledger – in his scruffy, shaggy-haired, drop-dead sexy Knight's Tale mode, not all cropped haired and straight-looking, of course – as a plaything.'

'Lu!' Doll and Mitzi howled in unison. 'That's not in the spirit of the game at all!'

'Tough,' Lulu gulped down her first mouthful. 'That's what I've wished for and oh, hey, Mum – this is great. Really great ... Go on then, Doll – what's your wish?'

Doll took a deep breath. She'd been wishing for so much earlier in the evening, hadn't she? Holidays, more money, sex ... They all seemed a bit too personal and grasping somehow. Oh, of course this was all a load of hokum, but if, just if, it worked. 'Well – getting married and having kids would be lovely – but there's fat chance of that at the moment, so to get things kick-started in the right direction I'll settle for wishing that Brett would show some impromptu romantic inclinations ...'

Lulu frowned. 'Oh, pul-ease! That's too disgusting to even contemplate. Postman Brett on the rampage – yuk! Still, if it's what you really want ... go on then – eat it or it won't come true.'

Doll looked down at the pie. Years of living with Brett had deadened her taste buds to all but the plainest of plain cooking. Even a touch of coriander was considered exotic in the bungalow. Oh, well. She took a mouthful of the pie. It tasted unusual, but certainly not unpleasant. The textures all blended into rich creaminess and even the spotty pastry melted in the mouth. She smiled and forked up some more.

'Congratulations, Mum – I think you've found your new

forte. Watch out Nigella, is all I can say.'

Mitzi went pink with pleasure and, staggeringly slightly, swapped Mott the Hoople for Abba.

The doorbell chimed faintly. Richard and Judy turned pale green eyes towards the hall.

'I'll go,' Mitzi said. 'It's probably Lav and Lob – they knew I was cooking and they'll be on the lookout for leftovers. Whoops! My legs have gone all tingly – must be too much of Clyde's parsnip and raspberry.'

Scraping her plate and surprising herself by reaching for seconds, Doll watched her mother make a sort of zigzag exit from the living room. 'I feel a bit woozy myself . . .'

'Mmmm, me too.' Lu rattled her braids. 'And this pie really is ace. Hey – you don't think it's this that's made us all light-headed, do you? You don't think Mum has really unleashed some sort of *magic*?'

'Don't be daft,' Doll tried to focus. 'It'll be Clyde's booze . . .'

They smiled squiffily at one another across the table, listening as Mitzi unlocked the front door. It was all very peace and love. Jigging gently, they joined in a very giggly duet of 'Gimme Gimme Gimme a Man After Midnight'.

The giggles suddenly died as they heard Mitzi scream.

Chapter Five

'Oh, my God!'

Mitzi clung to the bottom banister and gawped at Heath Ledger standing on the doorstep.

'I'm really sorry to have startled you,' he grinned at her, his teeth very white in the gloom. 'Are you okay?'

Mitzi nodded. The twinkly, floaty feeling seemed to have robbed her of her powers of speech. This vision in front of her, young, tall and beautiful, his perfect features tanned, his shaggy blond-streaked hair falling towards his dramatic- ally blue eyes, surely couldn't be real.

'Er—' she gurgled a bit, wishing that her legs would stop shaking '—um, yes, I'm fine, I think.'

'This is number thirty-five, isn't it?' Heath Ledger still looked concerned. 'Only I couldn't quite make out the numbers from the street.'

'Yes – that is, no,' Mitzi corrected herself quickly. Goodness – the poor boy was going to think she was doolally. What on earth was wrong with her brain? 'We're thirty-three. Thirty-five is next door.'

He grinned a bit more. 'Oh, right. Then I'm really sorry to have – oh . . .'

He was staring into the hall. Still clinging to the newel post for support, Mitzi turned her head carefully to follow his gaze.

To the loud background accompaniment of 'Gimme

Gimme Gimme A Man After Midnight', Lulu and Doll were shoulder to shoulder in the living-room doorway. They too seemed to have lost the power of coherent speech.

But not for long.

'Mum . . . are you okay? I mean—' Lulu's jaw dropped. 'Wow!'

'We heard you shout and . . . blimey . . .' Doll blinked. 'That was quick. She only wished for him a few minutes ago.'

'This . . . this – um – gentleman is looking for next door,' Mitzi explained. 'The Bandings, that is, not Flo and Clyde's.'

'Really?' Doll raised her eyebrows. 'Did something go wrong with the wish, then? What on earth would Lav and Lob do with Heath Led—'

'I'm so sorry to have disturbed you all,' he repeated, still smiling across Mitzi's shoulder towards Doll and Lulu. 'It may be too late to call on—' he scrutinised a piece of paper '—Lavender and Lobelia at this time of night.'

'They certainly go to bed quite early,' Mitzi agreed, forming her words carefully as her lips seemed to have gone numb, 'but if there's a light on in their front room you'll still catch them.'

'Okay, thanks. I'll give it a go. My apologies again. Goodnight.'

And with a long last look into the hallway, he disappeared down the dark path in a blur of faded jeans and much-washed black sweater.

Mitzi slowly closed the door. Of course he wasn't really Heath Ledger. Of course it was just a coincidence. Of course wishes didn't come true. Did they?

Lu exhaled heavily, rolling her Nefertiti eyes. 'Wow. Was he *fit* or *what*?'

'Very hot.' Doll raised her eyebrows. 'And Heath Ledger to a T. I reckon Granny Westward knew exactly what she was cooking up.'

Giggling, they all trooped back into the living room.

Richard and Judy were sitting on the table licking the plates clean. Mitzi hoped their wishes didn't involve the massacre of multitudinous wildlife to be presented to her under the duvet, still kicking, in the early hours.

'Anyone else want a drink? I think I need one.' Mitzi pushed her fingers through her hair, humming 'Waterloo' along with Abba. 'And I hope it wasn't the cooking, but I'm feeling pretty peculiar.'

'So are we,' Doll agreed, sitting down heavily and reaching for yet another of Clyde's bottles. 'But that may be because of the excitement of having a Heath lookalike on the doorstep rather than anything toxic you added to the pie.'

Lu still had a faraway look. 'Anyway, you only used herby things, didn't you? Granted not your usual spice-rack stuff, but nothing that could be classed as a banned substance. And don't half the royal family indulge in herbal remedies?'

'That's a recommendation, is it?' Doll laughed a little too loudly. 'Look at what it's done for them – there's not a normal one amongst them. Oh, crikey – I feel as high as a kite.'

'But it's not a nasty too-much-to-drink feeling, is it?' Mitzi frowned. 'It's sort of fizzy and floaty and rather lovely.'

Sinking into the fun-fur cushions on the sofa, she smiled to herself. Maybe the feeling was exactly what Granny Westward had intended. They'd had to find their own amusements in small villages even a few decades ago. Why wouldn't people spice things up a bit with one or two readily available hedgerow ingredients in their recipes? And if the rather potent results were then claimed as magical, where was the harm in that? It was only a bit of fun, after all. She really must study the book more closely and see what other entertainment could be found amongst its pages.

'Oh, my God!' Mitzi struggled to her feet. 'I must be mad!'

'What's up?' Lulu and Doll spoke together.

Despite her light-headedness, Mitzi was already at the living-room door. 'Me – I'm what's up. I've sent that bloke – gorgeous as he was – round to two elderly ladies at this time of night! Me! I'm supposed to be sensible and caring and keep an eye on them – and he could be a mugger or a rapist or a murderer or anything.'

'Course he couldn't.' Lu laughed. 'He was lovely.'

'And I'm sure there have been a lot of very handsome serial killers ...' Mitzi tugged at the front door. 'I won't be long.'

Because she could no longer feel her feet, the short journey down her own path and up that of the Bandings was a rather odd experience. However, clinging to Lav and Lob's porch, she leaned on the doorbell.

Eventually, Lavender, wearing a moth-eaten dressing gown and Celtic football socks, pulled the door open and peered across the security chain. 'Oh, hello, Mitzi. Are you all right? Your hair looks funny and your face is all shiny. You're not ill, dear, are you? Ah!' Lavender's eyes widened pleasurably. 'You're letting yourself go, dear, aren't you? You've spent one too many lonely nights with the gin bottle and have reached the cry-for-help stage. We knew it would happen before long. Come along in, dear. Lobelia and I will cheer you up.'

There was a lot of metallic scrabbling and Lavender flung the door open.

Stepping into the hall, which was fractionally colder than the autumnal night outside, Mitzi smiled. 'Thank you, but really I'm fine. I'm not alone, the girls are with me – we've had a lovely evening – but there was a young man at our door just now asking for you, and I thought I ought to come and check if he'd ... that is, if you'd let him in. Of course, I know you wouldn't, but—'

'Oh, yes we did, dear.' Lavender nodded happily. 'He's upstairs in the bedroom with Lobelia.'

Jesus! Mitzi whimpered. 'Okay, now don't panic. You

ring the police and I'll go up and see what I can do.'

'Why would we need the police, dear?' Lavender queried. 'We haven't got any more room. And anyway it would only be that rather dim Tom Hodgkin at this time of night – unless of course that nice young sergeant is on duty in which case we could perhaps squeeze them in and—'

'We're not inviting them to a damn party, Lav. It doesn't matter about the numbers. This could be serious. Just ring them and say this man has forced his way into your house and that he's taken your 82-year-old sister hostage and—'

'Lobelia is eighty-one and a half,' Lavender said crossly. 'And I'm seventy-nine. And she's hasn't been taken hostage. Are you quite sure you're all right, Mitzi?'

'Lav, look, you really should never, ever let strange people into your home. You know that don't you?'

'Yes, dear, of course we do. We're not senile, you know. But he's not a stranger. Dr Merrydew sent him. Because of our ad in the surgery. Good heavens Mitzi, surely you remember? We advertised for a lodger, dear. And he's here. Look . . .'

Heaving a huge sigh of relief, Mitzi realised that she'd been shaking violently. Her legs were really quite wobbly, so she sank down on the bottom stair, painted 1950s cream with a faded dusty runner in sepulchre brown, as Lav unfolded a piece of paper.

'There. See? A written recommendation from Dr Merrydew. This young man is newly attached to the hospital at Winterbrook and there's been an accommodation problem – his digs were double booked – and Dr Merrydew said he should try us. He's a paraplegic.' Lavender beamed. 'And his name's Shag.'

'*What?*' Mitzi tried to focus on the scribbled writing. 'No, no – this says he's a *paramedic*. And his name's Shay, Lavender. Shay.'

'Oh,' Lavender peered at the note. 'Yes, well, maybe. Dr Merrydew's writing is practically indecipherable. It's why everyone has to swap their prescriptions at the pharmacy. Do you remember when your Lance needed some ointment for his verruca and he got Mrs Elkins's Arthur's steroid cream instead? Didn't we all laugh? I mean, not too bad for your Lance of course, but absolute murder for Mrs Elkins's Arthur's haemorrhoids. And do you remember when—'

'Yes, yes . . .' Mitzi pulled herself to her feet. 'And I can see that everything's okay, even if it is a bit late for anyone to be looking for lodgings, but—'

Any further assurances were interrupted by Lobelia, beaming almost as widely as Lu had been, and the gorgeous Shay, making their way downstairs.

'Oh, Mitzi – lovely to see you. Were you feeling suicidal, dear? This is Shay Donovan, our new lodger. Mr Donovan, this is Mitzi Blessing, our next-door neighbour.'

They shook hands rather awkwardly.

'We've already met,' Mitzi explained to Lobelia. 'Lav'll tell you – anyway, I must get back.'

'Mitzi was worried that it was a bit late to be entertaining gentlemen callers,' Lavender puffed, bending down to yank her football socks up to her knees. 'She was worried about us – or so she said. To be honest—' she fluttered pale eyelashes in Shay's direction '—I think she was lonely. She's divorced, you know.'

Shay smiled at Mitzi with deep understanding. 'So are my parents. And you seemed to be having a fine time when I called.'

'We were,' Mitzi assured him. 'I'd cooked a meal for my daughters and—'

Lobelia hooted with laughter. 'Cooking! You? That's a turn-up!'

'Yes, I know – anyway, I was fine – but it just seemed very late for – er – Mr Donovan to be calling and I thought—'

Shay pushed his tousled hair away from his face. It fell back again. 'There was a mix-up – I was supposed to be sharing a flat in Winterbrook, arrived there tonight to find

59

people already installed, went back to the hospital to see if there was a temporary B&B in town, and your GP was there in the reception area. We got talking and well, here I am.'

'So I see,' Mitzi nodded, feeling mightily relieved. 'And now I really must go.'

'And I must feed our paying guest as he was expecting an evening meal at his previous digs,' Lobelia preened herself, pulling down the remnants of her shrunken cardigan. She beamed at Shay as she trotted towards the kitchen. 'Of course, supper isn't included normally, but on your first night we'd like to offer something a bit special. I can do you a nice fish-paste sandwich and a pickled cucumber.'

Mitzi tried not to laugh as Shay attempted to wear an expression of brave enthusiasm as he followed Lobelia.

'And,' Lob's voice echoed from the chill depths of the Bandings's icebox kitchen, 'as a welcome to your new home treat I can give you *two* slices of bread with your sandwich.'

'Bugger,' Lavender muttered as she opened the front door for Mitzi. 'Bang goes my bloody breakfast.'

Back in her own house, Mitzi was enveloped by the warmth and comfort and cosiness. Poor, poor Shay.

Doll and Lu were sitting on the hearthrug with Richard and Judy, and they all looked up expectantly. Giving them a quick résumé of why Shay was next door and being aware of Lu's eyes sparkling, Mitzi held her hands out to the fire. 'So, that's the Heath Ledger myth scotched. So much for Granny Westward's wishes coming true.'

'Oh, I don't know—' Lulu stroked Richard and Judy '—I think it's pretty cool, actually. Not the real thing, but as near as damn it. And you never know – oh, there's the door again. Maybe he's come back?'

'And maybe he hasn't,' Doll scrambled to her feet. 'I'll go – I need the loo anyway.'

Warm again, Mitzi curled herself into the cushiony sofa and closed her eyes. She still felt rather floaty.

'Christ!'

Lulu's shout made her jump. Opening her eyes, she blinked at the doorway. Doll, looking stunned, was standing just in front of Brett, who was hovering in the hallway wearing what appeared to be a black leather catsuit.

'Brett!' Mitzi scrambled to her feet. She still felt rather strange. 'Lovely to see you – um – Doll didn't say you were coming over.'

Brett smiled, looking very self-conscious. With a jolt, Mitzi realised that the black leather catsuit was actually tight black jeans and a leather jacket. He looked like the Milk Tray Man. Which was very odd as Brett's non-postman's-uniform wardrobe had consisted of beige chinos and even beiger polo shirts for as long as she'd known him.

'No – well, I thought that she may have had a little bit too much to drink to be able to drive, so I walked over so that I could drive her back . . .' He frowned. 'It was really weird, you know. I'd gone to bed, was asleep – and I had this really vivid dream that she needed me. I woke up, and just had to see her. Had to come over and get her . . .'

'But you've never collected her before, ever,' Lu sniggered. 'And why on earth are you wearing those pervy clothes?'

Brett, looking bemused, shook his head. 'Dunno, really. I haven't worn these for years, not since I gave up my motorbike – they seemed to fall out of my wardrobe and it was so urgent that I got here I didn't bother to look for anything else. They seemed to suit my mood . . .' He smiled gently at Doll. 'Anyway, darling, are you ready?'

'*Darling?* Blimey!' Lu looked at Mitzi. 'What did she wish for? Impromptu romance . . . Wow. This is scary stuff . . .'

'Shush,' Mitzi hissed. 'Whatever the reason, we don't want to spoil it. Doll love, you'd better get along home now . . . no, Lu and I will clear up in the morning . . . Off you pop. Both of you.'

Doll, still looking shell-shocked, allowed a solicitous

Brett to help her on with her coat. The fact that he seemed to want to kiss her all over as he did so made the process a little more awkward than usual. Lulu buried her face in Richard and Judy and giggled.

The goodbyes said, and having waved Doll and Brett off with a warm glow of happiness, Mitzi switched off the lights on the devastation in the kitchen and wandered back into the living room.

'Two out of three,' Lu untangled her feet from her long skirts and hauled herself upright. 'Not bad, Mum. Not bad at all ... And are you sure you don't want to clear this lot up tonight?'

'Positive. We'll probably feel a bit more normal in the morning after a night's sleep. But even I have to admit that Brett's behaviour isn't – wasn't – well, in character.'

'Poor Doll,' Lu shuddered, kissing her mother before wobbling across the living room. 'Thanks to Granny Westward she'll have to endure a night of passion with Postman Brett. Just think about it – no don't! I mean, Boring Brett and our Doll all loved-up! Yuk! Just shows – you really should be careful what you wish for ... Night then ... I'm off to dream blameless dreams about our new next-door neighbour.'

Alone in the firelight, Mitzi changed Abba for the Rolling Stones and trilled along with Mick and the boys generously sharing their '19th Nervous Breakdown'. Richard and Judy stretched in front of the fire, and Mitzi joined them on the rug. It had been a wonderful evening, although very, very strange – Shay arriving, and then Brett's totally uncharacteristic behaviour. And both so soon after they'd made their wishes. It was simply coincidence, of course. Nothing else. Funny though, and maybe, just maybe, there was something in this herbalism.

Over the weekend, she'd ring all the people who'd answered her Baby Boomer advert in the library, and arrange a meeting in the village hall. Booking the village hall would, of course, mean she'd have to face Tarnia

Snepps, and there would no doubt be the usual battle over who was really in charge. Tarnia, if she thought the Baby Boomers Collective might improve her image, would try to muscle in. As usual.

Mitzi tapped her fingers as Mick and the boys roared into 'It's All Over Now'. Perhaps she ought to study Granny Westward's recipe book more closely. There may well be something in the recipes to help her steal a march on the Botox Queen of Hazy Hassocks. Empowerment or something along those lines. Ginseng in the ginger nuts or caraway in the custard creams.

The phone rang. Groaning, Mitzi glanced at the clock. Gone midnight. It was probably a wrong number. Someone drunkenly wanting a taxi or a kebab delivery. Not bothering to stand up, she rolled towards the handset.

'Hello ... oh, Lance, these late-night calls are becoming a bit of a habit, aren't they? What's the matter? Is Jennifer listening in on the extension? She's where? Doing what? No, I'm not laughing ... honestly. But that's what you get for marrying someone from Chigwell. French manicures and facial detox weekends ... Hmmm ... What? No, I promise I'm not laughing ... what? Oh, don't be silly, Lance – of course you don't! Tomorrow? No, I don't think so – honestly. I'm very busy. Give me a ring in the week, okay? Sorry – goodnight.'

Irritably, she clicked off the phone and threw it under the cushions. Mick and Co. were warbling 'Under My Thumb'.

Mitzi cuddled Richard and Judy and sighed heavily. Bloody hell. Why had Lance chosen tonight, of all nights, to tell her how much he still needed and loved her?

Chapter Six

'I know it's a cliché, but I really, really hate Monday mornings,' Lulu grumbled as she burrowed deeply into the kitchen's avalanche cupboard, trying to find a matching boot. 'But then, if Mondays were part of the weekend I suppose I'd hate Tuesdays instead ...' She sighed heavily. 'What I really need is a life of total indolence.'

'Not unlike the one you have now, then,' Mitzi laughed.

'Not fair,' Lulu paused in her boot-sort to peer over her shoulder at her mother. 'Now you sound like Nasty Niall. It may not be a conventional career – but I work very hard in the shop and on fund-raising and awareness and – oh, and by the way before I forget, Doll says I'm to ask you if you're thinking of seeing Dad while Jennifer's away being buffed up. Because if you are, we want it put on record that we're not happy about it. Much as we love him, he's not to be trusted, Mum. If you take him back—'

'Of course I'm not taking him back,' Mitzi said. 'I'm not even going to see him. You know what your Dad's like. Without Jennifer there to mother him, he was just feeling lonely. And she was only being buffed up over the weekend. She'll be back today.'

'That's okay then.' Having resumed her hunt, Lulu broke off with a little yell of triumph as she discovered the boot, then sat on the floor to pull it on. Richard and Judy helped with the laces. 'Still, it was all a bit spooky. You know,

you wishing for someone to love you
– shazam! – Dad's on the phone sayin
'Pure coincidence,' Mitzi said firml
Dad always gets maudlin when he's lei
more then twenty minutes. But it was
Especially for you, with the gorgeous Shay
door.'

Lulu scrambled to her feet and opened the
'Yeah, far better for me than for poor old Doll   .ng to
endure Brett's amorous advances, that's for sure. Mind
you, I haven't caught as much as a glimpse of him since
Friday. He was probably just a pigment of my overheated
imagination.'

'Don't you mean figment?'

'After that Wishes Come True concoction I know exactly
what I mean.' Lulu grinned. 'Right, I'm off. Oh, sod it, it's
raining. I'll get soaked waiting at the bus stop.'

'Hmmm – not one of the things I have to worry about.
No more wet Monday mornings and getting into work
sopping wet and tearing round at lunchtime getting even
more sopping wet. I think I shall just spend the day
ensconced by the fire organising my first Baby Boomers
Collective meeting in the village hall – oh, and maybe
planning my next culinary surprise.'

'That's so cruel,' Lulu pulled a face as she rummaged in
the pile of back-door debris for a serviceable umbrella.

'Oh, I think the Baby Boomers are looking forward to
meeting up at last – and my cooking wasn't *that* bad.'

'It's not the cooking or the Baby Boomers.' Lulu looked
despondently at a selection of umbrellas with torn fabric
and bent spokes. 'It's the staying at home by the fire bit . . .
Oh, what the hell – I'll run to the dentist's and see if Doll
can give me a lift into Winterbrook. It'll be loads quicker
than the bus or waiting for you to get dressed and offer.'
She grinned. 'Plus it'll give me a chance to find out what
happened during the Love Fest. Bye!'

Doll had become used to her scrounging lifts in the Polo

...ement weather over the years. It always led to
...erly arguments about Lulu taking her driving test –
again. Having failed seven times and knowing that, even if
she could drive, she certainly couldn't afford a car, and not
being sure that as an almost-eco-warrior she should be
adding to atmospheric pollution anyway, Lulu always felt
the argument was very much stacked against her.

The rain was irritatingly fine and non-stop, so by the
time she reached the surgery Lulu's feet were squelching,
the hem of her trailing skirt was saturated, her Afghan coat
was giving off an even stronger aroma than usual, and
drops were dripping annoyingly from the end of every one
of her beaded braids.

'Drowned rat alert!' Viv the receptionist called out
cheerily, not looking up from her screen. 'Blimey Lu, that
coat pongs to high heaven! If you hang around outside
Patsy's Pantry with the rest of the rough sleepers, you'll
make a fortune.'

'Oh, ha-ha.'

Lulu sploshed her way towards the row of whey-faced
patients who, by the way they were all hunched together in
the furthest corner, clearly felt that having dental treatment
early on a grey and dark October Monday morning was not
high on their list of priorities. Perching wetly on the edge
of an uncomfortable chair, Lu wondered why dentists
always had awful furniture and harsh overhead strip lighting and receptionists like Viv. Maybe it was to fool people
into thinking things could only get better.

She picked up a copy of *My Weekly* and shook her soggy
braids out of her eyes. 'Is Doll in yet?'

Viv still didn't look up from her computer screen. 'Ages
ago. She and Mr J have got an early wisdom tooth. She'll
be free then until the new dentist arrives at about ten. I'll
let her know you're here.'

'Thanks.' Lulu plunged back into the magazine. She
always enjoyed reading Mitzi's copies when she could get
her hands on them. There was always a lot of retro-1960s

stuff in them. Lulu had always yearned to be a proper hippie.

The surgery door opened. The knot of waiting patients gathered more tightly together. Ignoring them – and their collective sigh of relief – Doll grinned at her sister. 'You're not getting into my car like that. That coat stinks like a sewer. Why on earth don't you invest in a mac?'

'I'll have a look through the stock when I get to work.' Lulu gave Doll a swift top-to-toe appraisal. Disappointingly there were no telltale signs of a passionate weekend. She didn't look even slightly ravaged. She looked, as always, neat, clean and sort of polished.

Doll shrugged. 'You are such a scuz-bucket! Can you just hang on there for a minute – I've just got to clear up a few things before Tammy takes over in my surgery.'

At the 's' word, the patients gibbered a bit more. Doll, in a swirl of pristine navy uniform and sensible shoes, vanished back towards the inner sanctum – but not before a menacing waft of antiseptic had blasted into the waiting room. Two of the patients crashed to their feet and headed for the door.

Their escape was hampered by a very tall, very wet man trying to get in. Lulu, having exhausted the instructions in *My Weekly* on the best use of black eyeliner and white lipstick to achieve the Dusty Springfield look, watched with interest.

The newcomer was certainly worth watching.

With cropped hair, a damp leather jacket, one diamond ear-stud and a sort of beautiful, craggy, dangerous Vinnie Jones face, he was head and shoulders above any of the usual Hazy Hassocks dental patients. Lulu had an almost-unfaithful-to-Heath-Ledger moment.

Viv was still immersed in her computer, leaving the man standing looking rather lost on the cream lino tiles.

Lulu smiled encouragingly at him. 'Hi.' She shook her damp braids away from her face in what she hoped was an attractive gesture. 'You might as well sit down and wait for her to finish. They have a really weird set-up here. The receptionist doesn't speak to her patients until she's finished playing her patience.'

The man gave a bit of a chuckle at the play on words and Lu warmed to him instantly. And he sat beside her. People often didn't, especially on buses, because of the Afghan.

Viv finished her card game with a triumphal flourish and glared at the newcomer. 'Yes? Your name? You can't just sneak in and sit there, you know. You have to tell me you're here and who you are.'

'Okay,' he nodded. 'Sounds sensible. I'm here and I'm Joel Earnshaw.'

Lulu gave him a further appraising glance from under her clogged-together lashes. Joel – nice name. Nice voice too. Deep and northern-ish. Being none too sure about dialects she couldn't tell if it was Lancashire or Yorkshire or maybe even Geordie.

'You haven't got an appointment!' Viv complained after scrolling through the appropriate page. 'Are you an emergency?'

Joel shook his head. 'I'm a bit early. I wasn't supposed to be here until ten.'

Viv pulled her skinny black eyebrows together. 'Well, I still can't find you here. You're not on my list. You're not an NHS swap, are you? Have you been sent to us from another surgery? This isn't a *benefits case*, is it?'

'No,' Joel said firmly. 'But now you come to mention it, I am very keen to see dental treatment available to all again. I don't believe that good teeth should be the sole preserve of the wealthy.'

The knot of quivering patients nodded as one.

Lulu clapped her hands. 'Oh, well done! I've been saying that for ages but no one listens.'

'Shut up,' Viv snapped at her. 'And you—' she flashed slitty eyes at Joel '—have no need to start spouting lefty cants in here! We give a good, honest, value-for-money service.'

'Glad to hear it,' Joel grinned. 'And before we get even deeper into the mire, maybe I ought to explain – I'm not here as a patient. I'm a dentist. The new dentist. Mr Earnshaw.'

'Oh!' Viv flushed russet. 'Why ever didn't you say so? You don't look like a dentist. And I thought you – he – was called Joe. Our nurse Tammy said you were called Joe.'

'Possibly she misheard,' Joel said gently, standing up and walking to the desk. 'My accent sometimes causes problems south of Watford. So, now we've got that cleared up, shall we start again?'

Viv was simpering and preening. Lulu smiled to herself as Joel Earnshaw turned on the charm. Lucky, lucky Doll – working with someone like him. Even the waiting patients – well, the female ones at least – had perked up considerably.

'Finished at last.' Doll tip-tapped back into the waiting room, pulling on a sensible navy raincoat and freeing the ends of her neat blonde hair from the collar. 'We should be able to get you to work before Mr and Mrs Pippin start advertising for a replacement.'

'They wouldn't do that,' Lulu said as she stood up. 'They've always said I'm totally irreplaceable. Well, that they'd never find anyone else quite like me – which is the same thing, isn't it? But Doll – look . . . no, *look*!'

'Why are you jerking your head like that?' Doll frowned. 'And why are you pulling funny faces? And why—'

'Doll,' Viv's voice dripped honeyed cream. 'Meet Mr Earnshaw. Joel. Our new dentist. Doll—' she fluttered her eyelashes at Joel '—is our senior nurse. She'll be working with you until you're settled in. Then you'll get Tammy.'

Doll smiled and held out her hand. 'Lovely to meet you. Sorry I wasn't around when you came for interview – and so sorry that I've got to leave you. I won't be long – an errand of mercy into Winterbrook – I'll be back in plenty of time for a quick run-through before our first patient arrives.'

69

Joel shook her hand, smiled back and murmured something friendly.

Lulu frowned. Why wasn't Doll all starry-eyed and breathless? Why was she simply her usual friendly efficient self? Why hadn't she at least blushed a bit?

'Come on then, sleaze-bag.' Doll was heading for the door. 'Let's get you to work.'

Still bemused, Lulu gave Joel Earnshaw a last glittering beam, and dripped in Doll's wake.

'What is wrong with you?' she exploded as the Polo swished through the Hazy Hassocks puddles towards the main Winterbrook road.

'Nothing.' Doll didn't take her eyes from the road. She drove as efficiently as she did everything else. 'I'm fine. Why?'

'But *him* . . .' Lu pushed her braids away from her eyes. 'Joel. Your new dentist. The man you are going to be working with in less than an hour's time!'

'What about him?'

'Dolores Blessing! You are beyond help!'

'Don't call me Dolores, Tallullah.'

They grinned at each other. Their real names – their parents' embarrassing flights of Hollywood fantasy – remained a dark secret between them, their closest friends and their birth certificates.

'But he's soooo cool!'

Doll changed gear. 'He's okay. A vast improvement on Mr Wiseman of course, and pleasant enough – and nowhere near as ancient as Tammy said he was. What do you reckon? Late thirties? But – he's not my type.'

Lulu gave a snort of disgust. 'No, well, he wouldn't be, would he? Not if boring old Brett the Postie makes you go weak at the knees.'

Doll giggled.

'Bloody hell, Doll – don't tell me you actually enjoyed being seduced by someone dressed in cheap black leather? Someone you know better than you know yourself.

70

Someone who cuts his toenails in front of you and picks his teeth, and probably does disgusting things under the duvet, and—'

'Yeah, okay,' Doll snapped. 'I get the picture. And yes, if you must know, I did enjoy it. Every minute of it. Brett and I have had one of the best weekends I can ever remember.'

'*What?* You mean, you and Brett ... *All weekend*?'

'Mmmm ...' Doll smiled dreamily. 'It was wonderful ... We only emerged from the bedroom to grab another bottle or two of plonk. We even had profiteroles and cream in bed. It's amazing what you can do with a profiterole.'

'Oh, yuk – far, far too much information!' Lulu pulled an agonised face.

Doll slowed the Polo as they approached the charity shop. As always there was nowhere to park outside it. She smiled soppily again. 'Brett and I couldn't bear to say goodbye this morning – it was like being sixteen again. All our old feelings were rekindled. And if I'm not pregnant after this weekend then there simply ain't no justice.'

Blimey! Lulu was stunned into silence. Maybe there was more to the Wishes Come True Pie than they'd imagined.

She was still pondering on the awfulness of her mother's sortie into cookery being responsible for Doll and Brett's amorous shenanigans as she dripped into the shop.

Dark and cavernous, smelling of age and decay and mould, with violently coloured 1970s crockery, 1960s plastic ornaments, and a trillion paperbacks vying for space with racks and heaps and piles of mainly unwearable clothes, it had been Lulu's workplace and sanctuary for five years.

'Sorry I'm late – had to wait for Doll to give me a lift because of the rain.' She shed the Afghan in a corner and grinned at her employers. 'Shall I put the kettle on?'

From behind the counter, Hedley and Biff Pippin nodded in unison. They looked more like siblings than husband and wife, both being short, rotund and wearing bifocals. They even dressed similarly in cords and check shirts. Biff, it was rumoured, had been quite a big name on the underground female wrestling circuit when Hedley had met her at an animal rights rally in the 1960s. It had been mutual attraction at first sight. They were easygoing employers, committed to their cause, and Lulu loved them dearly.

Over several cups of tea and while sorting through the black bags of donated clothes and bric-à-brac which was always left outside over the weekend, she told them about the Wishes Come True Pie – and the outcome – skipping the details of Brett and Doll's sexual marathon in case it horrified them as much as it had her.

'Maybe we could get your mother to make us something for our next animal rights rally,' Biff said, holding up a see-through nightie in purple nylon. 'We could wish for all the opposition to combust spontaneously.'

'Er – yes ...' Lulu paused in trying on a beige pac-a-mac. 'I'm not sure that Granny Westward's recipes have anything along those lines.'

'Don't you believe it.' Hedley puffed on his pipe which smelt even worse than Lulu's coat. 'Them old village women used to concoct potions for every occasion. Why do you think they was all drowned at the stake? Where do the basics for modern drugs come from? Plants, that's where. Take the poppy – such a beautiful flower – but it's responsible for most of the world's problems and—'

'Er – yes,' Lulu peeled off the pac-a-mac and cut short Hedley's rant. He had an unfortunate habit of turning into Tony Benn at every given opportunity. 'But I don't think Mum will be dabbling with anything that'll lead to a raid by the Drugs Squad. It's all hokum really.'

Biff shook her head. 'I think Hedley's right, dear. It's well documented that villagers used what was readily available to cure ills, alter minds, and make their entertainment. Mitzi may have stumbled upon something rather wonderful, you know.'

Lu folded a heap of two-ply cardigans in neon colours

into a neat display. 'Do you really think so? You don't think all those things would have happened anyway – without the Wishes Come True Pie?'

'Who knows,' Biff shook her pepper-and-salt head. 'The only way to find out is to get your mum to try something else. Make a few more meals from your great-gran's book and see what happens. If they don't work then maybe it was just coincidence – but there's only one way to find out . . .'

A dark shadow loomed in the rain-splashed doorway. Biff became instantly professional. 'Oh, goody a customer and loaded with bags by the look of it. Hedley, you make sure he buys something as well as dumping off!'

Leaving the customer to Hedley's killer selling techniques, Lu ducked into the back of the shop to scrunch up the black sacks and stack the cardboard boxes and put the kettle on again. The thought that Mitzi may be able to *make things happen* with her recipes was pretty laughable really. But then, look at Doll and Brett. No one in their right mind would surely want a 48-hour love-in with Brett without being under the influence of *something*, would they?

She nodded happily to herself. Maybe it would be fun to try one of the other recipes – maybe there was a proper love potion – maybe they could invite Shay round. She gave a little shiver of pleasure at the thought.

'Lulu, come and look at this lot!' Hedley's voice sliced through the delicious reverie. 'I know we say we'll never turn anything away – but honestly!'

Biff was kneeling among the piles of detritus spilling from the black bags on the floor. 'Couldn't even send most of this lot to recycling! Good lord, some of this is falling apart – and it smells awful. Who in their right mind would wear something like this?'

Lulu looked at the multi-layered, grubby and frayed frock. 'Er – me, actually. That's one of mine – and so is this! And this!'

She dropped to her knees and rifled through the bags. Everything belonged to her. Everything she possessed.

Everything she hadn't already moved from Niall's loft to Mitzi's house.

'Who brought this in?'

'Biggish bloke,' Hedley said. 'Youngish. Flash suit. Flash car outside. Flash young lady with him. He looked a bit familiar. Wouldn't bloody buy anything, though.'

Lulu scrambled to her feet and ran to the door. Niall's sporty Astra coupé was pulling out into the traffic. There was an immaculate redhead in a neat black businesslike jacket in the passenger seat. She was clutching a designer handbag and a matching neat black briefcase on her immaculate lap. Niall leaned from the window and gave Lu a mocking wave.

'Bye, Tallulah!' His voice rang above the steady pounding of the rain and the swish of the traffic. 'Dee-Dee and I thought we'd save you the trouble of removing the rest of your tat. This is where it – and you – belong. I hope we never meet again! So long sweetheart!'

Lu stared after the car as it roared off. Damn Niall to hell. It hadn't taken him long to find a replacement, had it? Not long at all, considering he had so recently sworn he'd love her for ever. Men! Fickle, pathetic and liars the lot of them! Lu sniffed a bit. And the woman in the car had been exactly what Niall had tried, and failed, to turn her into ... So – was her heart broken? She shook her head. No, bruised a bit and her pride battered, but nothing terminal ... And of course there was always Shay who surely wasn't fickle or a liar and who was a zillion times better than Niall. Maybe, she thought, turning back into the shop, now was exactly the right time to see if Mitzi's magic really worked ...

Chapter Seven

So far so good, Mitzi thought as she loaded the holdall. Had she got everything she'd need for the first Baby Boomers Collective meeting? List of names, yes; list of what was possible to achieve and what wasn't, yes; packets of biscuits to go with the tongue-stripping village hall tea, yes. Permission from Tarnia Snepps to use Hazy Hassocks village hall this afternoon, no; confidence, no; major butterfly attack, yes, yes, yes.

It had been a strange week: she hadn't expected Lu to have been quite so stricken by Niall's final goodbye, although of course Lulu had insisted it was hurt pride more than a bruised heart – nor had she expected Doll and Brett to be drifting around like love's young dream. However, thanks to the neighbours, and her friends, and the Baby Boomers, and Granny Westward's cookery book, Mitzi certainly hadn't had a moment to be lonely or bored. In fact she was beginning to wonder how she'd ever found the time to go to work.

And it had stopped raining. Now the end of October was rushing in with icy northern gales and brittle, nose-numbing mornings. The trees were being stripped bare and Hazy Hassocks was disappearing under a carpet of gold and brown and russet. More telling, Richard and Judy had abandoned the washing basket and were draped over the central heating boiler, a sure sign of bitter weather to come.

Happily humming along with Radio Two, Mitzi set out two mugs on the tray and opened a fresh packet of Hobnobs. It was Flo's turn to pop in for coffee and gossip.

'Come in,' she called hearing the knock on the back door, 'the kettle's boiling and – oh! What on earth do you want?'

Lance, looking a bit flushed and straightening his hair, grinned sheepishly round the kitchen door. 'Lovely warm greeting. Thanks, love.'

'Don't call me love.'

'No, okay, sorry – old habits and all that ...' Lance pulled out a chair and sat comfortably at the kitchen table. 'It's so cosy in here. Really snug after our all-white and stainless steel. I get quite nostalgic for the days of magnolia and Dralon. And you look – well – wonderful ... Retirement suits you.'

Mitzi made a little tsking noise of irritation. 'You know damn well the magnolia and Dralon went out of the door when you did. And you can cut out all the soft soap too. What's up? Had a row with The Harpy? Has she got you on detox again? You've only come round for strong coffee and a chocolate biscuit, haven't you?'

'Yes, well, no of course, not *just* for a chocolate biscuit ...' Lance shrugged out of his black woollen coat and relaxed. 'I was passing on the way back from one of the sites and thought I ought to call in and check that everything was okay.'

'Everything's fine, as always. And no longer your problem or responsibility. And yes, you can have gallons of non-decaff coffee and as many Hobnobs as you like. Okay?'

'Great,' he grinned at her.

Such a relief, Mitzi thought, as she turned away to re-boil the kettle, that the grin no longer moved her. For the best part of her adult life Lance's wide easygoing smile had turned her to jelly. It had taken a long time to recover from his deception. She'd never trust him, or any man, totally again.

He'd aged well, though. Not quite as well as she had, of course, but he was still lean and fit and handsome. And his hair was still brown and silky and he still had more than a touch of David Bowie about him. And his small building business was still buoyant, unlike so many others which had suffered in the recession. Handsome, gentle, kind, amusing and comfortably off. No wonder Jennifer the Harpy had found him irresistible.

No, she shook her head, she wasn't going to meander along that path – not ever again. She pulled her apricot sweatshirt down over her faded Levis and composed her face into a noncommittal smile as she handed him his mug of coffee. 'Two sugars. Or are you on to sweeteners now?'

'Not even sweeteners. Not while we're on the detox. Chemicals are out. Sugar is great, thanks. And you do look really terrific.'

'Thanks – I'm thoroughly enjoying my freedom despite my early misgivings. Have you heard from the girls?'

'Doll rang the other night and Lu popped into the office a couple of days ago. They seem okay. I'm glad Niall's finally off the scene – always thought he was a complete prat. However, they both told me your attempt at cooking had been successful – which worried me a bit.'

Mitzi flicked the tea towel at him. He'd always teased her about her lack of culinary skills. She sat opposite him, clearing away the clutter, nursing her own coffee mug, and shared the biscuits, chatting with ease about the forthcoming meeting at the village hall. They got on well as friends. They always had.

'Is this it? The recipe book they were talking about?' Lance stretched out his hand for the fragile collection of pages held together with an elastic band propped up against the flower vase in the middle of the table. He opened it carefully. 'Good God – this is amazing. Look at that handwriting – fantastic. And there are some real old-fashioned things in here . . . God! Suet puddings! Layer cakes! Pies! Pastries! Oh, I think I've just stumbled on nirvana.'

Mitzi giggled. 'There speaks a man who's spent far too long on pulses and brown rice and those awful bags of mixed leaves that everyone pretends to love. But have you looked at the names of the recipes? They're really quaint. That's the one we tried – Wishes Come True – and very tasty it was. A lot of them tie in with dates of the old festivals, see? I've been thinking of trying out something a bit special for Halloween. There's a really interesting one here – look . . .'

They pored over the book together.

'All Hallows Mallows?' Lance raised his eyebrows. 'Mmmm – I can see them going down well with the trick-n-treating thugs. And what's Mischief Night Cake? And Firework Frenzy? Hey, look at this one. You should knock up a batch of these for this afternoon.'

'Powers of Persuasion Puddings?' Mitzi frowned. 'Why? Do you think my Baby Boomers will need to be forcibly persuaded that they have the skills and opportunities to change their own lives?'

'Mitzi, love,' Lance dunked the last Hobnob in his coffee, 'I'm sure you could persuade them to do anything you wanted – no, I was actually thinking about feeding a bucketful of Powers of Persuasion to Tarnia . . .'

They laughed together. As they always had about Tarnia. Mind you, Mitzi thought as she headed to the kettle for coffee refills, Lance may well have a point. If Tarnia got wind of this afternoon's illegally arranged meeting she could turn very nasty indeed.

'How do you fancy doing a spot of home-baking?'

'Me?' Lance looked as though she'd made an improper suggestion. 'What, here? Now?'

'Right here and now – unless of course you have more important things to dash off to . . .'

'Nothing at all. Do you mean – make something out of this book?' Lance stood up and pushed up the sleeves of his pale-blue sweater. 'Great. Can't think of anything I'd like more. Right – what do we need?'

According to Granny Westward they needed – among other more prosaic things like flour, eggs and butter – carnation petals, ebony, gentian, ginger and grapes.

'Blimey, how much of that have you got in the larder?'

'None,' Mitzi said mournfully. 'Well, there might be some ginger but I'm fresh out of carnation petals. Used the last of it in sandwiches this morning.'

'You make a start on collecting together what you've got and mix up the other bits – the puddingy spongy stuff—' Lance clutched his car keys '—and I'll belt off to Herbie's Healthfoods and see what I can find . . . Shan't be long.'

And he wasn't. Again, the ingredients weren't exactly right, but as near as damn it. Rolling up their sleeves, the radio singing away, and aided by lots of coffee, they worked happily side by side at the table as they'd never done in all the years they'd been married. Richard and Judy sat up on top of the boiler and watched the proceedings with grave suspicion.

'You don't really believe in all this, do you?' Lance asked once the first batch of puddings were in the oven and the kitchen looked like the aftermath of an explosion in a bakery. 'That this odd concoction of herbs can actually – well – *do* things?'

'No,' Mitzi wiped a floury hand across her flushed cheeks. 'Not really. I don't believe in magic any more than you do, but I do think that maybe the odd combination of ingredients may have some sort of chemical effect on the brain. Or at least, they may have seemed to have done to a far more innocent generation than ours. Like copious amounts of alcohol or cannabis do now.'

'Maybe – but on the other hand,' Lance muttered, undoing the last packet of biscuits with his teeth, 'you may be tinkering with the black arts without being aware of it. Some of the stuff in these recipes is pretty suspect – and Lu told me what happened after the Wishes Come True Pie.'

Mitzi frowned. She hoped Lulu hadn't told Lance too much – especially what she herself had wished for.

'Coincidence, all of it. Probably all the Powers of Persuasion Puddings will do is give Tarnia raging heartburn.'

'Then they won't have been wasted,' Lance laughed. 'Right – are we ready for the next lot?'

They were just removing the first baking tray from the oven when Flo bustled in through the back door.

'Sorry I'm late, duck, but I had to help Clyde with his demijohns. He's got eighteen gallons of courgette and rose hip just on the turn and we'd have been awash with the bloody stuff if I hadn't waded in and helped him and – bloody hell!' She took in the domestic scene round the kitchen table. 'What's he doing here? You haven't gone stupid and taken him back, have you?'

Having closed the oven door on the second batch, Lance pulled a face. 'And I love you too, Flo. Clear a space and sit down.'

Laughing, Mitzi blew flour away from the kettle and reached for another mug. 'You can test the first of our puddings – seeing as Lance has eaten all the biscuits.'

Flo still looked perplexed. 'But you don't cook, Mitzi. And you certainly don't cook with *him*. And—' she glanced at the smouldering heaps on the baking tray '—they aren't puddings – they're overdone fairy cakes.'

True, Mitzi thought, they did look more like little glossy brown cakes. She'd thought they'd emerge in golden fluffy mounds. Still, they looked reasonably edible and smelled – er – okay. But there was no way on earth she'd let Flo know they were, well, *dabbling*. Fortunately Granny Westward's recipe book was well hidden beneath the tabletop debris.

'They're for this afternoon – my first meeting at the village hall,' she explained glibly, handing Flo a mug. 'You know how bad the committee are on providing refreshments. And Lance was here and well, got roped in.'

'Hmmm ...' Flo remained unconvinced, but bravely reached for the baking tray.

Mitzi and Lance exchanged glances.

Flo took a bite, gave a little scream and frantically fanned her mouth. 'H-h-hot! Bloody hot!'

Mitzi screwed her eyes up and held her breath. Whether the Powers of Persuasion Puddings did their trick or not wasn't uppermost in her mind. She'd be happy if they were simply edible. And anyway, it didn't hurt to experiment just a little. As Flo had been the most vociferous of her friends over Lance's infidelity and had only ever been icily polite to him for the last ten years, it was worth a try.

Watching Flo chomping manfully through the small brown cake, Mitzi silently willed her to be nice to Lance. Just a little bit pleasant. Not quite so acidic. Anything.

'There,' Lance said solicitously as Flo finished chewing, 'that wasn't too bad, was it?'

Flo swallowed, looked rather startled, then a beatific smile spread across her angular features. Her eyes crinkled and her lips twitched with mischief. 'Not bad at all. In fact, very nice indeed. May I have another?'

'Of course.' Armed with the oven gloves, Lance handed her the baking tray.

'Thank you,' Flo twinkled, flapping a coquettish hand at his arm. 'Wonderfully cooked and perfectly served. And by such a handsome waiter . . .'

My God! Mitzi clutched at the table. She's flirting with him!

'Er—' she snatched the baking tray from Lance. 'I think that'll do – otherwise there won't be enough left for this afternoon.'

Flo grabbed Lance's hand, fluttering her sparse eyelashes at him. 'Oh, go on, Lancie – just one more. Don't be mean.'

Lance shot a terrified glance at Mitzi, who gave an imperceptible shake of her head. Any more Powers of Persuasion Pudding and Flo would probably turn into full vamp mode – it didn't bear thinking about.

'Sorry,' she said firmly, 'they need to go into the tin

now. Lance . . .'

With an audible sigh of relief, Lance tipped the remaining cakes into the tin.

'What the hell is going on?' He hissed at Mitzi. 'What the devil did you do to her?'

'Nothing at all . . .' Mitzi muttered shakily. 'It was the puddings wot done it . . . Tarnia Snepps here I come!'

Chapter Eight

POWERS OF PERSUASION PUDDINGS

A cup of wholemeal flour
Half a dozen large eggs
A slab of best butter
Chopped carnation petals
A sprinkling of dried gentian
A good handful of pulverised root ginger
Peeled and sliced grapes – black
A generous measure of brown sugar
Three large spoonfuls of black treacle

Beat eggs, flour and butter in large bowl until smooth.
Add carnations, gentian and ginger.
Beat again.
Beat in sugar and treacle.
Fold in grapes.

Pour mixture into small patty tins.
Bake in a hot oven until well risen and dark brown and
*   steaming.*
Remove each pudding on to rack to cool.

Note: To invoke full powers of persuasion, the cook of the puddings (and no one else) must silently will the eater of the puddings to do their bidding. This is strong herbal magic so do this only with the best of intentions.

It was bedlam. Everyone seemed to be speaking at once. Mitzi, on the stage behind a trestle table which, among its many indentations, proclaimed that Dave luvved Kirsty '4ever', and something horrendously salacious about the vicar, peered into the body of Hazy Hassocks village hall with mounting trepidation.

Not only was it midnight dark owing to the granite clouds and howling gale outside, and the half a dozen 40-watt light bulbs inside, but it was also filled to capacity. True, half the people there were probably simply Hazy Hassocks residents who'd come along for a bit of a warm and a cup of tea, but even so.

The Powers of Persuasion Puddings were crammed into several Tupperware boxes behind Mitzi's chair. She wasn't sure she trusted them. The Wishes Come True happenings were easily explained – but Flo's miraculous change of heart regarding Lance? Could that have any sort of rational explanation? Mitzi exhaled. They'd been nose to nose over the kitchen table, giggling like schoolchildren when she'd left.

Maybe Granny Westward's herbal mixtures were really far more potent than any of them had realised. Maybe she should consign the recipe book to the attic where it belonged. Maybe she should – but she'd worry about that later. Right now she had other fish to fry.

'Excuse me!' Nervously, Mitzi cleared her throat. 'Could I have your attention please?!'

No one took the slightest notice. The sea of heads continued chattering happily to their neighbours. Owing to the poor lighting, Mitzi was unable to distinguish the features of those sitting more than four rows back, but she could see all her library cronies: Trilby Man was sitting right in the front with Sally and June and Mick and the rest, his hat rammed down to his eyebrows, a rather intimidating clipboard across his knees. Mitzi hoped he wouldn't ask any awkward questions.

There were a lot of strangers: she assumed these were the people who'd answered her Baby Boomers Collective ad and to whom she'd spoken on the phone. She wondered which one was Christopher – pyrotechnics and heavy metal? And Dorothy – snooker? But surely the Lily Savage lookalike had to be Ronnie – exotic dance?

Disconcertingly, the Bandings were also sitting in the front row. They had small tinfoil parcels on their laps and Day-Glo purple cycle helmets on their heads. Mitzi avoided their eyes.

She cleared her throat and hammered on the table with her fist. 'Excuse me! Could I have a bit of hush?!'

The babble died away. All heads turned towards the stage. Several people waved.

'Thank you,' Mitzi muttered. Goodness, she was nervous. Her mouth was dry and her lips had developed a sort of curling nervous twitch. She probably looked like a bad Elvis impersonator. 'Now – um – it's lovely to see you all, and I'm Mitzi Blessing, and as everyone knows why we're here today, I'll get straight to business ...'

'Actually, Mitzi, I don't know why we're here,' Lavender beamed up from the front row. 'Neither does Lobelia. We just followed Mrs Lovestick. We thought it might be a beetle drive. Like they have in the Snug of The Faery Glen on Thursdays after we've collected our pensions.'

'That's Wednesdays,' someone said from the back. 'Or it might be Tuesdays.'

'No, Tuesdays is housey-housey. Thursday is bingo.'

'Bingo is the same as housey-housey, stupid! And it *is* Tuesdays.'

'It'd be better if housey-housey was on a Friday.'

'Friday's Whist Drive! Allus has been!'

'Excuse me!' Mitzi almost screamed above the noise. 'Can we concentrate on the matter in hand? Thank you.'

Several people glowered. She ignored them.

'There, you've just listed the things that are available in the pub – and very welcome they are – so that's the sort of thing we want to get going here, isn't it?'

Complete silence. Clearly not.

'No, well, what I mean is, not the same as such . . .' She stopped. Her palms were sweating. She was beginning to flounder. 'No, we don't want to repeat what Otto and Boris have on offer at the pub, of course. Most of you are aware of those anyway.'

Trilby Man brandished his clipboard. 'Exactly. The stuff at The Faery Glen's fine for the old codgers who can't do much more than shuffle about and do a bit of eyes down and look in, but some of us wants more than that.'

'Excuse me!' Lobelia shot a viper look along the front row. 'To whom are you referring as an old codger?'

'If the cap fits . . .'

'PLEASE!' Mitzi thumped the table again, then scrabbled through her papers. 'Ladies and gentlemen! I have drawn up a list here of who is interested in doing what, and then here, on this second list, who among you is available to teach new skills. And on this list—' she held up a third sheet of paper '—I've done cross-referencing so that you can all get into groups and start organising yourselves into tutors and students.'

If she'd expected rapturous applause, she'd have been bitterly disappointed. Everyone simply stared.

'That's a bit complicated, Mitzi dear, if you don't mind me saying so,' Lavender adjusted her cycling helmet. 'And I can't read anything on that bit of paper from down here.'

'I've made copies for everyone,' Mitzi was close to tears. 'I was going to pass them along the rows – and it isn't complicated at all. Look, as an example, for all the people who said they'd be interested in learning ballroom dancing, you're listed here, then on the second list are those who can dance and would be willing to teach it and – and here,' she pointed to the third piece of paper, 'are the names of both sets of people so you can get together. Similarly, for those keen on forming a football team—'

'Yeah, yeah, we get the idea,' Trilby Man interrupted. 'Just get them bits of paper passed out and we'll do the rest.'

Mitzi shot him a grateful glance. Maybe there was something to be said for having a bossy-boots in their midst after all.

The organised rows erupted into chaos as the sheets were passed round, chairs were abandoned, and everyone started shouting at everyone else. Mitzi watched the confusion with a sinking heart. With hindsight it would have been far more sensible to give them name badges.

'Lavender's putting the kettles on in the kitchen,' Lobelia called up from the foot of the stage, 'seeing as we don't want to sign up for anything. We've brought our own sandwiches in case you forgot about food.'

Mitzi glanced down at the tinfoil package. Fish paste. She'd stake her life on it.

'Cheese salad,' Lobelia said. 'A terrible expense, of course, but Shay says it's important to have a balanced diet. And he knows because he's medical. You should take a leaf out of his book, Mitzi dear. You look very drawn. And your complexion is quite yellow. You haven't been hitting the bottle in your lonely moments, have you? Your liver is probably shrivelling to the size of a walnut as we speak. We understand about isolation, dear, none better. Mind you, now we've got young Shay, our lives have changed beyond recognition. You should get one.'

A resident paramedic? Not a bad idea.

'Where's the biscuits?' Lavender had joined Lob. 'I've made the tea and put out the plates and the doilies and the cups are on the trays – but there weren't any biscuits.' She looked accusingly at Mitzi. 'You did remember biscuits, didn't you, dear? We know how easy it is to forget little things when your mind starts to go.'

'Here—' Mitzi scrambled behind her chair, snatched at several of the Tupperware boxes, and passed them down from the stage. 'They're not biscuits exactly – they're sort of fairy cakes.'

'Oooh, lovely ...'

'Take one each and then share the rest round when you do the teas,' Mitzi said. 'You can't have them all.'

Goodness knows what might happen if the Bandings necked back the entirety of Granny Westward's weird mixture.

'And why are you wearing cycle helmets indoors? You did remember to lock your bicycles, didn't you? You know what the kiddies are like round here.'

'Goodness,' Lavender chortled, 'we didn't cycle here, Mitzi, dear. At our age? Whatever next! No, we walked.'

'Then, why ...?'

'Because Shay said they were imperative,' Lobelia said with a grave expression. 'He said he'd been to an RAC and that a little boy had been badly hurt because he hadn't been wearing a helmet and—'

'She means RTA,' Lavender broke in. 'She's useless at Scrabble. But yes, young Shay said everyone must wear cycle helmets. All the time.' She beamed up at Mitzi. 'You must get one, dear. It'd suit you.'

'Please just hand the cakes round,' Mitzi whimpered. 'And make sure no one takes more than one.'

The scrum ensuing in the hall still resembled a sort of lunatic Paul Jones without the music.

Lav and Lob, always happy in a crisis, scurried among the crowd dishing out tea and the little dark-brown cakes. The refreshments seemed to be going down better than the organising.

'Oh, for pity's sake,' Mitzi muttered, sinking down onto the chair again. 'Don't let this turn into yet another dismal Hazy Hassocks failure. Just let them sort themselves out.'

She wasn't quite sure what had changed, and when or

how, but something certainly had. The hall wasn't quite so manic. The noise wasn't quite so loud. And the heaving knot seemed to have miraculously separated into neat and orderly groups dotted through the village hall's gloom.

Blimey, Mitzi thought faintly, it worked.

And twenty minutes later it was still working. Coincidence of course. Again. They would have managed it without the Powers of Persuasion Puddings. Of course they would – wouldn't they?

Lavender and Lobelia, brown crumbs dusting their upper lips, seemed to have attached themselves to the cricket team. Looking on the bright side, at least they wouldn't have to shell out for the protective headgear.

Trilby Man, clutching a sheaf of papers, bounded up onto the stage. 'Any more of them crunchy cakes left, Mrs B? Went down a treat. No? Damn. Well, okay – this is what we've got sorted so far . . .'

Mitzi studied the lists. It all seemed to be extremely well organised. She was particularly delighted to see that her library friends had managed to find several things to do. And even some of the more odd requests from the phone callers seemed to have found a home. If it worked as well in real life as it appeared on paper, then Hazy Hassocks's grey army would have plenty to get their teeth into. The Baby Boomers Collective was – fingers crossed – practically up and running. Why on earth no one had thought about it before she had no idea. All they had to do now was arrange regular meetings each week to get the final details ironed out and follow up the progress. Wednesday afternoons would be a good idea. She'd suggest it later.

She beamed at Trilby Man. 'This looks really great. Now all we need to do is fix a time to meet for updates and things, and book the village hall for the indoor classes, say once or twice a week for each activity, and of course, find somewhere outside for the sporty stuff.'

'Snepps Fields would be ideal.'

Mitzi pulled a face. Snepps Fields were completely out

of the question. Tarnia guarded the use of the village hall with all the watchfulness and vengeful fury of Cerberus; trying to get her to agree to the hoi polloi playing rough games on her meadows would be absolutely impossible.

'Leave it with me. I'll have to speak to Tarnia about all this anyway.'

'Rather you than me,' Trilby Man said mournfully. 'And if you haven't squared it with her already, then we might as well kiss it all goodbye. The old bag has always squashed anything we've suggested before.'

'Yes I know but—'

'But nothing,' Trilby Man looked most disgruntled. 'What's the point in raising all their hopes—' he jerked his head towards the body of the hall '—only to tell them that they can't have their dancing and firework displays and football and heavy metal bands and—'

'They're going to form a heavy metal band?' Mitzi interrupted. 'Really? How lovely!'

'Yeah, well, may as well tell 'em not to bother now . . . or the dance troupe . . . or the ones what want to put on a musical . . .'

Mitzi gave a little groan. It all sounded wonderful. An over-fifties revolution . . . But if she couldn't persuade Tarnia to allow them to use the facilities it would all sink without trace and it would be her fault for raising hopes and – she looked down at the stage. A solitary Tupperware box lurked behind her chair. She smiled to herself. Could she? Should she?

Well, why not? It was worth a try, wasn't it?

'Just leave it with me,' she said firmly. 'I'll go and see Tarnia as soon as we've finished here. It'll be fine, you'll see.'

An hour later, sitting in her Mini outside Tarnia Snepps's house on the outskirts of Hazy Hassocks, Mitzi wasn't feeling anywhere near so confident. She'd left the village hall like some sort of conquering hero – they'd all been so delighted with the strides the Baby Boomers had made. And they were all now relying on her to secure the use of the hall and the land and the facilities so that their plans could blossom into reality. It was all down to her – and Tarnia Snepps.

Mitzi peered at the Snepps's mile-wide drive through the gathering gloom and sighed heavily.

As self-styled Lady of the Hazy Hassocks Manor, Tarnia had installed herself in a monstrosity that would more than do justice to the nouveau riche bad taste of a Premiership footballer. Having more money than sense, and more grandiose ideas than either of those things, she'd eschewed the centuries-old mansions and manor houses in the area and designed her own palatial abode.

Sprawling like South Fork at the end of a multicoloured gravelled drive, it was stuccoed and crenellated and adorned with curlicues and cornices and cherubs puking blue water from every surface. There were modern latticed windows and gilded lions and neon-bright flower beds even in late October, and some really tacky wrought-iron gates.

Tucking the Tupperware box into her basket, Mitzi shuddered as she left the cosy warmth of the Mini and headed for the intercom. A gust of icy wind took her breath away.

'Tarnia,' she called into the voice grille, 'it's Mitzi. Have you got a couple of minutes, please?'

There was a lot of crackling, then a foreign voice echoed through the darkening afternoon. 'Mizz Snepps is not at 'ome.'

Mitzi grinned. 'I know that's you, Tarnia. You never did have a clue about accents. Open these damned gates.'

'No. Mizz Snepps is not at 'ome to casual callers.'

'Suit yourself,' Mitzi shivered again. 'But remember I know all about Duncan Didsbury and the strawberry yoghurt.'

'Sod you, Mitzi Blessing!' The voice lost its Eastern European mystery. 'Five minutes – that's all.'

As she sprinted out of the gale back to the car, the

wrought-iron gates swung open to the tune of Big Spender, and Mitzi prepared to do battle.

Tarnia, wearing a size 8 velour tracksuit in gold and matching gold tinselly mules, opened the door herself, which was no surprise to Mitzi. The Snepps no longer had regular staff. Once the word had spread throughout the au pair network like wildfire, they'd had to resort to agency workers who did one or two shifts and then fled. Even the most desperate and destitute would-be domestic gave the Snepps a wide berth. Some of the more foolhardy locals came in to give a hand when the Snepps threw parties – but not often.

'Lovely to see you,' Mitzi beamed. 'So kind ...'

'Come in and stop being polite,' Tarnia snarled. 'You know I hate you.'

'Likewise.' Mitzi beamed again as she stepped into a white and gold and pink hall of the worst opulence money could buy.

Surely even Tarnia could see that fountains and statuary at the foot of the stairs were a little de trop? Especially the one with that hermaphrodite child standing atop a dolphin and peeing.

Tarnia, her short coal-black hair razored into vicious stand-up spiky layers by Justin of Rip-Off Hair-Care, her eyes widened by far too much Botox, her skin spray-tanned to an even orange, looked about sixteen. Whatever else she'd wasted money on, Mitzi thought, the plastic surgery had been worth every penny. You couldn't even see the joins.

'Shall we go into the library?' Mitzi ventured.

'Kitchen,' Tarnia snapped, click-clacking away across the pink marble floor.

Following her, Mitzi managed to avoid looking too closely at the Barbie-pink, trimmed, floor-to-ceiling mirrors, or the recently installed stained-glass window which dominated the stairwell and poignantly depicted the Beckhams en famille.

'Right,' Tarnia's voice echoed from the depths of a vast chrome-and-glass kitchen which had seen even less proper cooking than Mitzi's had. 'Let's get this over with. Marquis will be home soon.'

Mitzi stifled a snigger. 'Ooops, sorry. It just slipped out. This is me, Tarnia, remember?'

Tarnia glared. 'Which is why I don't want you in my house. But I suppose even that is preferable to having you standing at the end of my drive and screaming my private business to all and sundry. So, what do you want?'

'A cup of tea would be lovely, thank you.' Mitzi perched awkwardly on the edge of something Terence Conran could have had a hand in. 'I've brought some cakes.'

'I mustn't have cake. Atkins Diet. No carbs.' Tarnia gave Mitzi an up-and-down glance. 'Clearly not something you've ever heard of. You must be a good size 12. Still, it's so easy to let yourself go at your age. No, sorry. No carbs.'

Bugger. Mitzi tried not to look disappointed. 'Oh, these are very low carb, low everything . . . And they taste delicious . . .'

She tipped the remaining Powers of Persuasion Puddings on to the pristine table top. They still smelled rich and spicy and warm. Tarnia, clearly existing on a diet of not very much at all, turned from making tea in a transparent kettle, and weakened immediately.

'Oh, they do look – um – I mean . . . well, I suppose just one – before Marquis comes home and—'

'For God's sake stop calling him Marquis,' Mitzi giggled. 'I can't take it seriously, I'm afraid.'

Tarnia's lips puckered into a moue of anger. Her hand, hovering over the cakes, withdrew. 'How many times do I have to tell you that we've moved on, Mitzi. Marquis and I. We do not wish to be reminded—'

'No, no of course not.' Mitzi realised she'd have to eat a lot of humble pie if Tarnia was going to eat the Powers of Persuasion Puddings. 'I keep forgetting. I'm sorry.'

Mollified, Tarnia continued making the tea in a transparent teapot with transparent cups on a transparent tray. Of milk and sugar there was no sign. Oh, well.

It was all a far cry from their growing-up years, Mitzi thought. When she and Tarnia had been almost neighbours on the Bath Road Council Estate on the outskirts of Hazy Hassocks, classmates at Winterbrook Grammar School, and had both dreamed of being secretaries for record companies and marrying Scott Walker.

'So.' Tarnia slid her tiny frame onto one of the strange chairs. 'What do you want?'

Pushing the cakes forward and trying not to look over-eager, Mitzi explained about the Baby Boomers Collective.

'Absolutely not,' Tarnia sniffed, when she'd finished. 'No way. Not a chance. Okay? Now you can go.'

No, she couldn't. The cakes were still untouched. Mitzi steeled herself for a sip of the transparent tea.

Jesus! Jeyes Fluid!

'Earl Grey,' Tarnia said. 'Not cheap sweepings from the 8 'til Late's own label.'

'Lovely.' Mitzi smiled gamely. 'But why won't you let people use the hall and the fields and—'

'But I do. Only this summer Marigold Soames-Hartley had her Belinda's wedding reception in several marquees in the lower meadow, and the Pugh-Padgetts always have their charity functions in the village hall, and—'

'But they're not real villagers!' Mitzi put down her teacup. 'They don't even live in Hazy Hassocks.'

'No, they don't. And that's why they can use the facilities with impunity. They're the kind of people Marquis and I now associate with. They are our social equals. Our chums.'

'You mean they don't know that you lived on the Bath Road Estate or that your dad was a bus driver or that ... that Marquis was known as Snotty Mark at school and his dad is still the milkman in Winterbrook and his mum works in Tesco ... Or—'

'Exactly!' Tarnia's eyes flashed. 'Exactly! And why I want nothing to do with you, either! Why would I, having moved on from all that crap, want to surround myself with the dregs of the village who would take great delight in reminding me and my new friends – not to mention Marquis's business colleagues – where our roots actually lay? Why?'

Mitzi sighed. She'd known this would be Tarnia's reaction. It always had been. Ever since Marquis – no damn it! Mark – had got eight score draws on Littlewoods long before the lottery had been thought of, managed to make some sensible investments in vehicle leasing to multinational companies, and had built the Snepps's Bad-Taste Palace on the only decent bit of land for miles around. Ever since they'd discovered the deeds also covered the village hall.

It was an eternal stumbling block.

Mitzi shrugged. 'I don't think any of these people are the slightest bit interested in your past. Even those who remember it have got far more pressing things to worry about. All they want to do is spend their autumn years in enjoying themselves, using their brains, being useful members of society. They're our age, for heaven's sake – middle-aged – they don't deserve to be pensioned off and forgotten about.'

'Then they should have thought about that before,' Tarnia snapped, her fingers dabbing at some of the brown crumbs on the table top. 'And made plans for their futures.'

'Like you did?'

The crumbs hovered on a slim orange fingertip, then fell off. 'Exactly like I did.'

Oh, come on! Mitzi thought. Tarnia had never done a decent day's work in her life. She and Snotty Mark had married in the early 1970s because she was pregnant. They'd lived with Mark's parents until the birth of the second Snepps baby when the council had given them a maisonette. It was only when Tarnia was heavily pregnant with Snepps number three that Snotty Mark had jabbed his lucky biro into the right number of football teams.

'And how are the children?' Mitzi pushed the tea away. She might as well forget about the cakes. This was going to be another waste of time.

'Fine,' Tarnia said shortly. 'Wayne and Warren are directors of the company, of course, and living in Surrey. They're very busy with their own lives and families. We don't see much of them.'

'And Lisa-Marie?'

'Runs her own business in London. She rarely has the time to come home.'

'Strip joints, wasn't it?'

'Nightclubs!' Tarnia hissed. 'Nightclubs. Very classy. Lisa-Marie's training in – um – dancing stood her in good stead.'

'As did marrying one of her Middle-Eastern clients.'

'Get out!' Tarnia gripped the edge of the table. 'There's nothing you can say to me that will make me change my mind. Nothing. Not sob stories about the Hazy Hassocks saddoes, or threats, or blackmail! I do not want the plebs using my hall or my land! Understood?'

Sod it, Mitzi thought crossly. An insult too far.

'Okay. Fine. I should have realised that you wouldn't listen to reason. Compassion was never top of your list of attributes, was it?' She gathered the Powers of Persuasion Puddings together, then broke one in half and popped it into her mouth. 'Mmmm – delicious . . . such a shame you can't have one. No, no – don't waver. I'd hate to be responsible for you gaining an ounce . . .'

Tarnia took a longing look at the glossy brown cakes, shot out a slender orange hand and clenched her iridescent nails into the crumbly surface. Mitzi held her breath. With eye-watering speed, Tarnia crammed the whole thing between her pouting, collagen-enhanced lips.

Mitzi held her breath. What on earth was she doing? There was no way on earth that this was going to work. She waited until Tarnia's cheeks bulged. Her heart was thudding. Now? Should she? Oh, heck, why not? What was there to lose? Even if was all pie in the sky.

'There. Lovely isn't it? Have another – Snotty Mark need never know. Oh, yes, two or three. As many as you like ...' Mitzi said softly. 'And – and I really think you should change your mind about allowing the Baby Boomers to use the village hall and the meadows for their activities. Don't you?'

Chapter Nine

Two days later, Mitzi, snuggled in jeans and a fluffy purple jumper, curled her fluffy purple matching-socked feet beneath her on the sofa, and shifted the phone to a more comfortable position under her chin. As the rain rattled against the window and the midday sky darkened with racing storm clouds, the sumptuously coloured living room enveloped itself round her, and she truly relished not having to be at work. Not for the first time in recent weeks, she reckoned Troy and Tyler, and the bank's venture into youth culture had done her a massive favour.

'So,' Mitzi's voice echoed down the phone. 'What do reckon to a little get-together? Here, next Friday night? Just family, friends, the neighbours and maybe a few of the Baby Boomers.'

She'd known, it being lunchtime, that she'd catch Doll at home doing her housework. It was the way she'd organised her domestic life for years: not wanting to use noisy electrical appliances while Brett slept, not able to tolerate any mess or disorder, not allowing anything to get out of hand. It would be nice, Mitzi reckoned, if their new-found passion could include a bit of, well, loosening up on the domestic front too. There was something scary about Doll's obsession with all things clean and tidy.

'Sounds a nice idea,' Doll said, 'but – um – we're not really the sort of family that has parties, are we? I mean, friends round, yes – but this sounds like *entertaining* on a grand scale.'

Mitzi grinned into the phone, picturing Doll's perplexed face. Sadly, she could also picture her perched on the very 1970s telephone seat in the bungalow's hall. Hopefully, since the resurgence of the rekindled emotion, the bungalow was warmer than it used to be. That hall had been a virtual icebox.

'Oh, this won't be anything formal. Just a drop-in. There's some stuff I need to sort out before we have our next BBC meeting in the village hall, and I – er – just thought I'd try a few new bits and pieces from Granny's book and—'

'Are you sure?' Doll's voice sounded as though she was frowning. 'I know what happened with those funny puddings. Dad told me Flo only had one and he found himself almost having to fight her off, and they must have seriously addled Tarnia's brain if she's agreed to let you use the village hall for your shenanigans and—'

'Yes, well . . .' Mitzi cut in quickly, not wanting to think about the methods she'd employed with Tarnia, or the awful consequences for the BBC should she change her mind. She winced as, without warning, Richard and Judy crampon'd their way onto her lap. 'I'm not quite sure what happened there. The puddings may have played a part – but I doubt it . . . Anyway, the effects clearly aren't permanent. Flo hasn't got a good word to say about your dad again now.'

'Thank the lord for that. And are you sure about *Friday*? It's Halloween . . .'

'Mmmm . . . I had noticed. But I've found some lovely old-fashioned Halloween recipes which aren't doubtful at all. It'd be great if you and Brett could pop round – about eight-ish?'

'Doubt if Brett will be able to. He's doing a double-early on Saturday morning. But I'd love to come for an hour or so – especially if you're inviting Shay for Lulu as the in-house entertainment.'

'Don't be cruel. Since he arrived we've only caught glimpses of him as he flies in and out. Still, I'll include an invite for him when I pop round to Lav and Lob's in a minute, and hope he's not working next Friday night. His shifts are even worse than Brett's. Oh, and did you know that slimeball Niall has moved his new girlfriend into the loft?'

'Yes, Lu told me. Apparently she's his office line-manager and the affair's been going on for some time. All their friends knew, of course. Poor old Lu – I think Shay could be just what she needs, in more ways than one.' Doll giggled. 'Look I've got to dash or I won't have this hall hoovered before it's time to go back to work. Count me in for the get-together. See you Friday, then. Bye.'

Mitzi clicked off the phone, took another mouthful of coffee, shifted Richard and Judy into a less painful position on her lap, then dialled the charity shop.

'Oh, hello Hedley, it's Mitzi. Can I have a quick word with Lulu, please? Oh, is she? What, in Hazy Hassocks? Again? Goodness me. She didn't mention anything to me about it. She's with Biff, is she? Good – well, yes, in case things turn nasty, of course. No, it was nothing important. Just something I wanted her to buy on her way home. No, nothing drastic – just another loaf of bread – and she'd probably forget it anyway. Thanks a lot. Bye . . .'

The phone rang as soon as she put it down. She snatched it up again. Richard and Judy, who had spilled like liquid mercury into the space the phone had left, narrowed their eyes at it.

'Hello, Mitzi Blessing – oh, hello Lance. Your scarf? Did you? I haven't seen it. What colour was it? Oh, *that one*. The one I bought you the year – oh, yes, well – no I haven't seen it here. Maybe Flo picked it up and sleeps with it under her pillow . . . What? You have no sense of humour any more! Jennifer's what? Again? Is she old enough to need that lifted, then? Crikey . . . Me? Nothing much – just sitting by the fire organising my Baby Boomers and planning a few recipes for Halloween, that's all. Yes, it's a great life isn't it? What? Yes, of course if I find the scarf, I'll ring you – but my money's on Flo . . .'

Mitzi was still giggling as she hung up. Finishing her coffee, she idly flicked through the pages of Granny Westward's cookery book. Halloween, it appeared, was a major occasion in the home-cooking and village-ritual calendar. Not, of course, that Mitzi for one moment believed that this herbal-dabbling worked, but still.

'All Hallows Mallows,' she read aloud to Richard and Judy. 'As Lance said, they should be nice for the trick-or-treaters . . . Midnight Apples? Indigestion on a plate if you ask me . . . Oh, and look at this. If you light two dozen candles and sprinkle yarrow backwards into the flames you're supposed to see your one true love. Mmmm . . . well, maybe – especially if your one true love is a fire-fighter . . . I think—' she stroked the two grey silky bodies '—that this could be a lot of fun . . .'

'My mother's gone mad,' Doll muttered through her mask an hour later as she assisted Joel with the completion of a multiple-filling appointment. 'She's turning to witchcraft.'

The patient, prone and shackled in the chair, gave an involuntary twitch.

'Sorry, Mr Knowles,' Doll crinkled her eyes at him. Smiling with the lips was pointless because of the mask. 'Just a figure of speech . . . No,—' she raised her eyes to Joel again as she passed the loaded amalgam carrier '—I mean, she found this book that belonged to my great-grandmother, all herbal recipes and suchlike, and she's made some really strange concoctions from it – anyway, she rang me at lunchtime and invited me over for Halloween, and I know she's planning something else and—'

The patient jerked slightly.

'Sorry, Mr Knowles. The witchcraft isn't inherited and doesn't stretch to dental procedures. We're treating your occlusal cavities with the best your private health insurance can buy – not some herbal infusion and an incantation.'

Joel grinned. His very blue eyes twinkled. The mask made him look even more dangerous. Like a highwayman.

'Excuse me—' the surgery door opened and Tammy undulated in '—Mr Johnson says have you nicked our steriliser?'

Despite declaring him far too old to be fanciable, since Joel's arrival Tammy had taken to hoiking her uniform dress up to groin level and wearing long boots. She looked like a Principal Boy.

'No, we haven't,' Doll muttered. 'And I bet Mr J never used the word "nick" in his life. Viv's probably got it out in reception for steaming her pores. Sorry Mr Knowles – would you like to rinse?'

Tammy undulated out again, slamming the door. Mr Knowles missed the basin.

Joel flexed his shoulders and removed his mask. 'This Halloween party sounds like fun. There might be something similar on in Winterbrook, I suppose, if I bothered to look. I really ought to get out more, although I've got a feeling Halloween will see me in the flat watching Jamie Lee Curtis being scared out of her wits for the thirty-ninth time . . .'

Thanks to Tammy's less-than-subtle interrogation techniques, the whole practice knew that Joel was a Divorced-No-Kids. And that the ex-Mrs Earnshaw was merrily shacked up with Joel's brother in a Manchester semi.

'Why don't you come along to my Mum's party, then?' Doll said recklessly, helping Mr Knowles to his feet. 'Well, it's not a party as such, or so she says. Just a few people round to try out her new spells – er – recipes.'

'I couldn't possibly. Your mother doesn't know me. And I couldn't gatecrash a family-gathering—'

'Course you could,' Doll said as Mr Knowles scampered out of the surgery. 'Believe me, one more stray odd-bod at Mum's will be neither here nor there.'

*

'It's getting very dark,' Lulu said, pulling her Afghan more closely round her and blowing on her mittened fingers. 'And I'm sure people know we're here. And the cars all go through that puddle so I'm soaking and cold – and there hasn't been a sign of *them*.'

'It's more like December than October,' Biff agreed from her chunky crouching position behind the hedge. 'But don't be such a namby-pamby, Lu. What's a little discomfort compared with the mission we're on? Although sometimes, on days like this, even I wish we could do our undercover stuff in the summer months only.'

Lu looked askance at her employer. 'That'd be hardly fair on the animals, would it? Ill-treatment is probably at its height in the run-up to Christmas and just after . . .'

'It was a joke,' Biff said testily. 'And don't speak so loudly, Lu. We're supposed to be on a secret sortie. Silence is the key. Oh, bugger . . .'

Lulu giggled as Biff's mobile trumpeted Teddy Bear's Picnic into the murky gloom.

There was a lot of hissed conversation, then Biff switched the mobile off with a flourish. 'Hedley. Your mother phoned. Can you pick up a loaf on your way home?'

'That'll be for the pickled newt sandwiches.'

'What?' Biff adjusted her misted-up bifocals. 'I thought you were a committed veggie. Anyway, Hedley also said he's had a tip-off from our people in Fiddlesticks – the quarry is on its way.'

Thank goodness for that, Lulu thought, hoping she'd remember Mitzi's bread but somehow doubting it.

This front-line rescue service was a sideline of the animal welfare charity shop that Hedley and Biff had developed over the years. While Lu would do anything, anything at all, to rescue any animal in need, at the moment she was very cold and very uncomfortable, and beginning to become aware of the Afghan coat's antisocial aroma when wet.

103

There was also a tiny part of her that thought that they might very well be on another wild goose chase.

Hedley and Biff's underground network of informants were mostly over eighty, all slightly barking, and usually got the wrong end of every available stick. But because, on rare occasions, the intelligence had been correct and animals in sad and sorry states had been whisked away to live the life of Riley, Lulu knew she'd never refuse to accompany Biff on these missions.

However, she felt that this afternoon, squatting in a dripping privet hedge at the far end of Hazy Hassocks high street, on the flimsiest of tip-offs, with people and cars going past all the time and rush hour getting very close – well, such as the Hazy Hassocks rush hour was, of course – when they'd be visible to practically everyone, was probably not going to be one of their glory moments.

Biff and Hedley's narks in Hazy Hassocks's neighbouring village of Fiddlesticks were two elderly widows who had read far too much G.K. Chesterton and suspected everyone of everything. So far most of their information had been embarrassingly incorrect.

'Here they come!' Biff growled, squinting against the orange glow of the high street's halogen lamps. 'The silver MPV! Right on time!'

Lu pushed her beaded braids away from her eyes and exhaled. Her heart was thumping. There was a gnawing in her stomach as the adrenaline kicked in.

'Now!' Biff yelled, breaking cover and belting into the path of the silver people carrier. 'Let's get the bastards!'

Lu, emerging from the privet a split second later, screamed as the people carrier got Biff.

Biff rolled over and over into the centre of the road and lay still. The vehicle had slewed across the high street. People were running from all directions. The driver, an elderly white-haired man, sat there whimpering.

Shaking and crying, Lulu knelt beside the face-down Biff and tried to find a pulse, but the Afghan, the tears and her braids got in the way. She couldn't find anything at all through Biff's eighteen layers of clothing and Arnie-developed muscles. She did, however, find the mobile phone in one of Biff's parka pockets and snatched at it.

As she was probably the only person in the entire world who not only didn't own a mobile but was so non-techie that she had no idea how to use one, Lulu stared at it in despair. 'How do you use this?' she screamed up to the knot of people who were staring down at her. 'Can someone get an ambulance?'

Three people helped to remove the phone from her mittens. It was probably the last she'd see of it.

'Sod the ambulance,' Biff muttered from her prone position. 'Get them ferrets!'

'Oh, you're alive!' Lulu hugged Biff's massive shoulders in the rain-soaked gloom.

The crowd cheered.

'Of course I'm perishing alive,' Biff, still face down, spat out bits of twig. 'Just winded. Sodding leave me alone and get the ferrets, Lu!'

Sniffing back the tears and pushing her plastered hair away from her face, Lulu scrambled inelegantly to her feet, trampling her long skirts underfoot. Pushing the still-whimpering driver aside, she tugged at the people carrier's rear doors.

It was packed from floor to ceiling with cardboard boxes. At least the accident didn't seem to have dislodged them, Lulu thought. But there were no air-holes! The ferrets may well have survived the impact – but what if they'd suffocated?

Chewing her lips, she ripped the top off the first box . . .

'Oy!' The white-haired driver had staggered round to the back of the people carrier. 'What the blazes do you think you're doing?'

'Rescuing poor defenceless animals, you cruel bastard!' Lu screamed. 'We know what you've been up to! Collecting ferrets! Planning a nice little illegal line in rabbiting, no doubt! You can try to mow us down but you won't stop us! There – look! Oh . . .'

The box contained several dozen soft felt hats. Lulu reached for another box. More flat circles of felt. And another. And another.

The white-haired driver had been joined by a growing crowd of home-going Hazy Hassockers. They all stared accusingly at Lulu.

'Berets,' the driver said. 'B-e-r-e-t-s. Pronounced, in the French, as berrays. Not frigging b-e-r-r-e-t-t-s or frigging ferrets. Okay?'

'Er . . . yes . . .' Lulu nodded slowly. Bugger. Bugger. Bugger. No doubt the old dears in Fiddlesticks were as deaf as posts, not to mention not being up to speed with French pronunciation.

'I'm Jeffrey of Jeffrey's Millinery,' the white-haired driver said pompously. 'These are our new winter line. We've just collected them from our out-workers in Fiddlesticks. Perhaps beret liberation wasn't quite what you had in mind . . .'

'Er – no – sorry . . .' Lulu tried to smile placatingly, ignoring the dozens of berets soaking up the rain in the muddy gutter. 'An easy mistake to make – oh, shit.'

With blue lights flashing and sirens wailing, an ambulance was inching its way through the mayhem.

'Tell 'em to piss off,' Biff wailed, trying to sit up but, being hampered by the hefty layers of clothing, merely flailing around like a beached seal. 'I don't want no ambulance! Tell 'em!'

Lulu watched in silent horror as the youthful green-uniformed paramedics leapt smoothly from the ambulance and went to work on the still-protesting Biff. One of them, of course, was Shay. Despite the awfulness of the situation, she drank in the tall, lean, tousle-haired Heath Ledger beauty of him. Was there a more intoxicating combination than someone so gloriously male carrying out such a brave and caring profession?

Nasty Niall and Designer Dee-Dee were instantly forgotten.

'Excuse me, young lady,' Jeffrey of Jeffrey's Millinery tapped her on the shoulder, recoiling slightly as he got a full-on whiff of wet Afghan. 'You stay right where you are. The police are on their way too. They'll want to talk to you.'

Lulu nodded. She wasn't surprised. Still, Biff would be able to explain the mistake when they arrived, wouldn't she? Biff would be able to back up her story. Jeffrey of Jeffrey's Millinery might drop compensation charges, mightn't he?

Oh, double bugger.

Biff, still vociferously protesting, was being stretchered into the back of the ambulance.

Shay, making sure his patient was safely tethered, glanced across at her as he closed the ambulance's doors. His eyes lit up. 'Oh, hello. Nice to see you again. Guess what? Your mother's just invited me to your Halloween party. Cool.'

Lu perked up. Life wasn't all bad. What party? Who cared.

'Oh, great.'

Shay nodded. 'I thought so. It's my night off. Oh, and I've asked Carmel—' he indicated his tiny fairy-doll-pretty co-paramedic '—to come with me. That'll be okay, won't it?'

Chapter Ten

'Eye of newt – yes; ear of bat – yes; claw of toad – yes
...' Mitzi ticked off the ingredients on her shopping list.
'Well, okay then ... dried basil, figs, bananas, barley
water – yes; flaked blackberries, endive, tarragon – no;
fresh grapes, leeks, lemons – yes; liquorice – no; marjo-
ram, mixed nuts – yes; peppermint – no; pineapple, shallots
– yes; star anise, strawberries, thyme – no.'

Much to Mitzi's relief, unlike the previous ones, Granny
Westward's Halloween recipes had all seemed to contain
quite normal ingredients. Okay, so the Balm of Gilead had
posed a bit of problem, as had the rather worrying handwritten addendum about a sprinkling of betony being good
for curing elf-sickness. And as for the spikily crafted
suggestion regarding a good jugful of hemp seeds making
the party go with a swing!

'Apples, yes ... ebony, no. Ebony? *Ebony*? Possibly a
spelling mistake. Right – hazelnuts? A bit early ... Ah,
flaked poplar for astral transportation ... perhaps not ...
And pumpkins for decoration and the flesh for Pumpkin
Passion ... hmmm ...'

Realising that her monologue was quite loud and the list-
ticking was fairly flamboyant, she stopped abruptly and cast
a surreptitious glance around Big Sava.

Sod it. She was being carefully observed by a cluster of
people huddled round the bargain baskets. Mitzi gave them

a little smile, tucked the list into her pocket and, hoping she looked nothing like 'mad woman muttering to herself', trundled her trolley in the opposite direction. Anything still missing she'd probably be able to buy at Herbie's Healthfoods, and as before, could improvise with the remainder.

Feeling quite buoyant, she joined the queue at Big Sava's one and only open cash desk and slowly snaked forward. Even though it wasn't quite the end of October, Big Sava's tannoy was bellowing 'Santa Claus is Coming to Town'.

Mind you, as they'd had tinsel up since August bank holiday Monday, Mitzi wasn't unduly surprised.

They'd got on to Wizzard 'Wishing It Could Be Christmas Every Day' by the time Mitzi reached the till. She sang along with Roy Wood on the chorus as she unloaded her trolley.

'Fifteen punds and thruppence, Mrs Blessing,' Gavin the check-out boy sniffed. 'This stuff for your party tomorrow?'

'It is,' Mitzi handed over a twenty-pound note, unfazed by his insider knowledge. Hazy Hassocks was a small place and Gavin was one of Flo and Clyde's many grandchildren.

'Nan and Gramp says you're into cooking funny stuff since the bank sacked yer because you were too old to add up any more. It's all fruit and veg, innit? You ain't gone vulcan, have you? We gets loads of vulcans in here – won't touch meat nor eggs nor cheese nor nuffin. Daft if you ask me. I mean, what would you 'ave at Burger King?'

'Good point, Gavin. Maybe you should raise it on *Question Time*? And I wasn't sacked by the bank because I was too damn old. I took early retirement. Very, very early retirement. And no, I'm not a vulcan, nor a vegan, nor even a vegetarian. And what are you doing?'

Gavin was holding the twenty-pound note up to the light.

'Checking it.'

'It's kosher,' Mitzi smiled. 'Not one I made earlier – or even a little sample I helped myself to when I left the bank.'

'Can't be too careful,' Gavin sniffed again. 'Not with your family trouble.'

'What family trouble?'

Gavin leaned across his till and looked conspiratorial. 'I heard about your Lu being nabbed for a breach of the peace. In the 'igh street. In front of 'undreds of people. And then they didn't even arrest her, did they? It was so not fair! They just told her to run along home. Don't seem right somehow ... us lot on the Bath Road Estate would have been hauled up in front of the magistrates before you had time to blink.' He sighed heavily at the injustice.

'It was all a misunderstanding.'

'Yeah, well you would say that, wouldn't you? 'ere's your change. See ya later – and don't forget you can get extra discounts on the OAPs' specials. Oh bollocks, yeah – forgot – 'ave a nice day.'

'You too, Gavin.'

Outside, tucked away at the rear of the high street, the wind howled between the grey concrete buildings and blew tumbleweeds of empty crisp packets around Mitzi's booted ankles. Thumping her carrier bags into the back of the Mini in a corner of the Siberian wasteland that was Big Sava's car park, she groaned. Not only did she feel about three hundred and ninety but thanks to Lulu's brush with the law and the Hazy Hassocks jungle drums, the Blessings were now clearly akin to the Krays. And she still had the rest of her shopping to do. And she was bound to bump into umpteen people who would suck their teeth and tut in sympathy.

She locked the door and prepared to meet her doom.

The sycamores which lined the high street were whirling their little helicopter seeds in all directions. The green-gold leaves were eddying in the gutter. Putting her head down, Mitzi attempted to run the October gauntlet between Big Sava and Herbie's Healthfoods. Sadly, the Kray theory had travelled well, she discovered, as several people stopped her to offer blustery commiserations on Lulu's latest misdemeanours.

110

It was the trouble with living in a small community, Mitzi knew, although hopefully it would be a seven-day wonder. Lulu had seemed fairly unfazed by her 'don't do it again' warning by PC Hodgkin, and frankly, as Biff and Hedley managed to get into all sorts of peculiar situations thanks to duff information, a public caution was pretty good going. There would come a time, Mitzi was sure, when Lulu would be manhandled into the back of a police van and then the gossip mongers would really have a field day.

She hurried past Patsy's Pantry. There were far too many furry hats and paisley scarves and Pringle twin sets in there. Too many pursed lips. Too many loudly voiced opinions. She simply couldn't face a bevy of Torquemadas over an iced fancy.

It was with some relief that she stumbled into the tropical, overheated, spicy atmosphere of Herbie's Healthfoods without encountering any further sympathetic tutting.

Herbie, his halo of receding frizzed hair making him look like a septuagenarian Art Garfunkel, beamed at her. 'Lovely morning, Mrs B.'

Mitzi nodded as, with shopping list once more in hand, she scanned the pungently dark shelves for the remainder of the ingredients. Herbie thought every morning was lovely, even the most inclement ones. She assumed this was due to him having absorbed far too many happy herbs in his youth. At least he could be guaranteed not to comment on Lulu. The event wouldn't have permeated his permanently fogged brain.

'Ah – good choices,' Herbie said as she thrust her purchases across the counter. 'Lovely stuff for the Infernal Eve. That old Gran of yours must have really been in touch with the Dark Side.'

'I don't think so,' Mitzi said quickly. 'The recipes are simply traditional country ones for Halloween. For party games and things. We're not holding a seance or anything scary.'

'That's what they all say,' Herbie chuckled to himself

111

and popped various dried twigs, desiccated leaves and little phials of powder into his trademark bottle-green paper bags. 'Still, I suppose now you've retired you have to find something to while away the hours. Not much to look forward to at our age, is there? Not that I'd advise dabbling in the Black Arts as an alternative to cross-stitch – so don't blame me if you unearth something with this little lot that would have been best left slumbering . . .'

Mitzi almost flounced from the shop. Now she felt more decrepit than ever – and she certainly didn't want Herbie to put any doubts into her mind about the party food. She'd always enjoyed Halloween. In a completely non-witchery way, naturally. She'd loved it when Lu and Doll had been tiny and she'd dressed them in bin liners and black lipstick, and they'd called on Flo and the Bandings demanding money with menaces. Flo and Lob and Lav had pretended to be frightened and handed over Refreshers and Sherbet Fountains and everyone had been innocently happy.

Now that innocent enjoyment was somehow tarnished.

How dare Herbie hint that there was anything untoward in what she was doing? Cooking up a few traditional old-style party dishes surely wasn't the same as holding some sort of satanic mass, was it?

Having collected two oversized tangerine-orange pumpkins from the greengrocers, Mitzi was juggling with them and Herbie's carrier bag, and so, still feeling rather irritable, really wasn't in the mood for Trilby Man in full throttle. But while she was in the high street she felt she ought to check up on her Baby Boomers, even though they seemed to be managing very nicely without her. All they'd needed was someone to get the ball rolling and they were up and running, she thought, mixing her metaphors and clichés with sulky abandon.

Shivering in the cutting wind, and with her hair blowing spiky strands into her eyes and mouth, she shouldered her way through the heat-seeking crush into the Nissen hut library. Trilby Man was sitting alone at the radiator-table but had managed to drape a piece of greyish clothing over each chair to ward off invaders. He waved as he spotted her and began untidily folding away the *Sun*. 'Hello, Mitzi. Glad you dropped in. Just the ticket. Blimey – your face looks a mess. What's up? Are you crying?'

Mitzi sniffed. She'd probably caught something from Gavin. 'It's freezing out there and the wind made my eyes run a bit, that's all. It's probably smudged my mascara ...'

'Ah,' Trilby Man nodded again. 'It has that. You looks like that rocker bloke – whatsisname? Ah, yes, Gladys Cooper. You ought to tidy yourself up a bit. Easy to let yourself go when you're not gainfully employed and there's only the Grim Reaper to look forward to. Mind, what someone of your age wants with make-up is beyond me.'

Gritting her teeth, Mitzi dumped the pumpkins on the table and rubbed a finger at the smudged mascara. Then she remembered all the magazines said that you shouldn't be rough with the delicate under-eye tissue, so she stopped.

Thanks to Gavin, Herbie and Trilby Man she now felt fit for nothing but the Singing Cedars Rest Home.

'I was going to catch up on the Baby Boomers, but as you're on your own maybe I should come back later, or perhaps I'll just e-mail everyone tonight.'

'No need, duck. We're more or less sorted, but if you've got any hot news I'll pass it on. The others will be along shortly. You can have the *Mirror* 'til Ken gets here if you likes. No? Oh well, suit yourself. Look, sorry if I was a bit forthright just now. Probably why I've never been married. Calling a spade a spade don't go down too well with some of the ladies. They likes to be flattered – even if they are dog rough, if you gets my drift ...' He beamed at her. 'Anyway, at least you've got a nice new hairdo, duck. Been to Pauline's for a pensioner's cut, have you?'

'I'm a long way off being pensionable and – oh my God!' Mitzi caught a glimpse of her reflection in the window. She looked like Don King with a crimson rinse.

'No point trying to flatten it down,' Trilby Man said

comfortingly. 'It'll only end up like a bird's nest and look even more stupid. You leave it till you gets home, duck. After all, no one is going to give you a second look, are they?'

Fighting the initial urge to punch him squarely in the teeth, Mitzi conceded that he was probably right. Lulu turned heads. Doll was stunning. She was past it. Way, way past it. No one was going to notice her wandering along the windswept high street with a haphazard scarlet mohican, were they? They'd probably think it was a hat. A red hat. A Jenny Joseph red hat. Dear God – was she really that old? Was she rapidly turning into an old purple-wearing, red-hat-owning crone who wanted to learn to spit?

She glared at Trilby Man. 'No, I won't sit down, thank you. Can't stop. I'm off to my pensioners' lunch in the village hall. No, of course not really – it's a joke. Irony – or maybe sarcasm. Oh, never mind ... I just wanted to know if you got my last BBC update.'

'June and Sally did. The rest of us ain't up to speed on e-mails. Mind, it's handy having that Internet thingamabob here in the library. Not that I holds with it. It's not natural. Still, you're a bit of a silver surfer, aren't you, duck?'

'I think you'll find the silver surfers are more in their seventies and eighties, actually.'

'That's as may be,' Trilby Man looked almost jocular, 'but like I said, calling a spade a spade is my stock in trade so to speak and I bet's you're as grey as a weasel under that there dye of yourn.'

Bunching her fists into tight balls and counting to ten, Mitzi managed not to hurl herself across the table with a Paul Revere yell.

Triby Man continued to beam. 'So, thanks to you being a bit hot on the old laptop we all knows Mrs Snepps has agreed to let us use the village hall, and on what days, and we're grateful to you, duck. We're going ahead with a few of the indoor activities like we discussed. Want to see what we've got so far?'

As what she still really wanted to do was to hit him very, very hard, Mitzi's nod was curt and her smile was more of a bared-teeth grimace. Trilby Man didn't seem to notice. However, the list was impressive: quiz teams, music appreciation, a reading group, a writers' circle, an am-dram group, dance classes, a bridge and whist school, and an intermediate cookery course were all fully subscribed. In the warmer months, the list informed her, the Baby Boomers Collective were going to get together for various sporting activities and possibly rambling.

Mitzi noticed with some trepidation that Lav and Lob, despite their assurances they wouldn't get involved, had signed up for everything.

'That's lovely.' She pushed the paper back to Trilby Man. 'And the first sessions are booked for next week, I see. Well, you clearly don't need me any more, so—'

'Course we do,' Trilby Man asserted. 'You're our co-ordinator. Without you this wouldn't have got off the ground – and well, being honest, you're the only one who can negotiate with Lady Tarnia Muck, aren't you? We'll look forward to seeing you at the first meeting, okay? Now, if you don't mind me making a bit of a personal comment, duck – don't you think them jeans and that leather coat are a bit young for you? A bit mutton dressed as lamb, like? At your age you should be in a nice buff anorak and—'

With a whimper of fury Mitzi snatched up her pumpkins and whirled out of the library, leaving unheard the remainder of Trilby Man's unwise venture into Trinny and Susannah territory.

'Sod it,' she snarled as, hampered by the pumpkins, she caught the strap of her bag on the Aberdeen Angus-like handles of a toddler's buggy in the exit scrum.

The more she tugged, the more the buggy rocked and the more the toddler yelled.

''ere!' The toddler's mother stepped forward, thrusting a beringed nose under Mitzi's. 'You mind what you're at!

115

My little Paris is sensitive, bless 'im. Stop yanking! You'll 'ave 'im over!'

'Bugger Paris!' Mitzi muttered, still yanking. 'Bugger Gavin and Herbie and bugger most of all buggering Trilby Man! Ah!'

The buggy handles suddenly yielded up her bag strap with all the unleashed power of jet propulsion.

Mitzi and the bag and the pumpkins rocketed dizzily out of the library into the high street.

'Daft old bat!' Paris's mother yelled behind her. 'She ought to be in a 'ome!'

Feeling worse than she could ever remember since the silver wedding party and the Jennifer revelations, Mitzi gathered herself together, and tottered in the direction of Big Sava's car park. The gale was still screaming with icy fury, but the tears that prickled her eyes and trickled irritatingly down her nose were caused more by self-pity than the freezing wind.

She ducked her head down and, with a pumpkin under each arm, hurried past Patsy's Pantry. 'Bugger, bugger, bu – and oh, damn!' She cannoned off something large and solid. The pumpkins joyously escaped into the high street.

'Much the way I feel myself,' a voice said in amusement. 'Are you okay?'

'I'm fine but I've lost my bloody pumpkins.' Mitzi lifted her head. Her hair, whipped into even more of a Marsha Hunt Afro, got in the way of seeing. The man she'd walked into seemed about eighteen feet tall. 'I'm so sorry ... Wasn't looking where I was going ...'

'Me neither. Hang on – I'll get your pumpkins.'

Mitzi watched with deep gratitude and not a little embarrassment as the tall, dark-coated man nipped niftily in and out of the high street traffic, scooped down, and belted back towards her, triumphantly clutching both pumpkins like a double-fisted Martin Offiah.

He handed them to her. 'No damage at all. My mum

used to always have pumpkins on Halloween too. Hollowed out with candles inside. We thought it was magic.'

Was she old enough to be his mother? Possibly? She clearly looked it with her ravaged make-up lingering in the wrinkles that Oil of Olay hadn't yet obliterated, and the manic hair.

She smiled. 'Thank you so much. It's been one of those days.'

'I've had one of those years,' he smiled back. 'A single disastrous day would be bliss. Still, as long as you're okay.'

'Fine,' she reassured him again. 'And thank you. I hope the rest of your year is better.'

'So do I,' he grinned.

His teeth were remarkably white, Mitzi noticed, his bone structure sensational. And he had one diamond ear stud. Lulu would absolutely love him.

He was still grinning as he turned away and walked back up the high street. Mitzi watched him go with a feeling of acute sadness. For the first time since Lance's defection she'd felt a *tingle*. A real tingle. And it had to be caused by a man years younger than her who clearly saw her as on a par with his mother. Elderly. And dotty. And clumsy. And losing not only her pumpkins but also her marbles. And – oooh!

'Life,' Mitzi said out loud, pinching a phrase from her daughters, 'is *so* not fair!'

Chapter Eleven

The trouble was, Lulu thought, shouldering her way through the subterranean gloom of the charity shop on Halloween morning, that no one *understood*.

Everyone thought that she was upset about the brush with the law and the very public tussling with Jeffrey of Jeffrey's Millinery. Everyone, even Doll and Mitzi, thought she was embarrassed about her loss of face. Everyone thought she was *ashamed*.

And of course, she thought crossly as she thrust another handwritten 'Suitable For Halloween' card on a rail full of ancient black polyester frocks that smelled of encrusted talcum powder, what she really was, was heartbroken.

Okay, maybe that was a bit OTT. She and Shay had done no more than exchange a few smiles as they passed on their neighbouring paths, and had a couple of brief conversations in The Faery Glen, and once shared a gentle laugh together at the bus stop in Winterbrook over Lav and Lob and the cycling helmets. It was hardly a lifetime's commitment. But she'd had such hopes – and she fancied him sooo much.

It was – as she'd wished for – as if Heath Ledger had walked straight out of 'The Knight's Tale' and moved in next door. And now, she snorted in indignation as she untangled three wispy black shawls which reeked of moth-balls and mushrooms, at last he was going to spend the whole evening in her house – with some bloody little fairy-doll, do-gooding, lifesaving, paramedic called Carmel.

It was soooo not fair!

As another wave of people surged into the dark snugness of the shop, Lulu shoved her way back to the relative safety of the counter.

'I love Halloween,' Biff Pippin said, clutching a cup of vegetable Oxo which was steaming up her bifocals. 'One of our best times.'

Lulu nodded. The shop was always crowded at Halloween, and at Christmas and New Year, as people scoured the rails for suitable fancy dress costumes at a knock-down price. Unlike her, they didn't buy their year-round wardrobe from charity shops, and so never knew where to look for the best bargains on these one-off sorties. Biff and Hedley were demons at marking up tat on these occasions and making a vast profit for their animal sanctuary charities.

'What are you wearing tonight?' Hedley asked, pausing in changing the price on a black fedora with a filigree of cigarette burns on the brim. 'To your mum's party? It is fancy dress, I take it?'

'I don't think so,' Lulu looked doubtful. 'She didn't say so. To be honest I think it'll be a bit of a disaster.' A lot of a disaster, she thought darkly, if she had to spend it watching Shay and Carmel lusting all over each other. 'She's cooking. Again.'

The conversation was halted for a moment as half a dozen streaky-haired office girls gigglingly approached the counter clutching several long black skirts, two shawls and a 1980s halter-neck top in ebony lurex. As Lulu had had her eye on this top for Shay-snaring, her customer-service-smile was sadly lacking as she shoved it into the bag.

'No, we don't take Visa. Cash only. What? Oh come on – it's only a fiver ... No, sorry we can't hold it for you while you get some money. Too much demand today – sorry.'

'What on earth are you doing?' Biff snuffled through the

powdery bit at the bottom of her Oxo mug, watching as the streaky-haired girl left the shop empty-handed and Lulu shoved the halter-neck beneath the counter. 'That could have been a sale.'

'It still is,' Lulu said. 'To me. Um – well, as long as you can deduct it from my next week's wages. I'm a bit broke at the moment.'

Hedley nodded. The Pippins were used to Lulu's wage packet being mainly taken in second-hand clothes. 'So what were you saying about your mother's party?'

'Oh, just that she's cooking up some more of Great-Granny Westward's All Hallows Eve recipes. We'll probably all spend November in hospital with botulism.'

Biff shook her head. 'Don't be so damnably negative, Lu. It's one of the most magical nights of the year. Some of those old country recipes were specially written for The Dark Night of All Souls, you know. Mind, most of the ones I know seem to be love potions rather than raising the dead. Capturing the man of your dreams by chucking him backwards into a mirror. That sort of thing.'

'Sounds a bit violent, Biff, pet,' Hedley looked doubtful, as no doubt you would if your wife had spent all her professional life crunching other gargantuan females in headlocks and half nelsons. 'I understood it was more gentle physical fun. Like apple bobbing.'

Lulu said nothing at all. Her mind was shimmying off on a track of its own.

Love potions . . . capturing the man of your dreams.

She cheered up immensely. There was bound to be something along those lines in Granny Westward's book. Yessss! Take a few well-chosen herbs, blend in an ancient incantation or two, add the black halter-neck – and kerpow! – itsy-bitsy Carmel wouldn't get a look-in.

'Where's Mum?' Doll peered into the kitchen. 'Jesus! What are you doing?'

'Cooking,' Lulu looked up crossly, trying to cover

Granny Westward's book with a mound of apples, hoping Doll wouldn't noticed the saucepan of molten candle wax glugging on the cooker. Trust her to arrive early and start asking stupid questions.

'It stinks,' Doll said cheerfully. 'Really honks. What is it?'

'Just some last-minute – um – stuff.' Lu frowned. The wax – now melted with a whole mound of ancient Bronnley Apple Blossom bath cubes, stirred in because apple blossom was essential to the spell, but of course the real thing wasn't around in October, and either Granny Westward had lied about plentiful supplies of apple blossom on Halloween or global warming simply wasn't what it used to be – did smell very unappealing. 'No – don't touch it! It'll spoil.'

'I doubt that,' Doll wrinkled her nose. 'It reeks. Well, whatever it is, don't expect me to eat it.'

'It's not for eating, it's for decoration – and why aren't you tarted up? Why are you still in your uniform? It isn't fancy dress.'

'Isn't it?' Doll looked her sister up and down, then grinned. 'Actually, I haven't been home yet. I just popped in from the surgery in case Mum needed a hand with anything.'

'We're all under control, thanks.' Lulu now looked worriedly at the bowl of apple puree and herbs on the table. It was bubbling. All on its own. Like a geyser. She draped a tea towel over it before Doll nosied into that too. 'And Mum's gone to the hairdressers. She said she needed a bit of a spruce-up for the party.'

'Blimey—' Doll fondled Richard and Judy who had just emerged from under the table '—she'll be lucky to get an appointment anywhere tonight. The whole of Hazy Hassocks is being done up for the witching hour. Has she gone to Pauline's?'

'Guess so.' Lulu really wished her sister would bugger off. 'She didn't say. She seemed a bit vague, actually. I

121

think she's worrying about this party. Still, Pauline will always squeeze her in, so that should cheer her up. Why don't you go and see on your way home?'

'Yeah, I might. Are you're sure you don't need a hand here?'

'Really, really sure. Everything's under control.'

'That'll be a first,' Doll giggled. 'How many are we expecting?'

'Millions,' Lulu sighed. She really didn't have time to get involved in long-drawn-out conversations. 'Well, the neighbours, some of Mum's friends, oh you know . . .'

Doll nodded. 'The usual suspects in other words. Okay then, I'll see you in a couple of hours. Have fun.'

Waiting until Doll had slammed the front door behind her, Lulu picked up the recipe book again. Thank God for that – she was working on borrowed time as it was. Mitzi's impromptu visit to the hairdresser had given her the opportunity she needed to concoct a few love potions. Now Doll, being her usual helpful interfering self, had eaten into those precious minutes.

Right. Okay. On with the Apple Love Candles, then she'd tackle the Midnight Apples. Guaranteed to work every time – well, according to Granny Westward's handwritten notes anyway: *'guaranteed to work powerful love magic – but you must be very, very careful because . . .'*

Lulu decided to ignore the next bit that warned the use of Midnight Apples may border on manipulation. It was only a bit of fun anyway, wasn't it? She was pretty sure the black halter-neck top would do more for Shay than any amount of apple love magic.

She lifted the tea towel and peered at the puree and herbs. Mercifully, it had stopped bubbling but now looked and smelled like a foetid cowpat. Eyes watering, trying not to inhale, she pushed the bowl to the far side of the table. Richard and Judy, who had jumped up to investigate, backed away, spines arched, tails bushed into identical grey bottle brushes.

'It's okay,' Lulu assured them. 'No one's going to eat it. It's for the love candles, although I'm not sure about the smell being much of an aphrodisiac. Maybe it'll sort of evaporate . . .'

She yanked up her sleeves a bit more. She was having to modify Granny's instructions because the apple candles were supposed to been made weeks before the event – but then they hadn't had freezers in those days, had they? Surely all she had to do was gloop the puree into the molten wax, leave to cool, then shape it into – er – candley shapes and bung them in the freezer for half an hour or so?

The recipe book had said the candles must be pink, and had advocated a liberal additional of cochineal for the purpose. Lulu had bypassed this by melting down a dozen pink dinner candles from the living room, carefully removing the wicks and hanging them over the back of a chair for later use. So far so good – now for the Midnight Apples.

There were two love spells under this heading, both a bit iffy in Lu's opinion. The first love divination, according to Granny's book, was amazingly simple: it involved you holding an apple in your hand until it became warm, then, at the stroke of midnight, passing it on to the object of your desire. If they ate it they'd return your love. Easy-peasy.

Pretty sure that even if she managed to remember to hang on to an apple all night, by the time she handed it, sort of clenched and sweaty, to Shay he'd merely lob in the nearest bin, Lulu felt she ought to go for the second apple love spell as a back-up.

Of course, this one would have been so much easier if Shay's name had been Ian or Ivan. Carving his curvy initial into a relentlessly glossy Braeburn which kept skittering across the table was proving very difficult. The pile of discarded apples with zigzagged hieroglyphics jabbed into the skins was growing by the minute. 'S' was the trickiest bloody letter in the whole damn alphabet, Lulu thought, as she gouged away, remembering to leave enough room on the other side for her L.

By the time she'd finished, with a vaguely recognisable S and L, there wasn't much apple left, but still now all she had to do was remember the little incantation as she handed it over at midnight. She peered at Granny Westward's spiky writing.

'*I conjure thee apple by these names that what man tasteth thee may love me and burn on my fire as melted wax.*'

Blimey! Lulu raised her eyebrows. Granny Westward must have been a pretty hot babe in her day. She really wished she'd known her. This was great stuff.

Scraping the apple residue into a heap, making sure that the engraved apple and the smallish one she intended to clutch all night were put safely at the back of the crockery cupboard, she took a deep breath and began to tackle the love candles.

Richard and Judy fled to the washing basket as the fumes swamped the kitchen, and the whole procedure was far more tricky than she'd envisaged, but half an hour later, six squat, barrel-shaped, pink candles, complete with reinstated wicks, were sitting in the freezer.

The fact that they still smelt appalling, and had bits of lumpy puree and herb sticking out of them like a bad batch of Lincolnshire sausages, was neither here nor there. At midnight, when Lulu approached Shay with a double-whammy of apple magic, they'd dance and gutter and light the way to everlasting love.

'Christ Almighty!' the back door flew open. 'What the hell is going on in here?'

Lulu, still trying to reclaim the kitchen, bared her teeth at Flo. 'Just clearing up ... Er – Mum's not in and we haven't started yet ...'

Flo clanked several carrier bags into the mess on the kitchen table and proceeded to unload them. 'No, I know that. I've just bought the booze. I promised your Mum we'd do the drinks if she made the eats ... Crikey, Lu, she hasn't left you in charge of the food, has she? It'll be all rat dropping veggie rubbish. Our Clyde won't touch none of that.'

Ignoring this slur on her culinary abilities, Lulu looked at the ever-growing collection of bottles with mounting horror. There was an awful lot of elderflower and rhubarb, and swede and dandelion, not to mention parsnip and sloe.

'This is our special,' Flo said, flourishing a bottle under Lulu's nose. 'Rosehip and apple champagne.'

Lu's eyes lit up. 'Oh, right. Apple ... Apples are very important tonight, you know.'

Flo's eyes narrowed. 'Christ, Lu, you haven't got mixed up in that mumbo-jumbo, have you? Them cakes your dad gave me were bad enough, and our Gavin says your Mum was buying all sorts of weird stuff in Big Sava ... It ain't natural.'

'Actually, it is. Very natural. See, tonight, Halloween, is really Samhain – the end of summer in ancient religions. Samhain means the feast of apples and—'

'Spare me the details.' Flo frowned. 'It's all weirdo to me. Give me good old Halloween any day.'

'What with the witches and ghouls and ghosts and things?' Lulu laughed.

'Yes, well. They're proper. Right and proper for the occasion. You know where you are with them. All this new-age stuff fair gives me the heebie-jeebies – oh, there's someone at the front door. Shall I get it?'

'It's probably Mum back from the hairdresser,' Lulu said, wondering how ballistic Mitzi would go over the state of the kitchen. 'She's probably forgotten her key. I'll let her in – oh, and thank you for the drinks. I'll – um – see you later.'

Flo, not taking the hint, remained rooted to the spot.

Bugger, bugger, bugger, Lu thought, as she hurtled through the hall. She'd never get the kitchen back to normal and have a bath and do her hair and her face and squeeze into the black halter-neck in time. Why couldn't people just leave her alone?

She tugged the door open. The darkly icy night howled round her, swirling dead leaves into the hall with a dry rasping menace.

'Mum – look, I got a bit behind with stuff in the kitchen but it won't take five minutes and – oh my God!'

Lob and Lav stood beaming on the doorstep. 'Not too early, dear, are we?'

The Bandings, all in wrinkly limp black layers, with witches' hats atop the cycle helmets, pushed past her. 'Oh, how lovely and warm! And what a delicious smell! Is that pumpkin pie? Are we too early for the food, Lulu, dear? Only we didn't have any tea so as to save ourselves.'

'Er, yes, well, you are a bit early ... Mum isn't here yet and we haven't put the food out and well ... maybe if you'd like to wait in here with Flo ...' Lu ushered them away from the living room and into the bombshell of a kitchen.

Flo cackled with laughter. 'Blimey – look at you two! "Secret black and midnight hags" could have been written about you. And don't you look at me like that, young Lulu. I know me Scottish Play off by 'eart.'

Lulu had more than Flo's familiarity with the Bard to worry about. The Bandings had spotted the remains of the apple magic.

'Oh, lovely! Apples!' Lav clapped her Cyndi Lauper lace mittens together and homed in on the apple mountain. 'Are they for starters?'

'No they're bloody not,' Lulu hurled herself in front of the kitchen table. 'I – I'll make you a sandwich if you're that hungry.'

'Ooooh, super. Cheese and pickle would be nice, dear, thank you.' The Bandings clutched their pointy hats in excitement. 'And perhaps a small side salad?'

'Ill leave you to it, then,' Flo headed towards the back door. 'Tell your mum me and Clyde'll pop round about eight-ish. Oh, and be careful when you take the stoppers out of the swede and dandelion – it's a lively little vintage.'

Whimpering to herself, Lulu tugged out a sliced white loaf, piccalilli and the remains of the cheddar cheese. Bugger the Bandings! They were now going through the fridge with spindly fingers, exclaiming in rapture over half-empty tins of cat food and shrivelled cucumbers. She still had so much to do.

'I'll have to leave you in a second.' She pushed the sandwiches towards them. 'I need to get ready. Er – what time will Shay be arriving?'

'Oh, he won't be coming, dear.' Lob dribbled a mustard-covered gherkin down her whiskery chin. 'We told him this wouldn't be his sort of thing at all. All old fogies. He's taking little Caramel to the pictures instead.'

Chapter Twelve

PUMPKIN PASSIONS

Plenty of figs, chopped
Mashed bananas
Liquorice, cubed small
The mashed flesh of two large ripe pumpkins
A good handful of loaf sugar
Large spoonful of treacle
Mixed nuts, chopped
A handful of Balm of Gilead, powdered

Beat all ingredients together in large bowl with a wooden
spoon until dark and treacly consistency reached.

Spoon in small quantities on to baking tray greased with
best butter.
Bake in hot oven for half an hour until it takes on the
appearance of rich dark toffee.
Allow to cool before serving.

Note: All the ingredients in Pumpkin Passions have love
properties. They have been used in aphrodisiacs for
centuries. Pumpkin Passions can make the most sober
person behave in an unseemly and drunken manner. To be
eaten with the utmost caution.

Pauline, love her, had worked her usual magic, Mitzi thought, admiring her shadowy refection in the living-room mirror. Okay, so the image staring back at her was definitely enhanced by the fire glow and candlelight, but even so. . .

Gone for ever was the horrific Don King windswept look. The layers were now shorter, spikier and glossy chestnut rather than garish crimson. A long, jagged fringe swept across her forehead, and made her eyes look huge. It had knocked years off her. Even Lu had been impressed.

Before tackling the hellhole kitchen, Mitzi cast a last happy look round the darkened living room, with its deep jewel colours now embellished by the illuminated pumpkins on the window sills, masses of red and black candles, black cats, bats, witches on broomsticks, grinning tarantulas in gossamer webs and a dozen small luminous skeletons.

The party food, all from Granny's recipes, was piled high on every available surface, decorated by tiny ghosts and ghouls; Clyde's wine bottle mountain was glittering on the sideboard alongside a mass of mismatched glasses; the apple-bobbing tubs were set up on protective bin liners; Richard and Judy were perched on the back of the sofa purring in anticipation; and Mott the Hoople wavered sexily from the stereo.

Perfect.

The only flies in the festive ointment were of course the God-awful mess in the kitchen, with Lav and Lob in the middle of it twitteringly helping themselves to an early pint of cowslip and pea to wash down their sandwiches, and Lulu's unexplained gloomy mood.

When Mitzi had arrived home, Lu had made the complimentary coiffure remarks, cast evil-eyed glances at the Bandings, stormed upstairs and not yet re-emerged.

Putting it down to Lulu still feeling raw over the end of her relationship with Niall on a universal party night, Mitzi sighed. She'd assumed that once the girls had grown up the worrying would stop. Hah! She worried constantly about both of them: Lu because she was so flaky about men and everything else, and Doll because she wasn't.

Niall had broken Lu's heart and Brett would probably bore Doll to death. Men! Huh – who needed them?

Mitzi stopped dead in the hall. Blimey. She'd been using the 'who needs men' mantra for years – but suddenly it no longer rang true. She didn't need Lance any more, of course. She enjoyed his friendship and would never wish him any ill, but there was no *need*. However, the tall, dark, dangerous man she'd bumped into on the high street was another matter altogether.

He'd pressed buttons that had remained resolutely unpushed for ages. And she'd never see him again – and even if she did he'd only think of her as a sad old bat with wild hair, damp eyes, a red nose and an inability to hang on to her pumpkins.

'Sod it.'

'Language, Mitzi.' Lobelia teetered from the kitchen on her way towards the downstairs lavatory. 'You'll have to rinse your mouth out with some of Clyde's cowslip. Very tasty . . . ooh, have you got two staircases?'

'Just one,' Mitzi steered Lob carefully towards the cloakroom. 'And I really think you shouldn't drink any more.'

'I'll be fine when I have a – a—' Lobelia hiccuped violently '—oh, pardon me. No, I'll feel much better when we – hic – start on the food. No, no I'll be – hic – fine now, thank you – oops—'

'Don't lock the door,' Mitzi warned. 'And do you want me to hold your witches' hat?'

'No thank you.' Lob attempted to uncross her eyes. 'It's superglued to the – hic – cycle helmet and you know we *must* wear that at all times – whoops!'

The lavatory door closed with a resounding crash. Mitzi winced. Lulu really should have had enough sense to hide Clyde's booze.

The doorbell rang merrily.

'You get it – hic! – oh crikey! There goes my sock!' Lob

130

called happily from behind the door. 'I'll be – whoooo – quite all right, dear . . .'

Lavender, tripping over her drooping skirts, beat Mitzi to the door by a nanosecond.

'Come along in,' she breathed effusively, reeling slightly with her hat dipping towards her nose. 'Lovely to see you all! The more the merrier!'

Jesus.

Mitzi stared in horror as half a dozen of the neighbourhood yobs, baseball capped and hoodied to the eyeballs, trooped through the hall and into the living room.

'Cool,' the nearest one nodded to her. 'We was only going to ask for a fiver to stop us chucking eggs at yer door. This is wicked.'

They'd immediately homed in on Clyde's bottles, stuffing handfuls of All Hallows Mallows into their pockets, lighting cigarettes and jerking rhythmically to Mott the Hoople in the fire glow.

'No, sorry,' Mitzi started, just as the bell rang again. 'Oh, hell! Look! Don't touch anything! I'll be back in a minute and—' she flew out into the hall. 'Lav! Leave the door! Leave it! Oh, bugger!'

Too late. Lavender was ushering another batch of trick or treaters into the hall.

From behind the closed cloakroom door Lobelia was singing 'After the Goldrush'.

'We let ourselves in through the back,' Flo announced, emerging from the kitchen with Clyde in tow like the best Whitehall farcical entrance. 'Goodness, what a racket! We thought we'd be the first. And you look lovely. Black suits everyone – nice trousers. Bit tight maybe . . . Pauline's worked miracles with your hair, though. Through here, is it?'

The next half an hour passed in a blur. There seemed to be a constant stream of people marching into the living room, half of whom Mitzi couldn't remember inviting. Trilby Man and a clutch of the Baby Boomers, Biff and Hedley Pippin,

Herbie and all the old bags from Patsy's Pantry joined her friends from the village and the bank, the neighbours and the trick or treaters munching away at Granny's nibbles and knocking back Clyde's booze. Mott the Hoople's Ian Hunter was now at full husky volume. There was some dancing going on by the fireplace, and a couple she didn't recognise were struggling happily on the sofa. Lob was still in the downstairs loo singing 'Subterranean Homesick Blues' with the queue outside cheerfully joining in on the chorus, and Lulu remained in her bedroom.

'Bloody hell!' Doll's eyes opened saucer wide as she unlocked the front door and almost crashed into Mitzi who was carrying two full plates from the kitchen. 'Have I come to the right party? And wow, Mum, you look fab.'

'Thanks,' Mitzi thrust the plates at her daughter. 'It's got a bit out of control but so far everyone seems to be having a good time. Clyde's booze can always be relied on to loosen inhibitions.'

'What are these?' Doll peered at the plates. 'They don't look like cheese and pineapple to me.'

'Er – no, I think those are Autumnal Love-Nuts. And those are definitely Pumpkin Passions. And the little green ones are – um – oh yes, Stars of Venus – just lettuce and herbs and stuff, oh and celery and something else – avocado and liquorice I think. All good clean fun according to Granny and – good God, I didn't know Brett was coming. Hello, love, how – er – wonderful to see you here.'

Brett smiled and nodded. 'Hello, Mrs B. You look really different. Nice different, of course ...'

'Oh, of course,' Mitzi smiled warmly at Brett. She really wished he'd call her Mitzi or Ma or something. But she'd been 'Mrs B' to him ever since he and Doll were at school together and it was probably far too late to change now. 'Did you walk?'

'No, I drove. I won't be drinking because I've got to be at work early. So Doll can.' He hugged Doll with enthusiasm and scant regard for the piled plates. 'I couldn't bear to let her out of my sight. Not even for a couple of hours. Ooh, nice, cheese and pineapple.'

Mitzi watched as he helped himself to a handful of the Pumpkin Passions. Oh well. As he'd been behaving peculiarly ever since the Wishes Come True Pie, she assumed a bit of Pumpkin Passion wouldn't make much difference.

She watched them force their way, still entwined, into the living room. Were they really happy now? They certainly seemed so. Was that anything at all to do with Granny Westward's recipes? Did it matter?

The introspection was interrupted by the trick or treaters conga-ing out of the living-room door along with a few bank employees, Trilby Man and the BBC, Biff and Hedley, some of the neighbours and Lavender. The shimmying snake disappeared, high-kicking, into the kitchen.

'Mum!' Doll yelled from the living-room doorway. 'Mum, they're *stoned*! All of them! What the hell have you given them?'

'Nothing – well, just the party nibbles in Granny's book ... you saw the recipes. Just herbal things, little sweetmeats, nothing toxic.'

Doll still looked shocked. 'Don't give me that. I've seen enough chemical highs in my life, and this is like the last night of Glastonbury. Are you sure you haven't added something, well, you know?'

'Nothing,' Mitzi grinned. 'Just good old-fashioned herbs. Fun, isn't it? Oh, come on, love. Join in. Enjoy yourself. Whoops—'

The conga-snake reappeared from the kitchen and made its way up the stairs. Lobelia, hat intact but minus socks, having fought her way out of the downstairs loo, had tagged unsteadily on to the back and was kicking out of sync.

'Get out!!!!!' Lulu's voice screamed from her bedroom. 'Bugger off! All of you! Mum, what the hell is going on down there?'

'Just what I said,' Doll muttered. 'And why isn't Lu down here?'

133

'She's – um – still getting ready I think. Oh, that's a good idea, Brett. Give Doll something to eat to soak up Clyde's turnip and nasturtium. What? Oh, those are the All Hallows Mallows – totally organic and chemical-free. Honest ...'

There was a crash from upstairs and a lot of laughing. Mitzi, deciding to ignore it, ushered Doll and Brett into the living room. Richard and Judy scampered out and headed for the sanctuary of the kitchen and the washing basket. As she opened the door, Mitzi didn't blame them.

The fire glow, candles and flickering pumpkins were the perfect accompaniment for Juicy Lucy's sensuously spooky 'Who Do You Love?' which was now throbbing loudly from the stereo. Everyone seemed to be paired off, snuggled together, swaying.

Turning to make a comment to Doll, Mitzi blinked. She and Brett were suddenly entwined, gazing deeply into one another's eyes.

'Best leave 'em to it, duck,' Flo chuckled from the depths of the sofa where she was rather surprisingly sitting on Clyde's lap. 'Like I said, they needs a bit of a spark. This is a really good party. Come and have a drink.'

Elbowing her way across the room and helping herself to a glass of raspberry and celery and a handful of Pumpkin Passion, Mitzi was about to join Flo and Clyde on the sofa when the doorbell rang again.

'More bloody trick or treaters I bet,' Clyde gruffed through his moustache which was now tinged a sort of luminous green. 'Do you want me to sort the little buggers out?'

'I'll go,' Mitzi swallowed the last large chunk of Pumpkin Passion and swigged back her glass of wine. 'Hopefully Lav is still wreaking havoc upstairs with the conga-ers so I might be able to prevent this lot getting in.'

Crikey, she thought as she staggered out into the darkened hall, that wine is seriously strong. I feel quite woozy. I can see three front doors.

She fumbled with the door latch and eventually tugged it open a crack. 'Go away. Please. We don't want any more – oh!'

Dracula stood on the doorstep.

'Let me in, Mitzi. It's bloody freezing out here,' Dracula lisped round some very scary fangs. 'Oh, sod the things.' He spat them into his hand. 'What's going on in there? I mean, it looked dark from outside but I thought you'd had a power cut. The wind is playing havoc with the wires up towards Winterbrook which usually means—'

Mitzi blinked at Lance. 'Why are you dressed like Christopher Lee? It isn't fancy dress and you weren't invited, were you?'

'Do I need an invite to my own home – er – ex-home?' Lance frowned. 'And I didn't know you were having a party, did I? Oh yes, I vaguely remember you said you were having a little bash tonight for the neighbours, but I didn't expect – Christ! What the hell is that? Who's upstairs?'

'Half of the youth of Hazy Hassocks and a few other people.' Mitzi beamed. She wasn't sure she wanted to beam but her mouth gave her no choice. 'Anyway, now you're here you might as well come in.'

'Have you been drinking?' Lance stepped into the hall, patting his vampirish, gelled-back hair into place. 'And – is that dope I can smell? It is, isn't it? Mitzi, I thought we grew out of all that stuff during the early seventies? And what have you done to your hair?'

She beamed a bit more. Lance looked very handsome as Dracula. He had the right bone structure. And he'd been complimentary about her hair – well, almost. The beam upped a few degrees. 'If you weren't coming to my party, why are you all dressed up? It suits you, though. Bloodsucker.'

Lance looked even more shocked. 'To be honest, Jennifer and I are on our way to Tarnia's. She's having a Halloween Ball. I needed my white scarf to complete

135

the outfit. I left it here, remember? And as we were passing . . .'

Mitzi shrieked with laughter. It surprised her. She wasn't sure where it had come from. She hadn't been planning on laughing. The fact that Lance and Jennifer were going to a ball at Tarnia and Snotty Mark's bad-taste palace was surely no laughing matter. She tried very hard to stop, but couldn't.

'You *have* been smoking, haven't you?' Lance narrowed his made-up eyes at her. 'It always made you go giggly.'

It had, Mitzi admitted hazily to herself. Years and years and lifetimes ago when she and Lance had been very, very young, and hippiely in love. All that sort of recreational nonsense had come to an end when they married and got a mortgage and babies and responsible respectability, though.

'You look nice with make-up on,' she beamed at him. 'Even more like David Bowie. In his Ziggy days of course. And no, I haven't smoked anything at all. It's probably Clyde's wine – or maybe the Pumpkin Passions . . .'

'That bloody recipe book!' Lance was laughing too now. 'What on earth have you concocted tonight?'

'Masses of stuff and we're all having a lovely time. Much better than anything Tarnia can put on, I promise. You'd find out if you stayed, of course, but no doubt the Bride of Dracula would have something to say about that, wouldn't she? Ooooh – blimey! That was quick.'

Jennifer, white faced, black eyed, red lipped, wearing a strapless meringue wedding dress with realistic blood trickling from puncture marks in her neck and very pretty diamante-studded fangs, suddenly loomed in the doorway.

Mitzi blinked. Jennifer always gave her a shock. It was like looking at her own photograph twenty or thirty years ago. Lance had truly gone for the younger model.

'I'm not keeping him, Jennifer,' she smiled hugely. 'He's all yours.'

'I know,' Jennifer didn't smile back. It might be the fangs of course. Or the fact that she was freezing in the off-the-shoulder flimsy frock. 'I just wanted to make sure he was all right.'

The physical similarity was where it ended, Mitzi thought dizzily. Jennifer had no sense of fun whatsoever.

'He's fine. I'll just go and get his scarf – the one that Flo slept with, wasn't it? I found it in the washing basket so it might be a bit furry . . .'

She was still giggling as she lurched towards the hall-stand. Grabbing what she hoped was the right scarf she lurched back again. 'There we go. Give Tarnia my love won't you? And tell her I'll see her soon. Have a great time. 'Bye!'

She closed the door on them and almost immediately the doorbell rang again.

'Oh, sod off, Lance,' she giggled, tugging the door open again. 'Whatever you want this time it's no good – just sod off and – oh!'

Mitzi tried to rein in her grin and stop her stomach looping the loop.

The tall, dark, beautifully thuggish pumpkin-rescuer with the diamond ear-stud stood on the doorstep. He looked quite apologetic. 'Sorry, I'm not Lance – but I'm pretty good at knowing when to sod off. Shall I go now?'

Chapter Thirteen

Fighting a very out-of-character urge to drag him bodily over the doorstep, Mitzi managed to smile through her confusion. 'No, no – please stay, of course. Come in ... That is – um – you are here for the party, aren't you?'

He nodded. 'Coincidence, isn't it? If I'd realised that you were to be my hostess when I grabbed your pumpkins – er – well, no ...'

Mitzi trilled with laughter. She really wished she could stop doing it. Closing her mouth didn't seem to help much. She took a deep breath. 'Did – um Lu invite you?'

'Doll, actually.'

Doll? How did Doll know him? She hadn't mentioned it, had she? Mitzi's eyebrows rocketed into her hairline. And there she was thinking Doll and Brett were love's young dream and all that. Dark horses indeed.

He looked worried. 'Didn't she tell you? Hell – you must think I'm the worst kind of gatecrasher.'

'Not at all – I'm sure she told me but my memory's hopeless. Please do come in, it's freezing out there.'

'Thanks. Wow,' he stepped inside and looked round the navy-blue and gold hall with appreciation. 'Fantastic colour scheme. And—'

Anything else he may have been going to say was drowned by the conga-ers whooping and screaming down the stairs and vanishing back into the living room. A split

138

second later, Lav and Lob, who had become detached, splintered off on their own towards the kitchen.

The pumpkin rescuer grinned. 'This looks like my sort of party.' He held out his hand. 'I'm Joel. Joel Earnshaw.'

Joel. Nice name. Strong but unusual. It suited him. Names were so important, Mitzi thought, still slightly woozy. She'd always felt she'd never have fallen quite so much in love with Lance if he'd been a Cyril.

'Oh, right, yes – um, I'm Mitzi Blessing.' She shook his hand and immediately wished she hadn't. The electricity jolted her to the soles of her feet. Sure she was blushing, she yanked her hand away. 'Doll's mother.'

If he said something naff like 'never in this world!' or 'surely you mean sister?' she'd hate him for ever and ever and ever.

'That figures.' He grinned a bit more. 'And Mitzi? That's another fantastic Hollywood name. Great style. Doll told me about Dolores and Tallulah. Is it a family tradition?' Mitzi sucked in her breath and nodded, hoping that the manic laughter and inane grinning had stopped. Doll seemed to have told him an awful lot. Oh, dear. How long had this been going on? 'Well, yes. My childhood was made hell by it so I thought I'd inflict the same suffering on my kids.'

She laughed, reasonably normally, to show she was joking and this time Joel joined in so it wasn't too embarrassing.

Mitzi attempted to stop the laughing again. 'No, honestly. I'm not that cruel. They were just unusual names at a time when everyone was calling their daughters Kate or Sarah or Louise. And we thought they were pretty and original. And—' deciding that Joel was probably bored witless by the ramblings, she ushered him towards the living–room door' —anyway, make yourself at home - oh, er on second thoughts . . .'

The living room looked like a Bacchanalian Revel. Brett and Doll, it appeared, were revelling more than most. Juicy

Lucy, stuck on replay, was pulsating loudly to aid the gyrations.

'Hi, Joel!' Doll waved a bare arm from the depths of the sofa. 'Glad you could make it. You've seen Brett before, of course.'

Joel nodded politely at the half-clad Brett. 'Not quite so much of him, but yes, we've met. Er – hi.'

Brett raised a laconic hand in greeting. Mitzi sighed in admiration. How cool these youngsters were about relationships. Steering Joel away from the sofa, and making introductions on the way, she indicated the food and drink. 'Just help yourself. There's plenty of everything, and more in the kitchen.'

The conga-ers, clearly exhausted, were knocking back some of Clyde's more dubious mixture straight from the bottle. Everyone else seemed to be laughing. Joel, having helped himself to a glass of turnip and elderflower and a plate piled with Pumpkin Passion and All Hallows Mallows, had somehow squeezed himself on to the sofa with Doll and Brett.

Before Mitzi had time to worry about a *ménage à trois* breaking out in the living room, one of the teenage trick or treaters grabbed her round the waist and whisked her towards the dancing bit by the fireplace.

'C'mon, babe,' he grinned fetchingly from beneath his baseball cap. 'Betcha know how to salsa, doncha?'

Upstairs, Lulu put the finishing touches to her make-up. The conga-ers had disrupted the preparations somewhat, but now she was almost ready. As always, her bad temper had evaporated. Being moody took so much effort. She could never be bothered to stay grumpy for long.

So what if Shay had taken Carmel to the cinema? They'd have to come home at some point, wouldn't they? And because Lob and Lav lived in the eighteenth century they certainly wouldn't let him entertain ladies in his bedroom, which meant he'd be arriving home alone – and she'd be

140

waiting. Oh, not in a stalkery sort of way. Just in a friendly, neighbourly, why-not-come-and-join-the-party sort of way – and if, just if, it happened to be before midnight then all her cooking and conniving wouldn't have been in vain.

She swirled round in front of the mirror. Because there were mounds of clothes and junk everywhere, the view was somewhat limited, but what she could see was okay. The halter-necked top was a bit skimpy, but nicely balanced the long black-tiered skirt. And the black and silver beads and braids set her hair off a treat. Maybe she'd used a little too much kohl. Nah. No one could have too much kohl.

Right, she thought, closing the door on the devastation of her bedroom, all she had to do now was shimmy downstairs, slap on the smiley party face, trust in Granny Westward's witchery – and it might turn out to be quite a good evening.

Jesus!

Something musical of her mother's was rocking the house to its foundations. Ah, yes – Led Zeppelin. Mitzi really did have some peculiar tastes for an oldish person, Lu thought, wincing at the decibel level. And as she'd embraced these thundering bands for about forty years it was amazing that she wasn't as deaf as a post.

The living room, flickering dark, boomed and thudded. Shadowy figures were just about visible. Lots of them. Skirting the more obvious danger zones, Lu helped herself to a glass of wine and a slice of something glutinously black and treacly.

Blimey! Was that her mother dancing with a lad in a baseball cap? And Doll looking almost casual in black trousers and a white shirt that surely wasn't done up at all? And what was she doing on the sofa with Brett and – hell! *Joel Earnshaw?*

Downing the wine in one, and spooning the treacly goo into her mouth, Lulu circulated the party periphery. The music was pretty cool really, she thought, as her body seemed to liquefy and move with the back-beat. And the decorations were dead clever, all those candles flickering, all those little skeletons and witches and bats and spiders swirling in a gentle circle and . . . ooops!

'I'm so sorry,' she tried to disentangle herself from a group of Mitzi's Baby Boomers. A man with a trilby hat grappled with her for far longer than she felt necessary. The silky halter top slipped to an all-time low. 'No, I'm fine, thank you.'

Really, Clyde's wine must be an extra strong vintage. Usually it took more than one glass of it to make you see treble. She felt quite unsteady, and rather light-headed and all sort of warm and giggly. Not bad at all.

'Are you okay?' Doll, buttoning up her shirt wrongly, had staggered from the sofa and was weaving her way towards Lulu. 'Your eyes look funny. Have you eaten some of that p-p-p-pumpkin stuff?'

'Not sure. Was it black and sticky?'

'Don't know!' Doll shrieked with laughter, then clapped her hand over her mouth. 'Sorry – I haven't felt like this since – well, probably never actually . . . I need some water . . .'

Deciding that she was possibly slightly steadier on her feet than her sister, Lu grabbed Doll's hand and led her towards the kitchen.

Richard and Judy smiled happily up from their push-me-pull-you configuration on the stand-by food table and purred in blissful harmony. They'd probably eaten the Pumpkin Passion too.

With the door closed, the roar of the party dulled to an acceptable drone.

'So?' Lu poured Doll a haphazard glass of water and steadied herself against the draining board. 'What's going on out there? With you and Brett and Mr Sexy Dentist?'

The words all seemed to slur into one another.

'Nothing,' Doll emptied her glass and refilled it. Watering down Granny Westward's snackettes was clearly a good idea. She began to lose her bewildered look. 'I asked Joel to come along because he doesn't know anyone in Hazy Hassocks or Winterbrook and he's a nice guy. That's all. Why? Oh, come on! You don't think that we're – you know – do you?'

Using both hands on the draining board to stop the kitchen slipping away, and speaking with studied deliberation, Lulu shrugged. 'I'm not sure what to think. You've changed so much recently. Did I pronounce recently properly? Oh, good ... Er – no, you know, you and Brett ...'

Doll blinked. 'Yeah, well it surprised me too. And no, I don't think it was anything to do with the Wishes Come True Pie before you start down that road – oh—'

The kitchen door flew open and Lobelia, now with flashing devil's horns adorning her plastic witches' hat and the cycle helmet, skipped in, beamed at them, picked up a plate of sandwiches and skipped out again.

Neither of them found it weird enough to comment on.

Doll filled her water glass again. She spilled a lot of it and giggled. 'Look, all it took to sort us out was for Brett to start being a bit – well – unpredictable. That night he turned up here, behaving completely out of character, really impressed me. And well – ever since we've been making an effort ... you know, courting one another.'

'Courting? *Courting?*' Lu shrieked with laughter. 'What, holding hands in the moonlight and old-fashioned stuff? How boring is that!'

'Not boring at all, actually.' Doll smiled wistfully. 'It's been lovely. Trouble was, we'd been taking one another for granted for soooo long. After that night, we just started to make more effort and it was like, all sparkly and tingly again ... just like being teenagers ... We can't keep our hands off each other.'

'I'd noticed.' Lu fought the laughter. 'But what made him act like that in the first place? Wasn't it what you wished for that night?'

143

'Well, yes, sort of – but it had nothing to do with the Wishes Come True Pie.'

'Are you sure?'

'Oh, come on! You'd have to be mad to believe that. Oh, I know Mum thinks that's she's – well – magicking things with herbs and stuff, and I'm certainly not going to disabuse her of the idea. She needs something to make her happy. But me and Brett were far more basic than that. We must have come to the same conclusion at the same time. We knew we had to be more spontaneous, and then we just had to work out where we'd let things slide and what we wanted for the future.'

Lulu still wasn't convinced that Granny Westward's recipe hadn't played some major part in the Doll and Brett miracle. Probably best not to mention it, though. 'And you don't want Joel Earnshaw?'

'No. Well, he's bloody gorgeous of course, but no, I'm staying with Brett for ever and ever. Why do you want him? Jeeze – you do, don't you?'

Lu shook her head, the braids and beads rattling violently. 'No. I mean I think he's gorgeous as well. Vinnie Jones to a T and sexy as hell – but I've only got eyes for Shay . . . Who, before you ask, only has eyes for Carmel The Angel.'

'Bugger, then,' Doll said kindly, clearly trying not to laugh again.

'Ah – here you both are,' Mitzi opened the door allowing Led Zeppelin to boom in alongside her. 'I wondered where you'd got to. Everything okay?'

They both nodded and wobbled slightly.

Mitzi looked very bright eyed and a bit dishevelled. Stroking Richard and Judy, she then pushed them gently aside and picked up the bowl of apples. 'Need these for the apple bobbing – whoops – I think I'm a bit tiddly . . . Did you see me dancing the salsa with that Carl Fourboys from the Bath Road Estate? He said I was cool.'

'Mum!' Lu shrieked. 'He's only fourteen! He only knows "cool" or "wicked".'

'Does he? He said I was wicked, too. Now where are the spare dishes? And I'm sure I had loads more apples ...'

Knowing how many she'd hacked apart making the Midnight Apple spell – not to mention the love candles – Lu blushed. 'Er – I haven't seen any others. Anyway, do you think apple bobbing is a good idea? The state they're in out there they'll probably drown themselves.'

'It's traditional,' Mitzi stood on tiptoe to rummage rather giddily in the crockery cupboard for the dishes. 'Oh, look! There are a couple of apples in here. They'll do.'

'No they won't,' Lu lunged at them. 'Er – no – that is ... I think they're a bit – um – off.'

Doll and Mitzi were frowning at her.

'I mean – well ... You don't want them ...'

'Course I do.' Mitzi grabbed the apples before Lu could stop her. 'All contributions more than welcome.' She looked at Doll. 'And while you're here – you're not playing fast and loose with Brett's feelings, are you?'

'What?' Doll frowned. 'Of course not. I love him. He loves me. We're happier now than we've been for ages – why? Oh, God! You're as bad as Lu! You think I fancy Joel, don't you?'

'Well, he said you'd invited him. I thought it was all a bit, well, risky, having him and Brett in the same room at the same time and—'

'We work together,' Doll grinned. 'He's our new dentist. I invited him along because he's new to the area and was going to spend tonight on his own. That's all. Why? You don't mind, do you?'

'Mind?' Mitzi beamed a zillion-watt beam at them both. 'Oh, no. Not at all. He's – um – really rather charming. That is, for a dentist ... Fancy that ... A dentist ... Um – now I must try and sort out the apple bobbing as it's nearly midnight. And you two don't want to spend all night chattering in here. You don't want to miss it – it'll be fun – and for heaven's sake Lu, leave these apples alone! Let go!'

145

It was an unequal struggle.

Mitzi sailed out of the kitchen triumphantly clutching both the dishes and the apples.

Doll smiled. 'She's as high as a kite.'

'Good.' Lu was far more worried about the apples than her mother's herbal intake. Almost midnight. The love candles still reposed in the freezer, both her special spell Midnight Apples were about to be dunked, and Shay still hadn't turned up.

Doll finished her water, straightened her shirt and gave Lu a hug. 'Look, I know Niall hurt you, but lurching into another disastrous relationship really isn't the answer. Shay probably isn't the right one for you. Are you sure that you wouldn't like me to nudge Joel in your direction?'

'Quite sure. Under different circumstances I'd be delirious, but after the Heath Ledger wish I can't think about anyone other than Shay.'

'It wasn't really magic, Lu. Not what's happened to me or Mum or you. It was coincidence. All this stuff – all of it, tonight and all the rest of the recipes – it's only superstition and a fusion of herbs. Chemical not magical. Okay?'

'Whatever,' Lu said irritably. Her chemical-herbal-magical intake suddenly needed a boost. Normal everyday gloom was threatening to set in. She was in serious danger of sobering up completely, she had to light the love candles and she still wanted those apples back. 'Anyway, I'm going to help Mum with the apple bobbing. Coming?'

Mitzi set the apples carefully in the tub of water. The ones she'd found in the crockery cupboard were, as Lu had said, rather weary. She'd keep them for emergency supplies.

'Need a hand?' Joel appeared out of the gloom. 'Here let me take those apples. This is getting a habit – me helping you with fruit and veg.'

Mitzi handed over the two apples from the kitchen. Joel looked even more wonderfully saturnine in the flickering darkness: the candlelight shadowed across his cheekbones and made his eyes fathomless, the diamond ear-stud sparkled like a multifaceted star.

'Um – thanks . . .' She was careful not to touch him this time. It was no good at all going all gooey over him. He was far too young, and a dentist, and hadn't he likened her to his mother on that first meeting? Well, almost. And she'd looked terrible. And he'd been, well, *kind*. The way she'd always taught Doll and Lu to be kind to the older generation.

And now they were both rather drunk and being merely party-polite.

Free assured everyone that it was ear-splittingly 'All Right Now'. Clyde was playing air guitar with Lav and Lob and most of the trick or treaters.

Joel straightened up and smiled at her. 'This is one of the best Halloweens I've ever had. And certainly the best night out since I came to Hazy Hassocks. When I decided to make the break and move south I always knew it would be lonely, but nothing had prepared me for feeling quite so alone. But you—'

What difference she'd made to his solitary life, Mitzi was never going to discover.

Trilby Man shimmied between them, his hat pushed to the back of his head. 'Smashing bash, Mitzi. Lovely and warm. Funny food but plenty of it. We've had a great time. If you passes out, and you don't look too hot if you don't mind me saying, duck, don't forget – we're meeting in the village hall next Wednesday at six. So's we can get the meeting in before the fireworks.' He nodded at Joel. 'Mitzi's a prime mover in our Geriatrics Anonymous meetings. She was on the verge of losing it, you know, after she'd retired, but—' he nudged Mitzi painfully with his elbow '—we've proved that there's life in the old dog yet, 'aven't we, gel?'

Joel nodded politely. Mitzi, now officially labelled ancient, decrepit, a nodder and knitter, clenched her fists and willed Trilby Man to explode on the spot.

He didn't.

Mitzi glared at him, then clapped her hands. 'Form a queue for the apple bobbing! There's a small prize for every successful apple grabbed. What? No, of course not. With the teeth. It wouldn't be much of a challenge otherwise, would it?'

Everyone pushed and shoved their way into some sort of ragged, noisy line. They were clearly at that compliant stage of drunkenness where anything anyone suggests seems like the best idea ever.

Jimi Hendrix's 'Greatest Hits' had replaced Free. Purple Haze provided the perfect accompaniment.

In the untidy line, Doll had her arms round Brett and was whispering something in his ear. Lu, having lit some rather ugly knobbly pink candles which Mitzi had never seen before in her life, was squinting at the apples over Flo's shoulder. Mitzi, still hoping that Trilby Man would be the first apple-bobbing fatality in Hazy Hassocks history, cleared a space on the table for the clean dishes. There was still the Mischief Night Cake to cut and the cream to dollop out as a party finale.

Water was slopping all over the floor and the screams of laughter had become sort of gurgly. It was all going so well.

'Do you think you'll need these?' Joel was still clutching her spare apples. Maybe he hadn't heard all of Trilby Man's killer description.

The clock started to whirr towards the first of the twelve slow strokes of midnight.

'Doubt it,' Mitzi peered towards the bobbing tub. At least four of her friends from the bank and two of the Baby Boomers and Lavender had their heads under water. 'You can have them if you want. I mean, being a dentist, I suppose eating apples comes second nature to you. Good for the teeth, I mean. And—'

Lulu had suddenly hurled herself across the room, trampling most of the trick or treaters under foot.

'Noooo! Don't let him eat that apple! OOOOH – bugger! Which apple is it? Which one?'

Joel, having the remains of the apple snatched from his mouth by a frenzied Lulu, looked a little surprised.

Lulu swirled round and glared at Mitzi. 'He's been *holding* that, hasn't he? And you held it first and gave it to him. And now he's *eaten* it! At *midnight*! And you know what that means, don't you?'

Mitzi didn't have a clue. She felt that Lulu had probably gone mad.

'Where's the other one?' Lulu barked at Joel. 'The one with the bits missing? Have you eaten that as well?'

The apple bobbers, very wet, emerged from the tub to watch the entertainment.

'It's here,' Joel handed it over. 'Sorry. Didn't know it was your special apple.'

'Lu – what the hell is going on?' Mitzi felt she'd skipped a vital episode of her favourite soap. 'It's only an apple. There are plenty more – oh, now where are you going?'

Lu had heard the doorbell. And the clock was still slamming out the midnight chimes. She tugged the door open. Sod bloody Joel Earnshaw and her mother. If Granny Westward was right then they'd be fated to become the most mismatched couple since . . .

Shay stood on the doorstep. Carmel, looking like a little pink and white frothy fairy doll, stood wispily behind him.

'Hi,' he smiled. 'We made it . . . The film was crap and Lav and Lob's house is in darkness and we thought—'

'Here!' Lu shoved the engraved apple into his hand and grabbed at the sleeve of his leather jacket. Dragging him across the hall and into the living room, she fetched up beside the guttering Apple Love Candles. They still smelt like cowpats. The clock was booming its final chime.

'Eat it – please. Well, one bite at least . . .'

Shay, laughing, did as he was told.

Lulu, dredging up Granny Westward's words from deep,

deep in her memory, took a breath. 'I conjure thee apple by these names that what man tasteth thee may love me and burn on my fire as melted wax.'

Jimi Hendrix had moved on to the exceedingly sexy 'All Along The Watch Tower'.

Shay chewed thoughtfully. And swallowed. And grinned. 'Have you just put a spell on me?'

'Goodness, no! Of course, not!' Lu trilled happily. 'It's only a bit of party fun.'

Shay looked around the mayhem in the room with laughter in his eyes. Carmel sidled up beside him and glared at Lulu. The apple bobbers resumed their fun. Mitzi and Joel were dancing with Clyde and Flo, the Baby Boomers and the trick or treaters. Doll and Brett had disappeared. Lav and Lob, water dripping from the brims of their witches' hats, were hacking chunks off the Mischief Night Cake. Trilby Man, having inhaled a touch too much of the Apple Love Candles, was being sick in the coal bucket.

Lulu grinned to herself and her unknown great-grandmother and poured a large glass of celebratory raspberry and onion.

Chapter Fourteen

November the fifth was being wholeheartedly embraced by the Hazy Hassocks pyromaniacs. Outside the village hall the early evening sky was exploding with waxing and waning cushions of colour, while the ground shook with neutron-bomb-powerful detonations.

Inside the hall, sparks were also flying.

Trilby Man, clearly still a little fragile after Halloween, was wincing at the volume of several dozen people all shouting at once as he felt his way carefully between the noisy groups, handing out various pieces of paper and nodding in a concerned manner.

Lav and Lob Banding were trotting behind him, vociferously arguing they were a vital part of the am-dram group. Trilby Man was agreeing, over his shoulder, that yes, they'd signed up for am-dram as they had for everything else, but that the nature of the first planned production probably meant they'd be better as front – or even better still, back – of house.

The Bandings, now with haloes of black plastic adorning their cycle helmets where the witches' hats had had to be cut free, were insisting that they'd be perfect in the chorus line. They'd always done Gilbert and Sullivan when they'd been gels.

Amusedly watching the proceedings from the stage, Mitzi was even more convinced that she was no longer necessary in the Baby Boomers' lives. They'd needed someone to get them together, and keep them in touch, but now everything seemed to be up and running nicely.

The village hall was to be commandeered on Wednesday evenings for a general get-together, and on a neatly typed-out daily roster for the other activities. Tarnia's original agreement was believed by the Baby Boomers Club to be written in stone. Mitzi, sadly, knew better.

Maybe the Baby Boomers' activities would thrive without her, but Tarnia's letting of the village hall wouldn't. Another visit to Tarnia was on the cards, and soon, if the Hazy Hassocks over-fifties were to retain their lifeline.

She glanced at her watch. If she left now, she was bound to find Tarnia at home this evening, wasn't she? There'd probably be fireworks all round, and she didn't have any Powers of Persuasion Puddings tucked away in her handbag to sway things this time, but she might as well get it over.

On either side of her, June and Sally, flanked by several others of the BBC committee, were chatting happily. They'd all *loved* the Halloween party. Well, the bits they'd remembered. It had all been such fun and they really must do it again – oh, and if Mitzi had any more of her grandmother's country cooking recipes then they'd all be willing to pay her to make things for their own forthcoming parties if the spectacular effects could be guaranteed.

What, they asked, did Mitzi think about running a sort of Granny's party food outlet?

Mitzi, keeping her face impassive, murmured that it certainly sounded fun, she was flattered they'd all enjoyed the nibbles so much and she'd bear it in mind. However, a little squiggle of delight squirmed in her brain. A little frisson of excitement trickled along her spine. Cooking Granny's recipes for other people's parties? Why hadn't she thought of that before? Well, obviously because cooking per se had never been her forte – until now.

Why not? She wouldn't be going into *business* as such, would she? She wouldn't be a proper caterer. That sort of thing was bound to be accompanied by masses of Euro red tape and restrictions. She knew once you started manufacturing bulk food for resale in your kitchen the Brussels Bureaucrats were down on you like a ton of lardy cakes, followed closely by the HSE army and probably millions of other nanny state inspectors.

But surely, if she was just taking a few private orders.

She smiled delightedly to herself. Granny Westward's recipes could make a real difference to her life. The money would be very welcome to eke out her bank pension – it would, after all, be years and years and years before she qualified for any payouts to do with Old Age. And she'd be doing *something*. It might even be the start of a whole new career.

Trying not to grin too widely, Mitzi promised to let June, Sally and the rest have a list of Granny's recipes and a price list at the next meeting so they could chose what they'd like. She also decided it was best to wrap up tonight's meeting quickly so that everyone could get back to their own firework parties – and she could visit Tarnia.

'We've sorted out loads of things tonight, haven't we?' June said, reaching for her coat. 'This BBC thing was a brilliant idea of yours. Gives me a real purpose in life.'

'And me,' Sally agreed. 'It was great that you took charge like you did. I mean, we'd never have thought of it in a million years. It needed someone like you to take control and get it organised. Mind you, you were always bossy at school.'

'Was I?' Mitzi frowned. 'I thought I was quiet and diligent and—'

'Selective memory syndrome!' June laughed. 'You were always having Bright Ideas and organising stuff for us to do. Everyone hung on your every word. We all thought you'd end up as the first lady prime minister. No wonder Tarnia was so jealous of you.'

At the mention of the T-word, Mitzi flinched. She shook her head. 'Tarnia wasn't jealous of me, for heaven's sake!

153

She was my best friend at school. We were always together, remember? I was always in awe of her. I felt sort of – well – mousy and goody-goody compared to her. I really wanted to be like her. I wanted to be as devilish and foolhardy as she was.'

'While she,' Sally said, 'was dead envious of your popularity, your loyalty and your ability to see things through. You never gave up. Either on things or people. And yes, maybe Tarnia was a lot more *wicked* than you – but you got things done in a quiet and well, sort of kind but ruthless way. Everyone liked you, trusted you, relied on you – and they still do. You never let your friends down, while Tarnia didn't have any friends at all – except you.'

'She was the most popular girl in the school,' Mitzi protested. 'Everyone wanted to be her friend.'

'No they didn't,' June shook her head. 'Stone me, Mitzi. Don't tell me you never realised that even then people were scared of Tarnia's sharp tongue and cruel ways? They wanted to be in her gang so they didn't get hurt by her. She was an ace bitch even then. And Sally's right, she didn't have any *friends* as such, except you.'

Crikey! Mitzi blinked. It was getting on for forty years since they'd all left school, and she'd never known ... never realised.

'Oh, come on! You'll have me feeling sorry for her in a minute – and sympathy is about the last thing Tarnia needs! Anyway, I need to see her again about the things we've organised, and now's as good a time as any – so shall we call it a day?'

June and Sally nodded.

As well as the general activities, they'd also arranged a fund-raising Christmas Fayre, a one-off village Christmas party and show, and a Christmas Dinner for all those in Hazy Hassocks and surrounding areas who would be alone on The Big Day.

The ideas were coming in thick and fast, and the sense of community was being resurrected by the minute. It was exactly what Mitzi had wanted.

And Tarnia could put the kibosh on the whole lot.

Mitzi stood up and clapped her hands. As always, no one took the slightest bit of notice.

'Here,' June rummaged under the table, emerged looking a bit flushed, and passed her a whistle. 'This'll do the trick. Belonged to me ma. She used to be a dinner lady at the Mixed Infants, remember? Used it to bring the little buggers into line. Kept it as a memento. I always have it in my handbag in case of rape.'

Mitzi decided any comment here would be a mistake. She put the whistle to her lips and let out a lengthy ear-splitting shrill.

Bingo!

The uproar died instantly. With Pavlov's Dog reactions, everyone gawped at the stage. 'Er – sorry if that brought back vivid memories of lumpy custard and cold cabbage ... Thanks for your attention. I think we've done really well this evening but I'm sure we've all got things we need to get home for. I'll e-mail the minutes to the library so everyone can have a copy – and I'll see you here next Wednesday. Enjoy your fireworks.'

Several people clapped. Some nodded. Lavender and Lobelia waved.

Saying her goodbyes, Mitzi pulled on her gloves, turned up her collar and prepared to brave the relentless explosions outside.

Still mulling over the Tarnia revelations, Mitzi fumbled to unlock her car in the icy darkness. Intermittent rainbow explosions lit the sky and plunged the car park in and out of a kaleidoscope of colour and noise.

'Hang on a mo!' Trilby Man huffed and puffed out of the hall behind her. 'You going off to see Lady Muck Snepps now?'

Mitzi nodded.

'Ah, right. Well, can you tell her we'll definitely need the hall every Friday and Saturday from now until

Christmas, then, duck? And maybe a few nights in between? The am-drammers have decided on their little extravaganza, so we'll 'ave to 'ave plenty of rehearsals. There's not much time to get it right for the night . . .'

'No, the year's racing away. Still, if you're only doing a carol concert and festive readings or something like that it shouldn't take too much learning off by heart, should it? Everyone knows the Christmas Story and all the traditional carols.'

Trilby Man looked askance. 'Bloody hell, Mitzi. The vicar does the carol stuff and reading that old Yonder Star bollocks. Allus 'as. We don't want to tread on 'is toes, do we? No, we're going to put on a bit of a song and dance for the festivities. Show 'em in Hazy Hassocks that us old 'uns can still cut the mustard, so to speak.'

Mitzi frowned. There were a lot of would-be musicians, singers and alleged thespians in the Baby Boomers Club. But surely there wasn't enough time to regiment them into something too artistically elaborate for Christmas?

'That sounds ambitious . . . Er – are you going to organise it?'

Trilby Man nodded. 'Ah, I'm writer, producer and director. I like to adapt stuff my way, you know? I did a lot when I worked for the Water Board – did you ever see our production of *Oliver*? Brought tears to the eyes.'

Unable to visualise Trilby Man as Hazy Hassocks's answer to Cameron Macintosh, Mitzi trusted herself merely to nod again. 'That is, no, I didn't see it – but, um, yes I can imagine. So is that what you're going to be doing? *Oliver*?'

'Garn! No!' Trilby Man was scathing. 'This'll be even better'n that. Course, what I wanted to do was my version of *Titanic – the musical*, but I can see staging that in the village hall might cause a few problems . . .'

Mitzi clenched her teeth together.

Trilby Man beamed at her. 'So we've decided on *Hair*.'

Mitzi shrieked with laughter, then realising he was

deadly serious, managed to turn it into a coughing fit. 'Oh
... um ... how lovely ... right then, I'd better be off
now ...'

Shaking with held-in hysteria, she somehow managed to
unlock the car. She didn't let the laughter escape until she
was well on the way to Tarnia's.

Hair! The Baby Boomers were doing *Hair*?

Oh, God – she'd have to be careful on these narrow lanes
– she could hardly see through her tears of merriment.
Mind you, she thought, maybe slowing down wouldn't hurt
at all. The fireworks were glorious. It was like driving
through an extremely pretty war zone. The sky was sprin-
kled with flares and flashes and fountains of brilliant light,
and even with the car windows tightly shut and 'Beggar's
Banquet' roaring from the stereo, the explosions were
deafening.

Hair, though! Ohmigod! There wasn't one of them under
fifty! And fiercely loyal as she was to the creed of those
born in the after-the-war years having the right to express
themselves with gusto, even she'd have to draw the line at
all that grey and wrinkled flesh. And surely it was somewhat *acrobatic*? And the heating in the village hall was less
than efficient. Half of them would probably die of
hypothermia ... And ... Jesus!

What the hell had she started?

Mitzi's head was spinning. What an evening of revelations! The truth about Tarnia, a geriatric hippie musical,
and the Granny's Country Cooking thing. What a difference an evening could make. She turned up Mick and the
boys and sang along.

The short journey to Tarnia Towers became increasingly
lovely as more and more Hazy Hassockers ignited their
incendiary devices. Mitzi had always adored firework
night, and was intending to meet up with the rest of the
family on the village green for the annual effigy-burning. It
would have been nice to have made some food for the occasion, but after Halloween she felt it might be better to allow

both digestions and sensibilities to have a little time to recover.

Halloween . . . another revelation.

She allowed herself a little smirk of satisfaction. Everyone had said it was the best party they'd ever been to. After all that nonsense with the apples, Lu had danced until the small hours with Shay – admittedly with Carmel alongside them, but she'd seemed happy enough – and Doll and Brett hadn't emerged from the spare room until the following lunchtime, and Joel Earnshaw had stayed to help her clear up.

Not, of course, that she was harbouring any *ideas* in that direction – but it had been bliss to spend some time with a gorgeous man who wasn't her ex-husband. And the 'getting to know you' routine was always such fun. And because of the Pumpkin Passion and Clyde's wine, inhibitions had been shed so early in the evening, flirting had been de rigeur, and by the end everyone felt as though they'd known everyone else for ever.

Joel had said he might come along to the village firework display – so there hadn't even been that awkward wondering when, or if, she'd see him again – and she hoped he would. Of course, she could always go to the surgery, but as her next dental check-up wasn't for three months, and she was Mr Johnson's patient, and – more vitally – the last thing she'd want was for Joel to see her professionally, all prone and wild-eyed, with saliva and guttural utterances and far too much amalgam.

Not that she'd be *seeing* him as such, professionally or otherwise, she reminded herself as she pulled up outside Tarnia's filigreed gates. No, no doubt by the time Joel had sobered up he wouldn't remember much about Friday's party at all.

Still, thinking about Joel and *Hair* and her venture into becoming Nigella-with-Sinister-Herbal-Overtones would have to wait. Right now, for the sake of the Baby Boomers, she had – simply had – to get Tarnia on her side.

Scrambling from the car and shivering in the bitter darkness, Mitzi hurried towards the intercom.

Before she reached it, a squat figure trundled out of the shadows.

'You got an invite?'

Mitzi peered downwards in the darkness. Had Tarnia gone completely Lord of the Rings and started employing trolls?

The truncated bundle rocked on its heels. 'Intercom's deactivated. It's invites only tonight. For the firework party. So if you hasn't got one you can't come in. Oh, 'allo, Mitzi duck.'

A troll with special cognitive powers?

Trust Tarnia to go for the top end of the troll market.

'Er – hello?'

'It's me, duck. Gwyneth. Friend of your Lu's. And Hedley and Biff Pippin of course. You remember me, don't you?'

A fortuitous barrage of white light exploded overhead, giving Mitzi just enough time to pick out the octogenarian features of Gwyneth Wilkins, one of the Pippins' animal-rights, intelligence-gathering moles from the neighbouring village of Fiddlesticks. Gwyneth and her friend, Big Ida Tomms, were notorious for being more enthusiastic than accurate. They, apparently, had been solely responsible for the erroneous information which had led to Lulu's recent brush with the law.

'Oh, hello, Gwyneth,' Mitzi yelled over a Big Booma Bazooka Rocket. 'Nice to see you. I didn't know you worked for Tarnia.'

'Ah, well – I don't as a rule,' Gwyneth screamed back. 'But she's made a hefty donation to our Save the Voles group, so when she asked for volunteers to man the gates I couldn't say no, could I?'

Mitzi thought she definitely not only could but should, but chose not to say so. She shrugged noncommittally.

Gwyneth ducked as something whizzed overhead.

'Bugger me! That was a close 'un. What was I saying? Oh, yes, working for Tarnia ... Me and Big Ida did her Halloween bash as well – your Lance came to that, with 'is floozy, by the way – and we've been pencilled in for her next party in a couple of weeks' time and for her Christmas entertaining. She's very persuasive is young Tarnia ...'

Mitzi nodded. She knew Tarnia's methods only too well. Take advantage of the villagers while appearing to be doing them a huge favour. She'd been just the same at school. Maybe June and Sally had been right. Thinking back, Tarnia would break the nibs of your pens then offer you a lend of hers – at a price. Or she'd tear pages out of your text book then charge you a week's dinner money to share hers. Or spill milk all over your homework and make you pay to copy hers. Or ... oh, well, the instances were legion.

'I haven't got an invite,' Mitzi stooped down to be nearer Gwyneth's ears. She wasn't sure it would help much as Gwyneth was wearing a woolly headscarf beneath a man's cap with dangling earflaps. 'But I only wanted to see Tarnia for a moment. Village business. I don't want to go to the party.'

Gwyneth looked a bit concerned. 'Well, I don't know ...'

'You owe me one, Gwyneth. You caused our Lu an awful lot of trouble over that mix-up with Jeffrey's Millinery and the ferrets.'

'Ah ... Right ... Well, okay then, duck. Young Tarnia's still in the house getting ready. Party don't start in the Big Meadow until ten. Early-comers is in the stables 'aving drinks.'

'What stables? Tarnia's never been on a horse in her life, has she? Do they actually own horses then?'

'Search me.' Gwyneth shrugged inside the mammoth coat. It remained rigid. 'Shouldn't think so for a minute. They've got an orangery with no bloody oranges and a gazebo without hide nor hair of a gaz. So I doubts if they've got 'orses. Look, duck, if you wants to go in you'd

better go now. There's another car coming ... quick about
it – in you pop.'

Leaving the car outside the gates for an easy getaway,
Mitzi popped.

In the distance, the Big Meadow at the back of Tarnia's
Bad-Taste Palace was illuminated by a tower-block bonfire.
Shadowy figures were darting around, setting up the tubes
for the fireworks, with even more tending a massive barbecue. It made Hazy Hassocks's planned gathering on the
village green look very amateurish by comparison.

Tarnia, opening the door, was clearly not pleased to see
her.

'You aren't invited.'

'I know,' Mitzi yelled as the WMDs belonging to the
youth of the Bath Road Estate whined overhead. 'This is
just a flying visit. About the village hall and the fields ...'

Tarnia sighed. 'Oh, for heaven's sake. I haven't got time
to listen to all that again. I've agreed to you meeting there
– against my better judgement – haven't I? What more do
you want?'

'Something in writing – a year's lease of usage – or
something. Look, we've planned lots of things, especially
for Christmas—' Mitzi made a lightning decision to keep
the *Hair* revelation a closely guarded secret '—and everyone is really looking forward to it. I don't want you to
change your mind.' She closed her eyes as another WMD
exploded overhead. 'Could I come in for a moment?'

'No. I'm far too busy. We've got all the Rotary coming
tonight, and the council, and several titled people, not to
mention the Soames-Hartley and the Pugh-Padgetts and—'

'Duncan Didsbury and a vat of strawberry yoghurt?'

Tarnia turned pale beneath her orange skin. 'I knew I
should have burned that bloody Polaroid. Okay – but only
for a minute. And only in the hall.'

Once inside, Mitzi realised that tonight the hall and
Tarnia were a matching pair.

In tight pink leather trousers, gold high-heeled boots and

a white glittery bomber jacket, Tarnia could have been put on a plinth and no one would have spotted her. It would have been just like a tat version of *Where's Wally?* that Lu and Doll had loved so much as children.

'Oh, sorry.' Mitzi smiled at Tarnia. 'I didn't catch that.'

'I said, yes, I'll get our people to draw up a lease – but only if I can vet the proceedings first and only if your awful villagey things don't clash with anything I may have arranged.'

Blimey! Did the Powers of Persuasion Puddings have a lasting effect? Had Tarnia's brain been permanently addled?

Aware that she was gawping, Mitzi snapped her mouth closed. 'Oh, right. Yes, that'll be great. Thanks. I won't keep you any longer. Give me a ring when you've spoken to your solicitor and we'll get together to sign whatever is necessary. But – um – why the change of heart?'

Tarnia raked golden sparkly talons through her black spiky hair and looked smug. 'No change of heart, darling. By choice I wouldn't have the plebs within a million miles of my home. When you first came here and asked me about it – the day you gave me those rather nice cakes – I *was* dead against it. But later, when you'd persuaded me, and I had to confess to Marquis, he – clever boy – pointed out that it would go down well on our list of Good Works.'

'Good Works?'

Tarnia looked irritable. 'Oh, for goodness sake – you know. Charitable stuff. Being kind. Making donations. Improving things for the community. Being seen to be caring.'

'*You?* You and Snotty Mark? *Good works?*'

'*Marquis!*' Tarnia narrowed her eyes. 'And yes, why should that seem so odd? Look, for years they've handed out gongs and titles to bloody footballers and bloody pop singers and bloody people who work themselves to a frazzle for stupid charities – and what happens to us? We have great parties and have single-handedly raised the tone of the

162

area – and what happens each time the list is announced? Sod all, that's what!'

Mitzi concentrated hard on the pink tiles under her boots. If she laughed now it might prove fatal.

Tarnia's voice became even more strident. 'So – we're upping our profile. Your rubbishy village-hall stuff will do us a power of good – as long as you keep the riff-raff away when we have important people here, understand?'

Mitzi understood. Tarnia and Snotty Mark were aiming to become the Neil and Christine Hamilton of Hazy Hassocks. Once reviled, carefully rebuilding their public image, and if not quite aiming for canonisation, then definitely hoping for an honour of some hue.

If it wasn't so sad she'd laugh.

'I understand perfectly. I've always been a great believer in the ends justifying the means. Thanks ... Oh, and we're putting on quite a few Christmassy things so we'll need the hall practically full-time for the next couple of months. Will that be okay? Tarnia? *Tarnia?*'

'What? Yes, oh, yes – whatever ...' Tarnia was staring with ill-disguised delight at a tall black-haired man with very blue eyes who had just appeared in the doorway and who seemed rather dazzled by the golden pinkness of it all.

Mitzi raised her eyebrows. Tarnia's toy boy? Surely not – he was far, far too good to be wasted on the Botox Queen. Not as handsome as Joel Earnshaw, of course, but gorgeous nonetheless.

Tarnia had shimmied across to the newcomer and was clenching and unclenching her gilded claws in the sleeve of his leather jacket with the same sort of kittenish rampant delight as Richard and Judy displayed.

'All ready?' She batted the false eyelashes up at him causing a minor hurricane. 'No probs?'

'None at all.' He looked more scared than adoring. 'Everything's in place. So we'll be ready to go when your guests arrive, Mrs Snepps.'

Not a lover then, unless they were playing *Lady Chatterley*.

Tarnia, still fluttering, suddenly remembered that they weren't alone.

'Ah, Mitzi,' she was practically dragging him across the hall. 'Allow me to introduce you to my personal pyrotechnician. This is Guy Devlin from The Gunpowder Plot. He's planned my firework display for tonight's party: an hour's extravaganza – colour co-ordinated, choreographed, music-scored – one of the biggest in the area, isn't that right, Guy?'

Guy Devlin gave Mitzi a sympathetic smile and nodded again.

The Gunpowder Plot. Of course. Tarnia would have to employ the biggest fireworks maker and pyro-party-organiser in the south of England, wouldn't she? Tonight's display must have cost Tarnia and Snotty Mark thousands and thousands and thousands. And no doubt there were caterers in doing the barbecue. And waiters handing out vintage champagne. And a lot of hand-picked strangers feeling bored and being party-polite to one another.

It made the impending Hazy Hassocks village get-together – with their fireworks selection box purchased item by item over the recent weeks from Molly Coddle's Stargazer shop in Bagley-cum-Russett, and potatoes cooked in the embers of the bonfire, and more of Clyde's home-brew – seem suddenly cosy and friendly and very desirable.

Mitzi headed towards the door. 'Lovely to meet you, Mr Devlin. Tarnia, I'll be in touch about the hall – but thanks for agreeing. Let me know when the paperwork is drawn up. Oh, and enjoy your party.'

'Yes – yes . . . and you.'

Oh, I will, Mitzi thought, as she snuggled inside her coat and hurried down the drive. Believe me, I will. And I can't wait to see what other surprises tonight can spring on me.

Chapter Fifteen

It was probably far too soon, Doll thought, stretching out in bed in the mellow darkness.

The fluorescent flashes from outside the bungalow's bedroom window indicated that individual Hazy Hassocks fireworks parties were well underway. And they'd have to get up shortly and join in the communal jamboree on the village green. But not just yet.

She rubbed a slender bare foot along Brett's leg. 'Are you asleep?'

'No ... Just shattered ... Leave me alone ...'

She giggled. These afternoon-delight sessions had rejuvenated their relationship. But it was more than just sex. As she'd tried to explain to Lu, it was taking time to talk, to laugh, to rediscover one another. To spend time together, sharing stuff, making an effort, falling in love all over again. It simply meant *bothering*.

It had nothing at all to do with the Wishes Come True shenanigans.

She rolled across the bed and kissed Brett's shoulder. 'I'm going to grab a shower, then we really ought to put in an appearance on the village green.'

'Yeah, fine,' he smiled sleepily at her. 'But I'll probably fall asleep in my jacket potato. I've got to be up for work at four – as always.'

Sliding her white towelling dressing gown over her

naked body, Doll paused in the doorway and looked at Brett. She really loved him. She always had. She'd just taken it all for granted. They both had.

For twenty-five years they'd shared these village activities; first as children, then school friends, then as teenage sweethearts and finally as lovers. Twenty-five years. Her parents' marriage had only lasted that long – and she and Brett hadn't even started on that yet. They still had decades together. It reassured her to think they'd share the rest of a lifetime. They could so easily have thrown it all away.

'We won't stay long. Promise. I just love the village fireworks. And we've been going to them ever since we were kids, haven't we?'

Brett, propping himself up on the rumpled pillows, grinned. 'Yeah. Scary thought. An entire lifetime. And nothing much changes, does it? They still buy the fireworks from Molly Coddle, the vicar still gets overexcited and lets off too many at once, Clyde Spraggs still provides mulled wine that boils your mouth off, the jacket potatoes are always cremated. And everyone gets frozen feet and roasted faces and say they'll never do it again.'

They laughed together.

'You are happy, aren't you?' Doll asked. 'You don't want things to change?'

'Sweetheart, life is perfect. I know we've been through a rocky patch – but that's behind us now, isn't it? This is – well – like we used to be, and I have no intention of letting it slip back.' Brett reluctantly hauled himself out of bed. 'Shall I make a drink while you're in the shower? Tea? Coffee? Or would you prefer a glass of wine?'

Doll shook her head. 'Nothing for me, thanks. You have one, though.'

'Are you okay? You've been off-colour since—'

'Last Friday.' Doll laughed heading for the bathroom. 'Like the majority of the village. My mother is obviously in danger of turning into Lucretia Borgia.'

The bathroom, like the rest of the bungalow, had undergone

a small but miraculous transformation. Not only had the heating system been revamped so that it was always cosy, but they had daringly added a few splashes of colour.

True, the mainstay of the decor throughout was still very beige, but each room had been lifted by the addition of candles and flowers and a few softening ornamental touches in vivid primary or citrus tones. In the bathroom it was acid lemon and lime fluffy towels; the bedroom now had turquoise cushions and purple lampshades; the hall had been enlivened with hot pink, and the living room zinged with crimson rugs and cushions.

While the bungalow was still clinically neat and anti-septically spotless, Doll felt the warmth and new life in their relationship was now echoed in their home. She loved it.

Turning on the shower, waiting for it to heat up, Doll examined her reflection in the mirror. She looked pale. Her eyes were dark-shadowed. And Brett was right, she really hadn't felt 100 per cent since the Halloween party.

It was still too soon.

She stepped into the steaming shower. It *was* too soon, wasn't it? No, damn it.

Stepping out again, making sure the door was locked, and with strangely unsteady hands, she rummaged to the back of the bathroom cabinet and pulled out the narrow blue and white box.

'I'm not sure that I should like Guy Fawkes night!' Lulu shouted in Shay's ear as they stood in a huddle of Hazy Hassocks villagers on the green waiting for the bonfire to be ignited. 'I mean, I do like it because it's exciting and pretty and traditional and reminds me of being a kid – but I always feel so sorry for the animals. Poor things. They must be so scared. And the fireworks seem to get louder every year.'

Several rockets from the Bath Road Estate screamed their blazing trails across the sky to illustrate the point.

Shay, muffled in a scruffy, chunky knit, black sweater

and faded, torn Levis, nodded. 'And when I'm on November the fifth duty I always wonder how many kids with sparklers rammed up their noses I'll be rushing into A&E. But then again I wouldn't like to join the killjoys and ban it.'

'Me neither,' Lu said happily, thinking that he truly was the most devastating man she'd ever set eyes on, and that, after that shaky start on Halloween, Granny Westward's apple magic was sooo cool.

Okay, so this wasn't a date as such, but it was a huge step forward from chatting as they passed on their neighbouring doorsteps, or when she was queuing at the bus stop, or waiting to be served in The Faery Glen.

Shay had called round an hour earlier, saying that Lav and Lob hadn't returned from the village hall meeting and would they be okay, oh, and was Lu going to the firework party? Making sure that Richard and Judy were snug in the washing basket, the cat flap locked, the radio on to block the worst of the noise, Lu had grabbed her Afghan and been on the front path in a nanosecond.

Assuring him that Mitzi was still at the village hall too and that Lav and Lob would be fine and everyone would fetch up at the bonfire before long, they'd joined the groups of well-wrapped-up people all heading towards the green.

There was a lull in the detonations, so she smiled at him. There was a lot of ground to cover. 'I love all this continuity stuff, don't you? The security of having your friends and family round you. Knowing that each year the same people will be doing the same thing at the same time. Like tonight, and winter nights, and Christmas, and Easter, and summer evenings, and ... well, all of it.'

'Is that why you've never wanted to leave the village?'

She nodded. 'Guess so. I won't be living at Mum's for ever, of course. But I'll still look for somewhere to rent in Hazy Hassocks. Well, if I can ever afford anywhere on my wages ... I could never see the point of moving out of the area when everything I wanted was here. Although I did live in Winterbrook for a while – but that's only five miles away, hardly the other side of the world.'

'Mmmm. Lav and Lob told me about all that . . . oh, thanks . . .' Shay broke off to take two Pyrex beakers from a tray carried by Flo. 'Is it mulled wine?'

Flo grinned. 'Ah, you could say. Sprout and turnip with a touch of juniper berry. And a few spices. Boiled.'

'It's traditional,' Lu assured him, taking her beaker as Flo trotted away to inflict the wine in the next group. 'Clyde always makes it for the bonfire. So, what about you? Are you a world-weary traveller?'

'Very much so,' Shay sipped the wine. 'God Almighty!'

'An acquired taste.' Lulu grinned, wondering if mopping the front of his sweater would be a move too far too soon and deciding it wouldn't. She mopped quickly with her bunched-up mittens, fighting the urge to run her fingers along his ribs and across his abs and . . . she swallowed and snatched her hand away. 'And the beakers do tend to hold the heat.'

Shay laughed. He had a lovely laugh. And fabulous eyes. And the best body in the world. And Heath Ledger shaggy streaky hair. And a pale sexy mouth. And – oooooh.

Lulu's toes curled inside her tartan DMs.

She swallowed again. 'So, go on, you were telling me about your round-the-world travels.'

'I'm not sure I'll ever speak again.' He looked down at his beaker. 'Maybe I'll leave this to cool – if it ever does . . . And thanks for the rubdown . . . Right, yeah, I was an army brat. Always on the move. Dad had umpteen different postings; I went to umpteen different schools; we never put down roots; I never had any lasting friendships. I'd lived in seven countries by the time I left school. Then when he came out of the army, he and Mum went back to his home town in the Ring of Kerry – but Mum hated it. Couldn't settle. They divorced. He's still there. She's in London. They're both happy with new partners.'

Wow, Lu thought, nodding. A potted history. And it explained a lot.

'And the paramedic thing? Was that a lifetime ambition or something you drifted into?'

'When I eventually grew up, yes. I was a bass guitarist in a very heavy metal band during and for a while after university. We went pro for a while and did some really wild stuff.'

Wow, Lu thought. She could just see him: swaying sexily with his Rickenbacker in smoky spotlights, throbbing out the driving beat, his hair flowing, his body encased in skin-tight ripped denim and little else.

'I wish I could have seen you then. Did you have groupies?'

'Millions. It was an ace time.' Shay bravely took a sip of his mulled wine. 'But it couldn't last. We were going too crazy and I got a bit of a social conscience. Don't laugh, but I thought about joining the police – but I couldn't quite cope with having my hair chopped from waist-length to crew-cut overnight. The ambulance service wasn't quite so regimental about longish hair – so I shortened it gradually and here I am. I've been qualified for five years. I worked in London until my transfer here this year.'

'And – um – do you think you'll be staying ... I mean, will you be transferred anywhere else?'

He shook his head. 'No. I'd like to put down my own roots now. I've done the crazy stuff. And I've no desire to go back to the city. So, much as I love Lav and Lob, in the New Year I'll be looking for somewhere permanent to live round here.'

Yessss! Lulu mentally punched the air.

Of course there was a slight fly in the perfect ointment.

'And – er – Carmel? Are you and she—? I mean, will you—?'

Shay shrugged. 'We get on well together. We're a good team. She's a great girl. And surprising. Do you know what she's doing tonight?'

'No,' Lulu said, not really caring, just pleased that she wasn't there on the village green playing an ethereal gooseberry.

170

'She's helping with the bonfire night party at the children's hospice. She's on the Dreams-to-Reality team for terminally ill kids. Spends every spare minute with them.'

Lulu groaned. Oh, damn it. How could she carry on hating little fairy-doll Carmel when she was involved in something like that? It was only a step away from sainthood.

'That's wonderful,' she said quietly. 'She must be very special.'

'Oh yes,' Shay nodded. 'She is.'

Linking her arm through Brett's, Doll almost skipped along the dark smoky Hazy Hassocks lanes. The orange glow in the sky meant that the bonfire was already well alight. The fireworks wouldn't be long.

'Feeling better?' Brett looked at her. 'Are you really sure you want to do this tonight?'

'Absolutely. I feel fantastic now, thanks. Um – can I ask you something?'

'Unless it involves quantum physics or the meaning of life, yeah.'

'You know you said you didn't want things to change? Well, what about if I gave up work?'

'Do you want to?' Brett looked at her in some surprise. 'I always thought you were happy at the surgery.'

'Oh, I am – I just wondered what would happen if I had a bit of a career break for say a year. Could we cope? Financially?'

'I'm sure we could. We'd have to make a few cutbacks, but yes, if that's what you want I'd support you all the way, you know that.'

She smiled. 'Okay, that's great. And the other question. Do you want to get married?'

Brett stopped walking. 'What? To you? Or generally?'

'Preferably to me,' Doll grinned.

Brett pulled her against him. 'I wanted to marry you the first time I saw you – but as we were only six at the time and you'd just punched me for spoiling your skipping game

171

in the playground I thought I'd better wait a bit before asking you.'

'So, another quarter of a century on?'

'I still feel the same – but then again, it's never been necessary, has it?'

They'd turned the corner and were on the edge of the green. The whole village had turned out, as always.

'It might be necessary now,' Doll said softly. 'That is, if you'd like to go down the old-fashioned Hazy Hassocks route and have your baby born in wedlock.'

Arriving home from Tarnia's, Mitzi parked the car outside number 33, checked that Richard and Judy weren't terrified by Armageddon occurring overhead, and set off for the village green. The fact that Tarnia and Snotty Mark were aiming to be recognised by the Palace for dishing out largesse to the hoi-polloi had cheered her immensely; it could only be good news for the survival of the Baby Boomers Collective – although she still felt announcing *Hair* as the Christmas entertainment must be kept secret for as long as possible. However, the other activities, and particularly the Christmas lunch for the lost and lonely, would surely be embraced by the Snepps as a huge step forward on their way to Honourdom?

The bonfire, with its effigy now lopsided and sliding, was a roaring, dancing blaze of orange and red and gold. The faces surrounding it glowed in the reflection. The cold air was alive with expectation.

Exchanging greetings with each group, Mitzi moved towards the front of the crowd and over the heads spotted Lulu with Shay and some of her hippie-looking friends on one side of the bonfire, and Doll and Brett with Tammy and Viv from the dental surgery on the other. Both couples, she thought, looked extremely happy. She hoped they were. What more could a mother ask?

She'd experienced a stupid pang of disappointment when she'd realised Joel wasn't with Doll's dentistry gang. Of course he'd have said he'd be here tonight out of politeness, wouldn't he? He was a nice man; he wouldn't have left her after the party with 'thanks but no thanks'. He'd leave her to draw her own conclusions now.

For a split second, Mitzi felt very alone. In the middle of this huge crowd, most of whom she'd known all her life, she felt lonely. While she'd never been a rampant feminist, she'd always known she was okay on her own. She'd never been one of those women who had to have a man in their life whatever the cost. She'd survived well without Lance or any long-term replacement. But now, having spent some time with Joel, and felt that damn tingle, one half of a couple seemed a very desirable thing to be. And, she admitted to herself, she had been looking forward to seeing him again.

Bustling forward in the flickering light, the vicar shouted his usual greetings, made a sort of trumpeting fanfare through his teeth, and carefully manoeuvring the glowing taper, set alight the first firework.

The blue touch paper glowed. There was a mass intake of breath.

Nothing happened. The blue touch paper stopped glowing.

There was a mass groan of disappointment.

Ignoring all the safety advice, the vicar tiptoed forward, peered at the non-firework, and struck a match.

With a whoosh and a flash and a scream, the first of Molly Coddle's roman candles delighted the Hazy Hassocks crowd.

The vicar, minus an eyebrow and with a yellowish patch of hair, beamed triumphantly at everyone.

'What have I missed?' Joel forced his way through the crowd and pushed in beside her. 'Have they started on the sacrificial virgins yet?'

Mitzi, whose fingers and toes had been nearing frostbite, was suddenly suffused in a gloriously warm glow. 'No, but the vicar was close on being fricasseed. It's an annual event. We'd all be so disappointed if it didn't happen.'

173

The flames twinkled on Joel's diamond ear-stud. Mitzi found it amazingly sexy. It was so – well – unexpected. And it reminded her of all the unisex glam fashions of her youth. He was wearing the long black coat over jeans and a dark sweatshirt, and looked so gorgeous that Mitzi felt her stomach contract.

'I'm so pleased I managed to spot you,' Joel said. 'I've been wandering round and round this green for ages. Then I saw your hair. No one could miss your hair.'

Hennaed old hag? Was that what he thought? Oh, bugger.

'I love redheads,' Joel said happily. 'I even married one once.'

'I married a dyed blond who looked like David Bowie.'

Joel grinned down at her. 'No contest, then.'

The fireworks were whooshing and swooshing and exploding round them. The vicar, having escaped being blown up by his incendiary devices, was busily organising the Scouts and Guides on the far side of the bonfire, arming them with forked beanpoles.

'What the hell is going on over there?' Joel leaned closer to her, his breath warm against her ear, as a rank of Catherine wheels, going nowhere, stuttered and screeched on the spot. 'Is it some sort of rural initiation ceremony? I've never seen anything similar in Manchester.'

'They're hooking out the baked potatoes,' Mitzi laughed. 'They hand them round later when you're too frozen to care that they've stripped the skin from your mouth – always assuming that Clyde's wine hasn't done it first.'

'Do you fancy a proper drink?' Joel asked. 'Later? In a minute? I mean ... Well ... The Faery Glen is a nice pub and – er – of course, if you don't want to—'

'I'd love to,' Mitzi reigned-in her grin and fought the urge to caper. 'Ready when you are.'

The Faery Glen was quiet. A proper pub, being all genuine beams and bulging plastered walls and burnished brasses and worn polished furniture, it always offered a warm welcome.

Boris and Otto, looking bored, perked up behind the bar when Mitzi and Joel came in.

'Dead tonight,' Otto said. 'Everyone's at the fireworks. Be heaving later, no doubt. Nice to see you both. Er – are you together?'

Joel nodded. Mitzi, to her shame, blushed.

Otto smiled. 'Oh, right. Didn't know you knew each other, like. The usual, is it?'

'Pint for me, please,' Joel said. 'Mitzi?'

Boris bustled forward. 'Glass of red? Large?'

'Yes, please.'

Choosing a dimpled, copper-topped table beside the cavernous fireplace with its glowing logs, Mitzi slid off her coat and watched Joel chatting at the bar. No doubt Otto and Boris were digging out the minutiae of their friendship.

It was so long since she'd been taken out by a man that she felt quite nervous. Not that this was being *taken out*, of course. Just two people who knew each other slightly, being in the same place at the same time, having a drink. Two lonely-ish people, Mitzi added mentally. Two people who had very little in common except being divorced.

'Great pub,' Joel said, handing her the wine glass and shedding his own coat. 'I wish I lived in Hazy Hassocks – there's nothing as good as this in Winterbrook. They're all yoof pubs with lots of noise and music and games and screens ...'

'And you're too old for all that?'

'Sadly, yes. Awful, isn't it? Oh, not that I don't enjoy the music and the noise and the bustle. But much as I might think I still look eighteen, I'm always aware of the real teenagers staring at me with pity when I try to sing along with Nine Bob Note Rapper and His Wreckin' Crew, or whatever is playing on the juke box.'

Mitzi laughed. 'I stick with the Stones and Hendrix and

Mott the Hoople and Dave Edmunds – which are all probably way before your time.'

'Fishing?' Joel grinned. 'I'm forty-one.'

'Fifty-five,' Mitzi said, delighted that she wasn't quite old enough to be his mother after all. 'And don't we look good on it?'

'We do,' Joel raised his glass to her. 'Sensational. Here's to the older generation. May we never grow up.'

After that it was so easy to talk to him. Several drinks later, the pub rapidly filling up, they were still catching up on their various pasts, presents and hopes for the future. It was absolute bliss, Mitzi thought, having had slightly too much wine, to feel so relaxed.

'Hi, Mum.' Lulu suddenly loomed over the table. 'Hello, Joel. Can we join you?'

She pulled up a stool before either of them said a word. Bundling the whiffy Afghan under the table, she grinned at them both. 'Shay's just getting the drinks in. Have you had a good evening?'

'Great,' they spoke together and laughed.

Lulu nodded. 'All thanks to Granny's apple love magic of course . . . cool stuff. Oh, look – a family gathering!'

Mitzi craned her neck and could just make out Doll's neat blonde head bobbing through the crowds towards them, followed by Brett. It was lovely to see them, she thought. With his early starts they rarely went out in the evenings, and Mitzi hadn't expected them to come on to the pub after the fireworks. Things must be looking up for them.

'Hi.' Doll's beam outshone any of the fireworks. 'I'm so pleased you're all together. It saves having to say this more than once.'

Brett grinned at her and kissed the top of her head.

'Oh, pul-lease,' Lu pulled a face. 'Not in public!'

Poking her tongue out at her, Doll upped her beam. 'Mum, you're going to be a grandmother. Lu you're going to be an auntie. Joel you're going to be minus a nurse. Oh, and you're all invited to a wedding – on Christmas Eve . . .'

Chapter Sixteen

'When I asked you out for a meal tonight,' Joel whispered in the icy darkness of the village hall, 'this wasn't exactly what I had in mind.'

'No, I know. Me neither. I'm really sorry,' Mitzi whispered back, passing him one of Lavender and Lobelia's special sardine fish-paste sandwiches. 'But it's fun, isn't it?'

'And different,' Joel nodded in agreement. 'Which, since I've been in Hazy Hassocks, is something I'm beginning to get a taste for – unlike the sandwiches.'

Mitzi giggled just as the Dansette record player wheezed into Ragini, Rado and MacDermot's 'Electric Blues'.

The past week, since Doll and Brett's earthshaking announcement, had been one of the strangest of her life. Discovering she was to become a grandmother and being foolish enough to fall in love at precisely the same time, had turned her world upside down.

On Bonfire Night in The Faery Glen, Mitzi hadn't known whether to laugh or cry. Of course she was absolutely delighted for Doll and Brett, but – just when she'd been feeling all whimsical and girlish with Joel – the announcement couldn't have come at a worse time.

Of course, even then she'd known she was far too old for him. It was out of the question. Anyone with any sense would realise that. And he'd shown no inclination whatsoever in that direction. But after her Halloween party she'd allowed herself just a little dream or two of how it might possibly be if convention could be ignored and miracles happened and wishes came true.

Then came the body blow.

A *grandmother*.

Okay, it was very selfish, but just how *old* did that make her sound? However much she might think she was still twenty-two inside her head, and youthful in her outlook, her dress and well, everything – there was surely nothing more guaranteed to kill an embryo romance with a gorgeous younger man stone-dead than being called 'Gran'?

Sitting by Otto and Boris's roaring log fire that evening, hugging Doll and Brett and trying to take it all in, she'd realised she'd simply have to enjoy Joel's company. She'd have to make the most of his friendship, but there could be no more silly thoughts of reciprocal love. Her feet, which minutes earlier had been walking on air all the way from the village green to The Faery Glen, had been dragged back to the ground with a resounding thump.

Not that Mitzi's feet, or any of the rest of her, had stayed grounded for very long. Once the news of the baby and the Christmas Eve marriage had started to spread round Hazy Hassocks, she felt as though she'd been caught up in Dorothy's Kansas whirlwind.

With only six weeks in which to organise the wedding – very small, Doll and Brett had insisted, with the reception in The Faery Glen – and the BBC's festive activities, not to mention becoming a party purveyor of Granny's Goodies, Mitzi was more confused than ever.

For umpteen years when she'd been Mr Dickinson's right-hand woman in the bank, she'd managed to organise meetings and appointments and conferences and travel arrangements and holidays and seminars and a zillion other things. She'd kept Mr Dickinson's three diaries running smoothly. There'd never been a double booking, or a missed appointment, or a clash of any sort. It had all run seamlessly. She'd been efficient. Unruffled, calm and efficient.

What on earth had happened? Only a couple of months later and left to organise her own life, she'd gone completely to pot.

Oh, well, back to the real world, she thought – which at that moment was being alone with Joel in the darkened body of Hazy Hassocks's cold and cheerless village hall with a tinny version of 'Aquarius' now rattling through the lone speaker.

The first was lovely; the second was not so. . .

'I am sorry about this,' Mitzi said quietly. 'I'd really been looking forward to going into Winterbrook tonight and having a meal at Lorenzo's. My head's like a sieve recently. I'd forgotten all about the Baby Boomers auditions – and there was no way I could get out of it.'

'No problem,' Joel said. 'We'll go to Lorenzo's next time. And we can always get a takeaway later. I know you're up to your eyes in organising all the wedding stuff.'

Mitzi nodded. 'How's Doll coping at work?'

'Amazingly. Me and Viv and Tammy and Mr Johnson are frantic on her behalf, trying to get her to slow down and put her feet up. And she just laughs and says she isn't anywhere near that stage, and that both the wedding and the birth will be a breeze.'

'I know she's intending to work until the minute she goes into labour,' Mitzi hissed. 'And she probably will.'

The record player had moved on to 'Ain't Got No Grass'.

Joel grinned. 'She keeps telling us all to chill.'

'She's always been that way,' Mitzi said, bravely chewing at a sandwich. 'Cool, calm and collected. God knows what would happen if Lu was in that position. World War Three at least. And please have another sandwich. Go on, Lav and Lob made them specially.'

'Oh, well, in that case I suppose I ought to steel myself . . .' Joel helped himself from the depths of the silver wrappings.

Trilby Man, strutting in the hall's only illumination on the stage, peered crossly down at them. 'Can we have some 'ush in the auditorium, please! You're supposed to be writing this down for me, Mitzi, not nattering. We've reached a delicate point in casting – and you two rattling tinfoil and chatting and laughing like damn fool teenagers is putting us off!'

Mitzi and Joel exchanged glances and tried not to giggle again.

Of course, Mitzi thought giddily, Trilby Man was, for once, exactly right. She still felt just like a teenager in love. Madness, of course, and never destined for a happy ending, but blissful all the same.

She'd been more excited than she could ever remember when Joel had suggested the dinner date at Lorenzo's. And more disappointed than she'd like to admit when she'd realised it clashed with the casting auditions for *Hair*.

Of course there was no contest.

She tried not to look at the stage as the *Hair* LP skittered on to 'Sodomy'.

At least Joel had readily agreed to accompany her to the village hall. He'd said he'd been looking forward to spending an evening with her and while Lorenzo's may have been more pleasant, the village hall would suit him fine.

It was the sort of statement that made her fall in love with him even more, damn it.

So instead of the fat-candled and garlicky-herby-red-wine ambience of Lorenzo's, here she was on a plastic chair in the freezing mustiness of the hall, with an A4 notepad, her laptop, various post-it notes, scraps of paper, backs of envelopes, a million scribbled mnemonics, and of course, Joel, trying to juggle everything.

'Pass the foodie things to me,' Joel hissed, one eye on the stage and Trilby Man and a selection of the Baby Boomers who were being cast as The Tribe. 'No, not any more of those bloody sandwiches – who on earth mashes sardine paste with piccalilli? No, I mean the list of the recipes from your Gran's book and the prices. Thanks. Okay – so I'll type them up on the laptop while you sort out the wedding stuff and take notes for Mr Hitler-in-a-Hat up there.'

'Silence!' Trilby Man roared at them, as several of the less able BBC-ers and the Dansette wobbled through 'Hare Krishna'. 'We have artistes working up here!'

Mitzi stared very hard at the floor.

'Your shoulders are shaking,' Joel whispered. 'He'll notice.'

Mitzi bit her lips very hard and sniffed back hysterical tears. There was something unnerving about a dozen pensioners wearing hats and scarves and zip-up bootees and very tightly buttoned coats pretending to be youthful free spirits. And it could only get worse.

Lav and Lob, hippie bandannas tied rakishly round their cycle helmets, had made so much fuss about being left out that they'd been co-opted in as extras in The Tribe on the understanding that they wouldn't have to sing any of the songs with rude words.

'Lovely! Lovely!' Trilby Man clapped. 'That's The Tribe sorted, then! Mitzi – 'ave you got all the names down, duck?'

Mitzi nodded.

'Right. Good. So that's the lot. Now the main roles – make sure you gets 'em all in order ... Ronnie will be Berger, Christopher is Woof, and Sid and Philip will share being Claude because of the strenuous nature of the role. Beryl is Crissy, Doreen is Dionne, and Bernard can be Sheila because of his falsetto and wig. Oh, and hopefully Frank will be okay as Hud once he gets the all-clear re his blood pressure because of hanging upside down from that there pole in Act I ...'

Trilby Man's voice droned on. The Dansette was stuck on 'Ain't Got No ...' Mitzi scribbled. It became more and more obvious that this was going to be a disaster of epic proportions.

Joel, diligently tapping away one fingered on the laptop was trying hard not to laugh. 'I think I've nearly finished your list – you'll have to check the spellings on some of these things, though. But what on earth are Green Gowns? And Dreaming Creams? And who wants Dragon's Blood in their pudding?'

'God knows,' Mitzi started to gather together her pieces of paper. 'But someone might – it's supposed to be a love potion according to Granny Westward, so I just threw it in ... Thanks for doing that. I'll print out several copies when I get home and we'll see what happens ... Right – I'm more than ready for a drink.' She groaned as the Dansette hit 'Good Morning Starshine'. 'Let's get out of here before Trilby Man starts putting them through the song-and-dance bit and I really disgrace myself. You do fancy a pint at The Faery Glen, don't you? Okay, last one out of here buys the first round.'

Joel beat her to the door by a millisecond.

'Of course I'm delighted, darling,' Lance held Doll's hands in his across the scrubbed-pine table in his maisonette. 'Couldn't be more pleased. A grandpa! I still can't believe it ... And are you feeling okay? I remember how ghastly Mitzi was with both you and Lulu.'

'Hopefully I haven't inherited her morning-sickness genes, then. No, honestly I'm absolutely fine,' Doll grinned. 'It's very early days, of course, but you know me – strong as the proverbial herd of oxen.'

'Long may it last, love. And do you and Brett want a boy or a girl? Thought of names yet? And this wedding – I am going to give you away, aren't I?'

Doll laughed. 'Of course you are. It's only going to be a very small do, though. Church wedding at four o'clock on Christmas Eve then straight into The Faery Glen. And we don't mind if the baby's a boy or a girl – but one thing we are sure about, it'll have a very ordinary name. Jane or Ann or Susan or John or James – it will not suffer like I have!' She

182

looked round the very clean kitchen. 'Where's Jennifer? Have you told her that she'll be a step-grandmother at the tender age of thirty-two?'

'She didn't take it too well. Had to go off to the nail bar for restorative treatment. She'll be sorry to have missed you tonight – she's at her evening class at the moment.'

'Jennifer? Goodness, is she attempting to improve her conversational English?'

'Bitchy ...' Lance tried to look stern and failed. 'It's a ten-week course on skin buffing and something else she'll need to climb the beauty therapy ladder. Could it be colonic irrigation?'

'Possibly. Probably. Almost definitely.'

They smiled at one another. Doll really wished that the family hadn't been fractured. That her parents could have shared this wonderful news together. Still, it was something that Mitzi and Lance were now on such friendly terms. She'd probably never let either of them know that it was their divorce which had made her doubt for so long whether marriage to Brett was a good move. If Lance and Mitzi had remained together then they'd have probably tied the knot years earlier – baby or no baby.

Lance broke the silence. 'And what about your Mum? How's she bearing up about the Granny news?'

'Thrilled to bits, of course. She's threatening to learn how to knit.'

'I somehow can't see Mitzi with lots of wool and two-pointy things. She'd have someone's eye out. She's never been practical.'

'She's getting there,' Doll said defensively. 'She's learned a lot since you've not been around. Look how well she tackled decorating the whole house. And she does the gardening and can change plugs and mend fuses and—'

'Okay, okay. Point taken. Is she at home tonight? I might go round and commiserate with her. After all – grandparents – us! We're far too young. No, sweetheart, I'm kidding – but I'd like to see her, and Lulu, and raise a glass or two.'

183

Doll ran a forefinger round the rim of her glass of orange juice. 'It'd be a waste of time tonight. There's no one in. Lu's out on one of her animal rescue missions and – um – Mum's . . . well, she's out with someone else actually. At the village hall. They're sorting out the Christmas show.'

Lance stopped grinning. 'Oh – right. You mean – out with *someone*? As in a date? Do I know him?'

Doll shrugged. 'Not sure. Joel Earnshaw? Our new dentist? She's – um – well, they've been – um – getting to know one another and, er . . .'

Lance poured more wine into his glass. 'Oh, I see. Well, of course it's no business of mine if she wants to see someone else, is it?'

Much as Doll adored her father, she felt a rapid surge of anger. 'No it bloody well isn't! You left her ten years ago! You cheated on her, decamped with Jennifer – someone only slightly older than me and Lu – and you divorced Mum to bloody marry her, Dad! Your choice! Don't you dare criticise Mum for finding someone else after all this time.'

'I'm not . . . But has she? Found someone else? Is it serious with this Joe?'

'Joel – and yes, well, he'd like it to be.' Doll challenged her father with her eyes. 'He talks about nothing else but her at work. And they've got lots in common – including both being betrayed by someone they trusted implicitly. He's a great bloke and she deserves to be happy. So don't you dare spoil it. Okay?'

Lance downed his wine in one go and poured another. 'Well, I guess it was bound to happen one day. I just – well – you know—'

'Yes, only too well. You should never have had the affair with Jennifer. Never have left Mum. Still, you did, and however much you might miss and need Mum, you've just got to live with it.'

The silence ticked away in the spotless kitchen. Doll hoped her father wasn't going to cry. She'd been devastated when they'd divorced, but now even she could see that there was no chance of a reunion – and Joel would be simply perfect for Mitzi, if only she could see it too.

She finished her orange juice. Time to change the subject.

'By the way, Mum's going to be doing the catering for the wedding.'

'Christ!' Lance looked horrified. 'She can't! That's even worse than knitting. Whatever you say about her new-found skills, she'll never cope with fiddly formal stuff like vol-au-vents and petit-fours and things on sticks.'

'She says she's cooking up a traditional festive feast from Granny Westward's book.' Doll bit her lip. 'A combination of old-time Christmas and wedding fare.'

'Blimey,' Lance blinked. 'So we'll all be naked and chanting by six o'clock and calling on the various pagan gods of winter as we skip round the tables. You'd best ask Otto and Boris to have a few sandwiches on standby.'

Doll pulled a face. 'You're as bad as Lu! She thinks everything in that recipe book is magic. She reckons it was some sort of Sahmain apple love spell that got Mum and Joel together – not to mention her and Shay. Oh, and of course, the Wishes Come True Pie is totally responsible for my pregnancy and wedding. Complete crap. How many times have I got to say—'

'Say what you like,' Lance frowned. 'I know what happened with those Powers of Persuasion Puddings and Flo Spraggs. Never been so scared in my life! No, you ought to keep your mother well away from any of that magical cookery stuff if you and Brett want a smooth wedding.'

'When on earth has anyone in Hazy Hassocks ever had one of those?'

'Well, I think it's disgusting,' Lulu huffed into the folds of her vast multicoloured scarf in the freezing darkness. 'I've never heard of anything so vile!'

'Sssshhhhh ...' Biff Pippin, only her bifocals visible

between the pulled-down black bobble hat and the done-up black mackintosh, glared through the icy undergrowth. 'Keep your voice down. We don't want to alert the quarry. And what's so bad about your Doll and Brett getting married? They've been together longer'n most married couples after all.'

'It's not them getting married—'

'Well, surely it's not because they're having a baby? Good Lord, Lulu – I thought you were a free-thinking, hippie, live-and-let-live girl? No one's bothered about that sort of thing for years. Surely you haven't gone all moralistic?'

Lu sniffed. The cold was making her nose run. And crouching in the dark twiggy ditch was making her legs ache. And her teeth were chattering. 'No, it's not because she's pregnant either – although why she'd want to pro-create with boring Brett is beyond me . . . no, it's because she wants me to be a bridesmaid.'

Biff sniggered quietly. 'Bloomin' brave of her, if you ask me. And you don't want to?'

'What – me? In a meringue dress in some girlie colour? No bloody way! And – and—' Lu was almost exploding in her fury '—*and* she thinks I'm going to have my hair done! Done! You know – like . . . well . . . *done!*'

Biff chuckled. 'Bet you do it, though. Bet you trot down that aisle looking like a proper little lady. Don't matter how old you are, your mum'll make sure you're all scrubbed up on the big day. Mind you, your Doll's picked a bit of a daft date, if you ask me. Everyone'll be bushed rotten for Christmas after the celebrations.'

Lulu had thought much the same thing. Only the frighteningly organised Doll could possibly think that a Christmas Eve wedding wouldn't cause any additional stress to the already overloaded festive arrangements.

'Mum reckons she's going to be at the village hall on Christmas Day doing dinners for the lost and lonely with her Baby Boomers, so she's not having all the usual stuff this year. And Doll and Brett will be on honeymoon. It looks like it'll be me, complete with hangover, and Richard and Judy, home alone, with a nut roast and *The Great Escape*.'

'Oh, I love *The Great Escape*. It wouldn't be Christmas without it. And *The Sound of Music* and *The Wizard of*—'

'Good Lord, Biff!' Hedley spat. 'This is no time to turn into the *TV Times Quick!* Quarry approaching! Eleven o'clock!'

Squinting at her watch, Lulu shook her head. 'Nah. It might feel like eleven, but it's only nine-thirty. Cold enough to be damn midnight, though.'

'It's a directional indication,' Hedley hissed indignantly. 'Like the RAF used in the war.'

Biff and Lu exchanged raised eyebrows in the darkness.

'There!' Hedley pointed excitedly as a Range-Rover towing a trailer crackled across the farmyard's icy ruts and disappeared along the track. 'There they go! Now – we give 'em a few minutes to get out of sight then we move in! Okay?'

Biff and Lulu nodded.

Lu, knowing that tonight's intelligence had once again been supplied by Gwyneth Wilkins and Big Ida Tomms, was damn sure she wasn't going to be the first in. Not this time.

Tonight's stakeout was on the outskirts of Hazy Hassocks, at a remote and ramshackle farmhouse on the road to Fiddlesticks. According to Gwyneth and Big Ida, one of the farm buildings was being used for illegal puppy farming. If, by some miracle, this awful information happened to be true, then Lu knew it was way out of their league. The RSPCA would have to be involved immediately.

The Pippins would have to be very, very sure of their facts this time.

'Right,' Hedley said, pulling his cap down over his ears, and getting creakily to his feet. 'Let's go and see what sort

187

of bastards we're dealing with . . .'

With Hedley leading the way, they stumbled across the rock-hard ground in single file, their breath puffing out in smoky plumes and hovering in the brilliant white-cold night air.

The farmhouse was, as reported, dark, dismal and deserted. Surely, Lu thought with a shudder, no one could live there. The windows were cracked, the doors hung crazily from their hinges and creepers covered the crumbling walls. Maybe Gwyneth and Big Ida had got it right this time.

'Don't seem to me,' Biff muttered, 'that folks what drive Range-Rovers would be living in a hovel like this.'

'There's a couple of outbuildings over there.' Lu squinted through the darkness. 'Maybe we should look in there first.'

She had a really nasty feeling that they weren't going to like what they found.

Hedley crunched towards the first of the tumbledown barns and switched his torch on to main beam. The yellow light swept up, down and round. 'Nothing there. Nothing at all. Empty. Right – on to the next one.'

Lu followed in the Pippin's wake. She really, really wished Shay was with her.

Again Hedley shone his torch round the interior of the barn in an all-encompassing sweeping arc.

'Bloody hell!'

'What?' Biff frowned. 'What's going on in there?'

'Ring the RSPCA,' Hedley said gruffly. 'Now. Tell 'em it's an emergency. And Lu, you come inside with me . . .'

Chapter Seventeen

MISTLETOE KISSES

One dozen egg whites
One cup of caster sugar
Ground cyclamen bulb
Two good spoonfuls of lemon verbena
Pinch of ground nettle leaf
The merest pinch of crushed garlic
A good serving of vanilla

Mix together the cyclamen, lemon verbena, nettle, garlic and vanilla and set aside.
Whisk the egg whites in bowl with wooden spoon until mixture standing in stiff peaks.
Fold sugar into whisked eggs.
Gradually add the herb mixture to the egg and sugar mixture.
Do Not Beat Further.

Spoon small quantities on to baking sheets greased with best butter.
Bake in very hot oven until meringues have risen and are light golden brown on top.
Leave to cool.

Note: Real mistletoe is deadly poisonous. These are NOT to be made from real mistletoe.

Mistletoe Kisses are very strong love potions indeed. When eaten they will, over a period of time from one to six hours – whichever the cook so desires and suggests at the time of making – provide a powerful aphrodisiac. There will be a loss of inhibitions. There will be a feeling of powerful love for whomsoever is nearest. Mistletoe Kisses can cause unlikely people to lust and fall in love. Not to be eaten lightly.

There was no sound but the keening of the icy wind. The feeble light from Hedley's torch cast spooky shadows across blackened uneven walls and splintered beams. Lulu peered into the darkness of the towering, freezing, foul-smelling barn with mounting horror. Underfoot, the floor was matted with filthy straw. Hedley swung the torch in an arc, illuminating the interior of the whole building. The roof was almost torn away, leaving the barn exposed to the white-streaked sky and the biting cold. Despite this unintentional air-conditioning, the atmosphere was foetid. And the mould-encrusted walls were lined with makeshift wooden cages.

Squinting more closely as her eyes got used to the gloom, Lulu reckoned each cage was possibly six feet square, made of rough wood, with a padlocked hinged door and a small ragged chicken wire window.

Taking a deep breath, she moved carefully towards them. 'Oh my God!'

A heap of pleading brown eyes and pathetic furry muzzles were pressed up against each of the cage's chicken-wire fronts. Puppies. Dozens of puppies. All different breeds. And none of them were making any noise at all.

Lulu blinked back her tears, shaking with anger.

'Christ!' Hedley finally found his voice. 'Okay Lu, let's see what we've got. The RSPCA should be here pronto.

You know how to deal with this, don't you? Don't touch any of them. Just asses the situation.'

Sniffing back her tears, wiping her eyes on the raggedy cuff of her Afghan coat, Lu nodded.

In the years she'd worked with Biff and Hedley she'd helped in quite a few genuine animal rescues. Mostly they had been just domestic cases of ignorance and neglect and, after veterinary treatment, the animals had been cosily rehomed.

This was way, way beyond anything she'd ever experienced before.

'Is it – is it puppy farming?'

'Looks like it, though I've never seen anything on this scale before. Gwyneth and Big Ida must have picked up the right information for once.'

Walking slowly along the row of cages, Lu was aware that all the puppies cowered away from her. None of them growled. None of them whimpered. Their eyes were glassy.

'Sedated?'

'I reckon so,' Hedley nodded, his face grim. 'Bastards.'

There were possibly six or seven puppies to a cage. And at least twenty cages.

'Nice little earner for some sod,' Hedley said bitterly. 'Let's hope these little chaps are all alive.'

She looked again, not wanting to, knowing she had to.

It was impossible to tell. They all looked alive – just – and there were dirty bowls which may have once contained food and water in each cage, but whether any of the puppies would survive was another matter.

Wiping her eyes again, she took a deep breath. 'I think they're all okay. That is, I can't see any – um – bodies . . . oh, shit! Why do people do this?'

'Money,' Hedley said, taking off his glasses and scrubbing at his eyes. 'Big, big money. Bring 'em in from outside the country mostly. This time of year's great . . . advertise them as Christmas presents for the kids . . . bring the punters to see the puppies – just one or two, tarted up and undrugged of course, in some swish hotel foyer or rented room – punter falls in love, money changes hands – bingo!'

'But all the advertising about animals not being suitable presents—'

'Makes not a scrap of difference when little Campari insists that she wants a puppy this year. Very few people see the wider picture of introducing an animal into the home, Lulu, as you well know. It's all fluff and wagging tails and big brown eyes – but when little Campari gets bored it can't be simply pushed back into the cupboard, so we get another waif and stray – and the cycle starts all over again.'

Lu shuddered again. It was simply freezing in the barn. How could the puppies survive these temperatures? Why didn't the RSPCA arrive?

'So, even if they've had this sort of crappy start, they might go to good homes?'

'Who knows? Some may do. There's no vetting done, is there? They're cheap and disposable. Most of 'em probably end up in Battersea or the like before New Year's out. The ones what don't get sold to punters most probably end their days in some lab or other.'

Lu whimpered. This was too awful. 'And what about the mothers? Where are they? I mean, what happens to them?'

'Kept in whelp constantly until they're too old, then . . .' Hedley looked away. 'That's the end the RSPCA needs to tackle. And they might be able to if they catch the evil sods behind this lot.'

Lu stared upwards and blinked towards the ceiling. If she started crying now she'd probably never stop. She suddenly wished that bloody Niall could be here to see this. He'd mocked her animal rights work all the time they'd been together. Laughed at her for being involved. Been disparaging when yet another tip-off had failed to be correct.

But this! Oh, yes – Niall deserved to see this!

Hedley patted her shoulder. 'Come on, love. Chin up. We've contacted the right people. We'll do all we can for these little fellows – and hopefully put a stop to the buggers once and for all.'

Lu sniffed again and wiped her eyes on the knotted hairy cuff. Her feet and hands were aching with the cold. It was still unnervingly quiet in the barn. She longed to open all the cages and haul the dogs out and cuddle them warm.

'Cavalry's arriving!' Biff suddenly appeared in the doorway. 'They're coming up the lane. How bad is it, Hed?'

'Bloody awful. Worst I've seen. Let's hope the RSPCA have enough room for this lot – blow me!' Hedley narrowed his eyes at the crowds of uniformed people appearing behind Biff. 'How many did you phone?'

'Everyone I could think of. RSPCA, of course – said there was a barn full to make sure they came out in force. Oh, and all the emergency services – just in case, because I wasn't sure what we were dealing with.'

'Good girl. The police will probably need to be involved in catching the bastards behind this. Right—' Hedley became all officious '—over here, lads.'

Lu shrank back into the shadows as the various men and women in uniform swarmed in and took control.

It was all over very quickly. The puppies were removed from the cages, gently loaded into the RSPCA's vans and driven away. The police and remaining RSPCA officials exchanged a brief conversation with Hedley, as the fire engine, clearly realising it wasn't going to be needed, started to reverse up the rutted track.

Feeling sick, Lulu picked her way across the icy ground towards Biff. 'What's going to happen now?'

Biff wiped her bifocals on a mitten. 'Poor little mites will be checked over then kept in the RSPCA shelters and hopefully rehomed. They'll be okay. And a couple of the RSPCA blokes are going to hang around with the police to catch the buggers when they come back here. It might be a drop in the ocean but at least we'll have scuppered this particular little scam.'

Lulu nodded. It was something, as Biff said, but it was never enough.

The fire engine executed a neat circle at the end of the track, changing places with the waiting ambulance. Lu watched as itty-bitty Carmel, neat in her green catsuit and a bright neon jacket, jumped out from the behind the wheel. Didn't they have any other paramedics in Winterbrook? Why did Carmel always have to turn up looking like Kylie, only perter, with Shay in tow, when she looked her absolute worse?

'Guess there's no need for us to hang around any more,' Carmel said to Biff, having made short shrift of yomping over the icy ruts. 'No bodies to be patched and despatched?'

'None,' Biff replaced her glasses. 'Thanks for turning up though.'

'No sweat,' Carmel smiled then grinned at Lulu. 'I should have known you'd be mixed up in this. Shay said you were an animal activist.'

'Well, I don't fire-bomb labs or things like that,' Lulu bristled, 'but I do try to help animals as much a possible. They don't have a voice, do they? They need someone . . .'

Carmel looked slightly sceptical. 'Well, yeah, guess so. You're brave to get involved with something you believe in. So many people just pay lip service.' She grinned a bit more. 'I'll send Shay your love over the two-way, shall I?'

'What? Why? Isn't he with you?' Lulu peered towards the ambulance. 'I thought you were always together on your shifts?'

'Usually but not always. He's out on motorway patrol tonight. I'm paired with Augusta for local shouts like this one.'

Carmel waved towards the ambulance. Neon-clad Augusta, whose massive shoulders and wild curls seemed to take up most of the passenger seat, waved back.

Lulu decided not to join in the waving. She suddenly felt quite despondent that Shay hadn't been there to witness her moment of glory tonight. Especially after the ferrets-berets débâcle. She actually felt quite despondent that Shay wasn't there, full stop. The relationship, despite the apple magic, really wasn't progressing very quickly at all. She'd have to sneak another look at Granny Westward's recipes and find something to speed things up a bit.

Carmel scrunched away towards the ambulance again, swung herself up behind the steering wheel into the tiny gap left by the huge Augusta and, for one so small, manhandled the vehicle with surprising dexterity back along the track.

'Well, I don't know about you ladies, but I could do with a warm,' Hedley said, huffing on his hands. 'What say we all go back to the pub and have a snifter to cheer ourselves up and celebrate a job well done?'

'Not for me, thanks,' Lu said. 'I just want to go home.'

Just when she really needed someone to talk to, the house was empty. Still feeling shaky, Lulu turned the fire up to the hilt, switched on the television, and most of the lights, and headed for the kitchen to make herself some coffee.

'Blimey . . .' she looked at the heaps of papers strewn across the kitchen table, at the laptop, and the haphazard post-it notes. Mitzi had clearly returned from the village hall and gone out again. Quickly. Lu smiled. Probably with Joel. At least the Sahmain apple magic seemed to have worked well for them. Well, it would, wouldn't it? Inadvertently, Mitzi and Joel had got it exactly right on Halloween.

Richard and Judy squirmed happily from the washing basket and wove figures of eight round Lu's legs until she fed them. Idly forking tuna chunks into their bowls, she read Mitzi's notes. There were several recipes, a party plan, something bizarre to do with the Baby Boomers and *Hair* for heaven's sake, jottings about a Christmas Fayre, and a rather odd list of ingredients which could be for Doll and Brett's wedding feast.

195

'Your mum,' Lulu said to Richard and Judy as she placed their dishes on the floor, 'has taken the phrase "get a life" to whole new heights.'

It was actually rather dispiriting to think that Mitzi was forging ahead with this new life, and that Doll and boring Brett were now teetering on the cusp of changing their lives for ever.

Slopping water on to her coffee granules with one hand and burrowing under through Mitzi's notes with the other, Lulu eventually uncovered Granny Westward's book.

'Hah!' She grinned triumphantly at Richard and Judy who were far too involved with their tuna chunks to care. 'Now let's see what I can concoct to get myself a life and a man. Mum's not the only one in this family who can dabble.'

And tucking the book under her arm she headed for the living room.

Curled on the sofa, with the television softly babbling in the background, the fire and the coffee both warmed her as the puppy farm horrors started to recede slightly. At least the poor little things would be at the RSPCA kennels by now and being fed and cosseted. She'd ring first thing in the morning and see how they were doing.

Carefully turning the fragile yellowing pages, Lu scanned the recipes. Ah – this one looked interesting. Star Spangles. She peered at the spiky writing. According to Granny Westward, Star Spangles, when eaten immediately after cooking, along with the appropriate incantation, not only increased psychic powers and gave you amazing forces of astral persuasion, but also brought everlasting good luck. Sounded exactly what she needed. The only problem being that the main ingredient was something called 'badiana'. Where the heck was she going to get hold of that at this time of night? In Hazy Hassocks? Big Sava, even on a late-night opening, weren't likely to have early twentieth-century magical herbs on special offer, were they? And the only other likely place – Herbie's Healthfoods – would have been closed for hours.

Bugger. Lulu sighed in exasperation and riffled through the book again. There didn't seem to be any sort of substitute available, and none of the other recipes offered exactly what she was looking for. Maybe Herbie would still be open or stocktaking or something.

Determined not to be beaten until all stones were unturned, she flicked through Mitzi's address book and dialled Herbie's number.

After a minute of incessant ringing and just as she was about to hang up, Herbie answered.

'Um – hello. Sorry to bother you, and I know it's late. It's Lu, Mitzi Blessing's daughter, I wondered if you could help me—'

'If your mother has unleashed something nasty, then no,' Herbie said cheerfully. 'I've warned her about tinkering with magical herbs. In the hands of an amateur they can be lethal.'

'Er – no she hasn't. Unleashed anything that is. It's just that I've found this recipe and it needs a special herb and I wondered . . .'

Herbie inhaled noisily and giggled a bit. Lulu frowned. God! These old hippies never changed.

'So what is it then?' Herbie chuckled, his voice now slightly slurred. 'What noxious toxin are you Blessings planning to inflict on the village this time?'

'It's for personal use only,' Lu said indignantly. 'It's called badiana. I don't suppose you—'

'No I don't, but luckily for you I'm pretty sure your ma has got some in her cupboard. Left over from her Halloween party. She used them as a decoration. Saw them myself. At least, I think I did. Don't think I was hallucinating.'

'Really?' Lulu perked up, then remembered that Herbie was definitely stoned both now and at the party and possibly not to be relied upon. 'Why? Did you sell it to her?'

'Nope,' Herbie bellowed with laughter. 'You can get it

at any supermarket these days. People use it all the time since those poncey telly chefs started making it a must-have back in the nineties. It's star anise.'

Lulu frowned. 'What those little, orange, papery, Chinese lantern thingys, you mean?'

'That's the little devils,' Herbie giggled. 'The seeds have been used in traditional medicine for years and years – long before the poncey telly chefs got hold of them and—'

'Right, thanks,' Lu broke in before Herbie could go on full rerun. 'And – um – sorry to have disturbed you.'

'No problem,' Herbie inhaled again and rattled the phone clearly trying to align receiver and cradle. 'It's cool, man.'

As he eventually managed to disconnect, Lulu shook her head again at the appalling behaviour of the older generation. Still, stoned or not, Herbie had been more than helpful, and if there was miraculously some star anise left in the kitchen she could concoct the Star Spangles in no time. Smiling to herself, with Granny's book under her arm, she headed back to the kitchen.

To her delight, not only was there a bag of rather withered star anise in the larder, but all the other ingredients – eggs and sugar and cream – were also available. Star Spangles, it seemed, were sort of meringues using the badiana seeds. The star-shaped outer casings were to be kept intact to be used afterwards. Turning the oven on and removing the cream from Richard and Judy, Lu set to work, easing the seeds carefully from the little papery shells, careful, as per Granny's instructions, not to damage them.

After a bit of a problem separating the egg whites from the yolks, much to Richard and Judy's delight, the mixture was eventually whisked into stiff peaks, spooned into what Lulu imagined Granny meant by patty tins, and popped into the oven.

'There,' Lu said happily to the eggy cats, 'easy-peasy or what? And they only take ten minutes to cook – then I have to eat them while they're still warm and say aloud what it is I want to happen – oh, and I have to hold the starry bit in the palm of one hand at the same time of course. So, Shay had better watch out ...'

Richard and Judy, losing interest now the eggs had disappeared and the whipped cream was out of reach, gave her a disdainful stare and rippled silkily back into the washing basket to begin reciprocal grooming.

Ten minutes passed irritatingly slowly, but eventually Lulu had a tray filled with nicely risen, crispy, golden-tipped meringues. The anise seeds gave them a bit of a pockmarked look but she was sure it wouldn't spoil the flavour, especially not when sandwiched together with a good inch of cream.

'Okay,' Lu said to herself. 'One bite, then I'll say my bit and – oh, yes, balance these in my hand ...'

It was fortunate, she thought, that she was alone. The meringues were crumbly and extremely hot, the cream was melted and dripping, the empty star anise cases were fiddly little suckers, and her incantation came out in a sort of gurgled roar as she hopped around the kitchen fanning her mouth.

The intended 'Please let Shay really, really fall in love with me, and not be able to live without me, and let him realise Carmel is – um – okay, cute, but cute is temporary and commitment is forever – if that doesn't sound too Ricki Lake – and – um – oh, right, that we were meant for one another and let it happen soon – like – er – now, if that's not too greedy – oh, and yes, let all the puppies be okay and let the puppy farming stop and – well, just let me be as happy as Mum and Doll are, please ...' emerged as a mumbled, glottal jumble accompanied by a spray of meringue crumbs.

Gulping down the last of the very sickly Star Spangles and feeling rather strange, Lulu cast a look round the disgusting mess in the kitchen and decided that sitting by the fire for a while before clearing up might be a good idea, at least until her stomach settled down a bit. She also hoped that the powers which received the incantation would be able to pick the bones out of her mumbo-jumbo.

The television was still whispering to itself, and rather unsteadily Lu flicked through the channels. How long would she have to wait to know if the Star Spangles had done their business? That was one area where Granny Westward was never clear: the time span between cause and effect. The local newsreader, glossy haired and lipped, was looking serious and saying something about 'news just in'. Lu slumped on to the sofa then immediately rocketed to her feet.

'Ambulance taking motorway RTA victim to hospital involved in pileup . . . Emergency services on the scene . . . No news about further casualties . . . More as soon as we hear . . . Over to our man on the spot . . .'

And then some gruesome scenes of motorway carnage, with an ambulance skewed across the road, several worried policemen, a lot of gridlocked motorway traffic and a fat reporter looking suitably sombre.

'Nooooo!' Lu screamed. 'No! No! No!'

God, it was all her fault! The Star Spangle magic had made Shay lose concentration and now he was probably dead – and she'd never see him again and she'd never ever be able to live with herself and . . . oh shit!

There was someone at the door.

Whimpering, Lu staggered into the hall. It was probably Lav and Lob. They'd have seen the programme, or maybe they'd already been told what had happened as Shay's landladies and had come to break the appalling news.

With shaking hands, she eventually pulled the door open.

'Hi,' Shay grinned at her. 'I didn't wake you up, did I?'

Lu stared at him, unable to say anything at all. Was this a Demi Moore/Patrick Swayze, *Ghost*-type moment? Had his spirit drifted to her, drawn by the Star Spangle incantation? Did he not realise he'd just been killed?

'Lu?' Shay peered at her. 'Are you okay?'

She shook her head. 'You've had an accident. I've just

seen it on the news. You – you – oh—'

'Hey,' he stepped into the hall and pulled her into his
arms. 'Hey, come on angel. What on earth is wrong with
you?'

She was vaguely aware that his green paramedic uniform
felt warm and that somewhere she could feel his heart
beating. Maybe he was still alive. Taking a deep breath,
realising that she was still totally incoherent, she babbled
into his chest.

'Okay.' He pushed her braids and beads away from her
face and kicked the front door closed behind him. 'I think
I get the drift. Come on . . . come and sit down.'

He led her back into the living room. The crash scenes
were still being played out on the television screen.

'There,' he said comfortably. 'See. Not me. One of our
crews, yes, but no one badly hurt. We've all been told from
our central control. Walking wounded only. Minor injuries.
The telly always makes a drama out of a crisis. Yes, I was
working on the motorway tonight but my shift ended half
an hour ago.' He looked down at her and stroked her face.
'It's okay Lu, honestly. I'm fine. And you've just answered
a question I was going to ask.'

'I have?' Lulu muttered, wishing that he'd keep holding
her and stroking her and looking at her like that for ever
and ever.

He nodded. 'Carmel called me and let me know how
ballsy you were about the puppy thing tonight. I was so
bloody proud of you. I'd intended to come round as soon
as my shift ended anyway – but just a few moments ago I
had this really strong feeling that you needed me – I had to
see you straight away. Had to ask you . . . Needed to – um
– well, oh sod it – I had to know . . . to find out if you feel
the same way . . .'

Sending a hasty, silent 'thank you' to Granny Westward
and the Star Spangles and whatever else had made this
miracle happen, Lu nodded.

'Thank Christ for that,' Shay pulled her down on the

sofa. 'I wasn't sure how much longer I could go on doing the "just good friends" bit. I thought, after Niall, it was too soon for you, but I had to know . . . And now I do.'

'You do,' Lu said happily, snuggling against him. 'Oh, believe me you do.'

There was a moment a little later when they giggled over the wide distribution of the Star Spangle crumbs. And another when they rolled from the sofa onto the fluffy hearthrug and several of Lulu's braids got entangled with one of the Day-Glo furry cushions. And a brief interlude when an inquisitive Richard and Judy had to be ushered from the room.

Otherwise, Lulu thought in blissful ecstasy, that it was without question the most sensationally wonderful hour of her life.

'Oh, but . . .' she muttered much later when her reactions were slowly returning to normal. 'What about Carmel?'

'What about her?' Shay smiled lazily at her in the fire glow. 'She's my friend and my crew-mate. She'll be delighted for us. Just as I'm delighted for her and Augusta.'

'Augusta?' Lu squeaked. 'You mean . . . you mean that Carmel is—'

'Carmel's gay? Yes . . .'

'Pig!' Lu thumped him. 'You knew all the time and you let me think . . . let me think . . . well, you know—'

'Yeah,' Shay grinned and kissed her. 'I know. It was my insurance policy against looking like a complete prat if you didn't – er – reciprocate my feelings. But Carmel never fancied me. No, she fell head over heels in love the minute Augusta joined our station. Isn't that lovely?'

'Lovely,' Lu echoed, pulling Shay's remarkable body towards her again. 'Absolutely bloody wonderful.'

Chapter Eighteen

'But all I'm saying is you simply can't expect them to do it in the nude,' Mitzi yelled across the village hall hubbub to Trilby Man. 'Not in December. Not at their age. They'll catch their deaths.'

'Course they'll do it in the buff if they so chooses,' Trilby Man snorted. 'Damn me, Mitzi, you was the one what said there was life after fifty and we was going to prove it. Look, I ain't forcing 'em. They wants to go for full authenticity. 'Tain't nothing to be ashamed of. It's how it was written. We ain't going for titillation here.'

Thank the Lord for small mercies then, Mitzi thought, heaping a pile of well past their sell-by date Goya bath cubes in an attractive pyramid display on her trestle table. Titillation and the BBC's version of *Hair* in the same breath would bring the Trades Description Act down on Hazy Hassocks like a ton of bricks.

Trilby Man flexed his shoulders. 'We're going to be doing another run-through when this jumble sale diablo is over. You stopping to watch?'

'Er – no . . . I don't think so. I've got loads to do and—'

'You should, you know. They're very good. Raymond and Timothy have made us a lovely stage set of Greenwich Village, and Merle has got to grips with the lighting, and now that we've sorted out the acoustics you can hear every word of the lyrics even right at the back of the hall.'

Mitzi shuddered.

It was the day of the Hazy Hassocks Christmas Fayre. Actually it was nowhere near Christmas, being the last Saturday in November, but it was the traditional date for the villagers to turn out in their droves to buy tat for one another in good time for the festive season.

The village hall – decked with morose hand-gummed paper chains in sepulchre brown and dung green, and several sinister, cross-eyed, cotton-wool snowmen made by the baby class of Hazy Hassocks mixed infants – was buzzing. Mitzi, in charge of Bath and Beauty as always, had a zillion things on her mind.

The wedding plans were going well. She and Doll and Lu had been into Reading and bought The Dress. It was a classical, shimmering, white satin pillar with a white swansdown boa, long white gloves and a rather elaborate tiara. Mitzi thought the dress was ravishingly beautiful but probably far too summery. Doll had said her hot flushes which seemed to have taken the place of morning sickness, would provide more than enough inner warmth.

Lu had been amazingly acquiescent about her bridesmaid's dress. In fact, because of Shay, Lu seemed to be wandering about in a pink fluffy cloud all of her own. Speaking of which, she'd refused to wear pink, of course, or pale blue or lilac, but had been reasonably happy with dark-red silk and had even agreed to have some crimson beads mixed with holly and ivy in her braids. As they'd guessed, she'd totally refused to have her hair *done* for the occasion, but Doll had been happy to meet her halfway. Especially as Lu's beloved DMs were being replaced by some rather elegant high-heeled red satin stilettos.

Mitzi had spent ages over her Mother of the Bride outfit, settling eventually for a long medieval-style dress in emerald green velvet which made her feel a bit like Guinevere and set her red hair off a treat. Also, as one of the wedding recipes in Granny's book was Green Gowns, Mitzi had felt it was very apt.

204

Granny Westward's spikily written addendum hinting that Green Gowns, having aphrodisiac properties and therefore being suitable for weddings, had derived from the countryside expression 'give a maid a green gown' which in turn translated into making love to the local village strumpet in the fields, had amused her hugely. She'd shared the snippet with Richard and Judy but felt it was maybe a scrap of information too far for her daughters.

The vicar had agreed to fit the Christmas Eve wedding in late afternoon between the Carol Service and the kiddies' Christingle procession; suitable music had been chosen; Otto and Boris had been wonderful about having the self-catered reception in The Faery Glen; and Lance had said he'd foot the bill behind the bar – which, Mitzi thought, was brave of him, knowing the Hazy Hassockers' ability to consume alcohol at someone else's expense.

So really, apart from firming up which of Granny Westward's recipes would, alongside the already chosen Green Gowns and Dreaming Creams, provide the wedding breakfast, the ceremony was more or less done and dusted.

Which left *Hair*, of course, in a scary ten days' time, and the rest of the Baby Boomers' ever-growing activities, and her party food business, and the Christmas Day Lunch for the lost and lonely, and of course Joel.

Mitzi glanced at the clock. Quarter to twelve. Only fifteen minutes before the doors would be unlocked. There was already a queue outside, stamping its feet in the bitter north wind, and blowing on its collective fingers. Tarnia, who was opening the Fayre, should be here at any moment.

Suggesting they invite Tarnia as guest of honour had, Mitzi thought, been a stroke of genius on Joel's part. Tarnia, deciding it would be a wonderful opportunity to bring along the High and Mighties that she and Snotty Mark were desperate to impress as a tangible example of their multitudinous good works in the village, had accepted with alacrity. And it meant that activities in the village hall would be safe now for as long as Tarnia still angled for a gong.

Joel had said that New Year's Honours recipients were notified some time before the public announcement, so this may well be Tarnia's last chance to impress. Mitzi hoped Tarnia didn't realise it. It would be handy to get away with *Hair* and the Christmas Day feeding frenzy before Tarnia and Snotty Mark reverted to being the Sodding Snepps again and refused to allow the village access to the hall.

The Bandings, who were never allowed to run a stall, were helping Mrs Elkins from Patsy's Pantry price the clothes on Nearly New. As they were trying everything on – a slow process because of the cycle helmets – and admiring one another with squeals of delight, it wasn't progressing very quickly. Mrs Elkins shot the occasional venom-filled glance in Mitzi's direction.

Mrs Elkins had sadly taken umbrage over the rumours that Mitzi would be making and baking for village parties. She guarded Patsy's Pantry's celebration cake and gala pie takeout business with dogged tenacity. It had made not a jot of difference that Mitzi, over an iced fancy and what passed in Hazy Hassocks for a skinny latte, had assured Mrs Elkins there was room for them both, and Granny Westward's recipes wouldn't encroach on Patsy's Pantry's very specialised clientele. Mrs Elkins had remained unconvinced.

'Oh, please – no don't touch those.' Mitzi was dragged from her mental list-checking by the awful sight of Trilby Man trying to prise the lid from a small Tupperware box. 'They're mine.'

The box contained a few early prototypes of the Green Gowns and Dreaming Creams. Mitzi was going to pop them round to Doll and Brett after the Fayre was over to see what they thought. Of course they needed a bit of work: the Creams looked like lopsided and lumpy snowballs; the Gowns were rather livid green whirligigs – as Granny Westward said the colouring had to be natural, and only freshly collected and squeezed chlorophyll from juicy grasses would do, Mitzi felt she may have overdone the greenness. She certainly didn't want Trilby Man test-driving one and rushing off into the freezing meadows with the local tart.

'Putting a few choice bits away for yourself, are you? Stallholders' perks? Stocking fillers for the family? Ah, well, can't say I blames you, duck.' Trilby Man stopped trying to open the box and cracked his knuckles. 'Well, must get on. If you changes your mind about watching the rehearsal later you'll be more than welcome. And—' he peered at her '—have you done something to yourself again?'

Mitzi, pushing the Tupperware box out of sight and trying to hide a litre bottle of fluorescent purple Primitive Passion behind a row of talcs, shook her head. 'Not that I'm aware of. Oh, God – this isn't another of your cruel-to-be-kind homilies, is it?'

'Uh? Nah. Just there's a bit of a sparkle about you, if you gets my drift. Probably something to do with that thuggy looking dentist what you're knocking about with. Well, duck, you enjoy it while it lasts. He's far too young for you, of course. He'll be running for the hills the minute he sees you without your all-in-one.'

Mitzi bared her teeth and growled at Trilby Man's retreating figure. It was actually something she'd thought herself many times in the wee small hours when sleep eluded her. But she really didn't need Mr Tell It Like It Bloody Is speaking her worst fears aloud.

Reasonably trim as she was, and fit for her age, she knew that close up her body was definitely crêpey, definitely dimpled, definitely sagging southwards. Joel may well be happy with her clothed – but naked? Not a bloody chance!

'Christ!' Mitzi muttered to herself. 'Who am I trying to kid?'

'Talking to yourself?' Tarnia's drawl echoed from over her shoulder. 'You really ought to get out more, Mitzi. I knew once you'd retired you'd go strange. Living alone isn't natural.'

Mitzi looked at Tarnia and groaned. The Botox Queen, clearly going for the festive look, had eschewed her usual pink and was dressed in a tight scarlet 1960s-style suit – all nipped-in waist and pencil skirt – with stilt-high spiky black boots, and looked younger than Lu.

'Hi, Tarnia,' she forced a smile. 'You look nice. And I don't live alone. I've got Richard and Judy – and Lu, and Shay a lot of the time these days too.'

'You can't count animals or your hippie daughter and that scruffy retro boyfriend of hers. I've seen 'em together. They look like illegal aliens slouching round the village. You know exactly what I mean,' Tarnia batted inch-long blue eyelashes up and down Mitzi's body. 'You need a man. Mind, you really need to do something about yourself. It's probably too late to catch anyone worthwhile. You'll only end up with the sad and desperate ones – if you even get that lucky. No wonder you couldn't hold on to Lance. Mind you, young Jennifer takes care of herself, if you know what I mean. You can never start too early. I've exfoliated and moisturised every day since I was twelve.'

'Bully for you,' Mitzi muttered, really, really not wanting to hear about Tarnia's, and more especially Jennifer's, constant quest for eternal youth. 'And bully for Mrs Blessing Mark Two. Great abs and glutinous maximus apparently. Such a shame her workouts never stretched to her cerebellum. Have you got your speech ready?'

'Speech?' Tarnia raised her eyebrows. The rest of her face remained glued in place. 'I'm not making a speech to this lot. My people—' she waved a skinny, scarlet-taloned hand towards a clutch of overdressed and overfed people who were staring at Lav and Lob wearing most of the Nearly New stall with mounting horror '—only need to see me here, mixing with the riff-raff, being charitable. No, I'll just say I declare the damn thing open and hope to God I get out without catching some sort of infestation.'

Mitzi grinned. 'You'll probably be immune seeing as your Mum is running the tombola.'

Tarnia, who hadn't spoken to any of her Bath Road Estate relatives for years ever since she and Snotty Mark had won the pools, gave a little shriek. 'Jesus Christ! She isn't, is she?'

'Yep. Along with two of your sisters, Sharleen and Arlene, I think, and your Auntie Ada.'

'Dear God,' Tarnia shuddered. 'I hope they don't get rowdy when I start to speak. Still, I suppose I can always explain them away as jealous hecklers or inbreds or something.' She tried to furrow her brow and couldn't. 'Damn it all. I'll simply have to keep my people away from that side of the hall then – and don't you dare say a word.'

'Me?' Mitzi raised innocent and free-moving eyebrows. 'As if . . .'

'They haven't seen me, have they? The Dregs?'

Mitzi shook her head in disgust. 'I don't know and I don't care. I know they loathe you as much as you loathe them. It's none of my business. And those aren't for sale.'

Tarnia had picked up the small Tupperware box from the trestle table and was attempting to insert her talons under the lid.

'Why not? Aren't I supposed to purchase something to make it look as though I'm part of this sad affair? Oh!' The lid flew off with two of Tarnia's false nails. 'Shit! Bloody hell! What are these? Bath cubes?'

'They're sort of cakes. For Doll. Later. Not for sale.'

Tarnia's eyes stretched into what would have to pass for an expression. '*Your* cakes? Like those little brownies you made for me? I must say, Mitzi, crap as you always were at Domestic Science at school, you have improved recently. They were – um – rather special. Look, let me have these for my people. I've promised I'd buy something from this load of rubbish and I'd trust you more than the rest of the hoi-polloi. Look, there you are – fifty quid in your box – a fairish price for a few fancies, and for keeping your mouth shut about The Dregs being anything to do with me . . . Deal?'

209

'No ... Yes ... Oh yes, I suppose so,' Mitzi nodded. What did it matter? She could always make some more Dreams and Gowns for Doll, couldn't she? And fifty pounds was an awful lot of money for the village hall.

Tarnia stretched her mouth into a smile. 'I knew you'd see sense. Good girl. Now, let me go and find the others. And remember what I said about taking yourself in hand. Although forget about Atkins. It's so yesterday. I'll send you a copy of the South Beach Diet. It might help you lose your middle-aged spread.'

'Oh, sod off,' Mitzi muttered as Tarnia undulated away to be group-hugged by her cronies. 'Oh, God!'

The village hall doors had been opened and with a roar of giddy gusto Hazy Hassocks in buying mode flooded in.

'Wait! Wait! Wait!' Trilby Man, who had turned into Mr Ubiquitous, screamed into his microphone from the stage. 'You might be in, but you can't start spending yet! Put that down!!!! Down! Now! Right – I'd like to welcome our kind benefactor, Mrs Tarnia Snepps, to make the official opening.'

'Huh,' Mitzi muttered again, fighting a losing battle with a battered box of Tweed. 'It'll be Lady Snepps this time next year if she gets her way. Still, if it means the village retains the use of the hall I suppose I can live with that. But I'd still like to think my Powers of Persuasion Puddings played a small part in bringing about the change of heart.'

Tarnia, beaming beatifically at her cronies, teetered across the stage and wrestled the microphone away from Trilby Man. A few people cheered in a desultory manner. The whole of the tombola stall slow handclapped. Tarnia ignored them.

'I'd just like to say how lovely it is to see you all here today,' she cooed. 'And how pleased my husband and I are to be able to allow you to hold all these cosy village functions in our hall. We are, as you know, very aware of the importance of rural communities and will continue to do everything in our power to encourage this. Our home is

210

your home – well, no ... what I mean is, the village hall is on our land, but we magnanimously agree that you should share in it and—'

'That'll do, duck,' Trilby Man snorted as the tombola stall threatened to drown her out. 'T'aint the bleeding Gettysburg address. They just wants to get their hands on the crap. Wind it up, duck, there's a good girl.'

Thunder faced but still clinging to the mike, Tarnia nodded. 'So, all it remains for me to do is to assure you that these functions in the village hall will continue, and I hope you spend lots today which will swell the community coffers, and it's my great pleasure to declare the Christmas Fayre open.'

'Thank the flying figgit for that,' Flo Spraggs muttered as everyone ignored Tarnia and the village hall suddenly filled with the anticipatory roar of Hazy Hassocks in search of a bargain.

Never ceasing to be amazed at what rubbish people would buy, Mitzi was hectically busy for the next twenty minutes and the cash in her basin grew rapidly.

'Need a hand?'

Mitzi, pausing in selling an out-of-date foot balm grinned at Joel. She always grinned at Joel. She couldn't help it. Despite Trilby Man and Tarnia voicing her own dark doubts, she had no control at all over her mouth – or the rest of her body – when he was near.

'Are you sure? I mean – is this really your sort of thing?'

'Christ, no,' he squeezed in behind the table beside her. 'I've never been to a jumble sale in my life. Saturday afternoons in Manchester were spent at football or in the pub. This is something else. Yes, madam,' he smiled at an elderly woman wearing two coats. 'Bubble bath? The nice orange one? There we go – fifty pence please.'

'Very impressive,' Mitzi said. 'We'll make a stallholder of you yet.'

'Better than trying to remove a very reluctant wisdom tooth,' Joel said. 'Which is what me and Doll have spent most of our morning doing. Don't know which one of us was sweating most at the end.'

Mitzi winced at the mental image. 'Ouch. And what about the patient?'

'Oh, the patient was fine. Stretched out, warm, comfy, filled with local anaesthetic, in blissful ignorance. It was the staff who were going through the mill. Oh, by the way, Doll said to tell you she's going straight home to put her feet up. She doesn't think she can cope with this.'

'Wimps, my daughters,' Mitzi smiled. 'Lu has cried off too. She and Shay have gone to the RSPCA kennels to see those puppies again.'

'And are they still all loved up? Shay and Lu, I mean, not the puppies.'

'To the hilt,' Mitzi nodded. 'I'm pleased for them, of course, but it can get a bit much over the toast and marmalade.'

'Not to mention sticky,' Joel chuckled.

'Hello, young Mitzi,' Gwyneth Wilkins, wearing a massive, ground-dragging, herringbone overcoat and a woollen headscarf, trundled through the throng, with Big Ida Tomms in a trenchcoat and eyebrow-touching cloche towering behind her, and a snake of equally elderly ladies bringing up the rear. 'Good bit of work your young Lu did the other night with them pups. You should be right proud of her.'

'I am,' Mitzi nodded. 'And it was all thanks to your tip-off apparently.'

Gwyneth tried to look modest and failed. 'Makes a change for us to get it right, you mean? Maybe . . . but nice to know the dear little souls all survived and the buggers at the back of it have been nicked.'

As Gwyneth started raking through a basket of bath bombs with mittened fingers, Big Ida reached over her shoulder and scooped up a clutch of face masks. 'I'll 'ave these, love,' she beamed toothlessly at Joel. 'They'll do lovely for my godsons' stockings.'

Joel, to give him his due, made no comment, but bagged up the face masks and took Big Ida's money. 'Ida's godsons are both a bit Graham Norton,' Gwyneth whispered to Mitzi. 'Nice boys. Oh, and I must say it was well worth coming along just to see Lady Tarnia Muck doing the opening here. She's changed 'er tune since she and 'er Marquis decided to go for that there titular thing. I'm run ragged doing security for all the charity shindigs she puts on these days. We've been doing self-defence classes, me and Ida, so's we can cope if things turn nasty. Tai Kwon Do and a bit of kick-boxing. We've not quite got to grips with that, though. I'm thinking of taking on a posse to spread the load. Now – what else have you got here?'

'Lots of things,' Mitzi said, firmly pushing the picture of a whole horde of Fiddlesticks pensioners organising themselves into a sort of Charlie's Angels on Sanatogen to the back of her mind. 'And it's nice to see so many people from the other villages here for our Fayre.'

Gwyneth, whose chin only just reached the top of the trestle table, pulled a face. 'Oh, me and Ida always likes to come up to town to do our Christmas shopping. See, when you lives in Fiddlesticks, with its 'andful of 'ouses, if you buys at the local bazaars everyone knows who's given what. There ain't no element of surprise. We came over in the minibus with a party from The Bagley-cum-Russett Ladies League of Light.'

Joel snorted. Mitzi bit her lip.

'What about this for your Elsie?' Big Ida had reached across again and picked up the purple bottle of Primitive Passion, managing to jab one of the Ladies League of Light in the eye with her elbow at the same time. 'Oops, sorry Mrs Webb. Were you after this too? Have to be a bit quicker'n that, duck. What do you reckon, Gwyneth? Would Elsie like it?'

Gwyneth, her head on one side like a chunky sparrow, gave it some consideration. 'Hmmm, maybe. But our Elsie doesn't drink much now, does she? Not after that to-do with Clyde Spraggs's rhubarb and cowslip.'

'It ain't for drinking, Gwyneth,' Big Ida said scornfully, brandishing the purple bottle tantalisingly in front of Mrs Webb's watering eyes. 'It's for washing in.'

'It's not for washing in as such,' Mitzi intervened, valiantly trying to ignore Joel's hardly suppressed laughter. 'More for bathing.'

'Dat rules out your Eldie, den,' Mrs Webb snuffled, still dabbing at her eyes. 'She don't neber take all her clodes off at one go. Undlike some I could mention.'

Like a massive whirling dervish, Big Ida executed a neat groin thrust. Despite Gwyneth's doubts, the kick-boxing classes seemed to be paying off. Mrs Webb collapsed with a gentle sigh. Another member of the Ladies League of Light started going through her handbag.

'There,' Big Ida rubbed her hands together, paying for the Primitive Passion with a flourish, and powering her way towards White Elephant. 'That'll teach 'er not to cast aspirations.'

'Jesus,' Joel choked. 'Who writes their scripts? This is brilliant, Mitzi. Just brilliant.'

'We aim to please.' Mitzi wiped tears of laughter from the corners of her eyes. 'Oh, dear, poor Miss Higham's got them now.'

Miss Higham, next door to Mitzi on White Elephant, shot her a desperate glance across the trestles as Gwyneth and Big Ida started rummaging through her wares.

'You still walking out with that Aubrey, young Joyce?' Gwyneth asked chattily.

Miss Higham, all of sixty and blushing scarlet, nodded.

'Thought so. Her Aubrey,' Gwyneth loudly informed Big Ida, 'is in retail in Winterbrook.'

'Ah, it shows.' Big Ida studied Miss Higham's hand-written White Elephant banner which announced GIFTS FOR ALL THE FAMILY: PRETTY SAUCERS. SEASONAL FLOWER POTS. FESTIVE ROBINS GOING CHEAP. 'What's a festive robin?'

Miss Higham pointed to a heap of rotund brown things in a shoe box.

'I think you'll find they're just socks, Joyce,' Gywneth began kindly. 'Brown socks rolled into balls. Not robins. Can't see what's festive about old pairs of socks with – well – stuff stuck on 'em.'

'They're Christmas robins,' Miss Higham said archly, lifting one carefully from its confines. 'Handmade. I sewed all the little breasts on myself.'

Big Ida trumpeted with laughter and Mitzi knew she had to intervene before it ended in bloodshed. Not daring to meet Joel's eyes in case she disgraced herself, she pushed her way across to White Elephant.

'Look,' she said in what she hoped was a conciliatory tone, 'they may have started out as socks, but Joyce has worked really hard crafting them into robins. Look at the little lint breasts in – um – lipstick. And the beaks in – er – plastic, and their dear little pipe-cleaner legs.'

'Oh, give us half a dozen then,' Big Ida shrugged. 'They'll do for the neighbours' kiddies. Not that I'm convinced, mind. They still looks like socks to me.'

'But not to a child's imagination,' Mitzi said firmly. 'I might even buy some myself.'

Robins and cash rapidly changed hands and Mitzi scuttled back to Bath and Beauty.

'Oh, nice,' Joel said. 'Socks. Are they for me? A boy can never have too many socks – especially for Christmas.'

Mitzi punched him happily, pushed the festive robins into her pocket, and heaved a sigh of relief as Gwyneth, Big Ida and The Ladies League of Light trundled off in the direction of Nearly New.

'Fancy a cup of tea?' Joel asked in a brief lull. 'Or something stronger?'

'Oh, yes – thank you. A litre of Merlot would go down a treat,' Mitzi sighed, 'but as the village hall doesn't have a liquor licence – yet – tea will have to do. Two sugars please. And we could have had the Green Gowns with them but Tarnia's fed them to her cronies.'

'Shame,' Joel said cheerfully. 'You'll have to make some more just for me. I'll see if they've got some biscuits for dunking as a poor substitute, shall I?'

She watched him push his way through the crowd, luxuriating in the tingle. She loved him. It was foolish but irrevocable. And maybe, after Tarnia's warnings, she should have done without the sugars and definitely the biscuits, but what the heck.

A sudden rush of Bath and Beauty customers meant she had no time to ponder on it. She'd have to save it for later. Maybe the South Beach Diet, whatever it entailed, might be a good idea after all.

'Mitzi!' Tarnia thrust her way through the throng and screeched to a halt in front of the stall. Her face, if it hadn't been set in stone, would have been contorted. As it was, her eyebrows had disappeared into her spiky fringe and her mouth was slashed into a rigid rectangle like a post box.

'My people,' she waved an agitated hand towards the huddle in front of the stage, 'have just been abused by some of your – your riff-raff!'

Mitzi groaned. Lav and Lob? Clyde pressing his home brew? Trilby Man Telling It Like It Is? Tarnia's entire family giving away the dreadful secrets of her origins? There were so many options.

'I was giving them a swiftie tour of the hall,' Tarnia continued, 'as you do. And they were very, very impressed – so we went backstage to see what improvements had been made in the audio-visuals, and we were just having a cup of coffee and some of your nibbly cakes – those little green ones were so delicious they ate all of them and were asking for the recipe – and then . . . and then . . .'

Dear oh dear, Mitzi thought. 'And then what, Tarnia? Don't tell me old Baden Wiggins flashed his long johns at them? You know what he's like. He's been doing it all his life. Everyone just laughs – although I suppose it could be a bit unnerving for newcomers—'

'It was far, far worse than Baden Wiggins!' Tarnia spat. 'It was people ... people we went to school with – June and Sally and that funny Ronald who did embroidery a lot – with no clothes on! Not a stitch! And they were singing! Loudly! Some of the most disgusting lyrics I've ever heard in my life! My people were horrified. Horrified! I'm afraid I can't allow you to use the hall any more! This is too much!'

Mitzi closed her eyes. Bugger and sod. Why on earth couldn't Trilby Man have held off on the *Hair* rehearsals until after the Fayre? If Tarnia's High and Mighties were mortally offended it would certainly sound the death knell for The Gong and the village hall.

With no warning, Mitzi suddenly felt herself lifted from her feet. A pair of strong hands clasped her waist, a waft of clean skin and lemon shampoo and warm maleness enveloped her, and a pair of firm lips were kissing her very thoroughly indeed.

Out of practice and completely bowled over, Mitzi only hesitated for a split second, then she kissed him back. It was absolutely blissful. The tingle travelled from her toes to her head in a star-spangled fizz. On and on and on it went. The village hall and Tarnia and the roar of the crowd simply melted away.

'Oh ...' she gulped giddily when the kissing had stopped and Joel had returned her feet to the ground. 'Oh ...'

Tarnia, it seemed, wasn't even capable of an 'oh'. Her face was a study of shock and awe.

'Hello,' Joel grinned the melt-down grin. 'I'm Joel Earnshaw. Mitzi's lover. And you must be Mrs Snepps. How nice to meet you at last. I've heard so much about you.'

Still dizzy, Mitzi blinked. He'd *kissed* her. And she'd kissed him. At last. And it had been the best ever kiss in the history of kissing. A million, zillion times better than Lance. Ooooh.

Tarnia, still stunned, mouthed wordlessly. It was a wonderful moment.

'Er ...' Tarnia eventually gurgled, gazing at Joel with ill-disguised lust. 'I haven't heard anything about you at all. But it's – er nice to meet you too.' She nodded towards Mitzi, admiration battling with a million questions in her eyes. 'What were we talking about before ... before ...?'

'I've no idea,' Mitzi whispered. Her lips seemed to have been collagened. They felt as though they belonged to someone else. 'Um – it seems to have gone right out of my head.'

Tarnia, still looking unbelieving, did the post-box thing with her mouth again. 'Mine too. Er – you must both come to supper one evening. Soon. Very soon ... Mitzi, I'll ring you.'

Joel chuckled as she teetered away from Bath and Beauty. 'I overhead what she was saying about withdrawing her support. One of the things we were taught at college to get you out of a tight dentistry spot – always try to avert a disaster by causing a diversion.'

'Some diversion,' Mitzi said softly.

'But okay?'

'Bloody amazingly okay.' she tried to smile but her lips were still tingling. 'And it worked. Shame it wasn't for real.'

'What?' Joel leaned closer, the lights from the village hall dancing sexily from the diamond ear-stud. 'That kiss was as real as it gets for me. And about sodding time. Or do you mean about me being your lover? Well – we could always – bloody hell! Look at that!'

Mitzi, still floating, looked.

There was a huge schemozzle over by the stage. Tarnia and her High and Mighties were dancing around hugging and kissing and emitting little shrieks at one another. Trilby Man, the Bandings, Gwyneth and Big Ida, and The Ladies League of Light all seemed to be egging them on. Everyone else was laughing.

'Oh dear,' Mitzi said faintly. 'How very fortuitous. Another diversion.' Tarnia and her Great and Good entourage, now looked as if they were taking part in the love-in scene from *Hair*.

Joel shook his head. 'What the hell did you give them to eat? Sexed-up cookies?'

'Um – not quite. I mean, I knew the Green Gowns were supposed to have – er – aphrodisiac properties. I think I may have used a touch too much saffron ...'

'Maybe,' Joel tried to keep a straight face. 'That'd account for the group touchy-feely bit – but why are they all slowly turning bright green?'

Chapter Nineteen

'Then what happened?' Biff Pippin, filling the charity shop window with glittery evening dresses in Christmassy colours, paused in draping them ham-fistedly over some Barbara Goalen-thin headless mannequins. 'Did Tarnia have your Ma's guts for garters?'

'No way.' Lu posed in front of the cheval mirror admiring herself in a 1920s cocktail frock while being buffeted by various elderly people who, having collected their pensions from the Winterbrook post office next door, were searching for warm jumpers without too much moth. 'Mum was frantic that Tarnia would go all snippy and say they couldn't use the hall any more. But she didn't. She laughed about it, and her bigwigs all seemed to think it was the best fun they'd had in ages, and apparently none of them could remember a thing about the *Hair* rehearsal.'

'There's a mercy,' Biff mumbled through a mouthful of pins. 'Oooh, look at that fog out there. Getting thicker by the minute. A real pea-souper. Go on then – so Tarnia's still okay about the Hazy Hassocks hall is she?'

'Yeah. Tarnia actually rang Mum after the Fayre and asked for the recipe for the Green Gowns, without the face-paint effect of course, and some of the Bigwigs want Mum's recipes too for their parties oh and Tarnia asked Mum loads of questions about Joel, then she invited them both to go to dinner or something. I think Mum said it would all have to be after Christmas.'

'And did they all stay – er – amorous and green for long?'

'It wore off after a couple of hours, Tarnia said. Apparently all her cronies thought it was dead funny. You know what rich people are like – always chasing new experiences. I reckon Mum might have struck gold.'

Hedley bustled through from the back of the shop carrying a tray of tea and biscuits. He lifted it to head height as he negotiated the jumper-searching pensioners. 'Fog's getting thicker. Bit of a pea-souper if you ask me. Ah – that frock suits you, young Lu. Having it for the wedding are you?'

'I wish. Nah – my bridesmaid's dress is really normal and girlie – not bad though, considering. Actually I was wondering how much you were going to ask for this. Shay's taking me out tonight and I'd really like to wear something new – well, newish.'

'A fiver,' Hedley said.

'Done. Er – can you take it out of my wages, please? Only not this week because I'll need all my cash for going Dutch tonight and—'

'Have the frock on us,' Hedley beamed. 'You deserve it after that puppy-farming business, and me and Biff are so pleased that you're happy with Shay.'

'Thank you!' Lu pirouetted across the crowded shop and kissed Hedley's cheek. 'You are the nicest man in the whole world – after Shay of course.'

'Of course. And does this mean there's going to be a second wedding for your mum to cope with in the very near future?'

'Crikey – I hope not! Me and Shay are still doing the hearts and flowers falling in love bit. We don't want to spoil it with mediocrities like mortgages and weddings and – dear God – babies. Mind you, Mum might be a different matter.'

'Your mother? Remarrying?' Hedley coughed on his digestive. 'Well I never! You kept that quiet.'

221

Lu laughed. 'So did she! She doesn't realise it yet, but me and Doll are very hopeful. We think Joel would be perfect for her, and they're batty about each other.'

'Don't see the problem then,' Hedley caught the wayward dunked digestive with consummate skill. 'What's stopping 'em?'

'Oh, stuff like she thinks she's too old for him. His first wife didn't want kids and Mum reckons that he probably does and that she can't and—'

'Lot of bollocks,' Hedley snorted. 'Who needs kids when they can have animals? Me and Biff have been more than happy with our menagerie, haven't we, pet?'

Biff nodded vigorously. Pins ricocheted everywhere and two of the headless mannequins tumbled over. 'Young Mitzi is a fine-looking woman. And intelligent and amusing and – um – well, a damn good catch for anyone. And I'd heard from Big Ida and Gwyneth and loads of other people that your mum and the young dentist were canoodling at the Fayre. He gave her a right old going over, if you gets my drift.'

'Yuk!' Lulu pulled a face. 'Pul-ease!'

'Love and sex isn't just for them under thirty, young lady,' Hedley said, looking beadily at Biff. 'Where there's life there's hope.'

'Well I think it's dead romantic,' Tammy said, leaning her elbows on the window table in Patsy's Pantry. 'Joel's sex on a stick – for the crumblies, I mean. I wish my mum would get her hands on someone like him.'

'Your mum's been happily married to your dad for twenty-five years,' Viv snapped.

'Exactly,' Tammy sighed. 'Bor-ing.'

Doll, who still couldn't face tea or coffee, joined in the laughter and tried to look enthusiastic about her lukewarm drinking chocolate. She felt generally great. There was still no morning sickness, no peculiar cravings, but there was something about tea and coffee that made her shudder. And

222

the hot flushes were so embarrassing. She kept getting really weird looks, especially on cold, damp, densely foggy days like today when she had to rush out of the surgery into the high street and unbutton her uniform.

'Only three weeks to go 'til the wedding,' Tammy said enviously. 'Are you nervous?'

'Not at all. Well, yes a bit. About forgetting Brett's middle names or falling off my shoes going up the aisle or something like that. Not about the commitment.'

'And are we having a hen night?' Viv stared at her multiple reflections in Patsy's Pantry's selection of mirror tiles and patted a stray hair into place.

'Oh, goodness – maybe just a drink in The Faery Glen or something. As the wedding's so low key I can't see the point of going over the top.'

Tammy and Viv, who had obviously been looking forward to outrageous costumes, tequila slammers, male strippers and lashings of baby oil, looked rather miffed.

'Lunch!' Mrs Elkins bustled up to their table pushing a trolley loaded with gooey goodies. She glared at Doll. 'Surprised to see you in here eating my pastries. I thought you'd be out there touting your mother's so-called home-baking.'

'She's managing that fine all on her own,' Doll said happily. 'And that's all it is, you know. Old-fashioned country cooking. It's not magic. It's not witchcraft. And some of the stuff that has happened is because she's only a beginner and may have overused some of the herbs. That's all.'

'So you say,' Mrs Elkins growled. 'There's plenty of others in Hazy Hassocks that think your mother has stumbled on the elixir of youth and happy pills all rolled into one. They think she can make things happen with her cooking by adding – well – stuff. They can't wait to get their hands on her buns. She's no better than them drug dealers what hang around the Bath Road Estate. Hardened criminals most of 'em.'

Doll screamed with laughter. 'Oh, come on! The kids selling cannabis on Bath Road are mostly from the public school in Winterbrook – that's about as desperate as it gets. My mum isn't hanging out on street corners promising chemical rushes to the innocents – and she'll never be a threat to your business, believe me. I've tasted her stuff. It's not a patch on yours.'

Mrs Elkins looked mollified. 'Well that's as maybe – it's nice of you to say so . . . now who's the double Danish?'

'Me, please,' Doll said. 'I'm eating as much as possible while I can.'

'Crawly pig,' Viv and Tammy said in unison as Mrs Elkins and her trolley rolled away.

'Diplomatic pig, if you don't mind,' Doll poked out her tongue at them.

'It's probably about the only good thing about having a baby,' Tammy said, being rude with a chocolate eclair. 'You get to eat loads. Being pregnant must be the pits. What happens to your belly button?'

'It sticks out a lot more,' Viv said through the squirty jam stage of her doughnut. 'At least mine did. Why?'

Tammy lifted her uniform top. Several rings and two diamonds glistened in her navel.

'Flipping heck! If I were you I'd keep your legs crossed until you reach The Change,' Viv advised darkly. 'God knows what pregnancy would do to that lot. You'd probably explode and kill the midwife with the shrapnel.'

The door swung open and Joel shouldered in from the swirling midday gloom. All the twin sets and scarves turned and devoured him with hungry pale-lashed eyes.

He grinned across at Doll's table. 'Ah, superb. The whole surgery staff setting a perfect example to the patients. How much sugar is there in that lot? Enough to erode the enamel on every tooth in Hazy Hassocks, and then some.'

'Yeah, right,' Doll pulled out another chair. 'Sit down and shut up. What do want? The usual?'

'A mug of sweet milky coffee, two iced buns, a custard doughnut and a meringue, please. And I bet you never spoke to my predecessor like that.'

'Your predecessor,' Doll informed him after she'd given the order to a now smiling Mrs Elkins, 'was always so high on Novocain that speaking was rarely on the agenda.'

'Whereas,' Viv beamed at him, showing perfectly flossed molars, 'you spend all your time getting high on Mitzi Blessing. Oh, on her little cakes I mean, of course . . .'

Joel laughed. 'Oh, of course. And because I don't want to embarrass Doll, I'm not going to expand on the shenanigans in the village hall.'

'Bugger,' Doll said cheerfully. 'Anyway, Mum's told me most of it. The kissing thing was a bit of a brainwave.'

'What?' Joel frowned. 'Don't tell me your mother still thinks I was really only causing a diversion to save the village hall for her Baby Boomers? That it was all for Tarnia's benefit? Doesn't she realise that the kissing thing, as you call it, was for real?'

'No,' Doll picked up Danish pastry crumbs with her forefinger. 'I honestly don't think she does. Even though the rest of Hazy Hassocks can see it spelled out in letters twenty feet high, Mum can't.' She looked across at Tammy and Viv who were soaking it all up like the latest instalment of their favourite soap. 'And yes, this does seem a bit weird. Discussing my mother's love life – but I'm not selfish enough to think she doesn't deserve one.'

'With me?' Joel made a space on the table as Mrs Elkins arrived with his order.

'Of course with you. Mad as it seems, you know I think you're made for each other even if Mum can't see it.' Doll pushed her plate away with a sigh. 'Look, if the kissing thing and public declarations don't work, you'll just have to find some other way to convince her, won't you?'

Mitzi parked the car behind the bank and retrieved her handbag from the back seat. The short drive to

Winterbrook from Hazy Hassocks had been pretty scary due to the ever-thickening fog. She really hoped it wouldn't be foggy on Christmas Eve for the wedding. She'd always pictured Doll's big day as blue skied, clear, sunny and frosty. Fog would make everyone's hair frizz and completely ruin the photos.

The wedding was one of the main reasons she was here in Winterbrook. In the few days since the impromptu success of the Green Gowns at the village hall, she'd finalised the wedding breakfast menu. Of the more exotic dishes on offer, the Green Gowns were now modified – less saffron and far less chlorophyll – thus providing the right amount of spark without starting an orgy, and should also mean everyone stayed flesh coloured. The Dreaming Creams had become sleekly streamlined, and the Mistletoe Kisses were, well, okay, still in prototype form. The rest of the food was easily concocted from Granny's more basic recipes, and Otto and Boris at The Faery Glen had recently thrown in a proper wedding cake as their gift to the happy couple.

And after Tarnia's unexpected endorsement of her cooking she'd also managed to run off some rather nice little menus and price lists for Granny's Goodies on her laptop. Having scattered the flyers all over Hazy Hassocks, she now intended to leave them in public places in Winterbrook and see what happened. But first she was on a far more personal mission.

The bank, always gothic, loomed out of the yellowing fog like a Transylvanian castle. The lights were hardly visible. Mitzi shuddered and hurried inside.

She looked around the foyer at the stuccoed walls, carved wood and chandeliers. Whatever changes Troy and Tyler had brought to the bank's admin systems, nothing else had changed. Joining the snaking queue waiting for a counter position to become vacant, Mitzi felt rather uncomfortable. She'd been so loath to leave the bank, but now ... her life had changed in so many ways. She was liberated, fulfilled, happier than she'd ever been in her life. Troy Haley had unwittingly done her a massive service.

Hopefully she'd be able to return the favour.

Eventually reaching the counter, the clerk behind the toughened glass was a stranger. And about twelve and a half. And, according to her name badge, called Kelly-Jo.

'I want to close my accounts,' Mitzi said cheerfully. 'Both of them. Current and savings. I'm transferring them to the building society in Hazy Hassocks now they offer a banking service.'

'Right-oh,' Kelly-Jo said cheerfully. 'But you didn't need to come in y'know. The building society could take care of it online. All done on the Internet these days, right?'

'Yes, I'm aware of that. I'm not senile,' Mitzi said testily. 'I just wanted the satisfaction of seeing my accounts closed in person, of my last ties with this place severed.'

'You what?'

'I used to work here,' Mitzi said. 'I worked here all my employable life. They suddenly decided they no longer needed me. I am now in the happy position of not needing them either. So, can you arrange for the balances to be forwarded to my new bank accounts?'

'Yeah, sure.' Kelly-Jo tapped various numbers into her computer. 'I've only been here two weeks. It's okay. How long were you here?'

'Thirty-five years.'

'Frigging hell!' Kelly-Jo forgot all her customer-service training. 'That's, like, for ever!'

'It seems like that now, yes . . .'

Mitzi smiled to herself. It actually seemed like someone else entirely who had bustled in here every morning, neatly groomed, and worked diligently for eight hours a day, and then gone home – in the early years to Lance and the girls as youngsters, and then latterly to an empty house. But that grown-up, orderly Mitzi, with her routines and her ties and her worries, was a world apart from today's Mitzi with her

227

jeans and boots and chunky sweater, vivid red hair, sort of embryo herbalist business, village organiser, madly in love with a far-too-young but very sexy dentist.

'An' I bet you never even had computers,' Kelly-Jo said breathlessly, her fingers skimming over her keypad. 'Didja?'

'No, we had ledgers and scales and we wrote with pens and used typewriters and Roneos for copying and added things up with our brains and sometimes Comptometers—'

'Come again?' Kelly-Jo looked flummoxed. 'Blimey – it must have been like the Dark Ages.'

'Oh, it was,' Mitzi agreed cheerfully. 'All done? Lovely. Thank you very much – shall I just sign them? Okay. Now, would it be possible to see Mr Haley?'

'Troy? Yeah, sure. Take a seat an' I'll give him a bell.'

Mitzi sat and waited.

Chapter Twenty

'Come in quickly, Lulu.' Lavender, a scarf tied snugly round the cycle helmet and wearing mismatched mittens, pulled open the door. 'I'm surprised you ventured out tonight. The fog's very dangerous.'

'I've only hopped over the wall,' Lulu grinned. 'I don't think anything awful is likely to happen to me just coming from next door. Is Shay ready?'

'I'll just find out. Come in and sit down. Lobelia will keep you company.'

Lu shivered and pulled the Afghan more closely round her. 'It's okay, I'll go up—'

'You will not,' Lav said sternly. 'Shay knows the rules. No entertaining ladies in his room.'

'But he's not and I'm not – I mean, we're a couple now and I only wanted to hurry him up a bit.'

'You,' Lavender frowned, 'may have lax morals, but we maintain certain standards in this house. I'm well aware that Shay spends nights at your house. Lobelia and I, while afraid of the alternative, prefer to imagine that Mitzi puts him up in the spare bedroom.'

Lu grinned. 'Not a chance. But I accept you have house rules. Sorry.'

'That's all right. I was young once, you know. Not that Lobelia and I ever shared our beds with young men, of course. It was different in our day. We were saving ourselves.' She sighed. 'We might just have saved for a little bit too long ... Now you go into the sitting room and have a warm.'

Big, big oxymoron, Lu thought as she pushed her way into the mushroom and mustard room which was far more clammy and cold than the foggy night outside.

Lobelia, wrapped in several hand-knitted patchwork blankets, her football socks pulled way over her knees, was huddled in front of a paraffin stove which was giving off asphyxiating fumes. 'Hello, Lulu – oh, don't you look pretty. Is that a new frock I can see under your furry coat? I had one just like that when I was a gel. Are you and Shay going somewhere nice?'

'Just out in Winterbrook, I think.' Lu tried to stop her teeth from chattering and her eyes from watering. 'Are you sure you're warm enough? Why don't you light the fire?'

'Because we can't afford it. It's not easy living on pensions, you know. And our savings went years ago. If it wasn't for Shay's board and lodging money we'd be in dire straits. We'd be found dead in our beds, killed by cold and starvation. We often talk about it of an evening just to cheer ourselves up.'

Lulu sat as close as she could to the paraffin stove without being knocked senseless by the fumes and felt awful. She was so looking forward to moving in with Shay one day ... to renting their own flat in the village somewhere ... to share being together ... to being able to wake up and just stare at him as he slept.

And now, if he moved out of the Bandings, they'd be destitute. And she couldn't move in here and starve and freeze with him because Lav and Lob wouldn't allow it and – oh, bugger.

'Are you coming to watch us in *Hair*?' Lobelia asked, hitching up her socks with knotted purpling hands. 'Shay says he's swapped shifts so he can be there.'

Lu nodded. 'Wouldn't miss it for the world. I think it'll be the biggest laugh Hazy Hassocks has ever had.'

'It's not a comedy – is it? Maybe it is? That would explain a lot of things. To be honest, dear, I don't really understand it at all but it's got some lovely tunes and we've had such fun at the rehearsals. Very clever of your mother to galvanise us older people the way she has. The Fayre was really funny with everyone going green. Ah, here's Shay.'

'Hello sweetheart,' Shay pulled Lu to her feet and kissed her. 'Wow. Nice dress. Especially with the fake yak boots. Christ it's cold in here.'

'We were just saying,' Lob nodded at him, 'that your money and the extra lovely bits and pieces you buy us makes such a difference. We couldn't manage without you now, dear.'

'And I couldn't manage without you and Lavender,' Shay kissed Lob's cheek. 'It's like having two very special extra mums. Don't wait up for me – I've got my key.'

'We won't wait up—' Lavender, wrapping her scarf more snugly round her head, appeared in the doorway '—because we know you'll probably be staying next door. We don't approve, you know that, although we understand – but, and this has to be said, Lobelia, you know we've been worrying about it for ages – we're worried that you might want a reduction in your rent for the nights you're not here and—'

'Don't be daft.' Shay grinned at Lavender. 'You know I wouldn't do that. You know that isn't even on the agenda. Now you two keep warm and for God's sake put the fire on. I keep telling you I'll pay the bill. You can't sit in here freezing all night. It's like an icebox – and I don't want to be shovelling you into my ambulance with frostbite, do I?'

'God,' Lu said, her fingers entwining with Shay's as they scuttled down the path through the fog, 'I knew they didn't have much money but I always thought they were just, well, careful. I know Mum and Flo and other people in the street have always helped them out with food and stuff over the years, but I had no idea they were quite so broke.'

'Boracic,' Shay said as he unlocked the car and they both waved goodbye to Lav and Lob who were standing on the doorstep. 'And they don't eat properly and they won't use any heating – and I've told them over and over I'll take care of all the bills. Christ this fog's getting worse. I'm glad I'm not working tonight. Probably be a mass of RTAs.'

The heater kicked in almost straight away and Lu shrugged out of the Afghan and fastened her seat belt, then leaned across and kissed Shay properly.

'Ooooh – that's better. Couldn't do it in front of Lav and Lob. They'd already lectured me on my morals – or lack of them.'

'They're museum pieces,' Shay agreed after he'd kissed her back in a most satisfactory manner. 'And barking mad. But lovely with it. And now very much my responsibility.'

Lu nodded as the car inched forward through the fog. She wouldn't have expected anything less from him. Shay was a very compassionate man. It was one of the things she loved most about him – well, once you left out the phwoar factor bits of course – and she knew he'd never abandon the Bandings.

She giggled. Niall had left her for a designer-dressed corporate ladder climber – with Shay she was playing second fiddle to a pair of slightly crazy geriatrics.

'Maybe you could get them to drop the cycle helmets, though. I mean, I know they misinterpreted what you said about them having to be worn all the time but people laugh at them which is sad, and—'

'No way. Ninety per cent of body heat is lost through your head. At least while they insist on wearing the helmets at all times they stand some chance of surviving in that damn icebox.' Shay sighed. 'We'll just have to try and win the lottery for them. They'd qualify as a Good Cause all on their own.'

'Mmmm . . . if we could afford to buy a ticket in the first place,' Lu snuggled against him in the darkness, her hand on his faded denim thigh so that she could feel his muscles contract when he changed gear. 'Where are we going?'

'Lorenzo's – with a detour first.'

'Wow. Lorenzo's? Brilliant. Thank goodness I wore the posh frock.'

She always insisted on paying her way when they went out as Shay's paramedic's salary was as abysmal as hers was, so Lu did a quick mental calculation to see if her wages would stretch to a meal and a drink at Lorenzo's and decided they might – just.

She smiled across at him. 'We'll be able to take a really swish doggy bag home for Lav and Lob, won't we? And where's the detour?'

Shay didn't take his eyes from the road. The car's headlights seemed to be hitting a solid wall of fog. 'Wait and see . . .'

'The RSPCA kennels?' Lu leaned forward and peered through the gloom. 'Is this the detour? Oh, brilliant. We haven't seen the puppies for ages. I wonder if they've all been rehomed by now?'

Struggling back into the Afghan she shivered in the damp murkiness. Shay pulled her against him as they headed for the kennels' brightly lit office.

'Ah, hello. We were expecting you,' the receptionist beamed. 'And right on time too, despite this awful weather. Come on in.'

Lu pulled a quizzical face as they hustled along the corridor. Expecting them? Who was? They didn't usually have to make appointments. They usually just wandered into the kennel area unannounced.

The cages and runs, warm and cosy, were suddenly alive with dogs and cats, wagging tails, wriggling bodies in welcome. They all greeted Shay and Lu as old friends.

'Have all the puppy farm puppies been rehomed now?'

'Not quite all.' The pretty kennel maids were eyeing Shay with ill-concealed delight. 'But thanks to your callout, we've managed to close one huge enterprise down and that's led on to several others across the country. We've rescued dozens and dozens of bitches and their pups thanks to your tip-off. We're very grateful to you all. Ah, here's Roger.'

Roger, one of the local RSPCA inspectors, greeted Shay and Lulu almost as warmly as the four-legged inmates had done.

'Thank you so much for turning out tonight. Nasty weather. Right – is everything in order?'

'More or less,' Shay nodded. 'Just the one stumbling block which we discussed earlier but I've made arrangements to get that covered so ...'

Lu frowned. 'I'm not usually slow on the uptake, but could someone tell me if I've missed something here? A sentence? An entire conversation?'

Roger and Shay and the kennel maids all laughed. Lu was even more perplexed.

'Your young man here has arranged an early Christmas present, or rather several,' Roger beamed, handing her a chunky booklet. 'This is the first ... we're recruiting for trainees at the moment and ...'

Lu squinted down at the booklet. Then she squealed in delight.

'Application forms to train as an RSPCA Inspector? ME? Wow! That'd be just brilliant! But I can't! I mean, it's a career and I've never ... I mean – oh, what about Hed and Biff? I couldn't let them down ... Oh, and but – I can't drive and I'm rubbish with mobile phones and computers and—'

'All sorted out, sweetheart.' Shay kissed her. The kennel maids glowered a bit. 'If you want to do it, of course.'

'Of course I do!' Lulu beamed happily. 'More than anything. I mean, it's something I've always wanted to do but I never thought I could well, you know ...'

'You just need more confidence in yourself,' Shay said. 'You're a bit scatty, and disorganised and everything, and you play on it and everyone's always encouraged you to be the dippy one in the family – but underneath it all you're as sharp as a tack, and you've got the biggest heart in the world. You'll be the best RSPCA inspector in the world and—'

'You'll be perfect,' Roger broke in on the eulogy. 'Perfect. You match all the criteria, I know you have the qualifications, you're already involved in the animal welfare world, you've worked with us on many occasions. All you need to do is complete the forms and wait for the interview panel.'

'And my other Christmas present to you is a crash course – if you'll pardon the pun – of driving lessons,' Shay added.

'You can't afford them! I can't afford them! We're both broke.'

'I've got a nice little part-time job as barman at The Faery Glen in the New Year to fit in round my shifts.' Shay was grinning. 'Hedley and Biff are delighted and are more than willing to stand as your referees. To be honest they found paying your salary a bit of a drain – it'll mean more money for them to donate to the animals – and you can still help out there whenever you like.'

'Oh.' Lu's eyes filled with tears. She wasn't usually a weeper – well, not unless it involved animals, of course – but this was all too much. 'Oh, thank you. I don't know what else to say. Thank you so much.'

She kissed Shay and then Roger but passed on the kennel maids.

'But I won't have to have my hair cut off, will I? Will it fit under the cap?'

'The beads and braids may have to be calmed a bit but I'm sure you'll manage.' Shay was still grinning. 'And there is something else. Another present. I thought we should do all this before Christmas so as not to detract too much from Doll's big day.'

The kennel maids parted in a sort of Busby Berkeley movement.

Pip, Squeak and Wilfred, Lulu's secret favourites of the

puppy farm puppies, multicoloured, all gangly legs and liquid eyes, bounced up to her and all tried to kiss her at the same time.

'They were the leftovers from your rescue mission. They didn't sort of fit into any breeds. They haven't been rehomed, and I knew the love affair was mutual, so they're all yours – well, ours really. Your Christmas present from me—'

The tears really fell now. Pip, Squeak and Wilfred happily licked them away.

Emerging from a canine group-hug, Lu wiped her eyes, knowing the kohl and mascara would have run and made her look like a pierrot doll, and sniffed happily. 'But where are they going to live? Richard and Judy rule our place with iron claws, and—'

'With me. So they'll only be next door. Lav and Lob have readily agreed to let them move in. They love dogs, had loads when they were younger. And they'll be glad of the company when I'm on night shift.'

Lulu sighed. Now she'd have Shay *and* the puppies living next door. It was wonderful, of course, but how much more wonderful if they could all live together in a little cottage – maybe one of the tiled-roofed cottages on the village green. And she and Shay could organise their shifts so that they had time off together and take the dogs for long walks and come home to their own little nest.

'So,' Roger held out a hand and helped her to her feet, 'everything's sorted. Welcome to the RSPCA, Lu, I know you'll do well. The next training course starts in February, so we'll have plenty of time to discuss the ins and outs before then. And Pip, Squeak and Wilfred are staying here for another couple of weeks just until they're past their vaccination stage. I'm absolutely delighted, my dear.'

Sniffing back more tears, Lulu hugged him and Shay again, and the puppies. 'Thank you ... thank you all so much.'

'You are happy with all this, aren't you?' Shay emerged

from the mass attention of Pip, Squeak and Wilfred. 'You don't think I'm trying to become some sort of control freak, do you? You don't have to agree to any of it if it's not what you want.'

Lu threw her arms round his neck and kissed him. 'No, of course not. You've given me the shove I needed. It's all amazing. Brilliant. Honestly – I couldn't have asked for anything more.' Well, apart from a place of their own with roses round the door, of course. 'Now shall we go to Lorenzo's and really celebrate? And tonight it's all on me to say thank you again. You're simply amazing. You've changed my life . . .'

'You've made a considerable difference to mine too.' Shay smiled, pulling her even closer. 'I'd never considered falling in love with someone who looks like Elly-May Clampett and smells like a dead polecat.'

Lu grinned. 'You say the nicest things!'

'Oh, I can say even nicer things than that. How about – Tallulah Blessing, I love you even more than I love my Motley Crue CDs and I'd really, really like to marry you one day.'

Chapter Twenty-one

'Fog's still really thick,' Joel said, letting Mitzi's rich velvet curtains fall back across the window. 'But Shay and Lu must have made it through – it's at least an hour since they left. Where are they going tonight?'

'No idea,' Mitzi hopped around the living room trying to pull on her boots. 'Winterbrook probably. She had a new old dress on. And come away from the window and stop spying on people. You're turning into Flo. She's an ace curtain-twitcher.'

'I must admit I felt a bit voyeuristic earlier getting a front row seat for Shay and Lulu's snogathon.' Joel laughed. 'But there, I'm as nosy as the next person, you know that. And you look gorgeous – where are you taking me tonight?'

'Lorenzo's,' Mitzi collapsed on to the sofa and hauled at her boots. 'As it was my fault we had to cancel before.'

'That's great. But you don't have to—'

'I know I don't. But I want to. I really messed it up last time and you were such a star sitting freezing your bits off in the village hall munching sardine and piccalilli sarnies instead of munching your way through Lorenzo's luscious menu. Anyway, I have an ulterior motive.'

'Oh, God.'

Mitzi paused in zipping up and squinted at him. 'Crikey – do you know me that well? Already? Scary ... And as a special treat I'm going to drive so you can get roaring drunk if you want to.'

Joel sat in one of the fireside chairs. Richard and Judy clambered ecstatically all over him. 'Is that because you think I'm a pretty old-fashioned bloke?'

'A northern dinosaur, you mean?' Mitzi finally won the battle of the boots and stood up triumphantly. 'Of course. I know you think the man's the boss and the woman knows her place.'

'Aye. Kitchen and bedroom in that order,' Joel winked at her.

She threw a cushion at him. He threw it back. God, he was beautiful. They laughed together and Mitzi suddenly got the tingle from her toes zinging to the tip of her head. Damn. She actually *wanted* him. Right there and right now. Sex had been off the agenda for so long she'd almost forgotten what it was like to be engulfed in waves of hot lust. Oh, dear, wasn't it slightly distasteful at her age?

She peered at him to see if she'd given off embarrassing, telltale, hormonal signals, but he was still laughing and fussing Richard and Judy so she guessed not. Phew.

Ten minutes later, as she inched the car along Hazy Hassocks high street through the yellow swirl of fog with the hormones still rampaging, Joel looked across at her. 'You're sure you don't want me to drive?'

'I can do fog,' Mitzi said, staring straight ahead, chewing her lip in concentration. The density of the fog and Joel's proximity were twin distractions. 'I can do hazardous. Women are better at hazardous than men. They don't see it as a macho challenge.'

Joel chuckled. 'Okay. I'm not going to argue with you on that one – yet. But has it occurred to you that there might be a bit of a logistical problem here?'

'Where?' Mitzi inched the car on to the main Winterbrook road, using the verges as a marker.

'Well . . .' Joel relaxed back in his seat. 'I work in Hazy Hassocks and live – if you can call it that – in Winterbrook.

I drive my car to work. We're driving, in your car, to Winterbrook where I'm under instructions to become roaring drunk. Which means you can help me stagger into my soulless bachelor hovel at the end of the evening, but my car will still be in Hazy Hassocks which makes getting to work difficult in the morning. Unless you stayed over with me and drove me to work in the morning.'

'Can't leave Richard and Judy without their supper. And I've left the fire on at home. And probably candles.'

'Lu and Shay can see to all that.'

'They might forget. Or stay out all night or, well, anything. And – um – oh, I know . . . Doll could come over early in the morning and pick you up before surgery. She wouldn't mind.'

'Couldn't have that. Not in her condition. It might still be foggy in the morning. I'd never forgive myself for putting her at risk.'

'What a thoughtful employer you are,' Mitzi grinned, not taking her eyes from the solid sulphurous wall inches in front of the windscreen.

'I try,' Joel grinned back. 'So that means we'll have to drive back to Hazy Hassocks at the end of the evening and I'll retrieve my car from the surgery and drive, completely pissed, back to Winterbrook through this fog. Or—'

'Or you could stay over at mine – and sleep on my sofa or in the spare room.'

'Or not,' Joel said quietly. 'Which seems like the best option of all to me.'

Lorenzo's had pulled out all the festive stops. Eschewing their usual Italian decor, they'd gone for a virtual thicket of white and silver Christmas trees, with waterfalls of tiny white twinkling lights and silver frosted branches adorning the walls, and sequinned candles flickering on all the tables.

Mitzi, halfway through her seafood cannelloni with calabrese, sighed with pure pleasure. What more could a girl ask? Fabulous food, fabulous wine, fabulous surroundings and a more than fabulous man. A more than fabulous man who wanted to spend the night with her. And with whom she wanted to spend the night more than anything in the world. But not just one night. Not just a fleeting affair. She couldn't be hurt again.

'There's someone waving at you.' Joel broke into the dilemma of her thoughts. 'A young man. A very young man. Waving and grinning.'

'Oh, yes,' Mitzi waved her fork back across the restaurant in a casual manner. 'That's Troy.'

'*Troy?*' Joel wrinkled his nose. 'Look here, Mrs Blessing, it's clear that you have a penchant for younger men, but really – should he be allowed out on a school night?'

'He's a bank manager,' Mitzi smiled sweetly. 'He replaced Mr Dickinson when I was disposed of. The spotty oik beside him is Tyler. He replaced me.'

'No way,' Joel was staring unashamedly. 'He's nowhere near as sexy as you are. And – blimey – what are they doing?'

Everything she'd wanted them to do, Mitzi thought happily. The Mistletoe Kisses, had, as Granny Westward's book promised, loosened inhibitions and made everyone in sight seem desirable and irresistible.

'Um, well, I popped into the bank earlier. My friends, Moira and Evelyn, had told me that Troy and Tyler would be entertaining some of their biggest would-be corporate customers here tonight ... I – er – thought it might be a perfect opportunity to test drive the Mistletoe Kisses proto-type before Doll's wedding. Troy is such a kid, I knew he'd eat them, and hopefully share them with Tyler. They take about six hours to take effect. Which is—' she glanced at her watch '—just about now ...'

'Bloody hell, Mitzi,' Joel tried not to laugh and failed miserably. 'You mean, we're not just here to enjoy a romantic meal? This was your ulterior motive? You are a very, very wicked woman.'

Troy and Tyler, much to the horror of their suited and booted dining companions, were fondling one another's hands across the snowy white linen. Occasionally they'd break off in the fondling and kiss each other on the cheek. They did, Mitzi had to admit, look totally perplexed as they did it – but it was bliss to watch them make total and utter prats of themselves.

'A touch too much ground cyclamen bulb, as I thought,' Mitzi said, nodding. 'And possibly too much garlic – which of course I masked by using far, far too much vanilla – all of them, according to Granny, sure-fire aphrodisiacs ... Never mind, at least I'll know what measures to use for Doll's wedding now.'

Joel forked up some more of his saltimbocca, then dropped it back onto his plate as Troy, his eyes as pleading as a puppy's, leaned towards the most outraged of his dinner guests and tried to kiss him. There was a roar of affronted heterosexuality as the corporate guests rose to their feet as a man and stormed away from the table.

Mitzi bit her lip and stared at the tablecloth. It was cruel, yes, but wonderfully satisfying.

'Oh, look they've left their tortellini,' Joel said as he took a cheerful swig of Chianti. 'Revenge, being a dish best eaten cold, seems to be the only thing on the menu not being wasted. As a payback it was wonderful – but I really never thought you had a vindictive streak in you.'

'Haven't we all? I'm only human, and even the most ardent love and peace people can eventually be stirred to vengeful feelings, believe me. And I'm sure this little incident won't have dented Troy and Tyler's career opportunities too badly. After all, the Sex Discrimination Act will see to that. Even if all those suits assume Troy and Tyler are gay lovers with tarty tendencies, they can hardly use that as a reason for not doing business with the bank, can they? No, it was just an opportunity to test out a recipe – oh, and bring bloody, strutting, patronising Troy Haley down to earth.'

Joel chuckled. 'And do you feel better now?'

'Loads, thanks. Although as you know being dumped from the bank hasn't been the awful experience I'd imagined it would be. Far from it. I'm having more fun than I've ever had in my life. Still, two birds with one stone and all that.' She swallowed some more cannelloni. 'Oh – has seeing this bitchy side of me made you – um – feel differently about me?'

'Absolutely not,' Joel leaned across the silver foliage and the wine glasses and took her hand. 'Just makes you a more rounded human being.'

'Try something other than *rounded*.'

'Can't,' Joel grinned. 'Ouch.'

'Serves you right. I can kick like Thierry Henry when I'm angry. Now are you shocked?'

'Nope. I can do a mean Chinese burn – and I addressed my inner-bitch with my brother and my ex-wife too. Nasty, of course, but God, it made me feel great.'

Mitzi, who knew all about Joel's ex decamping with his brother, raised her eyebrows. 'Really? What did you do to them?'

'Oh, nothing as original as poisoning them with magical herbs and making them seduce everything with a pulse,' Joel smiled at her. 'But it was pretty unpleasant.'

'Go on then. Tell me. I'm all agog. I thought you were such a nice man.'

'Shows how wrong you can be about a lad then, doesn't it?'

'Mmmm. Maybe we're learning far too much about one another tonight.'

'We'll never do that,' Joel stroked her fingers.

Mitzi, feeling the lust stirring and the tingle starting, snatched her hand away, scattering a sparkling dust of sequins across the table, and quickly picked up her fork again. 'Go on then – tell me what you did to your wife and your brother.'

'Well, having access to my brother's house while they

243

were whooping it up for three weeks in Florida – he forgot to take my key back – I, er, broke eggs under the floorboards nearest to the radiators in their bedroom and sewed prawns into the hems on all their curtains. Oh, and I put kippers in their airing cupboard too and left plates of really niffy cat food all over the place then I turned the central heating up full bore and—'

Mitzi giggled. 'And you called me vindictive! What happened?'

'Oh, they spent a fortune on having the place fumigated for months. Never really got rid of the pong. They had to sell the house eventually but it took for ever and they lost a lot of money on the deal. I reckon they knew it was me, but as they'd caused a lot of trouble within the family by getting together, they never actually pointed the finger.'

'Here's to sweet revenge, then,' Mitzi smiled, raising her glass to him. 'And let's hope it's a one-off for both of us. Oh, damn . . .'

'Mitzi!' Troy undulated across the restaurant followed by a besotted-looking Tyler. 'How gorgeous you look! That purple top looks wonderful with your hair! You are one sexy lady!'

He'd kissed her passionately before she could move.

'Hey,' Joel laughed. 'Lay off my woman.'

Troy, looking slightly sheepish, let Mitzi go and kissed Joel instead.

Lorenzo's was riveted.

''ere!' Fredo, Lorenzo's third-generation owner, maître d', chef, meeter and greeter, wine buff and chucker-out, trundled through the designer decor. 'Nuff of that! Bugger off! I'm as liberal as the next man, but you can't force your attentions on people like that. Not in 'ere, you can't.'

Troy, looking appalled, muttered profuse and garbled apologies. Tyler giggled. Fredo, who looked more like a bouncer than someone who could cook up the most delicate dishes and embellish things with fairy wisps of spun sugar, grabbed both of them by the shoulder and ushered them towards the door.

'Goodnight, Mitzi!' Troy called cheerily as Fredo ejected him into the fog. 'Lovely to see you!'

Tyler, close behind, was still trying to hold his hand.

Fredo, making sure they'd skipped off into the pea-souper, held the door open as Lu and Shay came in. Mitzi gave a little groan.

'Let's order our zabagliones quickly,' she muttered. 'Much as I love Lu and Shay, I really don't want to share the rest of this evening with them.'

'Neither do I. But then they probably don't want to spend it with us either.'

Lu and Shay, looking very animated, rushed towards them.

'Hi, Mum. Hello, Joel. What a coincidence,' Lulu beamed. 'Are you celebrating as well?'

Lu, Mitzi thought, looked as though she was lit up from inside. It was lovely to see her so happy. And looking very pretty despite the Patagonian refugee ensemble. Her cheeks were flushed, her eyes sparkled, and the damp fog had teased all the braids into little higgledy-piggledy corkscrews.

'Not celebrating as such, no,' Joel said, having given the ice cream order to their waiter. 'More experimenting. Or at least, Mitzi was. I'm just an interested observer.'

Shay laughed. 'Seems to be the male role when you're involved with the Blessings women, doesn't it? Like being caught up in some sort of surreal whirlwind.'

Over the zabagliones and in spite of the waiter's attempts to show Lulu and Shay to their table, Lu told them about being sort of engaged, becoming an RSPCA inspector, and about Pip, Squeak and Wilfred, while Mitzi recounted the story of the Mistletoe Kisses.

There was much jollity and laughter and hugging and congratulations all round.

'But if you don't mind,' Shay said when things had

quietened down a bit, 'we'd really like to celebrate by ourselves this evening. We won't be making the engagement official until we can afford to do something about it, and we certainly don't want to steal Doll and Brett's thunder. So, as we've got loads to talk about, I hope you won't be offended if we don't share your table?'

'Not at all!'

'No, of course. We completely understand.'

'Ah, how sweet,' Mitzi said mistily, as Lu and Shay, totally engrossed in each other, were shown to their table in a silvery sparkling alcove. 'I couldn't be more pleased. She really deserves some happiness and he's a fantastic man. He'll be so good for her.'

'He's a lucky bloke, too. Lu's gorgeous, despite the dippiness, with a huge heart. They'll be great together.' Joel licked both sides of his spoon. 'So? Both your daughters happily settled before the end of the year, your witchy powers more than adequately endorsed, your Baby Boomers all occupied, Tarnia Snepps almost a bosom buddy ... what's next on the Mitzi Blessing agenda?'

His eyes were dark across the table. The myriad lights twinkled on the diamond ear-stud.

Mitzi dragged her gaze from his and looked across Lorenzo's again to where Lu and Shay were alternately toasting each other in Asti and kissing. The atmosphere was sultry, the darkness illuminated only by the silver sparkles and the flames of a hundred candles, scented with herbs and red wine, highly charged with lust.

She scooped up the last of her ice cream and finished her solitary glass of Chianti. 'Shall we go home?'

Chapter Twenty-two

First into work as usual, Doll switched on the waiting-room lights and scooped up the post from the mat. The previous day's fog had melted away, leaving Hazy Hassocks draped in a grey icy dampness. She loved it. It meant the hot flushes were far more bearable.

She left the post on Viv's desk, checked the answerphone for urgent overnight molar-agony messages – there weren't any – and headed for the usual morning ritual of cloakroom to tidy her hair, kitchen to prepare coffee for everyone, and then into the surgery to set it up ready for the first appointment.

She turned on the surgery lights and screamed.

There was a body in the chair.

'Jesus Christ!' Joel sat upright, cracking his skull on the overhead drill gantry. 'Shit!'

'What the hell are you doing here?' Doll gawped at him. Her heart was still beating a tattoo and an imminent hot flush had been instantly quelled by a wave of icy terror. 'You scared me to death! You look awful. Have you been there all night?'

'Yeah.' Squinting in the harsh fluorescent strip lights, Joel eased his feet to the floor and groaned. 'Don't ask.'

'Get real. Of course I'm going to ask. I thought you and Mum were going out last night?'

'We were. We did,' Joel winced as he ran his fingers

through the spikes of his cropped hair. 'We went to Lorenzo's. We had some great food and a great time and I had more than my fair share of Chianti – and please, please can I have some anti-inflammatories and a bucket of coffee?'

'Go and use the cloakroom first,' Doll advised. 'Stick your head in a basin of cold water. You look truly dreadful. Then I'll make you some nice strong coffee and sort out the pain relief and you can tell me all about it. We've got ages before anyone else comes in. And it's only Mrs Dobbs and her Duane for matching root canals first. They won't mind waiting.'

'I'm not telling you anything.'

'Oh-yes-you-are.'

Half an hour later, after Joel had regaled her with his version of the whole sorry story, Doll was more confused than ever. True, he had a killer hangover and so might have muddled the facts, but even so.

She'd have to go and see her mother. Mitzi must have had her reasons for behaving the way she had. But what on earth had gone wrong? They were so right for one another. Absolutely perfect. This was just awful.

Joel's account of the evening's events simply didn't make sense. Leaving out the débâcle of the ending of the relationship with Mitzi, where on earth had Shay and Lulu being engaged come into it last night? And Lulu actually getting a job – no, a career – and adopting *three* puppies? And as for the bit about a table load of all-bloke bank managers kissing and groping – well, it was all plainly ridiculous. 'I think you're still roaring drunk,' Doll said. 'And everything you've just told me is an alcohol-induced nightmare. It'll all become clear later, I'm sure.'

'It's crystal clear to me now,' Joel muttered, downing his third mug of black coffee and doing his tunic top up wrong. 'Crystal. Christ – how long does it take for this pain relief to kick in?'

'Twenty minutes. Shall I usher Mrs Dobbs in now? We

248

really ought to get her local going. Are you up to it?'

Joel nodded and flinched again.

'Best not let Mrs D or her Duane see your hands shaking when you're armed with the syringe,' Doll advised. 'And you've got your mask on upside down. Look, I'll go to Mum's at lunchtime on the pretext of talking about wedding stuff. I'll try really hard to be discreet and find out why she did what she did. Are you sure you didn't—'

'I didn't do anything,' Joel said sharply. 'And please don't cross-question your mother. She made her feelings absolutely clear last night. To quote the celeb pages, your mother and I are no longer an item. Right – wheel in Mrs Dobbs. No, Doll, I mean it. It's over. Not that it ever really got started. Just as well, really. Go on then – let's get to work.'

'You've got to be mad!' Doll sighed in exasperation across Mitzi's cluttered kitchen table. 'He's gorgeous! He's mad about you! You're mad about him!'

'Stop right there. Far too many mads. I don't know what he's told you, but we're not children. We don't need intervention from our best friend in the playground. Look, love, I made a mistake. It just wasn't meant to be.'

'Cobblers!' Doll snorted through her cup-a-soup, making little orange wavelets lap the sides of the Winnie the Pooh mug. 'Of course it was meant to be. He's hungover, miserable and as angry as a wet hen, and look at the state of you! When have you ever, apart from being ill, still been in your dressing gown at lunchtime?'

Mitzi sighed. She hadn't slept. And not sleeping at fifty-five really took its toll the next morning. It wasn't like being a teenager where the skin just snapped back into place after a sleepless night. And her head ached and her eyes were gritty and she felt grubby and achy. The sadness was a hard, immovable lump under her ribs. She felt truly awful and knew she looked it, not to mention puffy and grey and jowly.

'I'm not going into details,' she said firmly. 'It's none of your business.'

'Yes it is,' Doll gurgled through the remains of the soup. 'You're my mum and he's my employer and my friend. And I like – no, I love you both. Love, mother! Love. Don't you remember the L word?'

Mitzi laughed bitterly. 'Only too well. Which is the problem.'

'Oh, please! Listen to yourself! You're not going to tell me that because Dad dumped you for Jennifer the Harpy a whole decade ago you'll never fall in love again? That he was your one and only?'

Mitzi shook her head. She couldn't tell Doll what had happened the night before. Couldn't. 'Let's just leave it. Your wedding is only a couple of weeks away, Lu's just got unofficially engaged – surely that's enough romance for any family to be going on with?'

'No, it bloody isn't. You've lived your life through us for years. You've been ace. You've been the best mother in the whole world. Me and Lulu are grown up and sorted. Now it's your turn to have some fun. Some happiness. Some love.'

'I've got loads of love. I've got—'

'Don't you dare do that "friends and family and Richard and Judy" routine! Don't you dare! You know exactly what I mean.'

Mitzi sighed. She knew. 'Don't get so agitated, love. I had my reasons. Good reasons. And now we should be talking about the last few things for the wedding . . .'

'Sod the wedding!'

Mitzi smiled ruefully. 'You really should calm down. Your blood pressure will go through the roof.'

'My blood pressure is fine. I'm fine. The baby's fine. Brett's fine. The wedding is planned down to the last infinite detail. We don't need to discuss the wedding any more. We need to discuss why you and Joel are no longer together.'

250

'No we don't. And we won't.'

'Damn me, you're never usually this adamant,' Doll sighed, depositing her mug in the dishwasher and gathering her bag and coat together. 'I blame the Baby Boomers Liberation Movement. And you're really not going to tell me what went wrong last night, are you?'

'No. And don't try and worm it out of Lu, either. She knows nothing about it.'

'Par for the course. Miss Self-Obsessed is hardly likely to notice, is she? Now if you and Joel had four legs and a pair of waggy tails . . .'

Mitzi laughed. It sounded raw and scratchy. 'Please just let it go, Doll, love. I know it'll be awkward for you working with Joel, but for both our sakes, please don't subject him to the third degree.'

'Can't promise anything,' Doll said loftily. 'I'll just have to see what happens.'

Watching Doll sail down the dripping path and into her car, Mitzi sighed. She really wanted to go to bed, to retire to the bejewelled apricot opulence of her room, pull the duvet over her head, sleep for a week and wake up to forget that the embarrassment of last night had ever happened.

But she couldn't.

They'd driven home from Lorenzo's, slowly because of the fog, laughing and talking, with Jimi Hendrix at his most sultry in the background. The evening had been simply wonderful. Perfect. The tingle was still very much there. Just looking at Joel in the cosy cocoon of the car's dark interior had made Mitzi's stomach turn liquid with lust.

This happy state had lasted until well after they'd got into the house and lit lamps and poured wine and fed Richard and Judy. Joel had much admired the living room's Christmas decorations – all old family favourites brought out year after year and awash with memories, none of this trendy colour-co-ordinated designer stuff – and flicked through her CD collection and put a Stones compilation on.

They'd curled on the rug by the fire to the strains of

'Paint It Black'. They'd talked some more, and laughed a lot, and sort of snuggled together naturally in the firelight. He'd kissed her.

Mitzi blinked quickly, remembering.

It had been total bliss. She'd taken his face between her hands and simply soaked up his beauty. She'd never felt like this about anyone, ever. Not even Lance. The kissing had moved on to being interspersed with touching and stroking and whispering endearments.

Mitzi sighed, thinking how perfect it had been.

At last they were going to spend the night together. They'd make love. Joel would be there beside her while she slept and when she woke. The apricot and golden bedroom would no longer be her solitary sanctuary.

But the bedroom could wait. Right now they had the rug and the fire glow and one another.

There had been just one tiny, tiny niggle at the back of her brain: Lu and Shay. They probably wouldn't be home for hours, but even so there seemed something slightly distasteful about going to bed with Joel for the first time, with her daughter and boyfriend in the next room. It would be almost like an orgy. It would ruin the romantic idyll she'd imagined, worrying about being overheard, keeping doors closed. The relaxed spontaneity would be gone.

Joel had kissed her bare shoulder. 'You're beautiful. You're an amazing woman. I've never met anyone like you. You know how much I want you, don't you?'

Mitzi had nodded. She couldn't speak. It hadn't mattered. Nothing mattered then. Not the age difference or her wrinkles or her years and years of celibacy and being out of practice. Not even Lu and Shay. Not really.

Mick and the boys, with perfect timing, chose that moment to burst into 'Let's Spend the Night Together'. She and Joel had exchanged glances and laughed.

He'd kissed her again, then pulled himself into a sitting position and reached for his wine glass. 'Here's to you. To us. You're wonderful.'

She'd chinked her glass against his and giggled. 'So are you.'

And he was, of course. Gorgeous, funny, kind, generous. He was a man in a million as all the best magazines said.

Then things had moved on quite quickly and in the middle of all the emotional turmoil and the heady rush of lust, Mitzi had known this wasn't how she wanted it to be. She didn't want the rug and the fire glow, nor did she want the chance of being interrupted by Lulu and Shay. She didn't want to share this moment with anyone else.

However foolish, she'd always imagined, if it ever happened, sleeping with Joel in some nostalgic born-again-virgin sort of way. She'd wanted to go back in time, to when sleeping with someone you weren't married to wasn't accepted as the norm, when affairs were daring and exciting, when sex with a clandestine lover wasn't discussed as easily and publicly as new hairstyles and fashionable shoes.

She'd wanted the intimacy to be their secret; to be thrilling and audacious and memorable. She'd wanted to recreate that years-ago frisson of wickedness there had been about doing something so romantically reckless.

Of course there were advantages to the current openness, to the sweeping away of taboos, but even so, there had been so much magic in the sheer delicious sinfulness of it all.

She'd wanted to be seduced by Joel in her apricot bedroom and live the erotic and evocative words of Kiki Dee's 'Amoureuse' – like the first time. The first time with this very special man.

He'd sensed her change of mood.

'What's the matter?'

'Nothing ... It's just ... no, nothing. Really ...'

Joel had kissed her gently. 'I do love you, Mitzi. I hadn't planned to. Hadn't expected to. That's what makes it so wonderful. I never thought I'd feel like this.'

Neither had she. And that was the second problem. She

loved him. She didn't just want it to be tonight. She loved him and wanted it to be for ever. She didn't want a fleeting fling with Joel. She knew she couldn't sleep with him, give all of herself to him, only for him to leave her.

Losing Lance had broken her heart. Losing Joel would destroy her life.

She'd wriggled away from him. 'I'm not sure this is such a good idea . . .'

As soon as the sentence was uttered she'd known the words were all wrong. If she'd thrown a bucket of water over him she couldn't have killed the mood better.

He'd stared at her, hurt in his eyes. 'What? I mean . . . I'm sorry . . . I thought you wanted to . . . wanted me . . . Christ . . .'

'I did. I do . . .' Mitzi had mumbled. 'It's just – well, not like this . . .'

'I hadn't imagined we'd be spending the night on the floor either. Although I guess that's not what you mean is it?'

Mitzi had watched miserably as he'd reached angrily for his shirt.

'Not really. Look, Joel—'

'No,' his voice had been cold. 'You don't need to spell it out. I'm sorry. I'd thought you felt like I did. There's no way I want to force myself on you.'

'You're not. Of course you're not. Oh, God. Let me explain. Or at least try . . .' She'd pulled on her purple top. The buttons caught on her hair and the tears, so far held in check, spilled down her cheeks. 'Please, Joel . . .'

'Don't cry.' He'd scrambled to his feet and pushed his feet into his shoes. 'Please don't cry. We've had a great time – made each other happy. It would be crap to have it end in tears. I'm sorry if I got the wrong message. Gave out the wrong signals.'

'You didn't. It's me. I've ruined it. Please let me tell you—'

He'd grabbed his jacket from the back of the chair, making the Christmas tree rock violently and sending a

254

cascade of pine needles swooshing to the floor.

'Don't go. You can't go. You know – the drinking and driving and—'

'I'll be fine.' His eyes had been as brilliantly cold as the diamond ear-stud. 'At least we know where we stand now. I'm glad I didn't make even more of a fool of myself. No, I'll find my own way out.'

And Mitzi had watched him go, the sadness tightening in her throat, the loneliness engulfing her long before he'd slammed the front door.

Now, more than twelve hours later she felt exactly the same.

It had been all her fault. She was so out of practice with love game rules. Why, oh why couldn't she have been honest and just told him what she wanted? What she'd dreamed of? He wouldn't have laughed at her. Joel wasn't unkind. He would have understood, maybe even shared her romantic dreams, or at least pretended to. But not now. Now it was far, far too late. Because of her stupid dreams and ridiculous inexperience she'd done that unforgivable thing in a man's eyes – changed her mind at the height of passion. She'd hurt and insulted him. There would be no second chances.

Mitzi gazed at her reflection in the kitchen window. She looked every one of her fifty-five years and about a hundred of someone else's. Last night's make-up had creased into the crevasses, her eyes were baggy and dark shadowed with little globs of dried mascara clinging to her clumpy lashes like a pantomime dame's, and her hair was matted and tufty. Her skin seemed to be hanging in folds, almost touching the collar of her not-quite-clean, ancient, towelling dressing gown, the one she used for slobbing in, not the elegant cream silk one she'd planned to throw so casually over her nakedness for Joel's benefit.

'Jesus . . .'

Richard and Judy, emerging stretching from the washing basket in search of a second lunch, looked at her with unconditional love. She stroked them both, reassured by the twin-engined vibrato purrs.

'At least someone loves me – oh, bugger!' She looked up as the kitchen door started to open. 'Not Flo wanting coffee and gossip – not now. Oh, shit . . .'

'Nice to see you too,' Lance beamed at her. 'Dear God, Mitzi. Are you ill? You look really awful. Sorry if it's not a good time – didn't you get my message? Left it on the answerphone last night.'

Mitzi tried to shrink into a corner and glared at him. Of course she hadn't got his damn message. She hadn't looked at the damn phone. Last night she'd had other things on her mind, hadn't she?

'Go away, Lance. It's not convenient.'

'Then you should have answered my message. I said we'd be round at lunchtime to discuss a few things about Doll and Brett's wedding.'

We? *We?*

'I've managed to park the car,' Jennifer cooed, joining Lance in the doorway. 'It's such a funny narrow little road – oh, goodness Mitzi – have you got flu? You look dreadful!'

Mitzi tried to cram herself back even further into the darkest corner. It simply wasn't fair. Jennifer, dressed in pale suede, with a lilac cashmere scarf nestling round her throat, and long pale boots, exuded glossy radiance and elegant good-grooming from head to toe.

'She didn't get our message,' Lance said cheerfully, ushering Jennifer into the kitchen. 'Oh, nothing changes, does it? It's still a mess in here.'

Jennifer, staring at the clutter, gingerly pulled out a chair and inspected it for grime before sitting down. Richard and Judy immediately went into a synchro, arched-back, bushed-tail routine and hissed at her as they backed away through the remains of the cup-a-soups and crusts.

'I said it wasn't convenient,' Mitzi croaked, peeling herself away from the wall and staring venomously at

Lance and Jennifer. 'As you can see, I'm hardly ready for visitors and anyway—'

'Ooh, we're not stopping for long.' Jennifer's immaculately manicured pearly nails gathered crumbs together on the table top. 'We're off to London for a few days. We're staying at the Savoy and Lance is treating me to a shopping trip to Bond Street. As a birthday treat.'

Mitzi said nothing. Lance used to bring her service-station bouquets and a couple of drinks at The Faery Glen – when he remembered her birthday.

'I suggested we popped in,' Lance said, 'as Jennifer is going to buy her wedding outfit – designer, of course – and she didn't want to clash with yours.'

'How very thoughtful.'

'So,' Jennifer turned her perfect peachy face towards Mitzi. 'What colour are you wearing?'

'Green.'

'Green! *Green?* You can't wear green! It's sooo unlucky!'

'Only if you're the bride, apparently.' Mitzi tried to rearrange her hair and de-clog her eyelashes. 'And I like green.'

'Dear me,' Jennifer said, a smile tugging at the corners of her plump lips. 'How very retro. No problems about clashing there, then. And what about hats? Have you had one made?'

'I'm not wearing a hat. No one's wearing a hat. It's not that sort of wedding. It's only very small and informal.'

'You can't go to a wedding without a hat!' Jennifer looked as though Mitzi had suggested the entire congregation should go naked. 'I'm going to Philip Treacey for mine.'

'Excellent choice.' The kitchen door opened again and like a really, really bad dream, Tarnia appeared. 'Mine are all from darling Jasper of course, but Philip is a poppet as well.'

'What the hell do you want?' Mitzi growled as Tarnia

and Jennifer exchanged mwah-mwah kisses across the strewn table. 'You haven't been to see me since 1985!'

Tarnia, also looking perfectly groomed and glowing in baby pink leather trousers and a black biker jacket and boots, with her short black hair artlessly tipped in pink frosting, narrowed her eyes. 'Heavens, Mitzi. I hadn't realised you were ill. It's put years on you.'

'I'm not ill. I'm fine. I'm just not dressed for holding an open house.'

'At midday?' Lance laughed. 'You're really letting yourself go. No, okay, we'll leave you to sort yourself out. It'll probably take the rest of the day ... Anyway, we don't want to be late for dinner at the Savoy. And at least Jennifer will have a free hand in Bond Street now – no one else will be wearing green.'

'Green?' Tarnia shrieked. 'You can't wear green to the wedding, Mitzi! It's unlucky.'

'Only if you're the bride, apparently.' Jennifer got to her feet, inspecting the pale suede for crumbs and cats' fur. There were loads of both on her bottom but she couldn't see them. 'When we're back from London, Tarnia, I'll ring you about the Bancroft-Hulmes's drinks party, shall I?'

Tarnia nodded, and after another round of mwah-mwahs, Lance and Jennifer escaped.

'Don't look at me like that,' Tarnia said. 'I know this is probably a bit unexpected, but I was dropping some stuff off at the charity shop and thought as I was so close, I should just call in and ask if you've got any more of those little menu list things. You know, for your ancient country cooking foodie stuff. Marquis and I are planning a huge supper party for the charity commissioners in the New Year and, well, everyone is bored to tears with Nigella and Jamie, so I wanted to be the first to do something different.'

'They're around somewhere ...' Mitzi looked helplessly at the piles of clutter on every surface. 'I'll look for them later and drop them off to you.'

'That's okay. You look as though you should go back to bed. And have you thought of surgery, Mitzi? Or at least a chemical peel and a detox? We owe it to ourselves to keep young and beautiful as the song goes. And—' Tarnia pulled as much of a knowing face as the Botox would allow '—you'll never hang on to that absolutely divinely sexy young dentist if he sees you looking like the village crone.'

Feeling as though someone had just punched the air from her lungs, Mitzi tried hard not to crumple. 'No . . . probably not.'

'Tell you what,' Tarnia sang out, heading for the door, 'don't worry too much about your menu thingies. The ladies in the charity shop told me there's a bit of a Christmas show on at the village hall next week. No doubt you're involved – can't imagine why you didn't tell me about it – and Marquis and I will have to be seen to be there. So we'll pick them up from you then. Byeeeee . . .'

Chapter Twenty-three

DREAMING CREAMS

Two cups of icing sugar
One cup of the finest flour
Half a dozen eggs
Half a pint of fresh double cream
Handful of ground walnut
The rind and zest and juice of two lemons
A sprinkling of ground ginger
A handful of beggar's buttons
Crushed china berry
A pinch of allspice

Beat flour, sugar, eggs and cream together. Leave in a cool place.
Mix together lemons, ginger, beggar's buttons, china berry, and allspice. Grind small with pestle and mortar.
Whisk into cold creamed mixture.

Spoon into buttered patty tins.

Bake for three quarters of one hour in a moderate oven. The outside of the Dreaming Creams should be crisp and crumbly, while the insides should be of a soft and chewy consistency.

Note: Making dreams come true is easy with the right herbal magic. This combination is particularly efficacious. Dreaming Creams are made from a powerful country recipe which has been successful for generations. Whether spoken aloud or thought silently, dreams WILL come true if made while eating Dreaming Creams. These sweetmeats are traditionally used for wedding feasts.

'Maybe we should try and make some sort of love potion for your mum,' Brett said as he and Doll queued under lowering skies outside the village hall the following Saturday afternoon. 'From her recipe book. After all it's supposed to have worked for us – and for Lu and Shay, isn't it?'

Doll shoved him none too gently in the ribs and stamped her numbing feet. 'That's all rubbish and you know it is. Sadly, whatever went wrong between Mum and Joel is too far gone for a few herbs to make any difference.'

'But Lulu says she made some sort of wishing star meringues to finally hook Shay.'

'Yeah, right. Lu also says she can't understand why Mum and Joel have split up because they shared some really powerful apple love magic at Halloween and it can't have gone wrong. It's all hokum. As I've said all along.' She gazed up at the heavy sky. 'Do you think it's going to snow?'

Brett shook his head. 'Not according to the forecasts, no.'

It was only ten days before the wedding. The wind was screaming down from the Arctic, ripping at the flapping corners of the *Hair* posters outside the hall. The weather was getting colder and greyer by the minute, but the chances of a white Christmas were still officially about a million to one. Doll, who secretly relished the idea of walking from Lance's car to the church in a snowstorm, was very disappointed.

She was also more concerned about Mitzi than she was prepared to admit. Joel, she felt, could lick his own wounds in the sort of secretive macho way men always did. Sure, he wasn't usually afraid of being in touch with his feminine side, but this time confession sessions were clearly a no-go area. He'd simply refused to talk about Mitzi and Doll had given up trying to make him.

Mitzi, although professing to be fine, was anything but. She seemed to have shrunk back into herself, even more so than when Lance had first decamped with Jennifer. As she'd made such huge life strides recently, since leaving the bank, Doll found this rapid sliding backwards more than a little worrying. Doll knew her mother was desperately unhappy, but she too refused to discuss the break-up. Even Lu, obsessed as she was with Shay, the forthcoming career move, and Pip, Squeak and Wilfred, had noticed.

'Bloody long wait,' Clyde Spraggs muttered ahead of them in the queue. 'Like being in the West End.'

'You've never been to the West End,' Flo said tartly. 'And what's in that bottle?'

'Dandelion and rosehip with a touch of moonshine. Keeps out the cold.'

'Give it here then – no, don't let young Doll have any. She's carrying, remember?'

'Why aren't the bloody doors open?' Someone else complained at the head of the queue. 'We've been waiting hours and it's bloody freezing.'

The cry was picked up along the snaking queue. Any minute now, Doll thought, there'd be a Hazy Hassocks riot.

'Why are we waiting? Oh, w-h-y are we waiting?' someone chorused behind them. 'Why are we wa-i-t-ing? Why-oh-why?'

The discordant but mainly jocular vocal complaint was echoed over and over again as villagers from Hazy Hassocks, Bagley-cum-Russett and Fiddlesticks all joined in.

It was, Doll thought, probably far more tuneful than anything else they'd hear that afternoon.

'Are we going to be late?' Lu puffed as she and Shay, entwined as always, hurried across the village green. 'Doesn't *Hair* kick off at three?'

'No we're not and yes it does,' Shay said, his head down against the wind. 'It's only half-two and we'll be there in a couple of minutes – but I knew we should have brought the car. It's bloody freezing. I suppose this is where the Afghan comes into its own?'

Lulu nodded. It was. To be honest, the Afghan had always caused her a bit of a dilemma. Should someone as dedicated to animal welfare as she was really spend her life wearing the skins of dead, albeit long-dead, goats? As she'd always been very careful about not eating anything with a face or wearing anything other than man-made shoes, it sometimes bothered her. She'd always justified it to herself by saying the wearing of the Afghan was a living memorial to the animals which had given their lives for the vanity of man, and hoped that they'd forgive her.

The wind punched across the green in icy waves, and not for the first time Lu was delighted to be shrouded in the Afghan's impenetrable layers. She'd persuaded Shay to walk to the village hall because she was keen to map out the best routes for Pip, Squeak and Wilfred's future constitutionals. Neither of them had expected it to be quite so cold.

'Oh, look – Honeysuckle House is on the market.'

Shay looked across the green. 'It's not a house and there isn't any honeysuckle.'

'Pedant.'

'Looks nice though. A real cottage. Very tiny – probably only two up and two down? And the sign says it's to let, not for sale. Wouldn't it be nice if we could—'

'Yeah. Perfect.' Lu sighed. 'And the garden would be great for the puppies – not to mention being right on the village green for walks and stuff. The rent is probably affordable too, because it belongs to the vicar and he usually lets it out to deserving cases – which we are. Amy and Frank Worthy had it last – before the trouble. I didn't know they'd finally gone.'

'What trouble?'

'You don't really want to know about the trouble, do you? Yeah, you obviously do. Well, Amy and Frank looked like Mr and Mrs Middle-England. Retired. Rotary. *Daily Mail* and *Telegraph* readers. Pillars of the church. Genteel and impoverished. Just right for the vicar's good Honeysuckle House cause. Sadly, they spent all their spare time making videos for the discerning gentleman.'

'They made porn films?' Shay laughed. 'In that dear little cottage?'

'No, not in there. Somewhere near Epping Forest – they lived a perfectly respectable life in Honeysuckle House. But of course when it came to court and the *News of the World*, the vicar had to give them notice to quit.'

'Oh, of course,' Shay laughed again. 'This place is amazing. And why is the vicar a man of property? I thought they were supposed to give up all worldly goods when they took the cloth. Does he own a lot of property?'

'Just Honeysuckle House and his Harley-Davidson. He says they're his pension fund. Oh, but wouldn't it be brilliant if we could live there?'

They looked at one another and sighed. It would be perfect. But they couldn't even contemplate it because of Lav and Lob.

'Forget it,' Lulu said. 'I know it's out of the question. Anyway, we've got other things to worry about.'

'Your mum, you mean?'

'Mmmm. She's so unhappy. I hate seeing her like this. I can't imagine what went wrong. That apple magic is supposed to be infallible.'

'Sweetheart, maybe it was infallible in your Great-Gran's time, but not now.'

'Don't be daft. Magic is timeless.'

'Whatever. But even so, they looked really happy that night in Lorenzo's – it must have been something major to have changed things so drastically. Is she still not talking about it?'

'Neither of them are,' Lu said miserably as they slithered off the green and headed for the village hall. 'Me and Doll hoped they'd get together again at the wedding and at least talk to one another but Joel says he's not going now. Blimey! Look at that queue! Oh, great – Doll and Brett are near the front. Let's push in with them.'

Inside the hall, nerves were getting the better of the *Hair* cast. Trilby Man was racing around backstage, barking last-minute instructions, frightening the life out of everyone and getting in the way. Mitzi, who had peered out of the window at the immense queue, felt nothing at all.

It was very disconcerting, this ongoing feeling of total apathy.

'Right!' Trilby Man snapped behind her. 'Let's get those doors open. Are you sure you're okay for front of house, duck? You looks as rough as a badger's arse.'

'Thanks so much. And I'm fine.'

'And the half-time refreshments? Can you handle them, too?'

Mitzi nodded. They'd had a sort of co-operative arrangement over the refreshments with everyone in the Baby Boomers bringing something. Sadly, because no one bothered to write it down, they now had far too many sausage rolls and not enough cake. Lavender and Lobelia had provided sardine and mustard sandwiches. Mitzi had half-heartedly made some bits and pieces from Granny's recipe book. Nothing too controversial, of course, just some of her tried and tested recipes.

She hurried between the rows and rows of empty chairs, and flicked on the auditorium lights. The pain under her ribs was ever present, and her head felt as if it was filled with cotton wool. She missed Joel so much. They'd so looked forward to this afternoon, too. Joel wouldn't be here now, naturally. Or at the wedding. He'd already told Doll he'd decided to go back to his parents in Manchester for Christmas.

Pulling open the hall's double doors, Mitzi was almost knocked sideways by the twin onslaught of a northerly gale and several hundred cold people. Her request for tickets was lost in the raucous mêlée.

As they all streamed in, it was like her life in Hazy Hassocks flashing before her eyes. Everyone was there. Well, everyone except Lance and Jennifer because, on their return from London, they'd booked themselves a relaxing-and-tanning health farm break so that they'd look like the village's answer to Michael Douglas and Catherine Zeta Jones at the wedding.

Gwyneth Wilkins and Big Ida Tomms spearheaded the Fiddlesticks faction, and several members of the Bagley-cum-Russett Ladies League of Light had braved the cold and their unreliable minibus to make the three-mile journey. Herbie was there, and Hedley and Biff Pippin, and Mrs Elkins from Patsy's Pantry, and Carmel and Augusta, and Otto and Boris from The Faery Glen – and, well, absolutely everyone. Except, Mitzi noted sadly, Joel with the dental surgery crowd.

Doll and Lu hugged her. Shay and Brett grinned encouragingly.

'Are you sitting with us?' Doll said. 'We'll need you to explain what's going on.'

'It's all way beyond me,' Mitzi managed a smile. 'The original script was confusing – now our lot have got hold of it it's totally incomprehensible.'

'Nice music though,' Lu said. 'Are we allowed to sing along?'

'Oh, definitely. They're going to need all the help they can get.'

Everyone had already made a beeline for the front rows.

Mitzi, hoping that Joel might, just might, be there, had spread various belongings across six seats immediately in front of the stage.

'Great seats,' Brett said as they settled in. 'Who's the other one for – ouch!'

There was a huge sense of anticipation as the audience prepared to be entertained. As Mitzi had had the hot-air blowers on since first light, it was for once gloriously warm inside. Coats were shed and glasses retrieved from bags. The lights dimmed.

Everyone went 'ooooh'.

Trilby Man fought his way out through the lopsided curtains and everyone cheered.

'Lovely to see you all here,' he screamed into the microphone. The microphone, far too close to the amplifier, screamed back.

Everyone clapped.

'We're just waiting for one or two latecomers,' Trilby Man shrieked. 'Then we'll be underway. I hope you'll enjoy this afternoon's show, which is the first of many planned Hazy Hassocks am-dram productions. There will be an intermission between Act One and Act Two, and there are refreshments available at the back of the hall for those who—'

Too late. Mitzi closed her eyes. The audience, chilled to the bone in the queue, needed no second invitation. Chairs scraped back, and with a whooping rush, everyone clattered towards the food tables.

'For the intermission!' Trilby Man screamed helplessly. 'The refreshments are for the intermission – oh, bugger!'

Somewhere in the scrum for the food, with everyone piling their cardboard plates like mini Everests, Tarnia and Snotty Mark arrived. Trilby Man, spotting them from the stage, clambered down the rickety steps and ushered them to two reserved seats at the end of Mitzi's row.

'*Hair?*' Tarnia mouthed to Mitzi. 'I thought it was a panto.'

267

'It will be,' Mitzi mouthed back. 'Believe me.'

Tarnia was dressed in pink and gold and glittered a lot. Snotty Mark, who clearly didn't want to be there, was wearing a black Paul Smith suit and with his gelled-down hair looked like a funeral director.

'But, *Hair*?' Tarnia persisted. 'Is this suitable? I mean, my charity commissioners think it's all innocent fun for the village kiddies. I'm not at all sure this is an appropriate use of the premises.'

Mitzi shrugged. She really didn't care any more.

'Have a bun, duck,' Clyde Spraggs leaned over from the row behind and offered Tarnia his heaped plate. 'You could do with a bit of flesh on them bones.'

'Well, I really shouldn't – I'm on the Pratt Diet for the run-up to Christmas – but I'm starving and I'm sure one won't hurt.' Tarnia hesitated for a moment, then reached for one of the brown squashy cakes on the top of the pile. 'That's very kind of you. Mitzi, is this one of yours?'

Mitzi nodded, watching Tarnia's perfectly capped teeth sink into the Powers of Persuasion Pudding. Not sure now if it would work or not, she smiled. 'I'm sure you'll find that the charity commissioners will be absolutely delighted with this afternoon's production – and all the other uses for the hall. And I'm equally sure that you'll tell them about your continued and ongoing support for our projects, won't you?'

Mitzi was aware of Doll watching with suspicion, and Lu with encouragement. Tarnia finished the Powers of Persuasion Pudding and dabbed delicately at her lips.

She gave a stiff beam. 'Delicious. Absolutely melts in the mouth. You have remembered to bring your recipes, haven't you?'

Mitzi nodded and fished them from her handbag. Shay and Brett passed them along the row.

'Lovely.' Tarnia stretched her trout-pout lips into a smile. 'And of course I'll sing *Hair*'s praises to the charity commissioners. No problem. You've worked miracles in the village, Mitzi. Marquis and I are delighted to let you have the hall for as long as you want, aren't we darling?'

Snotty Mark grunted.

Lulu winked at Mitzi.

Tarnia wiped crumbs from her pink leather lap. 'You still look ghastly, though, if you don't mind me saying so. Such a shame you haven't taken yourself in hand, but there, we can't all have natural glamour, can we?'

Doll and Lulu sniggered.

Mitzi, surprisingly pleased that the Puddings could still work their magic, simply smiled back. She didn't care what Tarnia or anyone else thought of her appearance. What did it matter now anyway?

And if the Puddings could still persuade, she did wonder in a half-hearted manner how many of the audience had eaten her new recipe, Mistletoe Kisses, or the Dreaming Creams which she'd attempted again in the hope she'd be perfect by the time of the wedding, and if they'd have their usual effects.

But she didn't wonder for long.

With a drum roll from the stage, the lights went out, the footlights went on, the curtains rattled open, and everyone fell silent.

'What the hell is that?' Doll hissed along the row. 'Why is there a bloody great galleon in the middle of a park?'

Mitzi, who hadn't seen the final version of Raymond and Timothy's backdrop, shook her head in mystification.

'It's the *Cutty Sark*,' Shay whispered. 'It says so on it. And as the programme says the whole thing is set in Greenwich Village—'

Mitzi tried hard to stifle her giggles. Only in Hazy Hassocks could they have misunderstood *which* Greenwich. If she looked carefully she'd probably see the Observatory and the Meridian Line too – yes! There it was! Snaking away between the very English, painted flower beds. Oh, if only Joel could have been here to share this.

Several other people were chuckling loudly. Fortunately

the mirth hadn't reached the stage, where septuagenarian Sid as Claude, wearing an eiderdown, was sitting cross-legged, alone in the spotlight, his head bowed, his trailing acrylic wig slipping slightly askew. It was an awesome moment and stunned the audience into silence.

The silence, however, was merely momentary. As The Tribe made their first appearance, the village hall erupted into mass hysteria.

Even Mitzi, who was sure she'd never laugh again, managed a respectable chuckle.

The Baby Boomers, faces painted circa Woodstock 1969, wearing a selection of caftans, with nylon Afro wigs and beads, flowers and bells, shuffled on to the stage.

Lav and Lob had their wigs over their cycle helmets and waved cheerily to the front row.

Doll and Lulu were crying with laughter as The Tribe clumsily set up the altar, tried to start a fire with matches which wouldn't strike and had to resort to Sid's cigarette lighter, then discovered that no one had any scissors to snip off the symbolic lock of his hair, so tossed his entire wig into the flames.

There was a whoosh and a roar and a blinding flash.

A now bald Sid, who grizzled all the time about his arthritis and moved at the speed of a funeral cortège, leapt to his feet with a feral scream.

The Tribe, looking a little worried about the inferno, huddled towards the wings and spluttered into a half-hearted rendition of 'Aquarius' as Trilby Man clambered inelegantly on stage and threw a cup of coffee on the flames.

The fire went out, The Tribe shuffled forward, and 'Aquarius' increased in volume.

As someone had loaned a rather dubious surround-sound system, Galt MacDermot's music was at eardrum-splitting level. The audience, once assured they weren't going to be burnt to a crisp, joined in with gusto.

It was all uphill after that. The first act steamed on, with

270

no one in the audience having a clue what was happening on stage, the actors not seeming to care, and both having a whale of a time. The Baby Boomers' rendition of the title song was like watching massed ranks of aunts and uncles, very drunk at a wedding, having a go at karaoke for the very first time.

'Dance, damn you, dance!!!!' Trilby Man screamed from the wings.

The Baby Boomers tried their best. Given their age, they managed heroically. The movements were more robotic than sensuous; most of them stumbled on their caftans and several lost their wigs. Singing and dancing at the same time seemed not to have been a must-do at rehearsals. Ronnie fell over and Beryl, without her glasses, wandered off the edge of the stage and disappeared under the trestle table supporting the footlights.

'I think I'm going into labour,' Doll sniffed happily. 'I haven't laughed so much for years.'

Murdered song followed murdered song, flowers were strewn, Frank fell off his pole and had to be helped away, and Hazy Hassocks loved every minute of it.

Bernard, Doreen and Christopher tiptoed rather sinisterly towards the front of the stage. The sound system had 'Hare Krishna' on multi-replay. Hazy Hassocks was riveted.

'It's time for the Be-In!' Christopher shrilled. 'Tourists – come to the orgy!'

Hazy Hassocks was a bit slow on the uptake.

'They're taking their clothes off!' Tarnia screamed happily along the row.

They were. It was the most frightening thing Mitzi had ever seen. Thirty-plus pensioners stripping off to grey underwear, and in some cases even greyer flesh. Lav and Lob were resplendent in Vedonis. Thank the Lord, Mitzi thought, for the efficacy of the hot-air blowers.

'Come on.' Shay was on his feet, holding out his hand to Lu. 'We're the tourists. We're going to an orgy.'

He was out of his Levis and sweatshirt in seconds and

leaping onto the stage. Lu, in her vest and Sloggi pants, only seconds behind him.

'Blimey!' Doll raised her eyebrows at Mitzi. 'Shay's got a fantastic body.' She caught Brett's frown. 'Oh, not as good as yours, of course – but ...'

Once Shay and Lu were on stage, singing and dancing and loving in, Hazy Hassocks cottoned on quickly and needed no second invitation. Layers were shed along with inhibitions and chairs toppled backwards as the audience, in various stages of undress, charged forward.

Tarnia, giggling, had wriggled out of the sparkly pink leather and was skipping up the steps in a rather lovely set of Janet Reger. Snotty Mark buried his head in his hands.

'I'm not going up there,' Doll said. 'Not in my condition. And what exactly did you put in the refreshments? That love-in up there looks a bit too authentic to me.'

Mitzi nodded. It did. Lots of very unsuitable people were groping and slobbering over lots of other very unsuitable people. It was in danger of becoming a real orgy. The Mistletoe Kisses still needed a slight adjustment then.

'Come on, Mitzi!' Flo and Clyde Spraggs, wearing scaringly little, grabbed her hands. 'Up yer comes, duck!'

'No! I mean, I'm not going.'

'Course you are. It's all a bit of fun! Look at Hed and Biff! And Mrs Elkins – and young Tammy and Viv – and Gwyneth and Big Ida – oh, and look at Boris and Otto!'

Mitzi looked. 'Hare Krishna' roared, on stage the audience and players alike stalked and stroked and sang and snogged. Tarnia was chewing the face off a very young boy from the Bath Road Estate.

Mitzi hesitated. Did she have matching underwear? Did she care?

Tugging off her jeans and yanking her jumper over her head, with Doll and Brett's cheers in her ears, she rushed onto the overcrowded stage with Flo and Clyde. Her black bra and knickers weren't her best, but they were reasonably respectable and at least she'd shaved her legs.

It was, she decided, a whole lot of fun. And hadn't she read somewhere that Princess Anne had joined in on the Be-In during a *Hair* performance in the 1960s? Raising her arms above her head she swayed and waved and clapped and sang 'Hare Krishna' at the top of her voice. It was just like being at the Shepton Mallet Blues Festival in her youth. So what if her heart was broken? So what?

'That's the way to do it, duck!' Trilby Man shrieked in her ear. 'Give it all you've got!'

Mitzi glanced sideways at him. He was wearing nothing but his hat.

She shimmied away from him and ended up linking arms with Ronnie and Philip and going into a sort of Tiller Girl routine. The noise roared on; the auditorium was half empty; the stage was packed. Everyone was grabbing everyone else. The Mistletoe Kisses had worked their magic – again.

Mitzi grinned down at Doll and Brett who were clapping and singing in the front row. She couldn't see anyone else in the audience. Just a few faces, the more reticent villagers, dotted around in the gloom, all waving their arms in the air or clapping or singing.

All except someone standing alone at the back of the hall.

Someone who was watching her with an inscrutable expression on his craggy, beautiful face.

'Oh, bloody hell,' Mitzi groaned.

Chapter Twenty-four

It was the 23rd of December. A dark, grey, bitterly cold day. Mitzi's kitchen was a scene of devastation. Richard and Judy, covered in flour and icing sugar, were scuttling around the floor, tails erect, happily hoovering up everything that dropped in their path.

'Whose stupid idea was it to get married on Christmas Eve?' Mitzi grumbled.

Under the table, Richard and Judy chewed happily and said nothing. Hawkwind, throbbing from the CD player, didn't answer either.

In the days since *Hair*, Mitzi had managed to finish all her Christmas shopping, made sure absolutely everything was ready for the wedding, and tried to forget about Joel.

The first two had been easy, but not the third.

By the time the *Hair* Police had scrambled on stage to 'arrest' the orgy-goers, signalling that the official intermission had kicked in, and everyone had returned to their seats, Joel had gone.

Jesus! Mitzi was overcome by embarrassment again, simply remembering. Here she was, merely a few years off pension age, and he'd seen her, with baggy eyes and baggy skin, and without make-up and with her hair all anyhow, cavorting semi-naked in front of the entire populations of three villages.

Pride and self-preservation had prevented her from

274

asking Doll if he'd since mentioned her performance.

She sighed heavily and tried to concentrate on Granny's recipe book propped up on the table. The Mistletoe Kisses, Green Gowns and the rest were all done. All that was left was to bake the last batch of Dreaming Creams, defrost the remainder of the party food, take the whole lot to The Faery Glen, get to Pauline's for her mother-of-the-bride wash and blow-dry, and remember to smile at all times.

For a fleeting second, on stage in the village hall, she'd forgotten her broken heart and her anger at her own stupidity. Seeing Joel, dark and gorgeous, in the shadows, had deflated her euphoria as suddenly as a pricked balloon. And today, when the surgery closed its doors for the festive period, Joel would be driving home to Manchester.

'Silly cow!' Mitzi berated herself. 'You love him you had him and you let him go – all for some stupid romantic girlie whim.'

Hawkwind, showing no sympathy whatsoever, revved up into 'Silver Machine'.

Hair had been a stonking success. Act Two had gone down even better than Act One. The cast took curtain call after curtain call and the after-show party rocked on for hours. The aphrodisiac effect of the Mistletoe Kisses, so efficacious during the Love-In, had taken ages to wear off, and everyone was still very touchy-feely.

Mitzi had been moved to tears when the Baby Boomers had dragged her on to the stage and presented her with a huge bouquet at the end of the afternoon and told everyone none of it would have happened without her. That she had, with single-minded determination, shaken them out of their over-fifties lethargy. Mitzi Blessing, they proclaimed to the whole audience, had changed the lives of Hazy Hassocks's grey army for ever.

She too got a standing ovation, and hopefully only she and Lu and Doll knew all the tears weren't simply because she was awash with Baby Boomer emotion.

Tarnia, still trying to kiss everything in sight, had told

Mitzi it was the best day out she'd ever had and that the BBC could have the use of the village hall for ever and ever, and had been led away giggling by a stony-faced Snotty Mark.

At least something good had come out of it.

'Right.' Mitzi squinted at Granny Westward's scrawly writing. 'So we'll just leave this batch of Dreaming Creams mixture to cool, and I'll knock up a little pie for tonight.'

How long ago it seemed since cooking had terrified her. How many years had she wasted, defrosting ready meals, when she really had a knack for producing surprisingly edible recipes? And how long ago did it seem since she'd found Granny's cookery book and made that first Wishes Come True Pie?

Well, at least Doll and Lu had got what they'd wished for.

Tonight, she and Lu and Doll were going to have a girls' night in. Well, after Doll and Lu had had a swift drink with their friends in The Faery Glen as a sort of muted hen night. She'd declined the invitation to join them, saying she needed far more time than they did to pamper and primp and preen herself for the nuptials.

Surprisingly, they'd both asked her to make the Wishes Come True Pie for the last supper. Doll was staying overnight, at least giving some lip service to tradition, so that she could leave for the church from number 33 with Lance in the morning.

Tomorrow was all beautifully organised, and should be one of the happiest days of Mitzi's life, and of course it would be. Almost.

The dental surgery glittered with decorations, and Joel and Mr Johnson both wore Santa hats which probably scared the life out of the patients. Tammy and Viv had hopeful sprigs of mistletoe attached to their chests, and Doll wore flashing snowmen earrings.

The wind, still screaming from the north, made everything

rattle. The village shivered under the heavy grey clouds, and Doll kept looking hopefully for the first snowflake.

'It ain't going to snow,' Tammy said, hitching her uniform dress up another couple of inches and admiring her slim legs in opaque tights. 'The forecast says it's just going to be bloody cold. We never get white Christmases any more, do we? My mum and dad say they can remember them when they were kids. They used to go sledging and have snowball fights and get weeks off school. That's so not fair.'

'Doll doesn't really want snow,' Viv said. 'She'll freeze in her frock. We'll all have to wear thermals as it is.'

Tammy stopped admiring her legs and looked at Doll. 'Are you nervous now?'

'Nope. Not at all. Just really looking forward to it. I think it's because it's low key. Brett's parents got a bit sniffy over it being dumbed down, but they're okay now.'

Tammy grinned. 'And you really don't want any wedding presents?'

'Why would we? We've been together for ever. We've got everything we could possibly want. All we want is to have all our family and friends round us to help celebrate.'

'Ah, bless.'

Viv inspected her fingernails. 'What time are we meeting at the pub tonight?'

'Straight from work,' Doll still peered at the sky from the empty waiting-room window. 'And it's only a quick drink, nothing exciting. I want to spend this evening at home with Mum. She's cooking us a special meal.'

Tammy raised her much-plucked eyebrows. 'What? Like that stuff she made for *Hair*? That was cool. I had one of those meringues. It was better than Red Bull. You'll be as high as a kite when you walk down the aisle tomorrow.'

'It's not going to be anything like that. No herbal over-doses. This is just an old-fashioned pie. Me and Lu thought it would do her good to have something else to concentrate on.'

'Is she still ... upset about Joel – *you know*?' Viv gave the last two words heavy emphasis.

'Very much so. Such a shame. They were great together.'

'They were.' Viv patted her hair. 'And what about him? How's he? Any change?'

'No, he's much the same. I know he misses her. They're mad. He's going off to Manchester tonight. And he doesn't really want to because he might run into his brother and his ex at Christmas, and his parents won't take sides – he's just so bloody miserable.'

'No, I'm sodding not,' Joel, still wearing the Santa hat, yanked open the surgery door. 'I'm filled to sodding over-flowing with the sodding festive sprit. Surely you three have got better things to gossip about? And what's happened to my sodding two o'clock double filling?'

The surgery door slammed shut again.

'See?' Doll said. 'Broken hearted. Poor thing.'

'We're so looking forward to tomorrow,' Biff Pippin said, as they prepared to close up the charity shop for Christmas. 'Hedley and me love a wedding. We don't get asked to many. Mind, our social life is getting quite thrilling now thanks to your family, Lu. We had such a good time at *Hair*. Will it be like that, do you think?'

'Well, hopefully everyone will manage to keep their clothes on tomorrow,' Lulu giggled, folding up dozens of 'Suitable for the festive season' Tricel blouses. 'But the party afterwards should be fun.'

'Is young Mitzi doing the wedding food? Only we had some of those brownies she made, and they tasted wonderful. Not only that, but they made us feel – well – rather tipsy. Hedley had three and he was still laughing two days after.'

Lu grinned. 'Er – yes, she's making some of Granny Westward's specialities. Boris and Otto are doing the more normal stuff, though. She's cooking something special for us tonight too. I – well – I hoped that it might make things

278

better for her. With Joel, you know?'

Biff clearly didn't understand the implication. 'You're a kind-hearted girl. Nice of you to think that a good meal might take your mum's mind off that unpleasantness. What actually happened between her and the young dentist, then?'

'We still don't know,' Lulu finished her folding and putting away. 'That's why I want her to make the Wishes Come True Pie tonight. I reckon it'll make things happen.'

'Do you? Well I never ... D'you know, we're really going to miss you when you go off to join the RSPCA.' Biff polished her bifocals. She made it sound as though Lulu was joining the Foreign Legion. 'We'll get none of this gossip. But we're very proud of you. Very proud.'

Lu, suddenly feeling extremely emotional, scrambled over a pile of purple and pink geometric curtains and hugged Biff. 'And I'll miss you, too. Goodness – look at me. I'm not supposed to cry until tomorrow ...'

'Oh, it's lovely and warm in here. It's soooo cold out there. Still no snow, though. Can we do anything to help?' Doll asked as she and Lu piled into Mitzi's kitchen after their visit to The Faery Glen. 'Your hair looks great. Pauline's a star. Are we late?'

'Thanks – and not at all.' Mitzi looked up from wrapping things in cling film at the kitchen table. 'Everything's just on ready. Did you have a good time?'

'Lovely,' Doll smiled. 'Very civilised. Much better than having a full-blown hen night at a club and being made to wear L plates and having to dance with a male stripper.'

'Each to their own,' Lu muttered. 'Personally ...'

Doll pulled a handful of beads and braids.

'Did everyone go?' Mitzi said, not looking at Doll. 'All your friends – and everyone from the surgery – and, well, everyone?'

'Everyone,' Doll nodded, removing Hawkwind and slotting 'The Greatest Hits of Christmas' into the CD player. 'And yes, because I know you want to know, Joel's gone to Manchester. He left at four. He'll be there by now. I'm sorry, Mum.'

'Oh, there's no need to be sorry.' Mitzi tried to speak cheerfully. It was very difficult. She'd clung on to the hope that Joel might just change his mind. She'd even written him a Christmas card and bought him a small present, which was wrapped and hidden in her knicker drawer. She took a deep breath and tried to rearrange her face into calm acceptance. 'It's no surprise, after all. Right, are you both ready to eat?'

'We're absolutely starving,' Lulu said, hugging Mitzi. 'And you don't have to pretend with us, Mum. We know how you feel about Joel.'

'I know you do, love. But it's all history. I don't want to talk about it. Good God, Doll, put them down – you'll ruin your appetite. You're no better than when you were kids. They're for tomorrow.'

Mitzi reached for the last batch of cooling Dreaming Creams just as Doll crammed one into her mouth. They both laughed.

Bing Crosby crooned his way into 'White Christmas' from the CD player.

'Oooh, I'm dreaming of a white Christmas ...' Doll warbled, happily spraying Dreaming Creams crumbs down the front of her black sweater.

Lulu raised her eyebrows. 'You'd better be careful. You might just get one. Doesn't Granny Westward's book say those things make dreams come true?'

'She does,' Mitzi fastened the top more firmly on the box.

'Oh – you two and your witchcraft,' Doll grinned, popping the last morsels of the Dreaming Cream into her mouth. 'If the Met Office with their satellites and computers and twenty-first-century technology say there's going to be no snow, then there's going to be no damn snow.'

'You never know,' Lu insisted. 'Magic is far older and far stronger than technology.'

'Oh, pul-ease,' Doll pulled a face. 'Are we going to have this mumbo-jumbo all night?'

'Stop it, both of you,' Mitzi laughed, opening the oven and sliding out the Wishes Come True Pie. 'There! Just right – go on through to the living room. Everything's ready for you. Yes, take the CD player. And please try not to fight.'

'This is really lovely,' Doll said, looking round the darkened living room, illuminated by the fire glow, candles, and the Christmas-tree lights. 'Like it used to be when we were kids.'

Lu nodded. 'Same Christmas decorations, all the old things we've unwrapped year after year, and the tree lights are still the same, and the boss-eyed fairy . . .'

'And the Christmas music playing. I love "Winter Wonderland" more than any other song, I think. It conjured up so many lovely images when I was a kid. Do you remember Dad singing it to us?'

'Yeah, and making up his own words. And we laughed every time.'

'Bet him and Jennifer don't laugh much.'

Lu shrugged. 'His choice. His loss.'

Mitzi, poised to dish up the Wishes Come True Pie, smiled at them both. In the few months since they'd done this initially – sat down together in the cosy living room to sample Granny Westward's first recipe – so much had happened. For all of them. Most of it good.

It was kind of them to think they could recreate previous Christmases. They were lovely girls – but even she didn't think Granny Westward would give her a second shot at happiness. Not after she'd had it and chucked it away so spectacularly.

'Everyone got enough? There's more in the kitchen . . . Right, so who's going first with the wishing?'

'Doll,' Lulu said. 'After all, this is her last night of freedom. Anyone stupid enough to be tying herself for ever to Boring Brett deserves a last chance to escape. I reckon

281

everyone in the pub tonight was laying bets on whether she'll even turn up tomorrow.'

'Jealousy, jealousy ... sibling rivalry. How very sad.' Doll poked out her tongue. 'Well, last time I wished for Brett to show some spontaneity and get us out of our rut, and—' she laughed and patted her belly '—he certainly managed that. Oh, not that I believe the pie made a scrap of difference, but even so ...'

'Oh, for heaven's sake.' Lu jigged up and down in her chair. 'Just wish for a long and happy marriage and a healthy baby and let's get on with it.'

Doll scooped up her first forkful. 'Okay – of course I want both of those. And Lu's right, there's nothing else I could wish for ... so here goes.' She popped the Wishes Come True Pie into her mouth. 'Oooh, it's lovely, Mum. Um ... yes, then I wish that Brett and I will be together for ever and always happy and that the baby is perfect and has a – um – perfect life.' She swallowed. 'Not that I believe a word of this, of course. Go on then, Lu – you next.'

Lulu had no hesitation.

'I wish,' she mumbled round her first mouthful, 'that me and Shay and Pip, Squeak and Wilfred could have a home of our own.'

Mitzi looked sympathetically across the table at Lu. Granny Westward would have to pull out all the stops on that one. There was no way Shay would leave Lavender and Lobelia in the lurch. And no way that Lu could move in with them.

'Nice try, Lu. Let's hope it comes true.'

'It will,' Lulu said confidently. 'I mean, look what happened with Shay the first time. That was real magic. So go on then Mum – your turn.'

Mitzi sat silently for a moment. They were both watching her. She knew what they wanted her to wish for. She knew what she wanted to wish for herself. Did she believe in Granny Westward's magic enough? She sighed. It wouldn't just take a touch of herbal magic to make her dearest wish come true, it would take a bloody miracle.

'Go on . . .' Doll urged her. 'At least you believe in all this hocus-pocus. That must help.'

'Ssssh,' Lu admonished. 'You'll spoil it. Go on, Mum. Go for it.'

Mitzi lifted her fork to her lips. What did it matter? Lu and Doll wouldn't laugh at her. They wouldn't tell anyone how silly she was being.

She hesitated. There was no point at all in wishing for the impossible. She'd given up on impossible dreams a long, long time ago.

'I wish,' she said softly as Dean Martin wanted it to 'Snow, Snow, Snow' and Richard and Judy curled up to sleep among the presents under the Christmas tree, 'that tomorrow will be the happiest day of our lives.'

Chapter Twenty-five

Mitzi had always imagined, when the girls were tiny, that their wedding days would be oases of calm and dignity. That everyone would be drifting around in diaphanous wraps, looking very glam, casually sipping Bucks Fizz, saying, 'After you with the bathroom,' and giggling girlishly.

Nothing had prepared her for this mayhem.

Not even Dave Edmunds cheerfully intoning 'Crawling From the Wreckage' could calm her.

They'd never be ready in time. The morning and early part of the afternoon had already passed by in a roar of confusion. Flowers had arrived. The phone had never stopped ringing. Pauline had been in to give Mitzi a comb-through, Doll a re-style, and to thread the festive red and green ribbons, holly and ivy and other bits and pieces into Lulu's braids.

Surprisingly, Jennifer, in her beauty therapist's nylon overall and clearly an all-over Victoria Beckham brown since the health farm, had arrived to do everyone's make-up.

'My gift to you all,' she'd smiled vacuously. 'I know you were going to do your own but you really need a profes-sional on a special occasion like this, don't you?'

She'd taken over the living room with her cases and mirrors and umpteen brushes and pots and potions, worked

284

her magic, and eventually disappeared to pour herself into her wedding outfit.

Mitzi had been sure she'd have painted-in lines, bags, sags and wrinkles on her face and was surprised to find that instead she'd done an excellent job. For the first time in ages, Mitzi's face had a smooth, even pearly, appearance, practically line-free, her lips looked plump and smooth, and her eyes, darkened with earthy shadows and black mascara, looked huge and luminous.

Jennifer had, of course, turned Doll and Lu into Miss World contestants.

Then the neighbours had been in and out all day, offering advice and sandwiches, and getting in the way. Clyde had made a special white wedding brew – white roses, white turnips, white beans and cauliflower. Mitzi had taken a sip and emptied the bottle down the sink as soon as he'd gone. It had blocked the u-bend.

The afternoon was growing ever more gloomily dark. The wind continued to keen bitterly from the north, but there was still no snow and none expected, although Doll had glued herself to every weather forecast.

'Blimey, it's cold out there. Too cold for snow. How's everyone doing?' Lance appeared in the kitchen, a bottle of Bollinger in his hand. 'All under control?'

'Absolutely not,' Mitzi said. 'Mayhem, madness and bedlam reigns. Your buttonhole's here somewhere. The deep-red rosebuds there, look – under the cat food. You look great. Did you buy that suit in London? What a lovely colour. Old gold – and with that dark-red shirt and tie you look extremely festive.'

'Jennifer chose it,' Lance said, shoving the Bollinger in the fridge, then fixing the rose into his lapel, and trying not to preen. 'We've got co-ordinated outfits.'

Mitzi laughed. 'I might have guessed. Mind you, it was very kind of Jennifer to do our faces. A nice thought.'

'She does have them from time to time.' Lance pulled out a kitchen chair and sat down. 'And you look gorgeous.

Even in your dressing gown.'

'Thanks – but wait until you see the girls. They were pretty before but she's transformed them. Much as I hate to say it, Jennifer's very good at her job.'

'I know. Mitzi – your friend. The dentist . . .'

'Won't be here today. We're no longer together. So there'll be no awkwardness.'

'There wouldn't have been. I'm sorry it didn't work out.'

'So am I.'

Mitzi, who'd tried really hard not to think about Joel all day, felt her throat start to tighten. She looked away quickly.

'Are you nervous?' Lance said softly.

'Very. You?'

'Terrified. And a bit sad. I mean, I always thought, when the kids were young, that we'd be sharing their wedding day like proper parents. I know we are, but well, you know . . .'

Mitzi nodded. She knew.

'I'd better go and get dressed.' She looked round the kitchen. 'Will you be okay for a minute? The girls shouldn't be long. Lu's supposed to be helping Doll get ready – but no doubt it'll be the other way round.'

'No doubt.'

They exchanged smiles of friendship, fleetingly sharing a history and a lifetime of parental memories.

Half an hour later, Mitzi, feeling a million dollars in the mediaeval green velvet dress, slowly came downstairs again. Lance was lounging on the sofa in the living room, his face dark in the flickering firelight.

'Wow,' Lance gave an approving nod. 'Spectacular. Absolutely gorgeous. Very Queen Guinevere. And – oh, double wow!'

Mitzi turned and looked as Doll and Lulu came into the room. She sniffed back tears of love and pride.

Lu, in her dark-red slinky dress and with her festive hair

and her beautifully made-up face, had been transformed from eco-warrior to heart-stoppingly beautiful woman in a stroke.

Doll, blonde and elegant, looked as stunning as only a bride can. The dress skimmed and shimmered over her slender body, the tiara sparkled in her glossy hair, and with the swansdown boa and the long satin gloves, she looked like a fashion plate.

'Aren't we clever?' Lance looked at Mitzi as he stood up and kissed both the girls. 'To have produced such beautiful daughters? All your doing, of course.' He kissed Mitzi too. 'They inherited your genes. Let's drink a toast – to the three most beautiful women in Hazy Hassocks ...'

'Don't let Jennifer hear you say that.'

The Bollinger was fetched and the toast drunk and then there was the last-minute rushing backwards and forwards for purses and bags and trips to the loo.

'Shay's outside!' Lu peered out of the window. 'Time for us to go, Mum – oh my God! Doesn't he scrub up well? I'm not going to be able to keep my hands off him! Look at him!'

They all looked. It was the first time any of them had seen him in a suit. The sombre formal clothes on his rangy body and with his tousled streaky hair, were an incredibly sexy contrast. He looked, Mitzi thought, good enough to eat.

'We're a very glamorous lot, aren't we?' Mitzi said, trying not to think how superb Joel would have looked in his suit too. 'Okay then, we'll leave you two to it.' She hugged Lance and kissed Doll again. 'Good luck, darling. You look incredible.'

There was another round of hugging and kissing.

'Oh, by the way,' Lance said, 'just in case you're late back tonight, I fed Richard and Judy while I was in the kitchen. And put down some extra food and clean water.'

'So did I!' Mitzi, Doll and Lulu chorused.

*

287

In the December darkness, the church, decorated for Christmas, had an air of age-old mystery. Candles, hundreds of fat white candles, flickered, casting dancing shadows up the worn stone walls and across the ceiling. Holly and ivy twined everywhere, and the ends of the pews were garlanded with deep-red rosebuds and sprigs of mistletoe.

Mitzi, having left Lulu shivering in the dark church porch while Shay returned to collect the Bandings and the Spraggs, hurried down the aisle and made a brief diversion to the right-hand side where Brett and his family were sitting.

'All right? Not nervous?'

'I'm okay – I think.' Brett looked serious. 'She is going to turn up, Mrs B, isn't she?'

'Of course she is. She's on her way. And please, after today, could you call me Mum?'

Brett grinned. 'Not a chance, Mrs B.'

Smiling, Mitzi sat alone in the left-hand front pew and felt almost as though she'd stepped back in time. The colours of the Epiphany were vibrant, and the nativity scene – all worn wooden figures, the far-too-big star and bundles of straw – in front of the altar, was exactly as it had been when she was a child.

There was something very comforting about the sameness.

Merle, the organist and one of the Baby Boomers, was playing a selection of carols very softly, and peered round from her seat and grinned. Mitzi grinned back then smiled across again at Brett's family in the opposite pew. They looked as nervous as she felt.

The church began to fill very quickly. Mitzi kept turning round and mouthing greetings. Thanks to the vicar being a bit High Church, the air was rich with the scent of pine needles and incense, and the heating was going full bore. The velvet dress would have been a disaster with a more parsimonious parson.

Pews on both sides were now filled to bursting. It was like *Hair* all over again. Mitzi had a fleeting worry about whether there'd be enough food for this lot at The Faery Glen. She recognised nearly everyone, although some of Doll and Brett's friends were unfamiliar. And goodness – had Tarnia and Snotty Mark actually been invited? Their outfits were pure Hollywood and Tarnia's hat would have put Ascot to shame.

There was a rustling behind her as Flo and Clyde and Lav and Lob eased themselves into their seats. Mitzi swivelled round to greet them with mutual exclamations of 'Don't you look lovely'. Lav and Lob had, in deference to being in a place of worship, abandoned the cycle helmets and wore matching hats bedecked with glossy paste fruit and lots of feathers. The rest of their outfits were all limp lace, fingerless mittens and paisley layers – pure Hinge and Bracket.

Flo and Clyde, in drop-waisted suits with more than a slight aroma of mothball, looked as though they'd stepped from the pages of *Good Housekeeping* circa 1955.

Oh, and there was the dental surgery crowd: Viv with her short and stout husband who worked in the hardware shop in Winterbrook and who she always introduced at functions as 'Derek, my tiger', and Mr and Mrs Johnson looking very elegant, and Tammy in an unsuitable mini skirt and thigh boots holding hands with Gavin, Flo and Clyde's adenoidal grandson from the Big Sava check-outs – but not Joel.

Of course, not Joel.

Mitzi had made her own second wish last night, silently, but that wasn't going to work. Granny Westward said the wishes had to be spoken aloud – and she certainly hadn't made any mention of more than one wish. So, happiness all round was what she'd wished for – and who could ask for more?

Well, yes, she could and had, but she was a grown-up. She'd cope with the disappointment. And anyway, there was possibly something blasphemous thinking about herbal magic while in church. There'd probably be a thunderbolt.

'You look really nice.' Jennifer had slipped into the pew

behind Mitzi. 'I'm sorry I was rude about you wearing green. It's gorgeous with your hair and colouring.'

'Thanks,' Mitzi turned round, ducked under the brim of Jennifer's hat, and tried not to giggle. Jennifer was wearing old gold and dark red – exactly like Lance. They looked like Torville and Dean. 'And thanks for all your help today. You've made such a difference to us all. Look – don't sit there – come in here. There's plenty of room.'

'But the front pew?'

'You're Lance's wife,' Mitzi said without irony. 'He'll be in here when he's done the giving away bit. You should be with him.'

'Thank you ever so much.' Jennifer swapped pews in a designer rustle and a waft of bank-breaking scent. 'It's ever so kind of you.'

Merle suddenly cranked the organ up from a sotto voce version of 'Silent Night' and harumphed into 'The Entry of the Queen of Sheba'. Mitzi, turning with everyone else to watch Doll and Lance make their entrance, felt the tears gather and sniffed them back.

Doll, cool and controlled as always, looked radiant and beautiful; Lance was bursting with pride; and Lu was simply gorgeous.

Her family, Mitzi thought, as they reached the chancel steps beside her, was stunning.

She could smell the cold December air on them and feel their excitement. Brett's eyes were glowing with love as he stepped forward with his best-man brother.

Mitzi stood up with the rest of the congregation. The candles sparkled on the zirconias in Doll's tiara and on the sequins in her hair. Sequins? Had Pauline used sequins? On everyone? Including Lance?

Lu's eyes were huge as she leaned towards Mitzi. 'It's snowing!' she whispered. 'Really snowing! See – dreams can come true . . .'

Chapter Twenty-six

The Faery Glen was going to be bursting at the seams. After the wedding service and the photographs, the convoy of cars had snaked round the village green and along Hazy Hassocks high street. The snow, huge fat flakes tumbling from the darkness and still settling, had impeded the journey.

The village was fast disappearing under a white eiderdown.

'See!' Lu said delightedly as she clambered from Shay's car outside the pub, 'I told Doll those Dreaming Creams would work! Isn't this just brilliant?'

'Amazing,' Mitzi agreed, easing herself from the back seat where she'd been cheek by jowl with Lav and Lob. 'Cold, but absolutely amazing ...'

The Faery Glen was already crystalline-covered and the flakes were falling past the illuminated sign, faster and faster, huge goose feathers, swirling into a blur.

Doll had been ecstatic. The happy couple had been covered by snow as well as confetti outside the church, and the photographs had been taken in the nave.

'I'm dreaming of a white Christmas ...' everyone had sung as they slipped and slithered merrily down the church path towards their cars.

Shay, making sure Lav and Lob had been safely installed inside the pub, grinned at Mitzi and Lu from the doorway.

'Are you two coming in, or are you staying out there to make a snowman?'

'Tough call,' Lu grinned back, before teetering through the snow on her unfamiliar high heels.

Shay caught her in the doorway and covered her icy face with kisses.

Mitzi, with snowflakes settling in her hair, swallowed the lump in her throat and made her way towards the pub. Doll and Brett, Lulu and Shay – happy, healthy, in love. What more could any woman want?

Otto and Boris had worked wonders. The Faery Glen, already looking festive for Christmas, was a mass of wedding decorations: bells, banners and balloons, hearts and flowers, cascades of twinkling lights, white cloths over all the tables, the log fire roaring.

'We've put your food in with ours on the tables at the far end,' Boris said, pouring champagne into Mitzi's flute. 'Sort of mix'n'match.'

'Lovely,' Mitzi nodded. 'Thank you – this is wonderful.'

The wedding breakfast ebb and flow of laughter and dozens of splintered conversations rose around her. The entire congregation was there. The whole village and then some. She spoke to everyone. Doll and Brett, glowing with happiness, circulated. Shay and Lu didn't. They'd retired to an inglenook and were sucking champagne from each other's fingers.

'Super, Mitzi!' Tarnia shrieked, arm in arm with Jennifer. 'Super!'

'It is, isn't it?' Lance said, raising his champagne flute to her. 'Just perfect.'

'It is,' Mitzi agreed. 'And listen to that wind – if it's still snowing we'll have a whiteout by the end of the evening. This is better than I could ever have dreamed . . .'

Well, very nearly.

In an almost detached manner, Mitzi watched as the guests wolfed down the Green Gowns and the Dreaming Creams and the Mistletoe Kisses. She laughed to herself.

Hazy Hassocks on the razzle hardly needed any herbal help – the evening would probably degenerate into an orgy.

'Mind if we join you?'

Lu, lustfully immersed in licking Moët et Chandon from Shay's index finger, looked up irritably.

Carmel, holding hands with Augusta who was clutching a massively piled plate, was beaming at them.

'S'pose not,' Lu muttered ungraciously, squeezing round even closer to Shay so that Augusta's huge hips would fit into the inglenook. 'Are you enjoying yourselves?'

'Very much. It's a really great party and you look stunning,' Carmel said. 'And we won't – er – disturb you for long. We just wanted to ask you a question.'

'Fire away,' Shay beamed. 'The building of particle accelerators is my specialist subject.'

'Oh, ha-ha.' Carmel reached for a Green Gown from the top of Augusta's pile. 'No, we wanted to know if you'd heard of any places to live. We—' she smiled lovingly at Augusta '—want to be together. As you know we're both lodging with families at the moment, and well – er – things can get a bit difficult. We've both handed in our notice at our present places, but the house we were going to share has fallen through, so come the New Year we'll be homeless.'

Augusta managed to remove her face from the food for a moment. 'We'll take absolutely anything. Anything just so as we can be together. We just hate having to sleep apart.'

Shay and Lu nodded in sympathy.

'Actually,' Shay said, 'there's a cottage for rent on the village green and—'

'Noooooo!!!!!' Lu shrieked, clapping her hand over his mouth. 'No, there isn't! Look, wait here a minute! Don't move!'

Dragging a perplexed Shay behind her, she barged through the scrum of guests, stumbling on the stiletto-heels. Where was the bloody vicar? Oh, God, surely he hadn't stayed in the church to get on with the Carol Service had he?

Surely he'd have joined them in the pub for an hour at least? Rumour had it he was pretty keen on the communion wine.

'Ah! Got him!'

'What?' Shay blinked. 'Lu, sweetheart, what the hell are you doing?'

'Me? I'm not doing anything. My Mum's magic is doing it! As always ...' She grabbed the vicar's sleeve. 'Excuse me, could I have a word?'

The vicar, twinkly eyed and ruddy cheeked, had clearly downed a copious amount of Merlot.

'Would you like me to make it a double? Fit in a second Blessings wedding?'

'No thank you. Or at least, not just yet.' Lu smiled sweetly. 'We wanted to ask, is Honeysuckle House still vacant?'

The vicar nodded. 'Well, yes. As you know, I always look for suitable tenants and after the – er – problems with the Worthys I have to be very careful.'

'Would a paramedic and an RSPCA officer be considered suitable?'

'Eminently so,' the vicar nodded. 'Oh, absolutely – why? Do you know of such a couple?'

'You're looking at them.'

'Really?' The vicar's dissolute blue eyes sparkled. 'Oh, how perfectly wonderful. Yes, Lulu and – er—'

'Shay Donovan.' Shay held out his hand.

'Mr Donovan,' the vicar pumped his hand up and down. 'Well, yes, of course. I'd be delighted to have you as tenants – and the sooner the better. Do you want to have a viewing?'

'No, well, yes – but we'll take it. Now. Oh, and we'll have animals. Rescued puppies. Is that okay?'

'Perfectly,' the vicar beamed some more. 'I love all God's creatures. Not a sparrow falls and all that. Couldn't be more pleased. And you could move in, when?'

'Straight after Christmas,' Lu rocked on her stilt heels and kissed the vicar. 'You're a star. Thanks a million.'

'I hope you'll be very happy there.'

'Oh, we will,' Shay said dazedly as once again Lu dragged him through the partying crowd.

They found Lav and Lob lustily singing 'Oliver's Army' by the food table.

'Have you had loads to eat?' Lulu squeezed in beside them. 'And are you nice and warm?'

'Yes to both,' Lavender nodded. 'This is super. And what about you two?'

'We're fine. Lovely wedding wasn't it?'

'Beautiful. We cried all through it,' Lobelia sniffed happily.

'What we wanted to tell you,' Lu leaned towards them, 'is that we might have solved some of your financial problems.'

'Really!' The Bandings clapped their mittens. 'Oh, how wonderful that would be! But how?'

Quickly, Lulu explained that she and Shay would be renting Honeysuckle House from the vicar, but that they knew two paramedics – both girls – who'd love to share Shay's old room.

'So you see, you could have double the rent. Two people sharing the one room. And it would be all right because they're both girls, wouldn't it?'

'Double the rent!' the Bandings eyes widened in bliss at the thought of being able to afford food and heat. 'And two young gels in the house! Oh, what fun! But we'll miss you.'

'We'll only be on the village green,' Shay said reassuringly. 'You'll still see us every day. And you can come for your tea all the time. So is it all right? Shall I send Carmel and Augusta over?'

'Yes, please,' the Bandings chorused. 'Oh, this is the happiest day of our lives!'

'And mine,' Lulu grinned, as Shay's fingers circled lasciviously on her wrist.

*

The evening roared on. Those with young children and

Christmas Eve stockings to fill, had left. The remainder danced and sang and talked and laughed. It was, everyone said, the most magical night Hazy Hassocks had ever seen.

As all Granny Westward's delicacies had disappeared, Mitzi proudly felt that she might be more than slightly responsible for that.

She watched everyone partying, and felt suddenly lonely. Stupid. How could she be lonely among all these people? All her friends and family? But everyone had *someone*.

Then Doll and Brett, seemingly unable to prise themselves apart, had hugged her, and Doll had whispered that maybe there was something in the Dreaming Creams and the Wishes Come True Pie after all; and Lulu had skipped up, her braids all tangled and her dress covered in snow, and said she and Shay had been celebrating outside.

'The snow's nearly a foot deep already and still coming down. It's magical,' she'd beamed from ear to ear. 'Simply magical. And Doll's wedding has been perfect, and me and Shay and the puppies have got Honeysuckle House. Oh, this is just the best day ever! Not that it's any surprise. After all, we both know it's *really* magic, don't we? And as me and Doll have had our wishes come true, it's your turn now.'

'I've got mine, too,' Mitzi had said. 'I wished for this to be the happiest day of all our lives. And it is.'

Lulu had wrinkled her nose. 'Nah. Not that one. The other one. Your special wish last night. The one you didn't say out loud.'

Mitzi had watched Lu and Shay disappear through the gyrating crowd, and frowned slightly. How on earth had Lu known about that one? How could she possibly have known?

Nursing her champagne flute, Mitzi wandered to the window and gazed out through the leaded lights. The snow showed no sign of letting up. The wind had increased, whipping the storm into a cloud of white that swirled and eddied from every direction. There were already massive drifts in the car park and the cars themselves were all completely covered under several inches.

All except one.

Mitzi watched as the new arrival's headlights dimmed and went out, and then as the door opened and the driver stepped out into the blizzard.

'Brave,' she said to herself, 'coming out tonight in this ... oh, my God!'

Joel stopped for a moment under The Faery Glen's illuminated sign and looked at the pub. Mitzi was sure her heart had stopped beating. Was she dreaming? Had she conjured him up? She blinked. No, he was still there. The odd thing was, she realised, was that she was absolutely delighted to see him – but not entirely surprised.

Forcing her way through the manic crowd, including Trilby Man and all the Baby Boomers, who were now doing the 'Time Warp', Mitzi dragged open The Faery Glen's door.

Joel, who had obviously had his hand on the latch, almost toppled on top of her.

They stared at one another.

'You look wonderful,' he said.

'You look like a snowman.'

They smiled.

'Before we say anything else, would it be okay if I got warm? Thawed out a bit?' Joel indicated the log fire. The wind was howling down the chimney, making the flames leap and dance. 'I've had a hell of a journey.'

'You grab a seat. I'll get you a drink. And food.'

Within a few minutes they were knee to knee beside the fire, filled glasses and plates and another bottle of champagne on the table. Mitzi wanted to touch him, hold his hand, kiss him, feel his arms around her.

She managed merely to lean forward and look enquiring. 'I thought you were in Manchester?'

'I was. I came back.'

'Was it that bad?'

'Not at all. My parents were delighted to see me and my ex and my brother were holidaying in the Maldives.'

'So, why—'

'I have absolutely no idea. Except that last night, within minutes of arriving, I felt that I had to come back here. *Had to*.' He emphasised the words. 'Like there was some weird force telling me that I should be in Hazy Hassocks. Not in Manchester. It was bloody spooky.'

'Fancy that . . .'

'I've missed you so much.'

'I've missed you, too. It's been hell. I'm so sorry about—'

He leaned forward and placed his fingers on her lips. They were icy cold. They felt like fire. 'Don't. Not now. We'll do all the explanations and apologies later. I've been such a prat.'

'Two prats together, then.' Mitzi felt herself unravelling with love and happiness.

Joel drained his glass and filled them both again. 'Here's to Doll and Brett. And us.'

'Doll and Brett. And us. It was a shame you missed the wedding.'

Joel looked round the packed pub with everyone still whooping it up like billy-o. 'It was – but it looks as though I'm in plenty of time for the best bit.'

'We always save the best for last in Hazy Hassocks.'

Joel grinned. 'I saw you on stage in *Hair*.'

Mitzi felt the shame wash over her. 'I know. Please don't. I looked awful. Terrible . . .'

'You looked adorable.' Joel took the glass from her and put it on the table. Then he held her hands in his, his fingers stroking hers. 'You looked wonderful. Sexy, pretty, happy, absolutely bloody perfect.'

'But you left.'

'Of course I did. I was hurting so much because we'd finished. It was just bloody torture watching you, seeing you, loving you, wanting you – and knowing . . . thinking

– that you didn't want me. I'm a dentist. If I want torture I'll do my own root canals without anaesthetic.'

Mitzi sighed. 'I've been such a fool.'

'No fool like an old fool – ouch! – oh ...'

Joel's eyes met hers, and the wanting was mutual. He kissed her. Mitzi, melting with lust and longing and love, kissed him back.

'I love you.'

'I love you, too.'

He laughed. 'Not very original, are we?'

'Sod originality,' Mitzi giggled. 'I'm a traditionalist.'

Aware that Doll and Lulu had noticed Joel's arrival and the kiss and were nudging each other delightedly, laughing across the pub, Mitzi waved to them. They waved back.

'Do I have to wave?' Joel pulled her even closer.

'No. Just kiss me.'

He did and Mitzi sighed with total happiness. It was, without doubt, the happiest day of her life ... she'd got exactly what she'd wished for ... God bless Granny Westward.

The music suddenly stopped. The dancers didn't.

'Ladies and gentlemen,' Otto barked down the microphone. 'Just a little word. The police have phoned us. The roads are now impassable. The snow has drifted and they're expecting more. The good news is that we've definitely got a White Christmas. The bad news is that I'm afraid you're all going to have spend the night here.'

The cheers and whoops and screams of delight were deafening.

Boris took over the microphone. 'We'll keep the fire stoked up and we've got pillows and blankets for when you're ready to call it a day – or night. There's plenty of food and drink – so I hope you're all good friends because you're all going to be spending the night together!'

The screams of delight were even louder.

Joel grinned at her. 'This is sheer magic. It's all been magic since I met you. You've put a spell on me.'

'Moi?' Mitzi smiled blissfully. 'Not guilty.'

'But if were staying all night, what about Richard and Judy? Shall I see if I can get through the drifts?'

Mitzi wanted to kiss him to death. 'They'll be fine – more than fine. We all put down food before we left for the church. And the heating's on. They'll probably have a far more comfortable night than we will. But thank you for thinking about them.'

'I've grown – er – rather attached to them actually. And I didn't want you to worry.'

'I'm not worrying – about anything. So where were we?'

'About here, I think . . .' Joel kissed her. 'And – um – this isn't quite how I imagined we'd be spending our first night together.'

'Nor me,' Mitzi said softly. 'Which is a whole other story. Still, we'll have loads of time to do it properly, won't we?'

'We will.' Joel nodded. 'Loads of time. All the time in the world, in fact. Maybe even for ever and ever.'

'Happily ever after?' Mitzi snuggled against him. 'Sounds like a proper fairytale ending to me . . .'

Boris turned the music on again. There was a moment's silence, then, magically, The Faery Glen was flooded with the haunting strains of 'Witchcraft'.

Epilogue

Mitzi opened her eyes and stretched luxuriously amid the glorious cosiness of tangled white sheets, two blankets and a quilted eiderdown. For a fleeting, frightening moment she wondered where she was. Then she remembered and smiled.

There was no sound. Everywhere was eerily silent: a cushioned, uncanny, muffled silence. The unfamiliar room was filled with a muted white light. The heavy plum velvet curtains, not quite meeting, allowed a pale shaft to slide across the polished floorboards.

A strand of light across a bedroom floor.

She turned her head and smiled sleepily into the huge feather pillow. It was Christmas morning, it was snowing, and she wasn't at home, or alone.

Tentatively she inched her foot across the vast bed until it made contact with Joel's naked leg. Reaching out to touch another's skin.

Mitzi sighed with pure happiness.

Joel slept bedside her. She allowed herself the luxury of watching him breathing, naturally ravishing in sleep as so few people are after childhood. Breathing out as she was breathing in.

If this first love could be my last . . .

It was, and had been, everything – absolutely everything – she'd dreamed of. 'Amoureuse' to the last, sensual, haunting word.

Carefully, not wanting to wake Joel, she slid out of bed and waited to be frozen. Surprisingly, the room was blissfully warm, so she padded naked to the window and pulled back a corner of the thick curtain.

Overnight Hazy Hassocks had turned into Winter Wonderland. It was breathtakingly beautiful. Dawn was just breaking, a heavy yellow light over the hillocky whiteness, the snowflakes still falling slowly in a gentle haphazard way to rest on the drifts. Icicles, huge stalactites, hung from every one of The Faery Glen's windowsills, and the northerly wind still blew sub-zero temperatures across the village.

Downstairs, no doubt, all her friends and family were still sleeping under the piles of blankets and duvets provided by Otto and Boris. It probably wasn't the way Doll and Brett had expected to be spending their wedding night. Still, she knew they'd been offered a room on account of the special occasion and the pregnancy but they'd turned it down and carried on partying into the early hours with everyone else.

Well, nearly everyone else.

Joel murmured in his sleep. She turned and looked at him. God, he was gorgeous. He wriggled comfortably, flung his arm across her pillow and slept again as well he might, Mitzi thought with a flush of remembered pleasure.

And before he woke she'd have to lock herself in the en suite and repair some of the ravages. Where was her handbag? Oh ... how had it got up there? Had she thrown it? Kicked it? Crikey ...

Shivering a little from the arctic scene outside rather than the actual temperature, she grabbed Joel's sweater from the wild abandon of clothes on the floor. It was soft and slithered over her nakedness like a hug. As a makeshift peignoir – a word, she felt, which befitted a night of such wantonness – it would do perfectly.

In the bathroom, naked again, ablutions completed, Mitzi winced at her reflection.

Living 'Amoureuse' may have been wonderful last night with the shadows and the champagne and the heightened passions – but nothing, nothing at all, could disguise the devastation in the morning's stark snowy light.

Having no toothbrush, no toilet bag, no emergency supplies of Oil of Olay, Mitzi had scrubbed herself with The Faery Glen's oatmeal soap, cleaned her teeth with a cotton bud, and rubbed away the mascara shadows with a damp forefinger. Her hair was slicked back from the shower, and in the bathroom's unforgiving mirror every line, wrinkle and southward-slip of her body was thrown-up in exaggerated relief.

Dear God! Her bottom had cellulite on the cellulite!

She surveyed her body from every angle and shrugged. For her age and having had two children, it wasn't bad. It was her. She would always try hard to keep it trim and moisturised but time would, naturally, take its toll. She couldn't, and wouldn't, go down the Tarnia-route to eternal youth. Maybe Granny Westward had some concoction she could use to hold back the years. But then again, probably not. There hadn't been this obsession with personal vanity in Granny Westward's day, had there?

Ah well, it was her body, it was all she'd got, and she was comfortable with it. And anyway, Joel had seemed more than satisfied with it, hadn't he?

She grinned wickedly at her reflection.

Having darkened her eyes with kohl and a flick of mascara, and rubbed balm into her lips, she sprayed herself lightly with Opium. It had been the perfect scent for the wedding – it was probably too heavy for this morning, but it was sexier than oatmeal.

Slithering into the sweater again, Mitzi opened the bath-room door. Joel was still asleep. The bathroom activities hadn't woken him. She'd love to use the tiny kettle and make coffee but didn't want to disturb him. Instead, she sat on the wide windowsill and watched the snow.

The high street was unrecognisable in its new white and

silver sparkling livery. Somewhere in the distance a snow-plough was chugging, and the excited shrieks of children echoed through the silence. The church bells started to peal their chime of celebration across Hazy Hassocks. The vicar must have made it through the snow. How many of his once-a-year congregation would manage to be there this morning? Mitzi wondered, slipping and sliding their way through this fairytale landscape to give thanks for the age-old miracle.

Still, if this morning was ethereal, then last night had been sheer magic.

Joel had danced with her to 'Witchcraft', and they'd moved, close together, with no inhibitions. She'd felt happier than she ever had in her life. Doll and Lu had watched them dancing, and smiled hugely. And when later, in the middle of 'Do You Believe In Magic?', Joel had disappeared to the bar and had a whispered conversation with Otto and Boris, she'd simply assumed he was order-ing more champagne.

It had been a complete surprise when he'd held out his hand and led her away from the wildlypartying bar and into The Faery Glen's snaking, low-beamed corridors.

'Did anyone see us go?' he'd grinned at her.

She'd shaken her head.

'Good.'

Still holding hands, they'd climbed the narrow, oak-panelled staircase and Joel had unlocked a door at the end of the passage.

The bedroom – white-walled, low-ceilinged, criss-crossed with dark beams and decorated in rich plum and cream – was illuminated by tiny lamps.

'Oh!' Mitzi had looked at the sumptuously draped four-poster bed in amazement. 'Oh . . .'

'It's not the bridal suite,' Joel had looked slightly worried. 'Otto and Boris have reserved that for the happy couple if they change their minds, but it'll do, won't it?'

Unable to speak, Mitzi had nodded.

Joel had pulled her towards him. 'I've had plenty of time to think about why you – well, why we – well, what went wrong after Lorenzo's.'

'It was my fault. I was being stupid and I should have explained—'

'Nothing to explain,' Joel had bent down and kissed her gently. 'Not now. I wasn't too happy that night about the prospect of being interrupted by Lulu and Shay either. I'd wanted it to be special too. I guess in the lust of the moment the special bit got rather lost, but that's men for you.'

Mitzi had curled her arms round his neck. 'I thought you'd think I just didn't want you.'

'Oh, I did. For quite some time. It was your right to change your mind, of course, but I wondered what I'd done wrong. However,' he'd kissed her again, 'I'm a persistent sod, and I still wanted you, loved you, couldn't just walk away and forget you, although I gave it a damn good try. So, I'm trying to make amends for my macho-crassness now.'

'Thank you – it's fantastic.' Mitzi had looked around the room, and then up into his beautiful face. 'I don't deserve you. I – I did want it to be special that night . . . but there were other things as well . . .'

'Such as?'

'Oh, stupid stuff like it not just being a one-off and not wanting to be hurt and—'

'This is as real as it gets for me,' Joel had said. 'This is a forever commitment as far as I'm concerned. I've veered away from serious involvements because I didn't want to be hurt again, either. It was a huge risk for me, too. But one I was prepared to take because I loved you so much.'

Mitzi swallowed. 'But the age difference . . .? What if you wanted to have children with a new partner? What if—'

'Life's full of what-ifs, Mitzi. It's also very short. If you're given the chance of happiness, you can't ruin it by thinking of the what-ifs. And the age difference is minimal and totally unimportant. And no, I've never wanted

305

children. And stop making excuses. I love you.'

'I love you, too,' she'd sighed with relief and love and sheer happiness. 'So very much . . .'

He'd kissed her then, and she'd kissed him, and clothes had been shed with haste and happiness and heightened passions, and nothing mattered. Nothing mattered at all.

Vaguely, Mitzi remembered as they'd tumbled onto the four-poster's cushiony eiderdown, she'd thought one day she'd tell him about 'Amoureuse'. One day.

'Good morning.'

The night's blissful memories faded and she turned quickly from the windowsill. 'Good morning to you, too.'

Joel was sitting up in bed, looking as all men did after a night of passion – absolutely sensational. It wasn't fair, Mitzi thought, that women always looked wrecked while men . . .

'You look gorgeous.' He hauled himself out of bed, and padded towards her. 'Get back into bed and I'll make coffee. Oh – do you prefer coffee in the morning, or tea?'

'Coffee,' Mitzi giggled as he kissed her. 'Isn't that amazing?'

'Amazing,' Joel agreed, glancing out of the window. 'As is that. And this . . .'

She ran back to the bed and tugging off the sweater, rearranged the pillows and snuggled beneath the sheets, watching him, wanting him, loving him.

The coffee was surprisingly strong and hot. They managed to drink it while cuddling together, trying not to spill any.

From somewhere deep in the depths of The Faery Glen, Otto and Boris were awake and breakfast was being prepared. The mouth-watering aroma of frying bacon wafted up through the floorboards.

'Breakfast . . .' Joel kissed her damp hair. 'Would madam like it in bed?'

'Absolutely,' she grinned at him. 'And before everyone else in the village wakes up down there and rampages up here.'

'You'll have to wait just a little bit longer. Anyway, the door's locked and I've got both the keys. You're now at my mercy.'

'Oh, good ... I wonder if Doll and Brett will be able to make it to the New Forest for their honeymoon. Or if we'll be able to do the lost-and-lonely Christmas lunches, or—'

'Plenty of time to find out about that later.' Joel gently removed the coffee cup from her fingers. 'And as you well know, nothing's impossible. Not for you. Now can we prove that last night wasn't just the result of some pagan spell you cast on me?'

'Absolutely,' she sighed with bliss, wrapping her body round his as he pulled her towards him and kissed her. 'Oh, and happy Christmas.'

'Happy Christmas, Mitzi Blessing ...'

Author's Note

As I've said in my acknowledgements, HUBBLE BUBBLE was inspired by my Nan's sorties into 'magical cooking with natural ingredients'. This seemed to involve snatching strange, unrecognisable, growing things at first light – 'best with the dew still on 'em, duck' – from the hedgerows and other people's gardens. As her eyesight was iffy, and her culinary skills practically zero, we in the family were always careful to avoid any of her 'herbal specials'. Sadly her neighbours weren't so wary and she became – quite rightly – known as The Herbal Poisoner of Wessex Road.

The recipes included in HUBBLE BUBBLE are all based on dishes from my Nan's collection – but have been heavily fictionalised to fit into my story and will definitely make you VERY ILL INDEED – they are not real recipes or real magic. Make and eat them at your peril!!! You have been warned . . .

If you enjoyed *Hubble Bubble*, read on for a taste of Christina Jones's new book, *Fiddlesticks*, coming soon from Piatkus . . .

Prologue

'I still can't believe you're doing this. You must be mad. Even if you didn't want to leave with your Mum and Dad, you've still got millions of choices. You could travel the world, move to London, live by the sea – you could do, well, *anything*. Anything rather than this.'

'There's still time to change your mind, you know. We don't want you to go. We'll miss you. Why don't you stay here, get a nice little flat in Market Street – which is handy for all the nightlife and getting to work and for shopping—'

'Shopping! I bet you haven't even thought about shopping! What on earth are you going to do about shopping? There won't be any shops, or wine bars, or clubs, or well, anything, will there?'

'And hairdressers! Amber, have you even considered not having a hairdresser? You won't be able to get your artlessly casual Kate Winslet tousle with the blonde streaks and highlights and lowlights done in some hick-stick place, will you? If there is a hairdresser – which I doubt – it'll be someone called Cynthia who still does perms and mullets and uses hood dryers!'

'And work? Have you actually thought about where you'll work? It'll be all farming and wellies and mud and cack. You won't be able to sign on with an agency and pick and choose your office jobs there. You'll probably end up serving in the village post office – if they've got one and then only if you're very lucky and the postmistress hasn't got several hundred inbred relations waiting in line to grab the opportunity.'

'Or mucking out pigs.'

'Or driving a tractor.'

'Exactly. Listen to us, Amber. We're your closest friends. We've got your best interests at heart. You're only twenty-seven, and you're a townie girl through and through. Listen to what we're telling you. Who, in their right mind, would choose to leave town and go and bury themselves in some Godforsaken village when they've got everything they need right here on their doorstep?'

'Anyway, what do you know about actually living in the *country*? I mean, the country's fine for – well – looking at, but no one wants to live there, do they?'

'Amber does.'

'Amber's completely barking, then.'

Amber laughed and rather unsteadily raised her umpteenth glass of Chenin Blanc. 'Nice to know I've got the wholehearted support of my dearest friends. But seriously, this is what I want to do. I'm really looking forward to it.'

They all stared at her.

'This place? Is it scarily remote? Like Wales or Cornwall?'

Amber drained her glass. 'I've never been there, remember? But it's in Berkshire. Almost civilised. They have huge towns like Reading and Newbury and Bracknell and Ascot and—'

'Berkshire . . . Is that close to London?'

'Close-ish.'

'Oh well, maybe it won't be *too* bad then. And is it near Reading and Newbury and wherever else you just said?'

'Not that close, no. The nearest places are called – um – Winterbrook and Hazy Hassocks and – oh, yes – Bagley-cum-Russett.'

'Dear God!'

'When are you going?'

'Next week.'

'And you're going to be living with someone you've never met? Some mad old bat?'

'My Gran's best friend from when they were children, yes. She wrote to us when Gran died. We've been in touch ever since. And I'm only going as a lodger – not as some sad Jane Austen type companion.'

'Jesus, Amber. You're really going to live with a wrinkly, in a village, with no job, no shops – and no men?'

'After Jamie the last bit will come as something of a blessing.' Amber continued to grin. 'I've had enough of two-timing, spineless, commitment-phobic men to last a lifetime. In fact, it's one of the main reasons I'm going.'

They all pulled sympathetic faces. Jamie had broken Amber's heart, everyone knew that, but was that really any reason for her to up sticks and bury herself in the middle of nowhere with some very, very old lady she'd never met?

Normal women would make do with getting roaring drunk and then indulging in a bit of retail therapy before dusting off their stilt-heels and finding another, far better, man.

'I'll give you a month at the most. Then you'll be back.'

'A week. She won't last more than a week.'

Amber said nothing. What was the point? She'd made up her mind. It was all her parents' fault anyway. Well, and Jamie's of course. But mostly her parents.

Like all her friends, she was a SLAHWP: Still Living At Home With Parents. The lack of well-paid jobs and crippling house prices, and the fact she spent every penny of her salary before it arrived in her bank account, had seen to that. So when her parents decided to take early retirement and, overexcited by the surfeit of Change Your Lifestyle programmes on the television, chose to sell up and move to rural Spain, she'd been left with few choices.

At first she'd thought she'd move in with Jamie. They'd been together for nearly two years. It made sense.

Jamie, however, had nearly passed out at the suggestion and muttered feebly about being far too young to settle down and not being ready for that sort of commitment and, well, to be honest, Amber living in might just cramp his style.

Renting was out of the question on her own; house-shares were few and far between. Her sisters, Coral and Topaz, had been thrilled at the thought of living in a tumbledown goat shed about three million miles into the hinterland of Andalucia. Amber, who felt that luxuries like electricity, running water, drainage and a roof were fairly important, was simply horrified.

Then she'd had the letter from Gwyneth Wilkins, her grandmother's friend.

Why didn't Amber come and live with her for a while? Maybe just for the summer? Until she could sort out what she really wanted to do with the rest of her life?

Amber, still smarting from Jamie's rejection, and her entire family's embracing of the Spanish peasant lifestyle, had thought about it for all of two minutes and then said yes.

Her friends all looked at her sorrowfully.

'Well, when it all falls apart, don't say we didn't warn you.'

'It's not the other side of the world. You could always come and visit me.'

'Get real!'

'Yeah, well – we might . . . one day . . .'

'And what's this village-that-time-forgot called?'

Amber filled her glass again and smiled.

'Fiddlesticks.'